Prometheus Returns

ALSO BY REGINA BOGLE

Feeling Our Way: Embracing The Tender Heart

Redemption in the Dark: A Story of Heart and Soul

The Healing Light Series:

Chiron's Light

In and Out of Time

Prometheus Returns

Prometheus Returns

Regina Bogle

ISBN: 978-1-943190-39-3 (print)
978-1-943190-40-9 (eversion)

Prometheus Returns is a work of fiction. The resemblance of any character or aspect of the story to real life people or events is coincidental. Opinions expressed by the characters further the plot and/or invite reflection, but they are not intended as recommendations for any course of action or decision-making. Similarly, references to complementary healing methods have real life correlations, but they are in no way intended as a recommendation for any specific treatment or diagnosis. If interested, the reader is invited to explore their use by utilizing reputable sources, but please note that this includes seeking appropriate professional guidance when needed and taking full responsibility for one's own healing journey. However it is pursued, may healing abound!

Publisher's Cataloging-in-Publication data
Names: Bogle, Regina, author.
Title: Prometheus returns / Regina Bogle.
Series: The Healing Light Series
Description: Yachats, OR: Wild Ginger Press, 2023.
Identifiers: LCCN: 2023917537 | ISBN: 978-1-943190-39-3 (paperback) | 978-1-943190-40-9 (ebook)
Subjects: LCSH: Extrasensory perception--Fiction. | College students--Fiction. | Reincarnation--Fiction. | BISAC: FICTION / Visionary & Metaphysical | FICTION / Magical Realism | FICTION / Sagas
Classification: LCC PS3602.O4275 P76 2023 | DDC 813.6--dc23

Wild Ginger Press
www.wildgingerpress.com
Book & Cover Design by Bobbi Benson
Illustrations by Regina Bogle

To M. R. Bawa Muhaiyaddeen,
Sufi Sheikh,
and
Peter J. Prociuk, M.D.,
homeopath and physician to body and soul
True vessels of Grace and Healing
in service to the One

Prologue

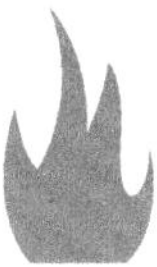

THE CAMPUS BELL TOWER GONGED the tenth hour as Promise made her way across the quadrangle that May morning. She lifted her gaze to appreciate the time-honored ritual and the vibrantly blue, cloudless sky doming the wondrous arrival of spring all around her. The end of her first year at Stella Maris University fast approached. This last week of classes offered the usual end-of-term challenges. She would do her best to meet them squarely.

The warmth of the day invited the donning of shorts and T-shirts in celebration of the season. Promise's recent Earth Day banner, now worn as a scarf, nicely complemented the green of her shirt and the reddish-brown highlights in her shining, long hair. She often wore it drawn back and tied with matching ribbon, especially when she needed to feel focused. This day required that of her in no small measure.

Promise had just left her psychology class, her second semester of the basics as required by her major. Today's topic, depression, had resonated too deeply, further challenging her need to maintain calm, clear thinking during her next class. She decided to tune in to her feelings about that previous discussion, knowing that if she tried to avoid them, they would reveal themselves to her in unwanted ways and moments. Despite her youthful nineteen years, she had to admit it: she knew all about depression.

What really perturbed her about the class involved the way her professor made it sound like a disorder in need of treatment. His lecture implied that something was seriously wrong with her. Was it?

Yes, she had experienced a somewhat steady, low mood for the past few months, difficulty falling asleep most nights, occasional crying spells, and little interest in the social gatherings her friends frequently invited her to share with them. But she still found beauty in the everyday gifts of Nature, loved running outdoors, had no trouble concentrating on topics that interested her, and felt seriously motivated to do something meaningful with her life – even though she had no clue about what that might be. Promise also acknowledged her sensitivity to other people's heartaches and worries. These weighed heavily upon her heart. Her professor made no mention of that....

Her reflections on her last class spilled into the content of the next one: Greek mythology. As part of her final grade, she would present the story of Prometheus to her classmates in less than one hour. She had grown up with this myth, mostly because her father really loved it and told it to her often. But the tale of Prometheus could not be fully recounted without mentioning the Centaur Chiron. As she walked to her next class, Promise found herself thinking about Chiron's role in setting Prometheus free.

Chiron suffered, as did Prometheus, but no one ever said they had a disorder that needed treatment. This left her with many questions. In fact, her entire first year of college left her with more questions than she had ever considered asking. The trusted adults in her life told her this was a blessing in disguise: an opportunity to explore the Unknown with humility. She wryly noted how they had *not* said it would be easy.

Promise arrived at her destination, a classroom in one of the older buildings on the other side of campus. Its art deco architectural style conveyed a sense of history, perfect for the liberal arts classes offered within its walls. Once in the room, she retrieved her notes and set up her thumb drive so that she might share the pictures and images she had collected to embellish the story of her namesake – at least, that's how her father described the meaning of her name. She hoped to honor them both – her father and Prometheus – and resolved to do her best.

When all the students had gathered and taken their seats, Professor Thompkins – a tall, slender man, well past his midlife – called their attention to the task at hand. He introduced their agenda for the class hour, then seated himself in the back of the lecture room, having graciously offered the podium to Promise. She rose from her place and assumed her position as pseudo-professor for the hour. After clearing her throat and sipping some water, she launched her presentation.

"Good morning, everyone. Today, I would like to share with you the story of Prometheus. Even though the narratives about him date at least as far back as the Bronze Age, around 3300 BC, it is highly likely that oral traditions spoke of the fire god long before that era. If ever there existed such an actual historical figure, his legend is now relegated to myth with numerous variations, dependent upon the tellers and their epoch in history. Despite these age-old origins, I hope to show how his tale remains particularly relevant for us in our modern times.

"According to the ancient Greeks, his saga naturally proceeds from their account of creation. In the beginning there was only Chaos, amorphous confusion in the endless darkness. From this great, chaotic nothingness emerged Night and Erebus, the incomprehensible depth of Death. This empty, silent, and dark stillness mysteriously and miraculously emanated Eros, the Love that embraces possibility, connects all things, and issues forth beauty and order. In the context of this potential, Light spontaneously came into being, creating Day and revealing Ouranos, the sky. Gaia, the Earth, next appeared. Ouranos and Gaia together created the first actual entities to manifest life in the way we humans know it. The ancient Greeks described the offspring of Heaven and Earth as monsters, the first several of whom were extremely destructive."

Promise shared some of her slides as she continued: "First, the hundred-handed, fifty-headed giants roamed the earth, followed by the Cyclopes, monsters with one large eye in the middle of their forehead. Then Heaven and Earth birthed twelve deities, later called Titans, who were just as strong and huge as their older siblings, although not all of them were as ravaging. One of those twelve offspring, Iapetus, became the father of Prometheus.

"Before we more deeply explore the story of Prometheus, it is important to understand the context within which he had to function. Ouranos, the sky god, had received a prophesy that his rule would eventually be overthrown by one of his progeny. Kronos, his Titan son – Roman name, Saturn – did, in fact, succeed in this regard. But Kronos, too, had received the same prophecy; he opted to swallow his children at the moment of their birth to preclude the loss of his sovereignty. His mate, another Earth Titan named Rhea, had other ideas, however; she saved her sixth child, Zeus, from this fate. Raised in secret, Zeus later challenged Kronos for the throne and won. This eventually established the Olympian gods as rulers, leading to the banishment of the Titans – specifically, all those Titans who did not help Zeus defeat his father.

"Iapetus, brother of Kronos, was a god of craftmanship and mortality. He and his mate, Clymene, procreated four sons: Atlas, Prometheus, Epimetheus, and Menoetius. Sources vary but most agree that these four gave life to human beings and shared the best and the worst of their traits with them: from Atlas, humans received strength and brash courage; from Prometheus, forethinking and cunning; from Epimetheus, afterthought and slow learning; and from Menoetius, action and violence.

"When Prometheus and Epimetheus were tasked with distributing gifts to the creatures they made, Epimetheus took all the scales, nails, sharp teeth, and fur for his animals. Consequently, few protections remained available for human beings. Prometheus reacted with compassion for his creatures. Having helped Zeus to oust Kronos, Prometheus still freely roamed Mount Olympus and the world below. He elected to use his forethought and cunning to safeguard his mortal humans, who struggled to survive upon the land."

Promise continued to show her slides. The subject matter now reflected environmental shifts on Earth's evolving landscape. She invited her classmates to reflect more experientially upon human origins.

"Perhaps we can take a moment to imagine the ecological conditions confronting our ancestors. Ice ages, floods, comet-strikes, volcanoes, earthquakes, scorching heat, and bone-chilling cold came and went over short or long periods of time with little predictability. By day, our ancestors also faced predators, needed to hunt for food, and had to determine which fruits, leaves, roots, and flowers brought nourishment and healing versus illness or possible death. By night, in the cooler darkness, they had no light other than that of the moon and the stars for guidance. No fire to warm them or show them the way. In the nocturnal shadows, the sounds of predators cried out all around them. Humans had to band together. The world was a potentially very dangerous place.

"With his capacity for forethought, Prometheus understood that humans would benefit from the gift of fire. Unfortunately, the god Zeus controlled the only source for this wonder, and he did not care to share it with mortals. He perceived those creatures as designed to be vulnerable and subservient to the gods and goddesses on Mount Olympus. Prometheus would have to use his craftiness to accomplish his self-appointed mission.

"He did so by tossing an apple into a gathering of goddesses with the announcement that it belonged to the fairest one among them. While they argued and fought over who that might be, and the gods egged on their controversy, Prometheus stole fire from the forge of the Olympian god Hephaestus and gave it to human beings.

"In a rage over the Titan's independence and trickery, Zeus had Prometheus chained to a mountainside, where he inflicted his wrath upon his prisoner through the daily visitation of his eagle. Like a vulture, it would peck out the Titan's liver by day. Each night, his liver would be restored in time for the repeated, daylong, devouring attack at next sunrise. This would continue eternally unless Prometheus divulged the name of Zeus's paramour, the one who had birthed the son destined to dethrone Zeus and all the Olympian gods and goddesses. Zeus had begotten many children by many different mothers; consequently, he himself was clueless in this matter.

"With formidable endurance of this daily torture, Prometheus rebuffed Zeus's demand. In response to the Titan's refusal, Zeus declared that only the offering of another god – one who would agree to sacrifice his immortality and descend to the Underworld – could free Prometheus from his chains and the eagle's daily ravaging.

"Despite the probability that his ordeal would never end, Prometheus held firm to his convictions. He did not relinquish his honor to Zeus's manipulative abuse of power. Prometheus maintained his own integrity. He did not respond to bribes. He did not give in to fear. He endured Zeus's punishment while holding onto hope.

"Coincident with the trials of Prometheus, the story of the Centaur Chiron – the immortal half-man, half-horse – slowly unfolded. Chiron had been accidentally wounded by Hercules' arrow, which had been dipped in the blood of the Hydra. Physical contact with the Hydra's blood afflicted immortals with eternal pain and killed humans instantly. Being half-god and immortal, Chiron therefore had to suffer eternally because, despite his proficiency as a revered healer and teacher, he could not heal his own wound. When Hercules later informed Chiron of Prometheus' predicament, the wise Centaur seized the opportunity and chose to offer his immortal suffering in exchange for the Titan's freedom.

"Zeus accepted Chiron's proposal. After sending the Centaur's soul to the Underworld, Zeus chose to venerate the renowned healer by raising his light to the night sky, where it continues to shine as the constellation Centaurus. Zeus also begrudgingly honored his decree: he set Prometheus free even while knowing that the Titan would strive to enlighten humans once again."

This part of the myth always brought Promise to tears, but somehow, with considerable effort, she managed to maintain her presentation persona on this occasion. She had never understood her reaction to this aspect of the tale. Her father, who would tell her this story whenever she asked, could never explain her tearful response either.

Promise took a deep breath before she continued: "This summary of the ancient Greek myth may seem quite fanciful to our modern ears. Yet, the element of suffering, the experience of seemingly endless unknowing, and the choice to protect and defend who and what we love, no matter how difficult, have implications for our lives today. Who among us can say that we might make the same choice Prometheus made? Or that Chiron made? Are we off the hook because we are mere mortals? Not gods and goddesses?"

Promise noticed that the occasionally glazed looks from her classmates as she told the story suddenly shifted to those of more rapt attention or irritation. She suspected those responses had everything to do with whether her listeners had already been touched by suffering or whether they worked hard to avoid it as best they could. In that moment, her previous class came to mind. She impulsively decided to challenge them further by asking the very questions that plagued her consciousness daily.

"I would like to add to our wonderings an experience I just had in another class on the topic of depression," she continued. "The professor identified several criteria that would earn a person a clinical diagnosis of disorder, to include: low mood; crying spells; hopelessness; helplessness; lack of interest in usual activities; problems sleeping, be it too much or too little; problems with appetite, usually too little but maybe the opposite; a sense of doom about the future; and, in severe cases, a wish to be dead.

"According to these criteria, we might wonder if Prometheus or Chiron, during their more difficult periods, might have been diagnosed as depressed by our modern-day psychologists. Would that change how we hear their stories? Would we appreciate their heroism? Their dedication? The courage of their choices to sacrifice something precious in service to a greater good? Perhaps the difference between our clinical diagnosis and these ancient tales involves a sense of meaning and purpose, laced with a dollop of hope. How does this impact our lives today?"

A profound silence filled the room for several minutes. Finally, Professor Thompkins rose from his seat and walked toward the front of the classroom. Promise had no idea what to expect. She managed to hold onto her own conviction that the questions she had just posed had value, even though she also simultaneously felt bewildered by her classmates' lack of response. Fortunately, their professor understood the depth of her reflections as well as the sometimes-limited capacity of young adults to join her in that kind of exploration.

He responded to the silence by saying, "Promise, those are very thought-provoking questions. Your deep understanding of this myth gives us all something to ponder. Thank you for your excellent presentation."

Promise blushed slightly as she nodded her thanks. She then gathered her notes and her thumb drive and returned to her seat. She had held her emotions in check as best she could, but she could feel them rising to the surface, imminently threatening to spill forth. Professor

Thompkins engaged his class with a less challenging discussion before he dismissed them for the hour. He then invited Promise to join him for a private conversation at his desk.

Professor Thompkins remarked, "That really was an excellent presentation, Promise. Your use of slides did much to engage more of our senses. I am also impressed by the depth of your thinking. I want to encourage you to explore your questions, particularly the ones about purpose and meaning, as you live life beyond this semester."

Feeling relatively speechless in that moment, Promise simply replied, "Thank you, Professor."

He continued, "You're welcome. You really do have a feel for the power of myth. You are a psychology major, correct?"

She found some words: "Yes, that's true."

Her professor thoughtfully added, "You may find that myth will inform your questions and deepen your appreciation of human psychology profoundly. You may wish to consider a minor in mythology. Just a thought…"

Promise regained enough composure to respond, "I really appreciate that suggestion, Professor. Thank you for taking the time to share it with me. To be honest, I am enormously grateful for this entire course. I sense it will have a major impact upon my life down the road. Thank you very much!"

"Again, Promise, you're welcome. That's why I do what I do. Purpose and meaning. May you find that as you go forward as well!"

Promise smiled. A tear glistened in the corner of her eye. She had been asking these questions about the purpose of her life, the reason for her sadness, the meaning of it all, since her early teens. Her mother validated her innate, sometimes intense, feeling sensitivities. Her Aunt Tara had taught her alternative, non-traditional ways of managing her extrasensory gifts and healing her heartaches. Her father often invited her to reason through her reactions, guiding her to deeper understanding. Uncle Alex added his own steady affirmations of love to the mix. Still, the barrage did not end. What did it all mean? Others did not seem so troubled. What was it about her life that needed to meet these challenges?

Promise truly appreciated that her professor extended himself in such a mentoring way. He affirmed her questions and her right to ask them while also inviting her to incorporate them into her quest for purpose and meaning. What light was she meant to share? She had always sensed that she had to do something important. But what?

She decided she would work to understand herself better, beginning with her past, then see what life brought her by way of guidance and adventures. She had no doubt that she experienced herself and her relationships the way she did for a reason. In that moment, she made a commitment to herself: she would work to discover that reason and honor it with her life.

Her professor's words were a gift to her; he had validated for her the importance of myth. She had been named after Prometheus, and she felt called to carry the light. Mythology in general would likely prove to be a great teacher, but this myth in particular – along with the spiral of leadership imprinted over her heart – offered clues to her past, present, and future. She promised herself she would explore them faithfully and hope for the coming of Light....

Part One

1

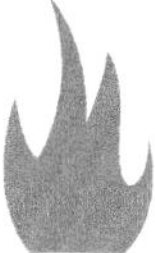

THE MORNING SUN'S WELCOMED RAYS streamed through the large windows in Peter's new home office. He sat at his desk amidst the room's dark furniture and bookshelves, gazing at the vibrancy of life outdoors. He still loved to watch Nature at work as winds blew, clouds floated across the sky, leaves budded on trees or swirled to the ground, and birds alighted on their feeders, which were purposely placed so that he might witness their comings and goings. On this particular Saturday, he had to review some financial reports. The beauty of the natural world kept his perspective and priorities in balance.

Three years had passed since the birth of his precious daughter, Promise. During those years, he and Brittany had enjoyed their previous home, also enveloped in the splendor of Nature. That setting had offered a solid beginning to their deepening relationship, forged amidst all sorts of challenges and struggles. Brittany still worked as coordinator for social services in the emergency department at St.

Raphael's Hospital, the inner-city healthcare facility where they first met. Even though the hospital's board of directors had rejected Peter's proposal for a holistic healing program, Peter found a way to midwife its birthing with the help of many friends and residents in the community. Now, the Rainbow Healing Arts Center thrived with a life of its own.

Fonzy, their golden retriever, had aged three years as well. He no longer engaged in puppy pranks, but his playful energy continued to require the attention of his human parents. Fonzy was also very protective of their latest addition to the family. The antics between the two of them often brought tears of laughter to Peter's and Brittany's eyes.

Having taken the moment to marvel at his life's unfolding, Peter then redirected his focus to the task at hand. With the door to his office ajar, he didn't initially notice that his three-year-old had quietly gained entrance. Not until he saw her curly, reddish-brown hair making its way along the far side of his desk, did he realize he had a special guest. Strangely silent for one so young, she came around to his side of the furniture. He watched her as she suddenly jumped forward and uncovered her eyes, exclaiming, "Peek-a-boo, Daddy! I see you!"

What could he do but smile broadly at her. The spiral birthmark on his jaw made a subtle shift in its shape as his face registered his delight with her game. Yes, he played it with her often, but this time she had initiated it. He marveled at all her milestones as only a proud, doting father can.

Peter reached for his cherub as he replied, "And I see you too!! Want a lift to Daddy's lap?"

She stretched out her little arms and waited for his massive hands to raise her to the best seat in the house. His six-foot-two-inch frame dwarfed her child's body while offering a warm and safe place to feel loved and cherished. She settled into his lap like it belonged to her... and it did!

Peter welcomingly asked, "What brings you here, young lady? Where's your mom?"

The sound of Fonzy's padded paws just outside his study announced her arrival. In the next moment, Brittany poked her head in the door, clearly looking for her little one and relieved to find her safe. Now that her daughter had mastered sufficient mobility, keeping an eye on her whereabouts proved more challenging. Peter winked at Brittany before he returned his attention to their precious child, awaiting her answer.

"Tell me the stawy about Pemus again, Daddy!" she enthusiastically replied.

Brittany's eyebrows arched quite noticeably as she made a comical facial gesture to Peter. He worked hard to ignore her, but he knew he would hear more about this later! For now, he would tell Promise the story of her namesake as a three-year-old might understand it. He figured he could embellish it as she got older and better able to appreciate the more challenging, complicated details.

Peter began, "Well, a long, long time ago, there lived a very powerful and smart Titan giant named Prometheus. He wanted to help people stay warm in the cold and be less afraid in the dark. He took fire from someone named Zeus, who got really mad about that. Zeus punished Prometheus for taking the fire without permission."

During this rendition of the tale, Peter said his hero's name very slowly, hoping Promise would eventually say it correctly and spare him Brittany's comments. Not yet, however.

His little one asked, "Why did Soos punish Pemus? Was he bad?"

The challenge of sharing this myth with someone so young impressed Peter once again as he struggled to answer her question. "No, he wasn't bad, honey. But Zeus was really mad. He didn't want to share."

"Mean Soos! Then what happened, Daddy?" she begged to know.

Peter decided to skip lots of details and go for the good part. "A kind Centaur named Chiron offered to help Prometheus get away and be safe. Then Prometheus could help his people and give them fire. The people were really happy, and Zeus didn't punish him anymore."

"So, Soos stawted to shaiwe his fiyeh? Like I'm leawning to shaiwe? When the new baby comes, I'll shaiwe my toys with her. I won't be mean like Soos!" Promise emphatically stated.

Peter beamed, not only with pride but with a sigh of relief. Brittany fully entered the room at this point with her eighth month of pregnancy offering a beautiful profile. The sight of her set Peter's heart aglow even as he also rightly anticipated her commentary about what she had just witnessed.

First, she said to Promise, "Come on, sweetie. We have to get you a bath." After Promise dutifully slid off Peter's lap and went to her mother, Brittany turned to Peter and said, "Pemus, huh? How would it be for her to tell everyone that's her name?!" The laughter in her eyes softened his reaction.

"It would have been temporary, my dear. Temporary!" Peter replied.

"Right..." She laughed as she reached for her little one's hand and guided her to the bathtub. Recognizing the ritual, Fonzy decided to settle himself next to Peter's bare feet.

Peter smiled a little sheepishly but filled with gratitude. Life truly offered many miracles, and three of them just left his study.

2

TWO WEEKS LATER, Brittany awoke feeling achy and "off"; she didn't know how else to describe it. Rising from their bed, Peter noticed her discomfort as he prepared to rendezvous with his coffeemaker. He groggily asked if she needed anything. Brittany thanked him for his offer even as she recognized that this state might last the whole of the day. He had an important presentation to give to a new group of potential clients. She resolved to keep moving, hoping the disturbance would pass.

Promise awoke early and played in her bed before toddling to her parents' bedroom. Her arrival coincided with Peter's plan to pursue a cup of coffee. Fonzy, who had slept at the foot of Promise's bed, accompanied her eagerly through the hallway in search of his food source. Peter laughed as the two of them approached him. He petted Fonzy and scooped up Promise, proposing to do the breakfast ritual for both of them if Brittany might like to rest. She thought about it for one long moment before holding firm to her earlier decision to engage her day as usual.

Peter registered mild concern but accepted her refusal. He did carry Promise, escorted by the tail-wagging Fonzy, to the kitchen, however. His percolating coffee awaited him.

Minutes later, Brittany followed them and did her best to create a cheerful impression. Peter left them to their morning routine so that he might shower and dress for his meeting. Promise, now settled in her special seat at the table, babbled her confusion as she detected something different about her mother. Fonzy stood at Brittany's feet, indifferent to her struggles, while eagerly waiting for his food.

Brittany began to prepare Promise's oatmeal, then she scooped Fonzy's food into his bowl. As she bent low to deliver Fonzy's breakfast, she doubled up in pain and fell to her knees. Promise's eyes opened wide as her small being registered alarm. "Mama!" she cried. "What wong?"

Brittany noted the alarm on her precious little one's face and winced a smile while trying to reassure her. "It's okay, honey. Our new baby is ready to come, that's all. Can you get out of your chair and go tell Daddy?"

With that, Promise did her best to wriggle out of her seat. She stood paralyzed for one moment, not knowing which parent needed her more.

Brittany said again, "That's good, honey. Now, go get Daddy."

Promise toddled toward the steps and climbed them one by one. She found Peter in his bedroom, having showered, now partially dressed. Peter looked up in surprise and noticed the alarm on her face. "What's wrong, sweetheart?"

"Mama said baby is coming. Mama said to get you!"

Peter quickly gathered Promise into his arms and negotiated the stairs as quickly as he could. He found Brittany still bent over in pain, on her knees, clutching her abdomen. Fonzy, having eaten his meal, dutifully sat beside her.

Peter gently delivered Promise to the floor, then ran to Brittany's side. This wasn't the slow progression that they had experienced with their first child's arrival. Delivery seemed more imminent. Peter worked hard to stay calm. He deftly lifted Brittany into his arms and carried her to the sofa. He then quickly called Brittany's midwife, followed by Tara and Alex.

Tara, hospice coordinator at St. Raphael's, graciously agreed to care for Promise that day. She would leave immediately to come to their home. In the meantime, Peter left Fonzy in charge of staying with Brittany while he carried Promise upstairs once again. He needed to finish dressing and collect what was needed for taking Brittany to the hospital.

Promise felt afraid. She babbled her distress. Peter tried to comfort her even as his own ability to concentrate struggled for mastery. Finally, he abandoned his efforts to multitask and turned his full attention to Promise. "Honey, Mama is going to be okay. Having a baby hurts a little at first. This is just part of Nature. Aunt Tara is going to stay with you. She can answer your questions. I am going to take Mama to the place that can take good care of her and help her get the new baby out safely. I have to pack a few things. It is all going to be okay."

Peter gave her a hug, then he decided to assign her a little job to distract her. "Why don't you get your favorite toys so you can play with them and Aunt Tara." Promise's face brightened. She loved spending time with Aunt Tara. She would pick her best fuzzy friends to enjoy with her godmother.

Peter left Promise in her room to fulfill her duties while he quickly gathered clothes and called to cancel his presentation. In contrast to their first delivery, their midwife had instructed him to bring Brittany directly to the birthing suite. Peter felt relief for the plan, but he also noticed the differences with some trepidation. Just then, their front doorbell announced Tara's timely arrival.

Peter quickly grabbed Brittany's bag and stopped for Promise on his way to the stairs. He met Tara at the front door, where they exchanged quick hugs before Tara took Promise and assured him that she would take care of whatever his little one needed. Peter's gratitude registered fully on his face as he left them briefly to put the bag and other needed items in the car. He then returned for Brittany, gathered her into his arms once again, and entrusted Promise and Fonzy to Tara's capable hands.

Brittany made sure to kiss Promise and reassure her that when she came home, Promise would meet her new sister or brother. At the last minute, between uterine cramps, she also remembered to tell Tara about the half-made oatmeal in the kitchen. Tara nodded her understanding and said, "Don't worry, Brittany. We will all be okay."

Promise added, "The baby is a gewl, Mama. I will shaiwe my toys with her."

Brittany and Peter looked quizzically toward their daughter and Tara, then to each other.

Peter tilted his head and said, "Maybe she knows things? Let's go find out!" With that he kissed his precious daughter and thanked their dear friend for her speedy arrival and care.

Peter and Brittany departed to welcome a new little one to their growing family. Promise and Fonzy watched them leave, not fully comprehending the moment. Tara sighed and took a deep breath. Another mystery was about to unfold.

3

"AUNT TAWA, that pink ball is pwetty!" Promise said while pointing to the orb on Tara's bookshelf.

"You like that?" her aunt asked as she reached to bring it to Promise's grasp.

Promise almost dropped it, not having expected it to be so heavy. She looked up at Tara with wonder.

After spending the morning with Promise and Fonzy in their home, arranging meals and playing with stuffed animals, Tara decided to take her charge to her own home for Promise's afternoon nap. Peter had called to address any last-minute questions and to express his concern that this baby's delivery seemed not at all like their first one. Tara could not mistake the stress in his voice. She did her best to reassure him, then contacted Alex to suggest that he stop in to visit if he had the chance. Tara could do nothing but wait and care for Promise. She returned her attention to her sweet little godchild.

"That's rose quartz, honey. It's a crystal."

"What is a cwystal?" Promise asked as she settled the heavy ball in her lap.

"Well, it's a special kind of rock. The earth makes it over a long, long time with lots of pressure...." She gently squeezed Promise's little arm as she said this, then added, "...and lots of heat. When we take it out of the earth and clean off the dirt, it becomes pretty like this!"

"When the new baby gewl comes, I will shaiwe this cwystal with her!"

Tara smiled. Oddly, she also had the unusual sense that Promise "knew things." Her little soul felt familiar in a vague, uncanny sort of way. Tara responded, "That's very nice of you, Promise. She may have to grow a little before she can hold it, so we will keep it safe on the shelf for when you both come to visit and she gets big enough. Okay?"

"Okay. I want to shaiwe my toys like Pemus."

"Pemus? Who's that, honey?"

"Daddy tells me the stawy, how he stole fiyeh from Soos! Soos wouldn't shaiwe!"

"Oh...Pemus! Yes, of course!" Tara grinned as she strongly suspected Brittany would have lots to say about that!!

They made a special napping place where Promise fell asleep rather quickly. Tara busied herself with household chores and called Alex, hoping he might have an update. Alex also worked at St. Raphael's, as an internist. He answered quickly and sighed before he reported Peter's news: the baby was experiencing fetal distress. They were in the process of delivering their child by C-section. Because Brittany had reached thirty-eight weeks gestation, the doctors were hopeful that all would be well for both mother and baby. Peter, on the other hand, seemed stressed enough for all of them.

Now Tara also sighed. Just then, Alex received a text from Peter. He shared the content with Tara immediately: their new little girl had arrived; she did well, considering all the concerns of the day. Brittany was resting comfortably, delighted to hold their new daughter in her arms. This time they had decided in advance to name their child, if a girl, Elizabeth, after Brittany's mother. Brittany and Lizzie would stay in the hospital for two or three days. Peter would be calling Tara soon. In response to this news, Tara's relief poured through the phone and met her husband's as they both laughed at themselves. Alex planned to visit Peter again within the hour.

Now that the tension had eased significantly, Tara wondered, How did Promise know she would have a sister? She had seemed certain of it. Tara had read about how some children seem exceptionally connected to the otherworldly realms, especially before the age of five. Would this special knowing persist beyond that point? Tara decided to pay even closer attention to her cherished goddaughter as she grew.

4

THE WARM SUNLIGHT OF AUGUST filtered through the treated windows of Brittany's sedan and challenged its air conditioning as she drove Promise and Lizzie to Tara's home. This Saturday morning marked a special occasion. Promise, now five years old, would experience her first day of kindergarten in just a few weeks. Brittany planned this as a shopping day for the big event. Tara had kindly offered to stay with Lizzie, while Alex and Peter escaped to the water to enjoy a sailing adventure together.

Lizzie, just turning two, had fussed most of the morning. Brittany had done her best to soothe her, running out of second guesses for what might be the problem. She had considered cancelling their shopping trip, but Tara encouraged her to bring Lizzie anyway. Brittany did so with the mixed feelings of motherhood.

As the three of them neared their intended destination, Lizzie started to cry. Brittany felt helpless and exasperated, needing to focus on the road while feeling simultaneously compelled to address her daughter's distress. Never expecting an answer, she asked Lizzie, "What's wrong, honey?" For some reason, Lizzie had not yet uttered her first word. This concerned Brittany as well and only added to her worry.

Typically, in such situations, Promise would answer Brittany's question on Lizzie's behalf. Today was no exception. Promise replied, "Her gum hurts, Mama. She is getting another tooth."

Brittany's forehead furrowed in amazement that Promise could know such a thing. This, too, had not been the first time. Once again, Brittany paused to wonder about her older daughter's uncanny perceptions. Despite the special, strangely familiar, unexplainable bond Brittany often felt with Lizzie – quite different from the more subtle but equally deep connection she had with Promise – her mothering abilities sometimes needed and appreciated the helpful clarifications that Promise's insights would provide. Even so, how Promise could ever consider that Lizzie might be teething astounded her. Why Brittany hadn't realized this in the context of her close relationship with her youngest puzzled her all the more.

Brittany had to ask, "How do you know that, Promise?"

She responded with the wisdom of a five-year-old: "I just do, Mama. I just know."

"Okay, honey. We'll tell Aunt Tara."

Upon their arrival, Brittany shared Promise's assessment with Tara, who, with Brittany's permission, rubbed her fingers along Lizzie's gums. Sure enough, Tara quickly identified the very spot where the second molar would soon erupt. She offered to rub her refrigerated mixture of cloves and olive oil on Lizzie's gums. She also prepared a cold spoon for teething and some chamomile tea to help Lizzie relax. Brittany sighed with relief. Tara smiled. Both felt grateful to have this bag of tricks available for just such occasions.

Lizzie had calmed almost immediately in response to the clove preparation. Consequently, Brittany felt more comfortable taking Promise on their appointed mission. They departed with hugs and

Tara's assurances that if anything problematic occurred, Brittany would be the first to know.

After Brittany and Promise arrived at the shopping mall, Brittany explained in more detail what they would do together during their trip. She identified the special clothes and supplies that Promise would need for her school days in kindergarten. Suddenly, a cloud seemed to pass over her young daughter's face. Brittany asked her about it.

For the first time, it occurred to Promise to ask, "Lizzie is coming to kindergarten too, isn't she?"

The question startled Brittany for a moment, then she quickly responded, "No, honey. Lizzie is still too little. She is not quite two years old now. She will have to grow big, like you, before she can go to kindergarten."

Promise suddenly looked very worried as she asked, "But who will tell you what she wants when I'm not with her, Mama?"

Brittany suddenly realized how attentive Promise had always been to Lizzie's needs. Maybe Lizzie didn't speak because she didn't have to! Still, how did Promise know what had been left unspoken? Her older daughter's inexplicable perceptiveness stirred even deeper wonder within Brittany's mothering heart.

Brittany directed them to a bench outdoors where they sat together while Brittany patiently explained, "Promise, Lizzie will be okay and you will too. But Lizzie has to learn how to use her words on her own. She will need them to make her way in the world. You both love each other very much – anyone can see that – but you each have to be your own person. Right now, for example, your gum is okay. You are with me, not Aunt Tara. You and Lizzie are both okay. When you go to kindergarten, Lizzie will be in daycare, and you will see each other when you go there after school."

"But, Mama, I tell them what she wants at daycare too! How will they know what she wants when I'm not there?" Promise asked with obvious concern.

Brittany's understanding of the situation only deepened. She comforted her older daughter with reassurance. "I will go to daycare one day with both of you before you go to kindergarten and watch what goes on. Then, I will go again after you go to kindergarten, and I will make sure the teachers know what to do for Lizzie. Would that be okay?"

Promise reluctantly nodded. Brittany now more keenly felt and understood the nature of her older daughter's efforts to ease her younger child's distress. The depth of it surprised her. In response, Brittany intentionally presented a lighter mood and worked to engage Promise in interests that would spark her enthusiasm for this huge transition. Later, she would discuss this with Peter, and together they would formulate a better plan for how to help their two girls cope with the upcoming changes. Clearly, both of them would need their parents' understanding and support.

Brittany held Promise's hand as her young one smiled and started to skip toward the store. Brittany reflected on it all with amazement. Parenthood offered one continuous challenge after another, interspersed with joys that exceeded any verbal description. Some days Brittany's head spun while trying to keep up with all the many permutations. Fortunately, her heart grounded her every single time. She simply shook her head, grinned, and skipped a few steps to join in the fun. Promise giggled. Together, mother and daughter shared a lovely afternoon.

5

PROMISE AND LIZZIE SAT CROSS-LEGGED together on Promise's double bed. They planned a sleepover for the evening: Lizzie would sleep with Promise in her room as a special weekend treat. The girls had grown even closer over the years. Promise, now ten, gladly continued to guide Lizzie, now seven, as they managed their many transitions. Last year, Promise and Lizzie went to the same grade school. This new school year challenged them with separation once again as Promise had to move on to middle school. These occasional sleepovers soothed their longings for special contact in many important ways.

Peter quietly poked his head into the bedroom, taking in the scene of his two daughters thoroughly enjoying each other's company. Promise's curls had straightened considerably as she looked more like her mother every day. Lizzie's locks still looped into all sorts of twists and turns, making their combing a major struggle for everyone involved. Their two reddish-brown crowns practically touched as they lingered over their game of Parcheesi. Suddenly, Lizzie's throw of the dice led to an eruption of glee. They didn't even seem to compete with each other. Promise thrilled with Lizzie's success.

As a consequence of their excitement, Promise noticed Peter's presence. Lizzie quickly turned to see her father grinning at them with pleasure. Both girls smiled in return before Promise took the opportunity to ask him once again to tell them her favorite story. Peter had developed an almost theatrical routine for it over the years so that it had become one of their frequent pastimes. He immediately swooped in as Prometheus, using the flashlight he happened to have in his hand as the torch of fire. The girls giggled as he continued.

When Peter got to the part about Prometheus chained to the mountain at Zeus's command, he fell to the floor and tossed the turned off flashlight to the side. Moaning and groaning, he described how Zeus's eagle kept pecking at his liver. He referenced Chiron, the wounded Centaur, standing in the corner.

Lizzie took the opportunity to ask, "What's a Centaur, Daddy?"

Peter jumped up onto his hands and knees and described his head as human and the rest of his body like that of a horse. He even tried to pretend he could swoosh his tail, which led to squeals of laughter. Fonzy responded on cue and stood next to Peter, wagging his own tail. The girls laughed all the more. Brittany could not help but overhear all the mayhem. She soon stood at the doorway, doing her best to witness the hilarity without too much interference.

Peter then described how Chiron traded his forever pain for Prometheus' freedom. He returned to the floor, quickly turned on the flashlight, then dramatically rose to stand triumphant, holding his flashlight torch on high once again. He then swooped toward the girls on the bed and asked them if they appreciated the firelight. Brittany turned off the bedroom lights to give them a real sense of its worth. The girls sighed in wonderment.

Peter hugged them both at once, feeling satisfied with his best performance ever. Brittany turned the lights back on and motioned to join them on the bed. Peter reached to include her as did the girls. Fonzy barked as he tried to jump on the bed as well. Their big family hug became the segue for tucks into bed with hopes that the girls would eventually fall asleep after all that excitement.

After their two cherubs had finally drifted off to slumberland, Peter and Brittany stood at the foot of Promise's bed, silently marveling at the miracles granted to them as parents. Yes, there were challenging times, some very difficult, but they had managed to face them together and to share the joy of these special moments. They knew the girls would grow up and perhaps never remember this night. Peter and Brittany would remember it forever, though, and hold this piece of their daughters' history in their hearts.

Sleep finally claimed the consciousness of everyone in the family, including Fonzy, who had never outgrown his snoring. He transported it freely from bedroom to bedroom as he made his rounds throughout the night. Peter and Brittany referred to it as their "nightly serenade." On this special occasion, Fonzy slept with the girls as part of their sleepover.

In the middle of the night, Promise woke suddenly from a terrifying dream. She simultaneously sat bolt upright and cried out, waking Lizzie in the process. Lizzie asked, "What's wrong?"

With tears in her eyes, Promise told her, "I just had the most awful dream! Daddy had a terrible car accident, and he got really hurt!!"

Lizzie, now also alarmed, begged her sister, "Let's tell him right now!"

Together they found their way through the dimly lit hallway, accompanied by Fonzy, who had woken to Promise's frightful screams and movements. They ran into their parents' bedroom with significant commotion, which readily roused Peter, then Brittany moments later.

Peter sensed their alarm and immediately asked, "What's wrong?"

Lizzie responded first. "Promise had a horrible, scary dream. You got hurt!"

Now Brittany and Peter both sat up and lifted the girls into their bed. Fonzy took his familiar place at their feet and curled into a comfortable position. Brittany brushed Promise's hair away from her forehead and noticed that she had been perspiring as well. Brittany responded, "Promise, honey, can you tell us your dream? Tell us everything you remember, okay?"

Promise gulped her distress. Peter held her close while he urged her to take a deep breath, then begin whenever she felt ready. He assured her that he was fine right now and that this was just a dream. She did as he suggested, then she hesitantly recounted her nightmare.

"Daddy, you were driving Mama's car up a big hill. Your car stopped running. You couldn't make it go. A big truck came rushing toward you from the top of the hill. At the last minute, it crashed into your car and hurt you!!! Daddy, please don't drive anymore!"

Peter looked to Brittany with wonder as he drew Promise even closer to his heart. Lizzie whimpered, having just heard all these details for the first time. Brittany held her tightly as well. Fonzy began to snore but no one noticed.

Somehow, Peter gathered his wits for a response. He realized that Promise was still too young to appreciate the symbolism of dreams. He had to keep his reassurance practical. He tried to maintain a sense of calm as he replied, "Promise, that does sound like a really terrifying dream. It's just a dream, though. It's not real. You can see that I'm just fine. I don't even usually drive Mama's car. Sometimes dreams are like fairy tales – like Captain Hook meeting the crocodile. They are not real. They just try to teach us a lesson."

He gently wiped away her tears. Promise gulped again. Peter suggested that she take another deep breath.

Promise asked, "So, what's the lesson, Daddy?"

Peter knew this was coming, but he hadn't formulated an answer yet. He quickly begged an angel for inspiration. "Well, I guess it tells us that when something really big and scary is happening and there's nothing that we can do about it, we should do our best to get out of the way."

Promise thought about this for a few moments, then sighed. "You mean like when the Rathmillers' dog barks really loud, we always cross the street to get away from him?"

"Yes, exactly!" Peter silently thanked the angel of inspiration as he realized that this explanation satisfied her. It seemed to work for Lizzie too. Brittany nodded this awareness to Peter as she felt her youngest relax in her arms. They decided to do a family sleepover for the few hours remaining in the night. Everyone settled to the tune of Fonzy's night music. The morning's sunlight would reclaim their day-consciousness soon enough.

The next morning, when Brittany and Peter had a few moments to themselves, Brittany reflected aloud on Promise's dream. Both she and Peter had noticed their daughter's tendencies to "know things" over the years. Brittany truly felt concerned.

Peter did as well but not to the same degree. He brushed the dream off as symbolic, reassured Brittany that he would drive carefully, and encouraged her to do the same with a wink. This made Brittany smile in that moment, but a nagging intuition persisted and perturbed her. She said a prayer to the angels on behalf of them all and did her best to go on with her day.

6

THE HOLMES-THOMAS REFRIGERATOR calendar registered the passage of two-months' time while life continued to offer its reliably unpredictable, distracting complications. The girls were fully involved in their new school year. Homework, projects, afterschool activities, and commuting shuffles interwove with Brittany's and Peter's work commitments. Halloween came and went, but not without the extra flurries of activity that accompany two school-age children. Lizzie wanted to dress up as Belle from *Beauty and the Beast*. In turn, Promise decided to be the beast; she liked the ability to growl in disguise. At the last minute, they decided to include Fonzy as a wolf. These preparations set the whole household in a creative tizzy.

In addition to all this mayhem, situations at the Rainbow Center sometimes required Peter's attention. His consulting endeavors also seemed to demand more of his time and energy. He did his best to keep up with it all, especially as he coordinated the girls' departure for the school bus each morning and picked them up from daycare toward the end of the day. He and Brittany sometimes made adjustments according to the nature of his work commitments. Extended family celebrations, someone's occasional cold, and Fonzy's needs added to the mix.

As part of his consulting practice, Peter had received a request for an in-person financial review at a telecommunications facility sixty miles away. He hesitated to accept the invitation, given the complexity of their lives at that point. Brittany assured him that she could manage her own schedule and provide the essentials for the girls during the brief period projected for this venture. The forthcoming monetary compensation would certainly help their budget as the holidays approached.

Consequently, Peter agreed to the company's proposal; they planned his first visit for the following week. Only later did Peter remember that he had also arranged for his car's required inspection on the same day. Attempts to reschedule the inspection would exceed the legal limit.

Brittany suggested that Peter keep both his appointments, with the telecommunications company and the mechanic, and that he use her car instead. With some minor tweaks to their daily routine, he could drop Brittany off at work and pick her up at her workday's end. If all went as planned, the girls would not be in daycare much longer than usual. Relieved to have identified a solution to his dilemma, Peter relaxed into his other commitments. Homework, projects, and social activities consumed most of their attention for the remainder of the week.

Thursday, the appointed day for jockeying all the chauffeuring rearrangements, finally arrived. Peter did his best to minimize the tensions related to the changes in their family's morning rhythm. Brittany had a more difficult time with it, but she realized that she had encouraged him to do this, so she did her best to accommodate the disruptions.

Promise seemed most challenged by the discombobulation of the morning even though she would be able to take her earlier school bus as usual. She was, in fact, the only one whose schedule held a measure of normalcy. Still, she responded to simple requests with irritability, fussing about things that normally wouldn't bother her. Both Brittany and Peter did their best to make sure that she did not have a fever or some other physical ailment; they could identify no other explanation for her obvious distress. They conferred and reassured each other that she seemed overtly fine and was perhaps just having an unusually difficult start to her day.

Despite her conspicuous attempts to forestall her departure, Promise eventually left for her school bus on time. Because Peter would be driving Brittany to work when he would have otherwise escorted Lizzie to her bus stop down the street, he decided he would also drive her to school. From there, he would set out for his appointment with plenty of time to spare.

Having transported everyone to their intended destinations, Peter programmed his GPS for directions to the distant town in the mountains. The sun shone brightly in the beautiful, cerulean, cloudless sky; its radiance glowed even more vibrantly as urban environs faded in his rearview mirror.

Peter appreciated Brittany's most recent choice of music and enjoyed the melodies as he made his way up a steep incline on the two-lane highway bounded by trees on both sides. Pines, oaks, red maples, birches – some ever green, some in their seasonal transition, some with leaves floating midair or already on the ground – greeted his vision. The sparse traffic offered little distraction. The blue tints in the sky ahead engaged him with a sense of awe as the foliage added its autumn contrasts to the panorama of color.

Peter's consciousness floated in the realm of beauty and music as he maneuvered the highway's ascent. His attention shifted suddenly, however, when he noticed steam rising from his hood and a plume of smoke trailing after him. There were no other vehicles on the road; he immediately assessed the state of his own automobile. Shocked, Peter realized that his engine's gauge had moved into the hot zone. He turned on the heater full blast, opened the windows, then quickly eased Brittany's sedan to the side of the road, where he turned off the engine and applied the emergency break to keep it from rolling backward. He got out of the car and circled it, trying to discern what had caused the problem. A significant puddle of liquid had already formed under his vehicle. Ruefully, he realized he would need to call for a tow.

Peter reached inside the car for his phone just as he heard, then saw a huge eighteen-wheeler ahead, rising over the road's highest point. It negotiated the apex, then barreled down the steep hill toward him at tremendous speed, arousing his alarm instantaneously. Even though the rig kept to its side of the roadway, Promise's dream came suddenly to mind. Without a moment's hesitation, Peter grabbed his phone and ran.

The tractor trailer precariously began to wobble. A tire blew out and the semi's massive frame swerved toward Brittany's car. The crashing sound overwhelmed Peter's ears as he quickly turned to watch their auto burst into flames. He stood there paralyzed in thought, word, feeling, and deed. His phone slipped from his hands and fell to the earth.

The rig finally stopped its prolonged skid. Somehow, its driver managed to escape from its cab before it, too, burst into flames. Peter eventually rallied enough to signal to the driver. Together, they phoned for help before they both dropped to the ground, their legs shaking uncontrollably, no longer able to support them upright.

Peter eventually called Brittany. He still struggled for words. Apologizing for the destruction of her automobile became the easiest thing he could say. Aghast, Brittany did her best to rally her resources. She reclaimed Peter's car from the auto mechanic, called daycare to explain that they would be late, then drove with her heart pounding to Peter's description of his location. Amidst the devastation of smoldering metal and gasoline fumes, fire engines, police cars, and towing trucks, Brittany found him at the site, still very shaken, having just finished his conversation with police. She ran to his arms; they embraced for a very long time.

When they finally had the wherewithal to leave the accident scene, Brittany turned to Peter and asked, "How did you ever survive this?"

Peter shook his head from side to side, still looking stunned. He humbly muttered, "Promise's dream... I remembered her dream. Before the tractor trailer even started to swerve, I knew to run away from your car. That *is* what saved my life."

Brittany's jaw dropped. They sat in silence together in Peter's car for several minutes before Brittany felt focused enough to begin the drive homeward. As their mental swirls slowly shifted from shocked silence to murmurs of thought, they each began to wonder, Do we tell her? How would Promise process the understanding that she had a sixth sense?

As their minds regained their capacity to formulate words, Brittany and Peter shared their confusion about what this might mean for Promise. They reflected on their daughter's unexplainable emotional state that morning. Had she sensed something ominous might occur that day? What might a ten-year-old understand and feel about having access to such information?

They quickly realized that they would have to comprehend all this for themselves first. Tara came immediately to mind. Not only did they want to help Promise; they also acknowledged that they had to personally recover from this trauma as best they could.

7

PROMISE WOKE EARLY FRIDAY morning, listening to the silence that permeated their home between bouts of Fonzy's snoring. She felt edgy. When her parents came late to daycare the previous day, they seemed upset, but they wouldn't say why. Even so, Promise felt greatly relieved to see them for reasons she could not explain. She tried to share her relief with them by comforting them with hugs, smiles, and an occasional joke, all of which seemed to help a little in the moment but not for long thereafter. She had numerous assignments that night, which she promptly completed on her own. She tried hard not to tax her parents further, so she helped Lizzie with her homework as well.

Now that Promise lay in her bed, conscious of the dim light before dawn, she felt her edginess intensify in anticipation of her day. In contrast, once everyone had awoken, she gratefully observed how her parents seemed both more animated and calmer after their night's rest. Promise overheard something about Mama's car needing repairs, so Daddy would be driving her to work again that day and taking Lizzie to school. Promise felt a momentary wish that she would not be excluded, but it didn't seem like anyone would be having much family fun in her absence. Everyone's mood seemed a little somber. Maybe her school bus offered the best option that day, after all.

Once at school, Promise met with several of her friends on the way to her homeroom, which also hosted her first class, math. Fortunately, she liked this subject. It helped her roving mind ground into logic. She did well in it, but she also sensed that her mathematical aptitude, along with her other talents, made some people uncomfortable. Consequently, she made it a point to discreetly help other students without emphasizing her gifts.

That morning, Mr. Higgins, her mathematics teacher, requested the assistance of a few volunteers to bring armfuls of books from the principal's office. Their new texts had just arrived, and he hoped to distribute them for use during their lesson once the five chosen students accomplished their mission. Promise raised her hand and was quickly selected along with four other classmates. Together, they immediately made their way to their appointed destination.

Christopher – a new student who had joined their class only a few weeks ago – accompanied them. He seemed very likeable even if a bit shy; Promise hoped to get to know him better over time. As they gathered to leave the classroom, she detected a swelling on his jaw, now also black and blue, which had not been there previously. Moreover, he seemed uncharacteristically subdued. When their group arrived at the office, their principal, Mrs. Greenwich, noticed his bruise as well.

As Christopher handed Promise some books, Promise suddenly experienced a vision of his father punching him. She stood back, horrified, her arms now loaded with textbooks, which she almost dropped. Christopher turned red in the face, significantly embarrassed by Promise's reaction, even though no words were spoken between them. Mrs. Greenwich observed this exchange and asked to speak to Promise privately.

"You seem upset, Promise. What is the matter?"

Promise looked into her principal's eyes and saw stress, firmness, maybe even impatience. As a result, she felt even more uncomfortable, but she also felt frightened for Christopher. She decided to share her vision with someone she hoped would be able to help him.

Promise exclaimed, "His father gave him that bruise!"

Mrs. Greenwich raised her eyebrows in serious concern. "Did he tell you that?"

"No, Mrs. Greenwich."

"Did you see his father actually hit him?"

Promise stammered, "No, no, Mrs. Greenwich. I just know."

Now, Mrs. Greenwich became angry. "Promise, you cannot walk around accusing people of such acts without creating all sorts of consequences that, I can assure you, you will not want to deal with. Just 'knowing' is not a good enough explanation! Do not repeat this story to anyone. Do you understand me? Do not spread lies either!"

Mrs. Greenwich might just as well have slapped her. Promise's face took on a scarlet hue. She struggled very hard not to cry. The horror of her vision now merged with the shame of her principal's admonishment. Her arms were still loaded with books.

Mrs. Greenwich then said, "Go back to class, Promise. I don't want to hear another word about this."

Promise mumbled, "Yes, Mrs. Greenwich," before she quickly retreated to the safety of the hallway. Christopher warily observed her on their way back to class. They spoke not one word.

Promise felt relieved that the fire in her face had subsided a bit by the time they returned to her classroom. Mr. Higgins had already begun the lesson, but he gladly paused to distribute the textbooks whose arrival he had long awaited. Promise faded into her seat. She tried to keep the frightening vision out of her mind's eye. Whatever they discussed in class that day never made it to her consciousness. She copied the homework assignment into her notebook and left the room quickly at the toning of the bell.

Promise somehow made it through the rest of the day, carefully avoiding the hallway near the principal's office. Thoughts of Christopher consumed her, but she had been warned to remain silent. Should she tell her parents? Mrs. Greenwich said not to tell anyone. The weight of this dilemma impacted the whole of her being. Her friends noticed her unusual retreat. She told them nothing. The weekend would save her from further contact with any of them. Hopefully, Christopher would be all right. Maybe a solution would come…?

8

WHEN THE GIRLS REUNITED at daycare that Friday afternoon, Lizzie immediately noticed that something bothered Promise. Attempts to uncover the cause produced no helpful results. Promise seemed sullen and withdrawn, which only upset Lizzie more. Peter came for them at the usual time, but he, too, seemed emotionally distracted. Lizzie started to cry.

Peter and Promise both responded immediately to her tears with an awareness that their own upset had now impacted someone else. Each of them decided to brave a more engaging face with hopes Lizzie would feel better. Still working to process the previous day's trauma, Peter hadn't noted Promise's contribution to the situation. Similarly, too preoccupied with her own shame, Promise had not appreciated her father's role in the matter. In response to their individual efforts, however, Lizzie stopped crying. For that, both Peter and Promise were grateful.

Next, Peter drove them all to St. Raphael's to pick Brittany up from work. She joined her family and immediately sensed something amiss, but no one provided the clue or invitation to ask about it. She presumed that the stress of the week lay heavily upon them all.

Brittany then explained to her daughters that she and Peter would be visiting with Aunt Tara and Uncle Alex that evening. She had arranged for Amy, their favorite sitter, to be with the girls during their absence. Peter would make pizza for the three of them, and they would have access to the new movie they had wanted to see. Hopefully, they would have a wonderful time. Lizzie expressed spontaneous excitement. Promise recognized that the moment required a pleased response. It seemed easier to provide it than to muddle through the shame and confusion related to her day. She said, "Great!"

Later that evening, Brittany and Peter sat in the kitchen at Alex and Tara's home. Alex worked at the stove preparing their food while Tara sat with their friends, who still seemed noticeably dazed by the calamity of the previous day. They had planned this dinner to provide Brittany and Peter the opportunity they desperately needed to process what had happened and to develop a plan for how to help Promise with her gift.

Tara sat quietly at their side, listening deeply to their narrative and distress. Clearly, the incident had its own trauma to heal. Peter was still quite shaken by the crash. Both Brittany and Peter expressed more concern about Promise, however. They described how their daughter had access to a "knowing" that had impressed them or surprised them in the past, but her foresight had always entailed more joyful, upcoming occasions or problem-solving activities; they seemed to involve Lizzie most often. This time, a nightmare had awoken her, frightened her – and Lizzie as well. Two months later, on the morning of the previously foreseen but thereafter forgotten event, Promise began her day feeling unexplainably distressed, and therefore inconsolable. Understanding this extrasensory experience incorrectly could make a ten-year-old afraid of her dreams, suspicious of her feelings, even uncomfortable living in her very skin. How might they help her?

Tara sat with them in silence for a few moments as she formulated her thoughts. She found herself reflecting on her own observations of Promise over the years, along with a nagging sense that some of this felt familiar, maybe even destined. She still could not resolve that intuition, but she did let it guide her response in the present.

She began, "This has so many layers to it. Let's deal with them one by one, starting with the abstract and then making it more personal and practical."

Everyone nodded their agreement.

Tara continued, "I know we four have talked about eleven dimensions in the universe in the past, but let's keep it simple for now. We have the tangible realm of our human experience; we also have the hidden realms – the ones we may sense via intuition, empathy, or dreams, or perhaps access with past-life regression, but which we cannot perceive with our five senses alone. Most people live their lives only aware of the tangible realm. Yet, we four have all experienced the intangible, mostly through dreams and intuitions, empathic pick-ups, and sometimes more intentional methods. We have done this as adults, however. We are capable of abstract thinking, so the hidden realms are easier to contemplate with our capacity for multilayered understanding."

Again, everyone nodded. Tara could sense that Brittany and Peter were beginning to relax as they realized there might be a way to help Promise.

Tara continued, "Promise is young, still too young to fully comprehend abstract thought, although she is precocious, bright, and clearly on her way to developing that ability. Most children begin to think abstractly around the age of twelve. I always chuckle when I remember asking a younger child, 'How did you sleep last night?' His answer, 'With my eyes closed,' truly reflected a more concrete level of thinking. You may both be noticing this subtle difference as Promise's comprehension diverges from Lizzie's understanding of similar experiences."

Peter smiled. He quickly reflected on how his renditions of the Prometheus myth had changed over the years and how he told it a little differently to each of his daughters when they weren't together. Yes, he still had to modify his storytelling for both of them, but Promise seemed to apprehend something still unseen by Lizzie. He chose not to interrupt Tara with his thoughts, however. Thus, she continued.

"Her developing capacity for abstract thought points to the possibility of talking with her most directly about her gift when she turns twelve or thirteen and begins to truly grasp the implications of what it can mean to be receptive to information from another, intangible realm. Still, we must also figure out how to help her handle it now."

Brittany agreed. "We do, Tara. She already senses that something dramatic has happened. She has observed that my car is gone, and she knows that I will be driving a rental. We've stalled the inevitable conversation by telling her my car isn't available for driving right now because it needs repairs, but we haven't said anything more. We have assured her that everyone is fine, although she can sense that Peter is still unnerved by the whole thing. I am too, of course, but not so much as he is. We need to tell her something more accurate without overwhelming her. Any suggestions?"

Tara nodded. "Yes, you are right, Brittany. She needs to know more of the truth so that she does not begin to doubt her own sensitivities. She needs to trust her inner signals and to know that someday she can learn how to interpret them more accurately. Without that inner trust of her own feelings and knowing, she will never feel safe or comfortable in her own skin. Until she can understand those messages for herself, she will need to know that she can share her perceptions with someone who will not criticize her for being crazy, too sensitive, or overly scared. She will need a trusted adult or adults to help her carry the information while also keeping everyone as safe as possible.

"Perhaps, Peter, you may want to tell her exactly what happened and that because she had her dream and shared it with you, it saved your life. Hopefully, she will then realize that her knowing can have a lifesaving purpose. The challenges will come, unfortunately, when the messages she receives confuse her or when people refuse to listen. That's when some support and training will be crucial for her. Perhaps you can tell her that when she gets old enough, you will make sure she receives what she needs in that regard."

"That makes perfect sense, Tara." Peter replied.

"But who will teach her?" Brittany asked. "Would you consider providing that for her, Tara?"

Tara smiled. For some strange reason, she thought of Alethea in that moment, how she had once told her that they had taken turns serving as each other's teacher across lifetimes. Why not for her godchild as well? She sincerely replied, "I would be honored to do that with her."

Simultaneously, Peter and Brittany both sighed with relief. Everyone noticed and laughed. Alex had finished the food preparation, so together they worked on setting the table and filling their plates.

Peter began to relax with the realization that perhaps this whole experience had happened for a reason. Promise would begin to appreciate that she had an extraordinary ability. His own trauma began to ease as he named a meaningful purpose for it all. He privately vowed that he would diligently help his daughter to recognize, understand, and value the preciousness of her extrasensory gifts as she grew.

9

AS THEY DROVE HOME, Peter and Brittany decided they would speak with Promise the next day while Lizzie visited with a friend. They hoped to eventually talk with their youngest as well, but they felt clear that Promise needed their attention first. They arrived home to find Amy, an attractive fourteen-year-old, comfortably slouched on the couch, her eyes glued to her phone. All seemed quiet upstairs. Fonzy, now thirteen and no longer as limber in his older age, apparently decided not to leave his post with the girls.

Amy seemed glad to see them. She immediately closed the app on her phone and rose to greet them. She described a fairly quiet evening, casually noting that Promise seemed much less engaged than usual. Lizzie tried to coax her sister along with some success but not much. They both went to bed without argument. Amy thanked Peter and Brittany for the pizza. She had nothing more to report.

Peter expressed his appreciation and handed her their agreed upon compensation plus a gracious tip. Amy smiled gratefully in response to his generosity and offered to be available any time they needed her in the future. Brittany and Peter acknowledged their own gratitude for her willingness to make an occasional night out possible for them. Amy lived in their neighborhood, so Peter made sure she arrived home safely. He returned to find Brittany completing what little cleanup was needed in the kitchen.

After they turned out the lights and proceeded upstairs, Brittany quickly sensed something amiss. Peter had peeked into Lizzie's room and determined that she was fast asleep. He gently tucked her blankets around her and planned to do the same for Promise. Instead, he found Brittany standing at their older daughter's bedroom door, left ajar, with a pained look on her face. Joining her, he immediately understood as he heard Promise crying into her pillow, trying not to be heard. Fonzy stood guard near the head of her bed as protector.

Peter and Brittany silently agreed that their intended conversation might take place sooner than they had anticipated. After gently knocking on her door, they entered together. Brittany turned on the bedside lamp as they each found a spot to sit on her bed near her pillow. Promise covered her head with her blanket and turned away.

Her parents exchanged glances of alarm. Peter gently removed the covers, took Promise into his arms, and put her on his lap facing Brittany. Promise covered her face. Peter asked her, "Honey, what's wrong?"

Promise cried out as she turned her face into his chest and tried to cover her head with her arms. Her anguish ripped their hearts in two. Brittany opted to empathically attune to her daughter's distress and thought she sensed intense shame. She silently mouthed the word to Peter. His brow furrowed in response.

He held his daughter close while Brittany spoke what she intuited Promise needed to hear: "Promise, honey, Daddy and I are here for you. You seem very upset. We want to help you feel better. Can you tell us what is upsetting you so much?"

Promise gasped between her sobs as if considering her mother's invitation before she vehemently shook her head to communicate her no response.

Brittany looked like she, too, might begin to cry, but she continued, "Sweetheart, I sense that something or someone has made you feel ashamed of yourself. I know these past few days have been difficult for you. Daddy and I were planning to talk with you about all that tomorrow. But this feels like something else, something worse than that. Am I right?"

Promise nodded her head in the affirmative, then sobbed again.

Brittany's and Peter's eyes met in a determined agreement to protect their daughter. Brittany continued, "Honey, Daddy and I want you to know that we love you very much. There is nothing that you, as a ten-year-old girl, could possibly have done to make you feel so much shame. There is nothing you might do that would ever make you a bad person, certainly not in our eyes. Did someone else make you feel that way?"

Promise seemed to calm a bit in response to her mother's comfort. Peter stroked her head and back to physically affirm Brittany's compassion. In the quiet of the next few moments, Promise nodded her head, yes.

Peter and Brittany sighed deeply, simultaneously. Peter's intuition peaked now. He asked her, "Did they tell you not to say anything to anyone about what happened?"

Promise again nodded her yes with her face still buried in Peter's chest.

He responded, "Well, I don't know who told you not to tell, but you need to know that you can always tell us anything. That never breaks a promise or goes against someone else's instruction. We are your parents. We are here to take care of you and to help you sort things out. That's how you learn. We are here to guide you and to keep you safe."

Brittany added, "There is nothing you can tell us that will make us love you less. We will help you to deal with this, sweetheart, whatever it is."

Another few minutes went by. Peter could feel his daughter's slender form relaxing in his arms. He nodded to Brittany. Together, they knew to patiently wait until Promise felt ready to share her story. Peter continued to stroke her back.

Promise finally turned toward them, her face soaked with tears. Brittany offered her a tissue and also gently wiped her young one's reddened, wet cheeks. Promise gulped a breath of air. Peter suggested she take a deep breath, then another. He could sense her deepening surrender to their care.

Trying to divine the best timing, Brittany ventured her softly spoken question once again: "Promise, can you tell us what happened?"

Promise couldn't help it; she gulped again. Peter kissed her forehead. Promise looked directly into their eyes now and felt their love for her. Their eyes were not at all like those of Mrs. Greenwich.

Promise nodded her yes. Then, pausing frequently, she replied, "This morning, Mr. Higgins asked for volunteers to pick up our new textbooks from Mrs. Greenwich's office.... I offered to go with four other kids.... Christopher, new to our class, came too. He had a bruise on his jaw, though.... When he handed me my pile of books, I saw his father hit him in his jaw! His father was not there with us, but I saw it just the same. I felt really bad for Christopher.... I didn't know what to do!"

Promise became more upset. The tears rolled down her cheeks. Brittany gently wiped them as she said, "That must have been really scary and confusing."

Promise nodded. "Christopher must have noticed the look on my face because he seemed scared. He backed away from me! Mrs. Greenwich saw the whole thing. She told me to come into her private office. Then she closed the door behind us, while everybody else waited for the secretary to hand them some books."

At this point, Promise's face turned scarlet once again.

Brittany immediately responded, "Honey, remember we love you. You have not done anything wrong."

Promise looked into her mother's eyes, then blurted out, "Mrs. Greenwich said I did! She said I shouldn't tell lies! That I shouldn't make up stories that will be too hard to deal with. She told me not to tell anyone else!" She lowered her eyes at this point, sobbed, then covered her face with her hands once again.

Peter and Brittany were aghast, wishing they could have had their planned conversation sooner. This was Tara's worst-case scenario. Peter drew his young, sensitive child closer and kissed the top of her head. Brittany gently stroked her daughter's arms. She softly but firmly stated, "Honey, Mrs. Greenwich doesn't understand. She did not help you. She unintentionally hurt you. You are good, Promise. You have a gift. You see things other people don't see, and it saved Daddy's life."

Hearing this, Promise lowered her hands and gazed directly at her father, arching her brow in confusion and wonder.

Peter more carefully explained, "Promise, do you remember the dream you had soon after school started? You saw a truck come down a hill before it crashed into Mama's car, which I happened to be driving in your dream?"

Promise nodded.

He continued, "Well, yesterday, I had to drive Mama's car to an appointment because my car needed an inspection at the shop. I was driving up a great big hill when her car broke down. I pulled it over to the side of the road and realized a hose had sprung a major leak. I would need to get a tow. Just as I reached inside the car for my phone, a great big eighteen-wheeler came barreling down the hill toward me. I remembered your dream and took it seriously. I started to run away from the car. The truck then blew out a tire and swerved. It crashed into Mama's car and set it on fire. Later, the truck caught fire too.

Because of your dream and your willingness to tell it to me, I knew to run, even before the truck started to swerve. That's what saved my life!"

Promise sat there, speechless. She looked to Brittany who simply nodded her confirmation as tears streamed down her own cheeks. They gave Promise a few minutes to appreciate the implications of their experience.

Brittany then added, "You were edgy that morning. We couldn't figure out why. None of us were thinking about your dream at the time."

"That's why I was so relieved to see you at daycare!" Promise exclaimed. "You seemed upset, Daddy, but I was so glad to know you were otherwise okay! I didn't remember the dream either."

Brittany added, "You probably don't remember that before Lizzie was born, you knew our baby would be a girl. You were just three years old then. Two years later, you were telling us at home and your teachers at daycare what Lizzie needed without her having to say a word. Do you remember that?"

Promise nodded with dawning recognition of something she had never put into words before. She asked, "So, what about Christopher? I saw his father hit him. Was that real?" She seemed genuinely concerned.

Peter replied, "It's hard to know for certain, honey, but we can try to find out. We are all just learning about the nature of your dreams, your visions, and your ability to know unseen things. I can do some exploring that won't get anyone into trouble. It is important to keep him safe while we try to sort out what's real and what's a warning. With warnings, we can make changes to prevent the bad thing from happening in the future. That was your gift to me yesterday. What's real would be something that is happening now or that has already happened. The fact that Christopher already had a bruise suggests it may have already happened. People can get bruised for lots of reasons, though. I will do my best to figure this out, okay?"

A tear rolled down Promise's cheek, but her face was no longer red. Brittany could sense her daughter's energy as lighter, less burdened, more relieved. She took the opportunity to add, "Promise, Daddy is right. We all need to learn more about this. When you get to be old enough – maybe in two or three years – you can meet with Aunt Tara, who can teach you more about your experiences and how to understand them and use them. In the meantime, please tell Daddy or me what is happening for you. We can figure out what is going on together. You do not have to bear this alone."

Peter reinforced this last point: "Promise, we really want you to know that you never have to face this alone. Okay?"

Promise nodded, then reached out to her mother for a hug. Brittany added several kisses to the mix before Peter got his turn for hugs and kisses as well. Relieved of her enormous burden, Promise lay back in her bed. Her parents tucked her in with another kiss from each of them, then she quickly fell asleep.

Peter and Brittany were now also exhausted beyond measure. As they made their way to their own bedroom, Peter quietly whispered, "Mrs. Greenwich will be hearing from me on Monday!"

10

SATURDAY AND SUNDAY PASSED rather uneventfully. During both afternoons, Brittany enlisted the help of her daughters to make luscious desserts in anticipation of their extended family's Thanksgiving feast later that week. In quieter moments, Peter privately contemplated how to best approach Mrs. Greenwich regarding his concerns for Promise and Christopher.

Monday dawned crisp and sunny. The girls had three half-days of school that week to accommodate the parent-teacher conferences scheduled during those afternoons. Peter had already arranged a time to meet with Promise's homeroom teacher. He made a call that morning to coordinate a discussion with her principal as well.

Fortunately, the appointments for Promise occurred soon after Monday's dismissal. Lizzie would be transported by bus directly from her elementary school to daycare, so Peter went directly to the middle school where he found Promise waiting for him as planned. With an affectionate smile, he invited her to lunch. She was thrilled about that, of course, but not at all about the meeting commitments that would precede it.

Promise stood patiently in the hallway outside her classroom while Peter met with her homeroom teacher. Peter rejoined her with a grin on his face. He quickly informed Promise that she had received a glowing report. This eased some of the tension between her shoulders, but the focus of the next meeting weighed heavily upon her. Peter understood this. He hoped, however, that Mrs. Greenwich would apologize to his daughter. He wanted a more complete healing.

Mrs. Greenwich's facial expression registered her surprise when she realized that Promise had accompanied her father. Promise felt immediately intimidated. Peter greeted Mrs. Greenwich cordially, then asked Promise to wait in the secretary's area while he and her principal had their discussion. Promise shyly nodded and, finding a seat, complied with his request.

Peter entered the principal's office. Mrs. Greenwich closed the door behind them. Promise tried hard not to fret.

Peter spoke first. "Mrs. Greenwich, thank you for seeing me on such short notice. I know you must be very busy, so I will get directly to the point. My daughter told me about what happened on Friday with Christopher. I know this may not make sense to you, but she does have an uncanny ability to sense things that are not obvious to everyone else. She is still learning how to understand this gift, as are we, her parents. She left your office feeling very shamed. I am hoping we can address this today and also ensure that Christopher is safe."

Mrs. Greenwich had years of experience talking with parents from every economic, ethnic, and educational background. Yet this particular parent's presentation of an issue – and the issue itself – had never crossed her desk. Her initial astonishment at seeing Promise in the waiting area only deepened now. This situation had become truly peculiar.

Mrs. Greenwich paused, considering how much she could legally and respectfully share with this parent, who clearly would not be bamboozled by vagueness or obfuscation. She decided that his point had serious merit and that his daughter's emotional well-being deserved and required an explanation. She took a risk while trying to honor the rules.

She replied, "Mr. Holmes, I sincerely regret the way I handled the situation last Friday. I hope you can appreciate how unusual this is. I am legally not at liberty to share any details with you, but if you will agree to keep this confidential, I will tell you what I can. I, too, am concerned about Promise – and Christopher. Will you agree to this?"

Now it was Peter's turn for surprise. He had not expected this to go as smoothly as her initial words seemed to suggest. He said for the record, "I will honor your confidence so long as it does not harm my daughter. That's the best I can do."

Mrs. Greenwich silently pondered his response for a few moments, then nodded her agreement. She continued, "After my encounter with Christopher and Promise Friday morning, I later learned that Christopher had shared with his teacher some information that supported Promise's insight. I do not know how your daughter knew. Nevertheless, we have followed our protocol for such matters, and we hope it will resolve for the best. That is all I can tell you."

Peter sat very still as he tried to process what this meant for Promise and how to best approach it. What could he tell her about Christopher? Only honesty would validate her experience. How would she manage that? It felt important for her to know that the adults in her world had taken measures to keep her classmate safe. She also needed healing for the shame she experienced. Not only would it impact her long-term relationship with Mrs. Greenwich and all future principals, but it would affect her sense of self and her psychic gift for the rest of her life.

Peter finally stated, "Mrs. Greenwich, thank you for sharing this with me. I am glad to know that strategies are in place to keep Christopher safe. Promise needs to understand that as well, and that you no longer think she was telling lies. She felt very shamed by your reproach. Nothing less will do from my perspective."

Mrs. Greenwich nodded in agreement. She replied, "Let's invite Promise to join us. I will apologize and reassure her of Christopher's safety. Would that be all right with you?"

"Yes, it would. Thank you."

Mrs. Greenwich rose from her seat, proceeded to open her door, then summoned Promise to come in. Promise seemed stunned and even more intimidated. Mrs. Greenwich realized she had used her principal's voice to issue the invitation. She softened it immediately and offered more encouragement: "Promise, please, come join your father and me. We have something we want to share with you."

Promise saw Peter wink at her, so she more comfortably entered her principal's office. She immediately went to Peter and planted herself next to him.

Mrs. Greenwich stayed on Peter and Promise's side of her desk and sat in the unoccupied chair. She began, "Promise, I regret the way I spoke to you on Friday. You took a risk sharing your experience with me. I want to applaud you for your courage and your concern for Christopher. In response to what you told me, I explored the situation more fully. I want to assure you that the adults are doing what they need to do to keep him safe."

Promise's eyes opened wide. She stood still at her father's side, speechless. The redness and heat that had threatened to resurface on her face subsided without a trace. Her principal now gazed at her with kindness in her eyes. Promise didn't know what to say.

Mrs. Greenwich sighed deeply as she finally recognized the sensitivity of this child standing mutely before her. She realized how painful their interaction on Friday must have been for her. She made a note to herself to be more attentive to this potential depth of feeling with other students in the future. She decided to take her apology one step further.

"Promise, I also want you to know that if, down the road, you have other experiences like you did with Christopher on Friday, I welcome you to share them with me privately. I do not want you to think that I will assume you are crazy or lying or anything bad. I will just need to quietly investigate to make sure everyone is safe and that no one is falsely accused or alarmed. Would that be okay with you?"

A tear fell down Promise's cheek as she nodded her yes. Peter put his arm around his daughter, who turned to hug him gratefully. He managed to keep his own emotions in check as he verbally expressed his gratitude to Mrs. Greenwich for her support.

She appreciatively responded to Peter, "You're welcome, Mr. Holmes. Thank you for bringing this to my attention. Promise is an excellent student. We are happy to have her here."

Promise shifted her stance to look more directly at Mrs. Greenwich. In that moment, she sensed that her principal really meant her spoken words. She replied, "Thank you, Mrs. Greenwich."

Upon the successful conclusion of their meeting, Peter and Promise left the office and promptly went to lunch. They opted for Promise's favorite restaurant. Her giggles returned as she enjoyed her special time with her dad. Peter sighed his private relief, then gave her more reasons to laugh. They enjoyed their time together thoroughly, bought something special for Lizzie, then picked her up at daycare.

The Thanksgiving holiday held a new spaciousness. This day's deep healing and reconciliation would meaningfully enhance their family's celebration of gratitude over the coming days.

11

AS THE CHRISTMAS HOLIDAYS swiftly approached, Peter and Brittany had many private discussions about their concerns for Fonzy. He was thirteen now; his gracious years had already exceeded the average age for a golden retriever. He rose more slowly from resting to standing positions, ate less food, managed the steps with noticeable effort, then gingerly found a way to rest once again. They had made numerous accommodations for him in his advancing years, ever so grateful for his presence. Still, they sadly realized that Nature would reclaim him as Her own in the not-too-distant future.

Promise and Lizzie had taken Fonzy's limitations in stride, only partially comprehending what their parents told them about the aches and pains of growing older and how he might not be with them much longer. As their parents tried to balance the reality of his impending death with a desire not to alarm their daughters, the girls remained blissfully oblivious until Promise had another dream.

Her vision woke her in the middle of the night, propelling her to tearfully negotiate the darkened hallway to her parents' bedroom. Lizzie overheard her sister's crying and followed quickly at her heels. Peter and Brittany groggily awoke, then snapped to attention at the sight of Promise's distress. They could still hear Fonzy snoring in her bedroom, where he lay at the foot of her bed.

Promise then shared her dream. "We are all having dinner together, laughing and having fun. Suddenly, we notice that we don't hear Fonzy's snoring. We look over to the corner where he is sleeping on his favorite cushion. He isn't snoring or breathing anymore. Daddy, you tell us he is gone."

Promise really started to cry at the sound of her own words. Lizzie did too. Peter and Brittany glanced toward each other, silently acknowledging that their daughter's dream echoed their own expectations. Would it happen just as Promise envisioned it? They could not know for sure.

Brittany and Peter invited Promise and Lizzie into their bed and held them close to offer what comfort they could. Peter carefully explained, "Girls, Fonzy is a very special dog and a very important member of our family. We all love him, and he loves each one of us. Sadly, dogs don't live as long as humans. He has already lived longer than most dogs do. There is a good chance that he may pass into Heaven soon. His love will always be with us, but his dog's body probably won't."

The girls cried even more. A tear trickled down Brittany's cheek as well. Peter did his best to stay centered, but his own heart felt near to sobbing. As he thought about all those times when Fonzy lay at his shoeless feet or retrieved a stick or sat by the bedside protecting the girls, his own tears began to flow. They cried together, locked in a family embrace.

Fonzy's snoring stopped; Brittany was the first to notice. Moments later, he joined them in Peter and Brittany's bedroom, tail wagging. Promise reached out her hand. He came to her readily. Peter carefully got out of bed and gathered Fonzy in his arms, then deposited him on the bedcovers, where he curled up and soon began to snore once again.

"He is still with us for now," Peter said with an appreciative smile. "We have the chance to treat him really well and love him as much as we can before it is his time to go. Shall we make the most of it?"

They looked to one another and spontaneously exhaled their answer, "Yes!"

Lizzie added, "Can we start right now by all sleeping together tonight?"

Brittany and Peter silently consulted each other, trying to read each other's face in the dim light. They both had long days to manage with the coming of sunrise, but this opportunity would not reliably come again. They nodded their agreement, then put it into words. They all found a way to be comfortable, then fell asleep to the sound of their night music, wanting to hear it forever but grateful for the now.

The holiday festivities included extra dog treats, more hugs and love pats, and frequent checks on Fonzy's needs and well-being. They were careful not to leave him alone for prolonged periods. They also included him in all their family rituals and photos. Fonzy loved all the attention. On New Year's Day, he seemed to perk up considerably. While Brittany made chocolate chip cookies in the kitchen, the girls played with him in the living room, creating mayhem during the televised football game, but Peter didn't care. He decided to get down on the floor himself, the perfect invitation for Fonzy and the girls to jump on top of him. Pandemonium reigned supreme.

Later, as they all sat at the dining room table, eating their meal and reflecting on the fun of the day, Promise suddenly sensed a loss that diverted her attention to Fonzy. Just as in her dream, he lay on his favorite cushion, now lifeless. Her facial expression and the tears streaming down her cheeks immediately directed everyone's attention to their loyal companion, who breathed and snored no more. Peter sighed, then rose from his seat, followed by Brittany, whose own face was now flooded with tears. Lizzie sat in shock at first, but she, too, soon began to cry. They gathered round him and sobbed their goodbyes. When they felt ready, they wrapped his body in his favorite blanket. Peter planned to bury Fonzy in the backyard the following day.

Brittany suggested that the girls find something they might want to leave with him in his grave. They each identified one of his favorite toys and added something of their own for him to remember them by. The next morning, Peter dug the hole, then they all gathered to gently set their furry beloved in his final resting place. Brittany said some prayers for Fonzy and for them, including that they would always remember their cherished family member and never forget his love. She hoped their love for him would send him on his way to Heaven and that they would see him again when it was their turn to join him.

Everyone helped to cover Fonzy with dirt, filling the hole again so that he would become one with the earth. They stood at his graveside as Peter reminded them that Fonzy would be with them everywhere; whenever their feet touched the ground, he would be part of their lives.

Grief-stricken, they returned to the family kitchen. Brittany made some hot chocolate and served it with her chocolate chip cookies while inviting each of them to tell Fonzy stories to honor his life. Before too long they laughed as they cried. She also made sure to tell them, "We are all going to be very sad – for the next few weeks, especially. It's okay to be sad. We will comfort one another. And we all have to remember that Fonzy isn't hurting anymore. He is really comfortable now, and everyone is going to be all right. Okay?"

Their reluctant, saddened acknowledgments made their way to one another's ears. The girls slept together that night. Amidst the stillness of heartache, life went on.

12

PROMISE SAT COMFORTABLY in her Aunt Tara's healing room, holding the rose quartz orb in her thirteen-year-old hands. She smiled as she palmed its smoothness and reflected on her memories of sharing it with Lizzie over the years. Tara joined her in the joy of those recollections even though she also sensed that a more troubling emotion lurked not far beneath her godchild's pleasant demeanor. Hopefully, Promise would trust her enough to share her deeper feelings. If so, Tara anticipated that a new chapter in their relationship would begin.

Promise, now an eighth grader, had blossomed into a very attractive teenager. Some of the age's awkwardness prevented her from noticing her own beauty as she occasionally found herself caught up in comparisons with her friends. Fortunately, she had discovered the benefits of jogging and singing to help keep her moods relatively even and her sense of self mostly intact – at least for appearances. Still, there were many occurrences that seriously challenged the stable persona she worked so hard to present.

The time had finally come for Promise to learn more about her abilities to sense the hidden realms. Tara had given considerable thought as to how they might proceed to explore such a daunting topic. It could easily become "heady," and that might be helpful at some point, but Tara had learned from her own years of practice that she had to honor the feelings first. With that awareness, she gently approached Promise's experience with respectful questions.

"Promise, I think you know that your mom and dad have shared with me how you sometimes have dreams and visions about things that no one else seems to be able to sense or interpret. I'm wondering what that has been like for you."

Promise looked directly into the eyes of her cherished godmother. Her gaze spoke volumes. Instead, she shrugged her teenage shoulders and said, "Sometimes, it's fun when I can impress my friends. Sometimes, it's hard when what I see is scary or sad. It's especially bad when the people involved don't want to know, or I have the feeling that I shouldn't tell them. Mom and Dad have been good about helping me figure some of this out. Still, I can't control it or predict it. It feels weird."

Tara nodded. "I'll bet it does! How do you make sense of it?"

Promise replied, "I can't, really. I figure that God wants me to warn some people, to keep some people safe, to help others, and sometimes just to know things, but when the people are strangers, or they don't want to know, I don't know what to do."

"That can definitely be difficult to deal with." In response to an intuition, Tara then asked, "Promise, I'm also wondering, do you ever feel sad, but you don't know why?"

Her goddaughter looked up suddenly and met Tara's eyes with recognition and surprise. "Yes, why?"

"Well, it may be that you also know things because your feelings tell you, even if you don't have a dream or a vision."

"Really?" Promised wondered aloud, feeling both interested and perplexed.

"Yes." Tara explained, "The sadness you feel – and it can be any feeling, for that matter – may belong to someone else, not you. *You* may not really be sad, although you do feel it. Often, figuring out who the sadness truly belongs to can free you from having that feeling. Has that ever happened to you?"

Promise paused. She thought about how she had left her home in a great mood last Tuesday. She met with her friend Megan, who smiled well enough and seemed fine. As they made their way to school together, Promise couldn't explain why she suddenly felt so unhappy. She found herself feeling like she wanted to cry, but she couldn't come up with a reason. Later that day, Megan shared in confidence that her mother had criticized her on her way out the door that morning, once again for something she hadn't even done. It upset Megan greatly. As soon as her friend acknowledged her own feeling, Promise's sadness left her. Promise shared this experience with her aunt. Tara sighed and smiled.

"Promise, it sounds like we will need to address this kind of knowing as well. Are you up for learning more about all this?"

Promise nodded with curiosity. She desperately wanted to understand herself better. But how might her godmother help her? She had to ask, "Have you ever had such feelings and experiences, Aunt Tara?"

Tara nodded. "Yes, Promise. It took me over thirty years to finally *begin* to figure out how I'm wired and what it's for. I didn't have anyone to help me in my youth. I'm guessing you've felt very alone and confused…?"

Tears welled up in her godchild's eyes, surprising them both. Embarrassed, Promise quickly tried to wipe them away.

Tara tried to reassure her, "When most people don't understand what you feel and how you know things, and maybe they react poorly when they get a hint of it, perhaps it makes you feel strange, like something is wrong with you?"

Promise seemed to shrink in stature right before her aunt's eyes. Tara's heart broke for her godchild's suffering even as she wanted to celebrate the possibility that this period of turmoil might come to an end.

Tara emphatically stated, "There is *nothing* wrong with you, Promise. Do you hear me? NOTHING!!! You have a gift. If you will share with me what you feel and what you experience, I will hopefully be able to help you make sense of all this. It will take some time, though. We can meet every few weeks, or as often as you like or need to. But I really think I can help you to not only understand your gift, but to figure out how to fit into the world with a sense of belonging. Would you like to do this with me?"

Promise gazed into the loving eyes of her godmother and knew in an instant that this was the answer to her prayers. Still, she hesitated. Tara sensed this and asked, "Do you have concerns about what we might do together?"

Promise paused and stared at her feet. She didn't know how to answer. Finally, she decided to confess, "Aunt Tara, will you tell my parents what we talk about?"

The question did not surprise Tara. She simply wished she had thought to discuss it directly. She honestly replied, "Only if you want me to – or if I'm really worried about you for some reason. In that case, I would tell you before I tell them. Would that be okay with you?"

Promise considered these conditions. "Okay."

"Can you tell me what you're worried about, Promise? It would simply help me understand better. Maybe it even ties in with what we will learn together. You know I love your parents very much, but from now on, you are my first priority."

Again, Promise paused. She mustered her courage and replied, "I know my dad wanted to name me after Prometheus. He thinks I'm a light bearer like my namesake. That's very kind of him, really, but I don't feel like one. Instead, I often feel dark and heavy. What if I fail? How will Dad feel? What if I'm not like Prometheus at all? Truth is, I really don't know who or what I am...."

Tears fell freely as she tried to cover her reddened face. In response, Tara felt her own heart break once again. She immediately went to Promise's side and held her in a warm embrace. They rocked back and forth for several minutes. Tara kissed her godchild's crown.

When Promise stopped crying, Tara pulled away to make direct eye contact with her as she gently said, "Honey, your dad loves you very much. He is a wise man and, yes, he really admires Prometheus. I am also certain that he really wants nothing more than for you to become who *you* truly are. Someday, hopefully, you will both have a conversation about this, but I will not interfere by telling him now. I promise.

"As for not knowing who you are, that is truly wonderful, believe it or not. And it also makes sense. When you are sensitive to so much information as it comes from the hidden realms through your dreams, visions, and feelings – and most of that information belongs to other people – how can you have figured out who you are at thirteen years of age? The truth is, at a much deeper level, we are all a mystery. That you feel like a mystery to yourself tells me that you are in touch with that deeper level. You are more than what everyone thinks you are. Because of that, though, they can't tell you who you are or what you are, although they may try. Your life can be an amazing journey of discovery as you try to come to know your own truth."

Promise sat very still in the silence that followed. She eventually asked, "So, how do I figure that out? How long will it take? And how do I live in the meantime?"

Tara smiled and patted her godchild's arms as she answered, "You live just as you are. You are thirteen years old. You love your family. You are in eighth grade. You jog, sing, and enjoy your friends. As for the rest, not everyone will understand, but then not everyone has to. You can share your questions with me as that feels right to you. I can certainly teach you some things, and we can learn about your deeper truth together if you like."

"Does this mean I have a secret life? Should I not share this with my friends?"

Tara replied, "You have one life, Promise. We all do. But none of us shares everything we think and feel with others. We always keep some things private. Many people feel badly about themselves, and that's what they keep private. You may have done this yourself at times. What's different is that you also sense things that other people can't experience directly. It may frighten some of them. Part of what you will need to learn is when and how to share your deeper truth with only certain others. This does not mean you are lying or bad. It only means that you are choosing to be private about some things. *Everyone* is private about some things!"

Promise sighed with obvious relief. Feeling much more comfortable about all this, she asked, "Aunt Tara, how will I get to know myself better? If people can't tell me, what can?"

"Well, your dreams can tell you. So can your feelings. But it takes understanding and guidance to interpret them. That's what we can do together."

Promise felt compelled to explore further: "So, do you mean that not all my dreams are about what will happen or what can happen to other people? Can they mean something else?"

"Absolutely, they can," Tara replied. "They simply tell you about what's unconscious, what's unseen and unknown at that point in time. Dreams can relate to the past, to the future, to a fear in the present that may or may never come true, to something forgotten, to something that *might* happen but won't necessarily, even to some part of yourself that your awareness needs to know. Sorting all this out can be a real challenge. It can take years of practice," Tara counseled.

Promise paused again as she more deeply pondered something that had confused her greatly. She eventually asked, "Can I tell you a dream I had last night? It seemed really strange to me. I didn't want to tell my dad because I think it's just about a piece of crystal he has on his bookshelf. It's just that the crystal was huge! It rose high in the sky. The sun sparkled through it and made a rainbow all around the buildings nearby; they were strange too, shaped like pyramids. How weird! People wore funny looking clothes, almost like the ancient Romans we learned about in class. Nothing bad happened. It just felt so real. Does this make any sense? Can some dreams be just weird? Or do they all mean something?"

Tara's facial expression could not hide her shock that Promise would have this dream. It so clearly paralleled the imagery that she, Alex, and Peter had dreamt when they first met many, many years ago. By sharing their dreams, they realized that they had experienced a prior lifetime together. Was Promise part of that lifetime? If so, who was she?! At this point, Tara couldn't know. She had to explain her reaction, though. Promise had already begun to emotionally retreat.

"Dreams usually do mean something, Promise. I'm looking surprised because this is the same vision that I had in a dream long ago. Uncle Alex and your dad also had similar dreams. We discovered that connection soon after we met. Honestly, I don't know what it means that you have also had this dream. I am glad that we will work together, though. Maybe between the two of us, we will figure this out!"

Feeling reassured that her confusion might be shared with respect, Promise responded, "That's what my dad always says!"

Tara added, "And he's usually right!"

13

TARA AND PROMISE CONTINUED to meet every few weeks as Promise blossomed into a beautiful fifteen-year-old who looked more like Brittany every day. Sophomore year offered her a new set of challenges, academically as well as socially, while she also tried to keep up with her gifted program's requirements and still participate in track and chorus. Dating became a hot issue among her friends. Their pressured invitations for her to join them, especially for school dances, weighed heavily upon her. Promise longed for a deeper relationship, but most of the boys her age would not react well to knowing her backstory. On some level, this still made her feel unlikable inside. Tara tried to help her godchild with only limited success.

Thanks to her aunt, Promise had learned Reiki as well as some energy exercises and a few additional strategies to assess and calm her inner, less conscious responses to complicated situations. Her aunt and her mother were also teaching her a tapping technique to help her deal with her emotionally overwhelming reactions. These practices all provided great benefit, but most of her friends thought them strange. She quickly learned to keep them to herself, which only added to her sense of isolation. She did her best to cope.

Tara noticed the stress that these social encounters presented to her godchild. She reflected quite often on this very real dilemma. Promise's challenge during this stage in her life involved the development of more personal autonomy and less reliance upon her parents as she forged deeper relationships with peers. This would lead to an increasing sense of independence while offering the support of belonging with friends. Independence and belonging – opposite sides of the same coin. Unfortunately, living into one of these conditions sometimes negated an experience of the other, like being able to see only one side of a quarter at a time. Tara understood, however, that these two qualities, as opposites, eventually needed to be held in conscious balance.

Instead, Promise was mastering independence at the expense of belonging. Tara reflected on her own history and recognized that she had not been able to find peace amidst these contradictions until, as an adult, she could identify friends who respected her gifts. Promise had not yet been blessed in this regard. Tara could easily attribute this lack to the mindset and developmental stage of her peers, who defined their belonging according to prevailing social norms. She could only empathize with her godchild's predicament and trust that their ongoing contacts with each other might offer Promise some consolation. Tara also said more than one prayer that Promise would hold on to hope.

As sophomore year progressed through autumn, then winter, spring soon arrived along with the beginning of track season and a flurry of galas and proms. Her friend Megan had begun dating a junior, so not only did the upcoming sophomore dance take over many of their discussions, but his junior status added that class's social activities to the mix.

In her excitement, Megan begged Promise to double date with her for the junior prom. Megan even asked her boyfriend, Steve, to find a date for Promise. Promise felt reluctant to spend the evening with a stranger, but she acquiesced to the expectations of friendship in the end. She told herself it would only be for a few hours. Not until the day before the dance, did she realize that Steve would be driving.

Peter reacted to this news with significant trepidation. Promise implored him not to make an issue of it, wanting so very much to please Megan and fit in with her peers. Peter and Brittany spent hours discussing this until Peter finally relented on the condition that Promise would call him should anything trigger her concern. Promise gave him her word on this. Peter also insisted that he be able to meet her traveling companions. Promise reacted to this with some apprehension, but she recognized it as best to agree. The teens made their plans.

When Megan, Steve, and his friend George arrived at the Holmes-Thomas residence, Peter greeted them at the door. He did his best to combine friendliness and intimidation as a gentle reminder that the young men should take very good care of his daughter. The fifteen minutes spent during this ritual couldn't pass fast enough for Promise. She sighed with relief as they all made their way to Steve's car.

Promise found George pleasant enough, even rather handsome. They enjoyed dancing together until his roving hands made Promise feel decidedly uncomfortable. She noticed that Megan had no difficulty allowing Steve's embrace full measure. Promise began to doubt herself as she observed many of her peers wrapped in the arms of oblivion. The chaperones clearly had their work cut out for them.

As the hours wore on, Promise realized that she had had enough. She excused herself for a restroom break and took longer than necessary while trying to strategize how to end the evening as peacefully and as quickly as possible. With only fifteen minutes left before the prom would conclude, she suspected that prolonged time in the car or a diner might be next on the agenda. She gratefully, silently thanked her father for his curfew. It couldn't come soon enough.

On her way back to the dance floor, Promise surveyed the room.

Upon seeing Steve, she suddenly envisioned the flash of an auto accident: Steve was driving as a rainy drizzle began. The road surface became slippery. He sped around a curve without accommodating for the weather. He lost control of the car. It spun and flipped. The shock of it left Promise aghast. She froze, caught in a time warp, suspended between two realities. No one seemed to notice.

The evening's event came to a close. Steve, Megan, and George were making plans for their next stop when Promise finally joined them. Megan accurately perceived her friend's level of distress and asked her about it. Promise stood motionless, seemingly unresponsive, while desperately trying to think.

Her mind assailed her with doubts: Did she have this vision because she desperately wanted to go home? What if she told them about it and nothing dangerous happened? What if she didn't tell them and an accident actually occurred? Given the potentially dire consequences if her vision proved correct, she felt compelled to share it, but the whole thing made her exceedingly nervous.

In the past, she had tried to tell Megan about some of her psychic experiences, but her friend often laughed as if Promise were trying to entertain her. Steve and George were total unknowns to her in this regard, and they clearly had another agenda for the evening. Still, despite these reservations, Promise knew she had to speak her truth. She resolved to do so, but first she inhaled deeply.

"Guys, I have to tell you that driving later tonight may be dangerous. It's going to start raining. Steve, you risk losing control of your car. If you do, it could be deadly. We should all go home now."

Having delivered her warning, she steeled herself as best she could for the forthcoming barrage. It came with a blast. Both Steve and George took offense, their reaction bordering on belligerence. Megan's eyes registered her disbelief that her best friend would ruin the evening in this way. Promise felt her face flare with humiliation, but she couldn't back down now; she felt the urgency of the situation too deeply. She begged them to listen, acknowledging that she knew her words sounded strange. She felt a strong knowing, however; it fueled her courage to adamantly assert that they would all meet a bad end if they didn't heed her cautionary advice. She insisted that they go directly home.

Steve lost all patience. He arrogantly stated, "I'm leaving now. We were planning to go to the diner after stopping somewhere to enjoy the city lights. I am still going along with that plan. Anyone who wants to come with me had better come now." Following his announcement, he turned and walked toward the exit door.

George promptly followed his friend. Megan stood paralyzed with confusion. She glanced toward Steve and watched the love of her fifteen-year-old life walking away from her. She couldn't bear it. She begged, "Promise, please tell me this is just another one of your stories. I have to tell you it's a bad one, at that. Let's go!"

"No, Megan, I can't, and you shouldn't either. Please don't!" Quickly realizing that reason would have no impact, Promise cried, "This night won't end well! Megan, please don't go! My father will drive us home. It's not safe to go with them!"

Megan threw up her arms in defeat, turned away, and walked quickly in Steve's direction. He waited for her at the door, gave Promise a profound scowl, then put his arm around his date and left Promise there to fend for herself. Tears flowed freely down her cheeks. People stared. She covered her face and ran to the restroom once again.

There, Promise called her father. Peter responded immediately and asked if she had a safe place to wait for him. She thought the front of the school building would be safe enough. He told her he would be there in minutes.

Brittany overheard their conversation with her own alarm receptors blaring. She had to stay with Lizzie, however. Peter assured her that he would call her as soon as he had Promise safely in the car.

Promise stood at the entrance to the school, alone, as peers filed past her. Chaperones also departed, not realizing what had occurred.

Peter arrived before they had even locked the doors, having challenged the speed limits whenever safety permitted. Promise quickly got into his car.

Peter took one look at her still tear-streaked face and gently asked, "What happened?"

She burst into tears. Her anguish was palpable. Peter knew immediately that there could be no good outcome to this story.

Promise exclaimed, "I had a vision. They are going to get into an accident! They wouldn't listen to me. It's going to rain, and Steve is going to take the curve too fast! The car will flip over!!" She began to sob.

Peter reached across the front seat and held his daughter tightly. He also wanted to honor his promise to Brittany. He reached for his phone and sent her a text. He knew the sound of Promise crying would unnerve her completely.

In truth, he also felt horrible worry. He did not know how to prevent this tragedy, assuming it would transpire exactly as Promise predicted. What would he do if he followed them to the diner? Could he reason with them? Could he take away the young man's keys? He doubted the latter, but he had to try something. Peter told Promise they would try.

Not knowing where else to look for them, Peter drove to the diner only to discover that Steve, Megan, and George had not yet arrived. Peter and Promise waited in the parking lot for over an hour. It began to drizzle. Promise became really upset. Peter held her hand and assured her that no matter what might happen, they had done what they could. All they could do now was pray.

After another half-hour of waiting in the pouring rain, Peter decided it was time to go home. En route, they encountered a traffic stop. They soon learned that an accident had closed down the roadway. Promise gasped. Peter cringed. They both knew simultaneously that a challenging curve lay up ahead. They could do nothing but hold each other and cry.

When they finally arrived home, they found Brittany tearfully waiting for them. Promise ran into her mother's arms and sobbed. Peter embraced them both; they all cried together. The news the next morning confirmed their worst fears. Steve and Megan had driven George home. Steve was dead at the scene. Megan had been admitted to the ICU at St. Raphael's with extensive injuries. The community was devastated.

Promise went cold deep inside. The passing days included Steve's funeral. Megan remained in the ICU, unresponsive that first week. Peter and Brittany witnessed the impact of this tragedy on their daughter, attentive to the obviously complex emotions she likely felt, while also suspecting that deeper, darker demons lurked just below the surface. What healing could possibly come?

14

DURING THE FOLLOWING MONTH, Promise socially and emotionally withdrew. She went to school but kept to herself. Many of her peers simply stared at her in the hallways between classes. Her track season ended with little luster; her coach didn't have the heart to let her go from the team. Her grades suffered from lack of class participation. She would confide in her parents only so much.

Promise maintained her connection with Lizzie, however. They had many sleepovers during which Promise would share more deeply how she felt: how she had failed her friend; how her "gift" was a curse; how no one knew how to relate to her now that George had told several of his classmates how Promise had predicted the tragedy. That news spread like an electric current in a swimming pool. Even Lizzie had heard rumors in her grade school. The sisters continued to share their feelings and experiences in the night's concealing darkness.

During one of their deeper exchanges, Promise confided that she felt at fault for the whole incident, for having agreed to attend the dance in the first place, for ultimately abandoning her friends to their fate. She wanted to shut out all psychic knowing for the rest of her life.

Lizzie reacted strongly, firmly stating, "Promise, if you had gone with them, they probably would still not have listened to you. You would have died too. If anything had happened to you, I wouldn't know how to go on. Mom and Dad would be devastated. And think about it: because you didn't go with them, George is still alive. We can only pray for Megan."

Promise saw the misery in Lizzie's eyes, matched by her own inner desolation. Lizzie reached out to hug her special, one and only sister. Promise did her best to seem comforted.

Meanwhile, Peter needed to consult with Tara. Watching Promise suffer the consequences of this tragedy bore down on his heart every minute of every day. He, too, felt at fault. He appealed to Tara, not for exoneration, however, but for guidance. Promise had resisted her meetings with Tara with excuses of headaches and fatigue. Peter knew better, but he didn't know how to help his daughter bridge the chasm surrounding her inner turmoil. He tried not to be selfish about it, but he needed her to feel better.

Tara listened carefully to Peter's doubts regarding his own decisions that horrible night. She explicitly reminded him that he had tried to balance the risks of teenage driving with his daughter's need for autonomy and independence. Promise had given him her word that she would call him if she needed him, and she had kept it. Peter also believed her when she told him about her vision. He even honored her concerns by trying to prevent the accident. Promise had received enormous validation from him and his efforts. Promise and Peter had done their best.

Tara also reminded Peter that other people had choices to make before, during, and after the dance. They made them. Their choices led to tragedy. Human life is filled with tragedies. Human life is not *only* filled with tragedies, however. Together, they agreed that Tara needed to meet with Promise. Tara would try to connect with her godchild once again.

This time, Tara went to Promise's track meet and approached her straightforwardly at its conclusion. Promise respected her aunt too much to shun her directly or to resort to seemingly less-offensive maneuvers of avoidance. Instead, she sheepishly gestured a hug in greeting and mumbled her thanks to her aunt for coming to her meet.

Tara didn't waste any time. She unequivocally made her point: "Promise, you've been avoiding me. I understand why. What has happened is incredibly painful, especially for you, and you probably want your psychic experiences to go away."

Promise raised her eyes to gaze into her aunt's. Tara recognized her godchild's agreement with her stated suspicions along with something else. She saw a strength that Promise had yet to acknowledge. Tara appreciated this insight. She would help Promise to consciously embrace her own capacity to survive and bear witness to life's heartaches and ecstasies. But first, they had to agree to meet again.

"Your psychic experiences are a part of who you are, Promise, part of your Mystery, part of your truth. If you shut them out, you might as well be dead, or go through life like the walking dead, the way you have this past month. You have a choice, Promise. You can continue to do that, or worse. Or you can make all this heartache mean something."

"Mean what?!" Promise cried. "Steve is dead, and Megan is probably permanently disabled! What can that possibly mean?!"

Tara persisted, "You have a choice, Promise. You have asked good questions. Do you have the courage to try to answer them meaningfully? If you really want to explore them, I can help you. If you want to give up and render this entire experience meaningless, you will have to do that on your own. I am here for you and will love you either way. The choice is yours."

Tara witnessed the flash of anger in Promise's eyes. A sign of life! Tara would dare to hope for the best.

Tara added, "Call me if you want to meet with me. I will be happy to hear from you."

Tara reached toward Promise and hugged her before she turned away. She would await her godchild's decision.

15

ONCE AGAIN, Promise sat with her Aunt Tara in her healing room. Two weeks had passed since Tara's visit to the track meet. Promise and Lizzie had talked often since then. Lizzie strongly encouraged Promise to accept their aunt's offer.

Fidgeting in her seat, Promise held the rose quartz orb in her hand, hoping to steady her inner turmoil's potential surge into her words and facial expressions. She didn't know what to expect from her aunt; more importantly, she didn't know what to expect from herself. It had been an incredibly difficult six weeks. The school year couldn't end soon enough.

Megan had regained consciousness. Many of her fractures were almost healed, but her doctors had yet to fully assess the scope of her brain injury. She barely recognized Promise during their first reconnection in the stepdown unit. Brittany had accompanied her daughter for that visit. The encounter proved difficult for everyone involved.

Megan's mother sat at her own daughter's bedside, often criticizing the staff for not being attentive enough. Promise understood in an instant why Megan had so often been upset. Promise also realized why Steve's affection meant so much to Megan. Promise struggled to contain her tears; she only managed it long enough to exit her friend's room.

Brittany spontaneously put her arm around Promise's shoulders. Without pausing to think, Brittany blurted out, "Is she always that nasty?"

Promise gazed up at her mother with deeper appreciation. "Yes," she replied. "Thank you for not being like that."

Brittany stopped and turned to hug Promise more directly. "I'm sorry if I *ever* sounded like that to you."

At the end of their hug, Promise wanly smiled. "Never, Mom. Thank you for being you."

The chrysalis state of Promise's retreat had begun to soften with Tara's confrontation at the track. Promise had made her choice. She would choose to *live* and figure out how to do it meaningfully in time. Hopefully, Aunt Tara would help her.

Tara began, "I suspect that we have many issues to address, the biggest being your ability to predict the accident in the first place. I'm sure it matters that they didn't listen to you. On some level, it probably also matters that they all talk about it now. There's your own grief at the loss of your friend. She may be alive, but you can't confide in her these days. And all those are just verbal descriptions of what must feel like unspeakable sorrow. Promise, I applaud you for reaching out to me, for your willingness to deal with whatever you can."

Promise sighed. Her tears flowed soon after. Tara welcomed them without comforting her godchild prematurely. Promise had some deep inner work to do.

Promise eventually admitted to her deeper feelings. "Aunt Tara, I didn't want to go to that dance in the first place. I only wanted to please Megan. As the evening went on, I didn't want to be with George anymore either, but I didn't know how to get away from him without making a scene. When that vision came, I thought I had made it up so I could go home! It scared me, though, because it could have been real – and it was!! Telling them created a scene anyway, and they all left the dance mad at me. Now Steve is dead and Megan is brain-injured. I've never had a real relationship with George, who is enjoying his place in the limelight, by the way. I feel like a freak, a very lonely freak!!"

Tara asked, "Promise, do you blame yourself for all of that?"

"Yes!" she cried. "Trying to please Megan had terrible consequences! I wasn't strong enough to say no from the very beginning. I should have said no! Why didn't I have the vision then?! Why did it wait until the moment when everybody planned to make out in the car? Nobody wanted to listen to me by then!!"

In the midst of Promise's emotional outburst, Tara did her best to remain calm and centered. She asked her godchild, "Has it occurred to you that they had that agenda from the very beginning? That the timing of your vision would make no difference on that score?"

Tara paused.

Promise could now see the truth of her aunt's words. "No," she mumbled.

"Then what possible benefit or invitation came from the timing of your vision that night?" Tara asked.

Promise looked bewildered. "I don't know.... It came at a time when I had another agenda. It served my desire to go home. It tested my willingness to reveal my inner experience for the good of someone else – at least, that's what I had hoped it would do. It made no difference, though!"

"Promise, it made a huge difference!" Tara affirmed. "George is alive because of you. And you are alive because you had the courage to listen to yourself." She persisted, "You felt your desire to go home. You felt the vision. Did they feel the same to you?"

"Well, no...," Promise murmured. After a few moments' reflection, she added, "My wanting to go home felt like a sentence ending with a period. My vision felt like a deep rumble, like a sentence with several exclamation marks and a roll of thunder thrown into the mix."

"Think about the time you had that vision of the boy being hit by his father. What did that feel like?" Tara inquired.

"It felt like thunder. It scared me like the vision at the dance. It scared me like the dream of that truck coming at Dad!"

"Yes. And please note the difference. You warned your dad and you warned your friends. You had no control over who listened and who didn't, and you never will. Your dad lives because you had that dream, you shared it with him, and he chose to listen. Sadly, your friends did not."

Promise looked at her godmother astounded. A tear of grateful acknowledgment flowed down her cheek.

Tara then wondered aloud, "I'm guessing you've had other scary dreams that did not come true?"

Promise answered, "I have...."

"Did they feel the same to you as that dream about the truck hitting your mom's car?"

Promise paused. "Not exactly, although it was more confusing. Some of my scarier dreams made me worry that I might see them unfold in outer life. They haven't, though. At least not yet. That dream of the truck took two months before it actually happened. How does that help me?"

Tara responded, "Well, I think all this is teaching you about your 'instrument.' Think of your body and your mind as a kind of thermometer, a device that registers information; for the thermometer, it's the temperature. You are trying to figure out what kind of information your system, or your instrument, registers. You are also trying to figure out how to read its scale."

Tara continued, "Regarding the visions, it sounds like your body responds differently to thoughts and wishes versus visualizations that could come true."

Promise nodded with dawning recognition.

Tara added, "Your dreams may be more confusing because they have such direct access to all sorts of unconscious information, whereas your visions, which have only occurred during the day, seem much more specific. We will have to pay more attention to your dreams to see if we can better understand what they are trying to communicate to you. In the meantime, though, perhaps you can more carefully tune in to your body's guidance to sort out the validity of these revelations?"

Promise reluctantly smiled. "What a painful way to have to learn, Aunt Tara!"

"I agree with you there, Promise, but your visions seem to involve painful experiences, so perhaps there is no way around this. The real challenge for you is to remember, even while you are feeling the pain, that you are also a Mystery that is beautiful. You may have to exhale the sob of heartache and the sigh of beauty in the same breath at times. Nevertheless, it will be very important for you to not lose sight of your own beauty, the beauty of your mysterious soul."

"But what if I haven't seen that beauty yet?" Promise sadly asked.

"That may be one purpose of your life, Promise, to discover your own beauty. I see it, but that doesn't matter except to offer you this invitation. Your journey may require you to explore the darkness, that of others and your own, to find your own beautiful light. Then, having found it, your task may be to honor it and learn how to see it in others as you feel so called. This may make no sense now. I can only tell you that you have much beauty worth discovering. I hope you will choose to honor that path."

Promise seemed confused, but she also felt infused with a new sense of hope. She responded, "Aunt Tara, I promise not to dodge you again. Thank you for your faith in me."

Now Tara reached for her godchild with a hug. "You're welcome, honey. It is an honor!"

16

THE MONTHS PRECEDING high school graduation involved numerous special occasions and the typical anticipation of the spectacular. Promise marveled at how all that excitement quickly transitioned into an eerie quiet in the days that followed. In the stillness of an early June afternoon, she appreciated how a gentle breeze could spread the sun's warmth even in the shade. She sighed deeply as she gazed upon the beauty all around her.

Promise lounged in a generously cushioned chair on her home's front porch. A book lay opened upside down on her lap. Her only companion – a young golden retriever who had joined their family two years ago when his owner, an elderly neighbor, could no longer care for him – curled up at her feet. Everyone else in her family had work, meetings, or extracurricular activities to attend. They would return one by one in an hour or two. Promise used the time to reflect on her high school experiences and how dramatically everything would change at summer's end.

Her peers seemed to have forgotten the tragedy of her sophomore year as the following summer's escapades rolled into the happenings of their junior year. No longer able to attend school, Megan had begun her slow road to a limited recovery, sequestered in a rehab program. Promise tried to visit her friend as often as she could, but it proved too difficult for both of them.

Megan felt guilty and angry with herself. Her wordfinding, now limited, could not adequately express the complexity of her feelings or reactions to Promise's attempts that fateful night to save her from her current suffering. Megan's emotional outbursts intensified during and after her friend's visits. Promise could do nothing to help; after returning home from these encounters, she often sobbed into the night. Eventually, her parents helped her see that she could do no more.

Promise continued her meetings with Aunt Tara. She learned more about how to discern her own reactions to people and situations. She developed a feel for how to interpret her dreams and found herself wanting to learn more about the deeper human psyche. During her junior year, she tentatively decided to pursue the academic study of psychology. She and her parents began to explore colleges and universities that had earned good reputations in her chosen field but that also offered a broad range of studies in case she changed her mind down the road. Together they narrowed the selection down to three schools. Promise hoped to apply for scholarships, so she completed the recommended preparatory courses.

The excitement of Promise's senior year included Lizzie's attendance at her high school as a first-year student. The girls were thrilled to have this year together, perhaps for the last time in their lives. Promise shared her hard-earned wisdom to ease Lizzie's anxieties about the transition. Lizzie appreciated her sister's guidance and respected her accomplishments. She, too, decided to try out for the track team. It seems they both inherited their mother's propensity for athleticism and speed.

As her senior year progressed, Promise sat for the college entrance exams, applied to her three chosen schools, took their tours, and engaged in the festivities specifically associated with her last year of high school. No one registered surprise when she was accepted for admission to all three schools. All three institutions even offered her financial assistance in acknowledgment of her academic achievements. Deciding which school to attend provoked significant inner turmoil, however. One of her concerns involved how close or far away she would be, especially from Lizzie. Lizzie had her own feelings about this as well.

Promise reminisced about how this paralleled their earlier separations, which occurred before she went to kindergarten, then middle school, then high school. Unfortunately, Lizzie somehow remembered those times as well; they never got easier for her. The anticipated separation now would be no less difficult. Lizzie had come to rely on Promise's presence, and not just for practical reasons. Their bond had grown stronger through the years. Promise did not want to hurt Lizzie in any way.

Consequently, Promise finally decided to attend the local college, even though it had not been her first choice. Her parents, having witnessed her range of emotional responses to the different schools during their tours and subsequent discussions, rightly suspected that Promise might once again sacrifice her own interests to maintain the bond with her sister. Brittany planned to intervene, much as she had twelve years earlier, when Promise had a dream that made everything quite clear.

Promise smiled as she remembered her Aunt Tara listening intently to the details of her dream. Two young children played on a beach. The sun glowed beautifully as it prepared to set beyond the distant waves. Few clouds filled the evening sky, but a faint star seemed to trail the sun as it hovered over the horizon. That star grew brighter, more brilliant than the sun, then it transformed into the shape of a woman. It floated through the air toward the children and gently landed on the sand in front of them.

The star woman turned to the older of the two children and handed her a starfish. It, too, glowed like the starry light. She said to the child, "Follow the starfish. It will take you where you need to go." With that, she faded into sparkles, then disappeared. The starfish sparkled as well, but it didn't leave the child's hand. Instead, it transformed into a creature of the sea. The children stared at their gift in awe. The star in the sky grew brighter as the sun began to set. Their mother came for them. The children showed her the starfish. Then Promise awoke.

As Promise finished relating the dream, her Aunt Tara smiled broadly before she launched into asking her usual, discerning questions. It quickly became clear that this dream did not predict her future; it offered her guidance. Its symbolism was uncanny. Aunt Tara asked her, "What can you also call a starfish, Promise? Think about the names of your chosen schools."

"Robertson Johnson College, Stella Maris University, Merriam-Rogers University...." Promise shrugged with confusion. Those names didn't seem associated to her dream at all.

Not having had much exposure to Latin, Promise needed her aunt's assistance. Tara then explained, "*Stella* means 'star'; *maris* means 'of the sea.' Does that help any?"

Promise's eyes opened wide. Actually, that school had sparked her greatest interest. She appreciated the friendliness of the faculty and students, the relative safety of its locale, and its beautiful setting on the outskirts of the small city named Dunkirk Hollow. Unfortunately, being the farthest away, it required a three-hour drive to get there. Spending time with Lizzie would be most difficult, limited to holidays and family visits. The sadness that filled Lizzie's eyes at the mere mention of Promise possibly choosing Stella Maris had effectively nixed her decision to attend that university.

But the star woman in the dream had said, "Follow the starfish. It will take you where you need to go." What did that mean? Aunt Tara once again reminded Promise that she had a choice. The option to ignore the wisdom of her dreams had proven itself to be a poor one over the years. If Promise elected to heed its advice, however, she would have to resolve her conflict about leaving Lizzie. Later, when Promise shared her dilemma with her mother, Brittany used this as the doorway to a deeper discussion between them.

Now that Promise could hear her mother with seventeen-year-old ears, Brittany's words could convey more meaningful layering. She emphasized the cherished bond between her girls and how she hoped it would sustain them throughout their lives. Once again, however, she had to stress that they had separate lives, their own soul paths. No matter which school Promise chose to attend, Peter and Brittany would continue to support Lizzie in whatever way they could. Lizzie found her way when she was little and through all their separations since then. Now, Brittany assured her, with so many more resources available to her, Lizzie would find her way again.

Lizzie also had their canine companion to keep her company. Promise smiled as she remembered how her family had agreed to have Corkie live with them when Mrs. Rafferty's health declined and she could no longer provide the care he needed. They often took Corkie to visit Mrs. Rafferty until she passed on several months later. Not long after that, in an attempt to vent some other-related frustration with humor, Peter called him Quirkie. To everyone's surprise, their pet responded to that name, so everyone called him Quirkie thereafter.

Lizzie and Quirkie had a special bond. Knowing that brought Promise a measure of comfort as she tried to make her weighty decision. She considered the advice of her trusted adults very carefully alongside the dream, which continued to hold its power within her. She finally chose Stella Maris University, hoping that Lizzie would eventually understand.

After Promise notified the university of her acceptance, Lizzie grieved for the whole month that followed as if someone had died. The adults rallied around her sister to help her see the wisdom of letting Promise experience what was best for her. Fortunately, by the end of her first year, Lizzie had also carved a niche for herself with the track team and had made many new friends. Their separation would still be difficult for both Promise and Lizzie, but they could finally accept it as an important part of their lives together. They planned to make the most of the summer and to email, text, or video with each other every day after Promise left. Promise wistfully reflected on this with a simultaneous sense of sadness, excitement, and peace.

Her reminiscence came to an end when Quirkie suddenly raised his head from slumber as he sensed Lizzie's presence moments before she arrived home. She enthusiastically joined Promise and her furry best friend on the front porch, where she proposed they have a picnic and play a game together. Promise quickly agreed to the idea, glad to have Lizzie's company for as long as their paths would allow.

17

SUMMER FLEW BY, or so it seemed to Promise, who wanted to savor every minute. When the time came for her to purchase the needed supplies and pack for a semester away from home, she often found Lizzie hiding out in her room with Quirkie at her side to console her. Sometimes Promise intervened; sometimes she didn't. She had come to accept their impending separation as a necessary process that they would need to negotiate alone and together.

Meetings with Aunt Tara seemed more important than ever as Promise realized she would really be on her own once she left for college. Tara had offered to be available by phone if needed, but they both knew things would be different. Promise had to stretch her wings and discover how her gifts and sensitivities would fare in a larger world. Tara made sure to encourage her apprentice to honor herself above all else and to trust her inner knowing no matter what others might tell her. Promise recognized the wisdom of her aunt's advice; it was her own ability to follow it that she doubted.

Moving into the dorms offered its own layer of chaos. Promise tried to keep her nervousness in check as Peter easily lifted heavy boxes and suitcases up the flight of steps to her second-floor room. Fortunately, her roommate, Melissa Walters, arrived at the same time so that they could quickly negotiate who would take which side of their shared space. Melissa impressed Promise as a practical, straightforward kind of person. Her energy felt easy to be around. Promise liked her immediately and breathed a sigh of relief.

Promise remembered the moment of parting with her parents and Lizzie as especially difficult. The mixture of excitement and sadness definitely drifted toward the grieving end of the spectrum for several hours after they left. Promise tried to focus on unpacking boxes and decorating her new abode in a way that soothed her soul and calmed her mind. Melissa chatted merrily throughout the process, having matter-of-factly decided that the phase of saying goodbye had passed and that this phase of settling in deserved her utmost attention.

Promise soon learned that her blonde roommate enjoyed playing field hockey and hoped to make the university's team. Tryouts for new students would take place the next day, interwoven with first-year orientation; classes would not begin until the following week. Melissa reluctantly admitted that she had gained a little weight over the summer from all the partying she had come to enjoy. She expected to lose it quickly with the upcoming sports season. Her athletic, five-foot-seven-inch frame suggested that she might be able to accomplish her goal – until they went to the dining hall where Promise witnessed Melissa's food choices in action. It would be an interesting semester.

Promise did her best to manage her unsettled emotions in response to all the non-stop stimulation and novelty by working out at the track on a daily basis. The consequent endorphin flood helped calm her nerves. She purposely waited a few days before she called her parents and Lizzie, hoping to give them a cheerful report.

Her schedule of classes required that she awaken early most

mornings. This worked well for her because Melissa and most of her dormmates slept well past sunrise to recuperate from their late-night parties. This pattern would also later accommodate their all-nighters to finish papers or study for exams. Promise kept to her own schedule, though, doing her best to fall asleep in the midst of the mayhem so that she might appreciate the solitude of the morning hours and begin her days in peace.

Despite their differences, Melissa remained friendly and accepting. Somehow, she did make the hockey team, which actually helped their communal sleep schedule overall, at least for the fall season. Promise continued to enjoy her runs on the outdoor track whenever the weather permitted. One sunny, mid-autumn afternoon, an uninvited companion maneuvered to join her.

Lost in thought, she hadn't noticed the quick approach of earth-pounding steps trying to catch up with her. A tall, fair, slender yet muscular young man with reddish-brown hair started to run alongside her, matching her pace. She suddenly tuned in to his presence and glanced in his direction. His attractive, smiling face led to a longer gaze. She instantly felt a sense of familiarity about him that confused her greatly. Her perception didn't feel harmful to her in any way, however, so she decided this experience might be safe to explore further.

He smiled more broadly in response to her visual interest and began with a polite introduction. "Do you mind if I run with you? I don't want to intrude if you'd rather zone out."

Touched by his sensitivity to that issue, Promise responded, "Not at all. May I ask, why do you want to?"

"Very direct, you are!" he exclaimed. "I like that. Okay, I'll be direct too. Besides the fact that you are beautiful, I see you running here almost every day. You keep a good pace and go for the distance. I get bored easily and welcome the company, but I know that not everyone does. My name is Lugh. What's yours?"

"Promise. Is that Lou for Louis?"

"No, actually, it sounds the same but it's spelled L-u-g-h. He's a god from Irish mythology; the name of his Welsh counterpart is spelled L-l-e-w. They have different stories, but I especially like that he had incredible aim and multiple talents, to include intelligence and the capacity to handle a spear. Personally, I've decided to practice archery instead."

Promise responded with a quizzical smile.

Lugh quickly added,"My parents are heavily into Celtic mythology. My name, at least, sounds normal. My sisters, Cerridwen and Maeve, didn't fare as well."

Promise laughed. As they continued their run, she had to ask,"So, do you hunt with your bow and arrow?"

"Sometimes," he responded."I really prefer the challenge of hitting a steady target squarely."

Promise didn't like to hear about the hunting of animals. She knew very little about it, but the images of Fonzy and Quirkie came readily to mind. She suddenly wished that she hadn't agreed to run with this archer.

Lugh sensed her emotional shift and commented,"You are opposed to hunting, Promise?" When the look on her face confirmed his suspicion, he continued,"I don't need to talk you out of that, but I must remind you that there is such a thing as the food chain. We all have to be nourished by something. Even if it's plants, we have killed something before its natural end. To me, it's really about the respect we bring to the process of taking a life and how we treat the offerings of that sacrifice afterwards. To my way of thinking, the Native Americans had the right idea: to give thanks for the gift of the life and to meaningfully use as much of the remains so that everything is honored and nothing is disrespected or wasted."

Promise gazed at him more intently in response to his explanation. It jarred her previous perspective and gave her something to ponder, even if it made her uncomfortable."I'll think about that" was her only response.

She had come to the conclusion of her run and had to get ready for her afternoon Honors English class. She slowed down, so Lugh did as well.

He paused. He hoped to spend more time with her, but he sensed it best to keep the invitation simple. He asked, "Can I run with you again sometime? You can always say no if the moment doesn't suit you."

Their eyes met in such a way as to send a strange sensation down Promise's spine. It wasn't uncomfortable, really. Actually, it felt comforting and familiar…and all the more strange! Caught between the discomfort of his hunting philosophy and the ease of the weird feeling, Promise could only respond, "Okay."

She tried to be polite, but her smile registered her confusion. She backed away before she turned and left, lugging her confusion along with her to her next class.

18

PROMISE KEPT TO HER SCHEDULE of running on the outdoor track, even if a bit self-consciously at first. She surprised herself as she registered feelings of disappointment when she did not spot Lugh on the field. She found herself scanning the turf and the bleachers for his presence. She laughed at herself and eventually resumed her more usual preoccupations as she jogged.

Two weeks later, Lugh did join her for a run. She learned that he majored in anthropology, hoping to focus on the social and cultural aspects of human communities in the far distant past as part of a doctoral program after graduation. As a junior, he was currently exploring his longer-term options and visiting programs that seriously interested him. He seemed fascinated by the collective human mind.

When Promise shared with him her intended major, he seemed genuinely interested. Their conversations took on a lively turn. Promise found herself feeling progressively more comfortable in his presence. They ran together several times more before the end-of-semester crunch, even coordinating a run together as their class schedule concluded. Exams and other commitments would continue to require their presence on campus for at least one more week.

During that last week, Promise finished her final papers for her Honors philosophy and English courses. Exams in biology, introductory psychology, and German induced their own degree of stress, which only added to the tension she felt regarding the deadlines for her papers. Once these requirements of early December came to an end, however, Promise set her sights on returning home for the holidays. She couldn't wait to see everyone, including Quirkie.

Peter came alone to bring her home because Brittany and Lizzie had important commitments at their work and school, respectively. Promise hugged her father wholeheartedly and felt his love for her in return. They talked the whole way home, sharing stories about the family and her campus experiences. Before too long, Quirkie's antics dominated their conversation.

When Lizzie arrived home, she and Promise embraced for a very long time, laughing all the while, thrilled to be together again. Despite their prior, relatively brief reunion over the Thanksgiving break, Lizzie still had much to share, so they planned a sleepover for that very night. Quirkie could not be ignored, however. He foisted his body between their legs and groaned for attention from each of them. Brittany's return home from St. Raphael's interrupted their laughter.

Brittany's maternal heart glowed as she reunited with her daughter and held her close. A mother's love for her child – simultaneously ephemeral and intense, yet impossible to describe – claims its place in everyone's consciousness during such precious moments. Promise surrendered to the peace of reconnecting with her familiars. She truly felt at home.

With a few weeks remaining before holiday festivities officially began, Promise used the time for Christmas shopping and reconnecting with her high school friends. She also planned a meeting with Tara and enjoyed sharing her deeper reflections with her aunt once again. Tara immediately noticed a growing maturity in her godchild. They spent several hours catching up on the events of their lives and their more relevant concerns. With relief Promise reported that she had not had any visions of disaster, nor any visions at all, for that matter. She had been preoccupied with all the adjustments of her first semester and gratefully welcomed the break.

Promise thoroughly enjoyed the visits with extended family, all the dinners and parties with them and her friends, even the jogs with her mother and sister, sometimes with Quirkie in tow. Peter's schedule offered considerable flexibility for the holidays, so Brittany took some vacation time from work to fully participate in their family adventures. Lizzie's life had become more active socially during her sophomore year. This holiday interlude offered them the increasingly rare opportunity to enjoy their family camaraderie. Peter and Brittany treasured this time, recognizing that life would offer them fewer occasions for these special reunions as the years marched onward.

Promise met with Tara once more before she returned to Stella Maris for her second semester. They were discussing her upcoming courses: this semester would include the continuation of her psychology, biology, Honors English, and German classes along with an elective in mythology. Promise hoped that a greater exposure to the symbols of myth would better help her understand her dreams.

At the mention of her dreams, Promise spontaneously remembered the one she had dreamt the previous night. She asked if she might share it with her aunt because it made no sense to her. Of course, Tara readily agreed.

"I am standing in a huge garden of many flowers. The grass is an incredibly luscious green. The sky is bright with the sun's glow overhead. I walk toward a plant that seems interesting to me. When I get closer, I notice that it has many yet unopened buds that are almost ready to bloom. They begin to blossom one by one, each one fully flowering before the next one starts to open. The first one, a rose, is a beautiful pink. I expect them all to be pink, but they're not! The next one is yellow. The one after that is white. The next one is red. Then one is blue. The following one has two colors combined in pink and white swirls. Another is an orangey color, and yet another is black. I am amazed and want to point this out to someone, but no one is there. It is the only bush like it in the whole garden.

"What can this dream possibly mean, Aunt Tara?" Promise asked.

Tara paused to allow the symbols to settle in her subconscious. She asked Promise, "What do roses mean to you?"

Promise reflected, "Not a lot, really, other than that they mark special occasions and are especially pricey on Valentine's Day…."

Tara considered this and said, "Well, your associations seem to suggest a connection to ceremony and love. Your dream's imagery also portrays the presence of diversity on a single bush, an unusual feature to this degree. I've heard of rosebushes having two colors, maybe, but not as many as in your dream. It would appear that this bush of many colors is meant for only you to see. It's obviously not a literal dream. If it has any predictive value, it must surely be symbolic."

Promise shook her head, the lingering confusion still obvious on her face.

Tara added, "It will be interesting to see if this makes sense to you over time."

Promise nodded. Moments later, Alex's arrival home diverted their attention. He hoped that they might invite the Holmes-Thomas family for dinner that evening. Tara and Promise enthusiastically agreed and helped with preparations. Promise forgot her dream in the context of further festivities and her anticipated return to school. She would come to understand it soon enough.

19

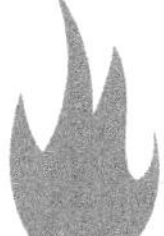

JANUARY'S BITTER COLD took everyone by surprise. That it extended into February pleased no one. Sports activities that typically pressed for outdoor workouts shifted to the use of the indoor facilities, where coaches reserved blocks of time for their teams. This made Promise's use of the campus gym's track more complicated. Fortunately, the breaks between her classes accommodated the track's availability most days without too much difficulty.

Having mastered the rigors of her first semester, she knew better what to expect of the second. She looked forward to her mythology class in particular. It did not disappoint her expectations.

Two weeks into the new semester, Lugh encountered Promise on the indoor track. She greeted him warmly. They shared the highlights of their holiday adventures as they jogged together along the course. Lugh explained that he had met with a Celtic shaman, hoping to gain a more experiential understanding of anthropology. In response to this comment about a concept so foreign, Promise asked him to describe what he meant: What was a shaman? What did they do together? And how did that relate to his major?

Lugh appreciated her interest. He launched into the topic with enthusiasm, defining a shaman as someone who travels in consciousness to unseen realms by entering a trance state. He or she converses with beings or spirits on the Other Side, then returns to this realm of awareness with important information to share. Historically, many shamans from various cultures relied on mind-altering substances, like ayahuasca or mushrooms, to achieve their shift in consciousness. Alternatively, some used dancing, drumming, or other trance-inducing methods. The shaman he visited preferred the latter-mentioned approach.

Lugh continued his explanation by noting that he had joined six other interested newcomers for this introduction. Their instructor guided them in the ways to form a sacred circle using lit candles, blessed water, seasonal fruits, and purifying incense to symbolize the four elements. Together, they called in the four directions – East, South, West, and North – and learned about the goddesses and gods associated with each one. Then they focused on the center of the circle, known as Sovereignty in the Celtic world. Lugh was surprised to discover that his namesake actually represented the energies of the West, which in the shamanic sense related to ancestors and visions. He excitedly noted that their host and teacher, Dylan, told the group a great story about the god Lugh.

Having been introduced to the ancient roots of mythology in her class, Promise couldn't help but consider the powerful depths that myth evoked in her, even as a young child. To meet someone whose parents had named their children after mythological gods and goddesses interested her greatly. She wanted to hear the myth, in part because she simply loved stories, but mostly because she wondered how it might reflect Lugh's character and, if it didn't, how he felt about having that name. Promise responded with enthusiasm, "Lugh, please tell me the story!"

He appeared delighted to have elicited such interest, and, of course, he wanted to share it. He began, "Once upon a time... I guess that really applies to fairy tales, not myths, but it sounds good!" They laughed.

He continued, "...in the ancient days of Ireland, two supernatural beings from opposing dynasties mated to end their long-term feud. Cian of the Tuatha Dé Danann partnered with Ethniu, daughter of Balor, the leader of the Fomorians. Cian and Ethniu had several children, one of whom was Lugh. Their son developed numerous talents as he grew. During his youth, the battle between the dynasties had also resumed, and the Fomorians were in control. When Lugh came of age, he wanted to join the Tuatha Dé Danann, so he traveled to Tara, the seat of their royal leader. To be accepted into their numbers, King Nuada had to first grant him an audience.

"When Lugh knocked at Tara's gate, the doorkeeper refused to admit Lugh unless he had some unique skill that he would use to serve the king. Lugh told him, 'I am a swordsman.' The doorkeeper replied, 'We already have plenty of those. Go away!' Lugh returned and knocked again. The doorkeeper repeated his question. This time, Lugh replied, 'I am a smith.' Again, he received the same answer: 'We already have a smith. Go away!' Lugh returned again and again with a different response each time: 'I am a builder.' 'I am a harpist.' 'I am a poet.' 'I am a historian.' 'I am a sorcerer.' 'I am a craftsman.' 'I am a hero.' Each time, the doorkeeper's reply was the same.

"For his final attempt, Lugh knocked and said, 'I have all these skills together. Do you have anyone like that?!' Ultimately stumped, the doorkeeper granted Lugh admission. At last, he could meet with the king, who welcomed him to join the Tuatha Dé Danann. In his bid to gain the respect of his fellow warriors, Lugh challenged their champions to compete with him. They accepted his dare; he bested each one in turn. As his own fame mounted, Lugh also observed how the Tuatha Dé Danann had resigned themselves to their oppressed state. He suggested to the observant King Nuada that they consider battle instead. The king eventually agreed and appointed Lugh commander-in-chief of his troops.

"Lugh led the Tuatha Dé Danann into a fierce clash with the Fomorians during which King Nuada was killed. Following this, Lugh faced his Fomorian grandfather, Balor, on the battle field. Balor had a poisonous eye that killed anyone it gazed upon. It supposedly took four soldiers to open and hold Balor's eyelid in place to wreak that devastation. With excellent timing, Lugh aimed his slingstone at Balor's just-opened, perilous eye, killing him instantly. The Tuatha Dé Danann won the battle, and Lugh became king. He is remembered during the Celtic feast of Lughnasadh, which is celebrated on the first day of August each year to mark the beginning of autumn."

Lugh, the anthropology student, smiled brightly as he brought his myth to conclusion. He quipped, "So, how's that for a yarn?!"

Promise stood agape, marveling at the tale itself along with his entertaining talent for storytelling. "It seems you have inherited your namesake's capacity for history! That was fascinating! How is it for you to be named after someone so multitalented? Does his story resonate with your own life experience?"

"Ah, what a deep, personal question! I should not be surprised that a psychology major would ask me that. Truth is, I'm not sure. For one thing, the Irish Lugh was a supernatural being, a god of sorts. I would never claim to be that. Many talents? Maybe. I don't want to get my ego all caught up in this, though."

"That's probably wise." Promise contemplated whether she would share her own confusion regarding her name and her namesake. Lugh looked at her quizzically, so she decided to take the risk.

She faltered, however, by stating the obvious: "You are looking at me funny."

"Sorry. It's just that your last comment hints at more than your words. What deeper thoughts will you share with me?" His face conveyed his interest and reassured her.

"Okay," Promise responded. "My name reflects the compromise my parents made at my birth. My dad wanted to name me Prometheus. Are you familiar with his story?"

"The Greek god who brought fire to humans, then was punished by Zeus for having stolen it from Mount Olympus?"

"Yes," she confirmed, then added, "My dad is enthralled with the concept of the light bearer. I sometimes wonder if I can ever live up to his dream."

"Prometheus was also a god, like Lugh. Maybe a name is meant to inspire us, not define us. I think they were both associated with light, by the way." Lugh grinned.

Promise gazed at her companion with new eyes. She responded, "Really? I appreciate your story and your reflections. Thank you!"

She paused. Suddenly, her dream of the rosebush and the many-colored roses came to mind. She felt it strongly: the dream related to Lugh. She tried to hide her shock, unsuccessfully as it turned out.

Lugh immediately asked, "Okay. Something else is going on in that head of yours. Care to share?"

Promise felt embarrassed; her face had never provided a good mask for that emotion. With a blushing countenance, she replied, "I don't know why I'm turning so red, but I suddenly remembered a dream I had, that's all. It was about a rosebush with lots of different colored roses. It's silly, really."

Lugh comforted her, saying, "It's not silly at all. I don't dream much, but I know some people take them very seriously. I try not to criticize things I don't understand."

Promise breathed a sigh of relief and felt the color of her cheeks cooling in response.

Lugh continued, "You know, I very much enjoy talking with you. I am wondering if you might be free to continue this sometime. Maybe this evening?"

"I promised my roommate I'd attend an indoor hockey match

tonight; she's on the team. Would you care to go to that?" Promise suggested.

"I don't know much about hockey, but I'd be happy to join you. You can explain the game to me."

Promise admitted, "Actually, I don't understand it very well, other than trying to get the ball past the opposing team into the net. We'll probably talk about other things – if we can hear each other, that is!"

Lugh laughed. "Great! Tell me where and when to meet you, and we'll have an adventure."

Promise laughed as well. "Okay, then!" She gave him the details. They parted company. As she walked away, she mumbled to herself, "What have I just done?!"

20

LUGH MET PROMISE OUTSIDE her dormitory building, and together they walked to the athletic facilities one block down the street. The chilled vapor of breath trailed their every word, mostly small talk to calm Promise's nervousness. She couldn't explain to herself her feeling reactions toward Lugh. She remembered her Aunt Tara's advice and simply accepted them. Shaming herself for her feelings, no matter how confusing, would only make it worse.

Promise and Lugh soon entered the warmth of the indoor stadium, where many students had gathered, looking for something to do besides study on a cold winter night. They found seats on Mel's side of the bleachers. Promise made sure to wave to her roommate and cheer her on. Promise then explained to Lugh what Mel had told her: the area of play would be smaller than what is typical for field hockey. Another difference included the side-boards used to define the sidelines so that the ball wouldn't leave the pitch. Consequently, the players had to act quickly and think several plays in advance. Their coach encouraged

Mel's team to sharpen their skills by engaging in this activity every winter.

The game commenced. The sounds of running feet, audience rumbles and shouts, and referee whistles filled the airwaves. Promise and Lugh gave the match their undivided attention for several minutes before they realized that they didn't understand the rules or the referee calls. Mel's team did score a goal, however, and they shouted and clapped along with the rest of the fans.

Attempts at more serious conversation proved pointless amidst all the ambient sounds in the gym. Lugh leaned toward Promise and asked her if she might like to go to the local diner for hot chocolate to warm up after the game. Promise smiled and nodded her yes. She welcomed the thought of a quieter space and didn't feel quite ready to part with Lugh.

Toward the end of the match, as tensions ran higher and exhaustion took its toll on the players, a member of the opposing team lost control of her hockey stick. The swing hit Mel directly in her lower abdomen and doubled her over instantly. The referee called a timeout. Promise immediately sprang to her feet with concern.

Others in the bleachers stood as well. Lugh's height gave him the better vantage point. He described Mel as clutching her gut and rolling on the floor for several minutes before she could relax enough to lie still. Her coach and the team's athletic trainer had rushed immediately to her side. After another few minutes, Mel was able to stand with assistance. The crowd cheered for her. The owner of the offending hockey stick clearly felt remorse for her lapse and approached Mel for forgiveness. When they patted each other and smiled, the crowd applauded once again. Mel did not play for the rest of the game.

Before Promise could consider pursuing her plans with Lugh, she wanted to check on Mel. Her roommate readily assured her that she was fine. She might have some black and blue marks for a week or two, but she didn't want to interfere with Promise's date. Mel planned to go back to their room and rest. She insisted that she felt much better and that Promise would be very bored watching her sleep.

Reluctantly, Promise left the athletic building with Lugh after Mel's teammates assured her that they would escort her roommate back to their dorm and tuck her into bed. Lugh understood Promise's ambivalence and offered that they be very attentive to time. Promise appreciated his sensitivity and found herself relaxing once again. She silently noted how he often made her feel more comfortable.

At the diner they indulged in hot chocolate and brownies while they talked more about Lugh's shamanic experiences and how they dovetailed with Promise's understanding of the human ego. Trance seemed to take a person beyond awareness of the egoic self. Despite the historical immaturity of traditional psychology as compared to the ancient roots of shamanic consciousness, Promise had the distinct impression that proponents of her academic major would label the trance experience as disturbed, if not pathological. Given Lugh's assessment that shamanic wisdom offered great benefit to the community, this triggered some questions, maybe even some doubts, about her chosen field of study.

Once again, Lugh had invited her to think beyond the conventional world. She appreciated his larger perspective. She even wondered if her own experiences of dreams and visions had something in common with shamans. She hoped one day that she might share this with him and hear his perspective on the matter. For now, however, she kept this aspect of her extrasensory perceptions to herself. She had faced too much disapproval to share this just yet.

They walked back to her dormitory building in the street-lit, bitter cold. In a shadow near the entrance gate, Lugh paused and Promise with him. He gazed into her eyes with tenderness and respect, then asked, "May I kiss you good night?"

Taken aback by his thoughtfulness and sensitivity, Promise smiled and readily responded, "Please do." If it weren't so cold, they might have lingered longer. A gust of wind ended that fantasy, eliciting laughter instead.

Before they parted, they planned another time to run together, meeting outside the indoor track to determine if an outdoor experience might prove to be an option. Promise smiled once again as she waved her good night. Lugh smiled at her in return, making sure she entered the sanctum of her dormitory. He then quickly made his own way to his off-campus apartment. Both felt warmer despite the weather. Promise found Mel asleep. She appreciated the silence to more quietly enjoy the glow of her evening with Lugh.

Several days later, Promise and Lugh met as agreed. Delighted to realize that their chosen day had turned into a warmer surprise, they welcomed the relative quiet of the outdoors and jogged to the track. They conversed as they ran round and round the oval, discussing the evolution of human consciousness from anthropological and psychological perspectives. Lugh acknowledged how much he appreciated their conversations. Promise agreed wholeheartedly.

As they slowed their pace, Promise suddenly felt a painful, burning stitch in her right lower abdomen. She bent forward slightly, instinctively clutching at her side, as she simultaneously had a vision of Mel lying in her bed, feverish in the night. Promise kept hearing the word "appendix." Her face registered her distress.

Lugh had to ask, "Promise, are you all right?"

Promise realized at this point that she could easily stand up straight, that her right-sided pain belonged to her visionary experience, and that she herself felt quite fine. Lugh stared at her with utter confusion. She had to tell him *something* by way of explanation. Just as suddenly, her high school friend Megan's disbelief flashed before her inner eye and once again broke her heart. She gazed at Lugh, daring to hope for a better response.

"Lugh, I've hesitated to tell you this, but I sometimes have visions. They don't happen often. Actually, this is the first one I've had this whole school year. I just felt and saw my roommate feverish with appendicitis in the middle of the night. I am really worried about her."

Lugh's surprise and disbelief could not be mistaken. He stood there, speechless, not knowing how to respond. He really liked Promise. He had just been talking about shamanic out-of-body experiences. Here she was having one, perhaps, and he didn't want to believe her; he couldn't even say why. Consequently, he said nothing.

Promise couldn't control the tears now flowing down her cheeks. She backed away saying, "I'm going to go, then. I need to check on Mel. Bye..."

She turned and walked away. He let her go. That made her cry all the more, but he didn't see. He couldn't see. He did not want to look.

21

PROMISE DID HER BEST to conceal her feelings as she made her way back to her dorm. She found Mel there, looking somewhat pallid. Promise immediately felt even more worried, but she tried her best to be discreet.

"Mel, are you okay?"

"I'm fine, maybe a little tired, that's all. Why?"

"You look a little pale to me. I'm just concerned," Promise said, minimizing her true feelings. "Do you need to go to the health center?"

"No! What makes you think that?!" Mel exclaimed.

Promise was taken off guard by the reactivity of her roommate's response. She tried to soften it by saying, "Well, you were hit with a hockey stick just a few days ago. I understand if my suggestion seems a bit dramatic. Maybe we should just call it an early night?"

"You can, Promise, but I've got a commitment for dinner with the team," Mel seemed more than a little testy. Promise wondered why, but she knew better than to ask at this point.

Not minutes later, some of Mel's teammates stopped by. She really did not look well to Promise; Mel seemed to be pushing herself, hoping she would just feel better. Raw from her experience with Lugh, Promise opted to remain silent and attentive to what might unfold.

Once everyone left the room, Promise closed the door and let herself cry the tears that had wanted to flow after she left the track, now even more profusely. Lugh's facial expression, flat and unresponsive, combined with his silence, stung her in a very wounded place. She had allowed him to enter her inner sanctum. She could not pretend this did not hurt.

She skipped dinner that evening and fell asleep in her clothes. She never heard Mel return to their room. Midway through the night, she awoke with a start for reasons she could not explain. She immediately thought of Mel, however, and quietly got out of bed to check on her.

Promise thought she heard her moan, so she turned on a lamp and went to her roommate's bedside. Aghast, she realized Mel had an evident fever; she seemed in significant pain, clutching at her abdomen, but unable to engage in any meaningful conversation. Promise ran for the residence hall staff.

At three o'clock in the morning, Promise knocked as forcefully as she dared on her hall monitor's bedroom door, awakening her from an obviously deep sleep. Groggy, with hair askew, Carrie opened her door after a minute or two.

Promise exclaimed, "Carrie, come quick! Mel is really sick. I think she has appendicitis. She needs to go to the hospital. She is feverish and can't respond well to anything I say to her. Please come quick!"

Carrie gathered her wits and her robe and followed Promise back to her dorm room. With one look at Mel, Carrie agreed that they needed to call an ambulance. Most of the students slept through the arrival of the EMT's, who efficiently transported Mel to the local hospital's emergency department. Promise accompanied her roommate as the vehicle's lights flashed the announcement of urgency to other drivers on the road. Carrie told them she would follow in her car and notify Mel's parents on the way.

Once at the hospital, staff asked Promise for whatever medical history she could provide. Promise knew little about that, other than that Mel had been hit in her abdomen during a hockey match not quite a week ago. She hadn't seemed quite right since then, but she hadn't complained of anything in particular. Still, Promise felt it important to let them know her suspicions. "I think she has appendicitis!"

The nurse furrowed her brow, looking directly at Promise as she wondered how a college student would think to diagnose someone in such acute distress. She said nothing, however. She really didn't have to. That look was becoming all too familiar. The nurse wheeled Mel to an examining room, leaving Promise on her own in the lobby. Fortunately, Carrie appeared moments later with Mel's medical information and consent papers. She assured Promise that Mel's parents were on their way.

Carrie asked to speak with Mel's nurse to provide the needed medical background. Afterwards, she, too, was dismissed to the waiting room while the doctors and staff completed their evaluation. Fortunately, Mel's family lived within an hour's driving distance to the university. They arrived in a state of urgency and worry. Mel's mother quickly approached Promise and Carrie for an update, while her father went to inquire at the reception desk. Promise shared what information she could. At this point, she made no mention of her suspicions.

Within the hour, Mel's parents returned to thank Promise and Carrie for calling the ambulance. A surgeon had been called; he planned to perform emergency surgery to remove Mel's inflamed appendix. They hoped to avoid more serious complications. Mel's parents promised to be in touch.

Carrie clearly wanted to go back to sleep as soon as she could. In the dark of the morning, Promise could only accept the offer of her transportation with gratitude. She doubted that she would sleep, however. The day's events had taken their toll.

The next morning, sunrise greeted Promise's exhaustion after she somehow managed to doze for perhaps an hour or two, at most. She knew she would never be able to attend her classes with any measure of competence. Instead, she opted to try sleeping another few hours, then jog to the hospital, hoping to visit Mel.

Fortunately, the temperature that day made such a venture possible. Promise arrived at the hospital's main entrance and quickly ascertained that she would find Mel on the surgical unit in a private room. Having gotten the needed directions, Promise found her way and stood outside Mel's closed door, wondering how best to proceed.

Suddenly, the door opened and a tall man in a white coat stood before her. Promise immediately shuddered for reasons she could not explain. She looked into his eyes and detected arrogance, lust, and shock, all of which made her feel even more vulnerable and alarmed. Oddly, he also seemed confused. He had already given her a visual once-over; his facial expression intimated that he had seen a ghost. He finally smirked and moved to brush past her. She quickly got out of his way.

Now that Mel's door stood open, Promise took a deep breath and tried to shake off the disturbing reactions just stirred in her by that man's presence. She entered Mel's room and felt immediately relieved to find her roommate relatively alert, even if a little groggy from the anesthesia for her surgical procedure.

Mel had only recently awoken. She greeted Promise with a smile. "It seems I have you to thank for saving me from a very bad outcome. I should have listened to you and stayed in our room last night. Thanks, friend!"

"You are so welcome, Mel. Are you going to be okay?" Promise asked.

"Yes, thanks to you," her roommate replied. "They will likely let me go home tomorrow if all goes well today. I probably won't be back to campus for a week or two, though. I'll miss the end of the indoor hockey season!" Mel clearly was not happy about that.

Promise had to ask, "Who was that man who just left your room?"

Mel replied, "The doctor. It seems he has a decent reputation as a surgeon, but I have to tell you he gives me the creeps."

Promise concurred, "He gave me the creeps too. Maybe you can switch doctors?"

"I don't think Dr. Roland will take too kindly to that! I watched him with a nurse earlier when he thought I was still sleeping. Let's just say that he does not handle rejection very well!"

Promise responded, "Well, what's most important is that you feel better. Stay in touch with me while you're gone, will you?"

"Absolutely, I will! Thanks again, Promise."

Mel's parents returned to her room at that point. After another round of their expressed gratitude, Promise thought it best to leave. She departed the hospital warily, hoping not to encounter the infamous Dr. Roland on her way out. She did not like the way she felt in his presence. She could not get far enough away from him, in fact. Something about the aura of the man alarmed her. She made a mental note to herself: never need a surgeon while attending Stella Maris University!

22

AFTER MID-FEBRUARY'S TURMOIL had passed, the rest of the semester significantly dulled in comparison. The weather did improve by mid-March so that Promise could reliably return to the outdoor track for her daily jog. She really valued the release it provided and privately noted how much it helped her mood. She needed it; happiness proved elusive as winter slowly transitioned into spring. Promise did her best to cope, however, and her grades once again announced her success in at least one area of her life. She could not deny that Lugh's reaction to her vision about Mel continued to hurt her deeply.

Mel eventually returned to campus, and Promise did see Lugh from afar on the track a few times. On all but one occasion, he pretended not to notice her and departed quickly. When he could not dodge her presence, he conveniently joined some friends, let her pass him as she ran by, and simply nodded his greeting. His message couldn't be clearer. Consequently, Promise did what she could to refocus her attentions with only moderate success. She wondered if they would ever speak again, if he would ever explain his sudden change of interest and behavior. In the absence of that explanation, she could only attribute the striking difference to her extrasensory gift. Honoring herself for having it became progressively more difficult.

On a brighter note, Promise really appreciated her mythology class, much to her surprise. She also discovered that some branches of psychology actually value myth's contribution to the healing of the human psyche. Unfortunately, Stella Maris offered a traditional program; its psychological tenets did not incorporate a more expansive, mythological point of view. With some disappointment, Promise realized that she would have to explore the integration of these two subjects on her own.

Her enthusiasm for this endeavor peaked in response to one particular myth; it spoke to the wounds Promise incurred as a consequence of sharing her visions with others. The ancient Greeks told the story of Cassandra, the mortal daughter of the king of Troy. Her beauty attracted the romantic attention of the god Apollo, who gifted Cassandra with second sight in an attempt to court her interest. When she refused his advances, he cursed her. Unable to rescind his gift, he broadened it to include that no one would ever believe her prophecies.

Before the ensuing Trojan War – during which the Athenian warriors hid in their gigantic, constructed, wooden horse, then entered Troy and overtook the city in battle – Cassandra had foreseen it all and tried to warn her family. No one listened. Ultimately, Athens conquered Troy, and Agamemnon, the Athenian leader, claimed Cassandra as his prize before he and his men departed for home. When his fleet finally docked on his native shore, Cassandra foresaw her own death at the hands of Agamemnon's angry wife. In her despair, she ran willingly toward his castle to meet her tragic end.

Cassandra's tale resonated deeply within Promise's own soul. She understood what it felt like to foresee the future and have no one believe her. She silently thanked her parents and Aunt Tara for not siding with the skeptics. Without her cherished loved ones, she might have easily succumbed to Cassandra's fate. Instead, she dared to hope she might fare better. Her inability to imagine how or why, however, challenged her hope significantly.

Promise went home for spring break and socialized with a few friends, but many of them had their weeklong vacation at different times. Lizzie had to focus her energies on her challenging sophomore year curriculum, plus track season had begun. Consequently, Promise went for long runs on her own and a few shorter ones with her mom. She also visited the Rainbow Healing Arts Center and took a few classes to spark her interest in something, anything. Classes on flower essences offered her a remedy combination that included Gentian, Star of Bethlehem, and Walnut. She tried yoga and liked it. She hoped all this would help.

While jogging with Brittany, Promise shared the tale of her encounter with Mel's doctor. Brittany's own sensitivities went on high alert when her daughter described the man as tall, arrogant, and creepy. Her alarm intensified exponentially when Promise expressed how she felt when he looked at her, especially when she added, "as if he had seen a ghost." Brittany took an intentional, deep breath before she asked his name. At the sound of it, her face went white. Promise noticed. They stopped running and faced each other.

Promise said as statement, not question: "You know him!"

Brittany looked hard at her daughter, not knowing how much to share. She did emphatically state, "Yes. Long ago. Please, stay far away from him!"

"I look a lot like you. Did he figure that out, I wonder?" Promise felt a deeper knowing that answered her own question.

"Did you tell him your name, by any chance?" Brittany asked.

Promise honestly responded, "No. We didn't talk at all. He would have walked right through me if I hadn't stepped away quickly enough. Do I need to be concerned, Mom?"

Brittany tried to be reassuring without lying. She had learned long ago that minimizing or distorting truth to her daughters, especially Promise, only led to worse consequences. With this in mind, she said, "I don't want you to worry, Promise. Your dad and I will see what we can find out. You won't have to deal with any of this alone, okay?"

"Okay. But what is the backstory? Why are you so alarmed?" Promise had to ask.

Brittany reluctantly decided to be honest with some serious editing thrown in: "He tried to hurt us in several ways for a year or more before you were born. His malevolence has reached across lifetimes, in fact. We had made an agreement with him that he would not work within one hundred miles of us, me especially. That agreement didn't anticipate that you would go to school outside that geographic range. Who would have thought you would wind up in the same town?!" Her voice drifted. Brittany had already shared more than she wanted to. She suddenly became very silent.

Promise sensed that her mother would say no more. She appreciated the information, however, even if limited. It confirmed her impressions. She remained hopeful that she would not have to have any contact with that surgeon ever again.

Following this revelation, unbeknownst to Promise, Peter and Brittany had several long conversations about their former nemesis. Peter experienced an edginess that he had not felt since those long months preceding notice of the lawsuit against the Rainbow Center. During that time, he had accurately sensed that something ominous would happen. That lawsuit subsequently went to trial, covertly subsidized by a pharmaceutical company in league with the infamous surgeon.

Fortunately, justice prevailed those many years ago, but Peter and Brittany fully recognized that hurting Promise in some way now would offer Mark Roland an ideal opportunity to retaliate against them. They had not anticipated this. Peter planned to consult with Angela Rilken, their attorney during those court proceedings. She had since become a family friend, helping Peter with legal matters as needed.

Meanwhile, Promise returned to Stella Maris University for the conclusion of her second semester as a first-year student. She no longer looked for Lugh on the track. She simply tried her best to enjoy the company of her roommate, who had recovered well from her appendectomy and returned to the hockey field soon after. Promise had to prepare a presentation for her mythology class, so she applied herself to the task with serious commitment. Prometheus had played a prominent role in her own life. She wanted to do justice to the Titan and her father, who obviously loved this god's story.

With only days left before the semester's end, Promise delivered her talk on Prometheus to her class, complete with slides and reflective points for discussion. Her professor's response to her project warmed her heart. His words of encouragement and his suggestion – to more seriously consider taking additional mythology classes while she pursued her psychology degree – led to deeper musings as she walked back to her dormitory.

So often, her psychology classes seemed to focus on labels and definitions, all based on statistical averages for what "most people" might think, feel, or do in the course of daily life. Those measures guided the parameters of normality; everything outside those parameters earned the stamp of abnormal – to include the intellectually challenged as well as the genius. Promise felt seriously constrained under these conditions, especially when those very statistics predicted a future of doom.

Mythology, on the other hand, offered multiple layers of interpretation. Each level of understanding opened a doorway to different possibilities. In this context, nothing was abnormal, really. A myth's characterization of an aspect of human nature left room for integration and evolution. The myths themselves seemed to evolve over time, in fact; Lugh's discussions about anthropology confirmed this. While reflecting on these legends, Promise felt herself come alive.

These ruminations about her chosen focus of study contributed to an ever-increasing sense of inner confusion. She realized that she might ultimately change her major as a result. She wanted to discuss this with Aunt Tara and her parents after her return home for the summer. During these months, she planned to work as the evening and weekend receptionist for a local medical center. Hopefully, she would have many opportunities to explore the concerns, curiosities, and questions that sometimes begged not-so-softly for attention in her mind and heart.

After all her classes had ended and she had completed the papers and presentations and taken all the exams, Promise returned to her dormitory for the last time. She still had to pack her possessions before Peter came with his SUV to take her home. As she passed the dormitory gate and the security office located there, Ralph, one of the guards, greeted her with a wave and an invitation to speak with him privately. She quickly went to his post.

"Promise, there's been a delivery for you!" He maintained discretion, not sure how this parcel might be received. He handed her a bouquet of roses, a dozen, each of a different color.

Promise received these with obvious surprise. The notecard attached immediately drew her curiosity. She thanked Ralph graciously and quickly found a quiet, secluded bench to open the envelope.

The notecard read: "Dear Promise, I've been an idiot. Please forgive me. Can I call you? Lugh." His phone number was included below his name.

Promise sat dumbfounded, relieved, tearful, curious, angry, thrilled, all at the same time. She took a deep breath, pulled out her phone and texted the number given: "Thank you, Lugh. They're beautiful. Yes, please do. I'm packing to go home right now. Will be free in a few days."

He texted back, "Would Thursday afternoon work? I'd really like to speak with you – I have some explaining to do."

She texted in reply: "That would be perfect. And yes, you do! Thanks again."

Promise smiled broadly, feeling better than she had in months. That would be perfect, indeed!

Part Two

23

AFTER PETER ARRIVED at Promise's dormitory and they had exchanged their affectionate greetings, they worked together to load his SUV with Promise's books, small refrigerator, clothes, and other possessions. As they prepared to drive away, Peter intentionally asked, "Promise, would you like to drive home?"

Promise looked up quizzically, then smiled broadly. "Sure!" she replied before adding, "Maybe I can get my own car and drive back and forth on my own from now on?"

Peter responded with a twinkle in his eye. "Are you reading my mind, or does this just make some sense?!"

"It makes lots of sense to me, Dad!!"

As they made the three-hour trek home, they discussed how Promise would pay her part of the automobile's expenses, how much her parents would contribute, and what kind of car might suit her best. Promise had already saved some money for this very venture. She also realized that she would need a part-time job near SMU's campus next fall to manage the ongoing fuel and maintenance costs. No matter. She looked forward to the independence that having her own vehicle would bring.

During their conversation, Peter also highly recommended, expected, that Promise would take a self-defense course during the summer months. Promise registered her surprise at her father's suggestion, then asked him directly, "Does this have anything to do with Dr. Roland?"

He grimly nodded. "Yes, it does, but it also doesn't hurt for you to know how to protect and defend yourself. None of us can foresee what life has in store – well, maybe you can, sometimes. I just want to feel assured that you know how to be safe. Your mother appreciated learning these skills long ago for various reasons, to include her own greater self-confidence. I'm hoping you will too."

Promise allowed her father's spoken words and unspoken feelings to settle in her being. She recognized the wisdom of his suggestion and decided she would comply. She asked, "Is there a particular kind of self-defense practice I should learn?"

Peter shook his head and replied, "There are many good ways to keep yourself safe. The best is the one that makes you feel most comfortable. I appreciated wrestling, but I don't think that's for you, necessarily. You can explore various modalities, like Tai Chi, Aikido, karate, or more specifically focused self-defense courses. I just hope you will learn something that makes you feel capable to meet an opponent on your terms and that gives you an edge in risky situations. It will allow you to think better on your feet and problem-solve in the moment, rather than get caught up in fear. That in itself is an important aspect of the whole process."

"Okay, Dad. I'll explore my options. Thanks for your care."

"You're welcome. And thanks for yours!"

Now that Peter had fulfilled his major conversational agendas for their trip, he tuned in to the scent of roses. He asked Promise about that. She smiled cryptically, then responded, "Someone owed me an apology."

Promise offered no further explanation. Peter sensed the value of leaving it be. Promise appreciated his discretion. They moved on to other topics.

They arrived home and somehow unpacked the SUV without stepping on Quirkie's paws, which, in his enthusiasm, often wandered close to their own feet. Lizzie had a track meet that day, so they planned to surprise her by attending. Brittany also arranged to join them there after work.

Lizzie noticed Promise in the stands before she began her two-hundred-meter sprint. She waved to her sister enthusiastically. Promise returned her greeting with a huge smile and their team's symbolic gesture of success.

At the sound of the gun, Lizzie sprang off the starting block and seemingly flew down the track. She clearly had inherited the greatest capability for speed in their family. Promise and their parents wholeheartedly cheered her on and jumped to their feet as she crossed the finish line first. Her team's excitement capped the event. Lizzie accepted their cheers and compliments gratefully, sneaking a peak in her family's direction to notice how they witnessed her accomplishment. They beamed and waved in response to her glance. That night, they celebrated with dinner at their favorite restaurant. Peter and Brittany took a moment to silently, gratefully share their awareness of another sweet reunion. It joined the many memories already collected in the archives of their hearts.

Promise had a few quiet days to herself before her new part-time job would demand her attention. She organized her bedroom to accommodate the things she brought home from SMU, made sure her roses had enough water, and contemplated her upcoming conversation with Lugh. She couldn't imagine what reasoning he might use to justify his avoidance of her all semester. She finally gave up trying. She decided that she would let him explain and see if it made any sense to her heart. She wanted this to work out with him, but she prepared herself for the possibility that it might not.

On Thursday afternoon, Lugh called just as he had said he would. Even though she had been checking her phone frequently, hoping not to have missed this connection, Promise startled at the sound of the ringer. She collected her wits and answered simply, "Hello." He responded with his own greeting. Promise thought she detected some sheepishness in his voice.

After Lugh engaged in some preliminary small talk, inquiring about her trip home, he got to his point. "Promise, I want to apologize for the way I avoided you most of last semester. You didn't deserve that. Admittedly, I was freaked out by your report of having visions. I didn't understand why. I have to ask, did Mel have appendicitis after all?"

Promise replied, "Yes, Lugh, she did. She was able to have surgery in time. She did well."

"I am happy to hear that. Your vision made that possible?" he asked.

"I think so. Everyone appreciated the timing for her arrival in the emergency department. They don't know about the vision, of course." Promise's tone reflected her unresolved feelings about how others had responded to her gift over the years.

Lugh heard that clearly. He replied, "Promise, again, I am really sorry. It must be hard for you. It sounds like my reaction is not the first insensitive response you've had to deal with. I've had to do some deep soul searching. I now realize that how I've handled this has had everything to do with something inside me, not your gift per se. I felt shame and guilt, maybe even grief, for reasons I have yet to understand. Fortunately, I do know now that those feelings were not caused by you. I have to figure them out for myself. But I don't want to give up a relationship with you, in whatever form it may take, just because I can't deal with my feelings. I want to deal with them without hurting you anymore. Will you forgive me?"

Promise held the phone to her ear, speechless. She hadn't imagined this outcome at all. Tears welled up in her eyes. Something healing had just begun. She sighed into the phone, then suddenly empathized with how he might hear it. She quickly asserted, "Yes, Lugh, I forgive you. I appreciate your apology. I've missed talking and jogging with you. But I have to ask you: Will my having visions continue to freak you out?"

"Honestly, I don't know," Lugh confessed, "but I do hope to handle it better. I'm interested in the visionary experience as an anthropological phenomenon, after all! I've been talking to Dylan, the shaman I mentioned to you. He suggested that maybe I'm dealing with a past-life memory related to having visions of my own. Many people were burned at the stake, women mostly, but I could have been a woman in the distant past. In any case, that's my new focus. I want to discover the roots of my discomfort. Speaking of which, I want to plant a seed with you.

"Dylan has scheduled a Lughnasadh celebration at a retreat center relatively close to your home, I think. It would be a daylong event on Saturday, the first day of August. I'm wondering if you might like to attend it with me. I'd be happy to pick you up and bring you home at the end of the day. You don't have to answer now, but I hope you will think about it. You can let me know any time before the date."

Promise felt a surge of curiosity and an intuition that her participation would prove helpful to her in sorting out her recent confusions. She had wanted to ask Aunt Tara about shamanism, in any case. She also wanted to see Lugh again. She replied, "Lugh, that sounds really interesting. I will think about it and get back to you."

"That's great, Promise. I ask nothing more...other than maybe you will let me call you during the summer? August feels like a long time from now!"

"I would really like that, Lugh. I'm starting a part-time job on Saturday, but I'll be around during the weekdays before five o'clock. Staying in touch would be great!"

"Thank you, Promise. I will do better. I will add one more colored rose to my bag of talents!"

Promise laughed. "The roses were lovely, by the way! Thanks again!"

They hung up their respective phones, each breathing a sigh of relief. More adventures together were in the air. Despite the miles between them in that moment, they each inhaled deeply, hoping to accept graciously whatever would unfold.

24

PROMISE SETTLED INTO HER NEW summer routine. She awoke early with everyone else, then sent them onward to their day's commitments before she jogged, took Quirkie for walks, ran some errands, or did some chores around the house. She read whatever indulged her curiosity at the time and loved the exploration. Weather-permitting, she went to the local swim club where Lizzie worked as a lifeguard once school ended for the summer. Promise's work hours began at five o'clock each afternoon and often extended into the evening, typically nine-thirty, sometimes later. Once she finally had her own car, her newfound sense of freedom and independence infused all her activities with a greater sense of purpose and ease.

Twice weekly, Promise also attended Aikido classes, having chosen this approach to satisfy her father's request that she learn to physically defend herself. She appreciated his concern and valued the opportunity to feel more confident, especially if confronted by the likes of Dr. Roland. She chose Aikido because she valued its founder's philosophy:

"To injure an opponent is to injure yourself. To control aggression without inflicting injury is the Art of Peace." Morihei Ueshiba, she discovered, had trained with several martial arts masters in his homeland, Japan. In his later years, he developed Aikido to encourage the spiritual and character development of its practitioners. He aimed for harmony within the individual as well as in the world. Promise studied the art seriously. Its principles resonated within her on a very deep level.

Unfortunately, Promise's work schedule didn't allow much overlap with her Aunt Tara's ongoing full-time employment. Her godmother joked that she would never retire. Promise suspected that her aunt's status might soon change, however, as Uncle Alex increasingly made more overt comments about traveling together before this lifetime passed them by. Not having made that transition formal yet, Tara did carve out a few Sundays to meet with Promise instead.

They sat together in Tara's healing room on a particularly sunny, hot, Sunday afternoon in early July. Promise couldn't help herself: she reached for the rose quartz orb and held it appreciatively, now more attuned to the loving energies it readily conveyed. They had been talking about Promise's confusion regarding her major during their last few meetings. The topic came up once again as Promise found herself resonating deeply with her explorations of myth and the spiritual focus of Aikido, not so much with the textbook discussions of psychological diagnosis and practice. She asked her aunt for her perspective.

Tara reflected on her goddaughter's observations, then harkened back to one of their initial conversations. She replied, "Promise, do you remember when we spoke of your sense of self as Mystery? How no one in the world can accurately define you because they can only respond from what they know? Your soul dwells in Mystery, the realm that mythology and spirituality humbly attempt to approach and understand while always realizing that there will be more to discover. Psychology deals more with the knowns of human consciousness, the ego's role in the midst of survival. Perhaps this is why you struggle with the topic now?"

"Aunt Tara, that makes perfect sense to me. The question is, what do I do about it? Do I continue to learn psychology because there's some value in learning more about the ego? Or do I change my major to something more suited to my quest to humbly understand what I can of the Mystery? That's my dilemma. Thanks for helping me name it!"

Tara nodded before she added, "Just to be objective, one could argue that immersing oneself in a traditional model and gaining some expertise in it could provide more credibility for those who seek their wisdom from institutionally approved authorities. On the other hand, wisdom is wisdom. Those who speak it are appreciated by those who can hear it. Resonance with the deeper truth needs no credentials to pave the way.

"Having said that, there is the work of Carl Jung, a psychiatrist from Switzerland who passed on more than half a century ago. He focused on the transcendent aspects of the soul in his quest to understand the human psyche. Dreams, myths, astrology, I Ching, and other broad perspectives informed his own journey and the theories he formulated as a result of it. I do need to mention, though, that his work is not taught in mainstream psychological circles.

"It's also important to add that the learning that leads to wisdom usually comes by way of some painful experience. Choosing to pursue a field of study that does not resonate with one's soul could fit that requirement, especially if one chooses that path from a fear of disapproval. Eventually, however, that fear would need to be faced and addressed in order to grow wise. Obviously, there is no simple, absolutely correct answer. No matter what you learn, though, you can't go wrong. It's what you do with it that counts."

Promise allowed her aunt's words to penetrate her being. They brought some measure of peace. She decided to continue on her current academic trajectory while also exploring mythological studies more deeply. She also took this opportunity to ask her beloved mentor about shamanism. Immediately interested, Tara tilted her head and raised her eyebrows, quickly admitting to her respectful but limited knowledge of the subject. She asked Promise to describe more about what prompted her question.

Promise explained, "Well, I've met someone – a senior now, I guess – who is majoring in anthropology. He runs on the track, and we've gotten into many conversations at this point about the interface and the differences between his major and mine. I am fascinated by the evolution of human consciousness, and he – by the way, his name is Lugh, after an Irish god of many talents – he notes how most myths have several versions, often depending upon the culture that tells them. He is exploring shamanism, an ancient practice, it seems. He has invited me to attend a shamanic ceremony to celebrate Lughnasadh at the beginning of August."

Tara smiled. "Perhaps he had something to do with the colorful rosebush dream?"

Promise blushed. Tara respectfully pretended not to notice. Instead, she replied, "It sounds very interesting. If the invitation feels right and appealing to you, it might be something worthy of pursuit?"

This time, Promise smiled and sighed with a relief she hadn't realized she needed. She did want to experience the shamanic ritual after all, but she hadn't decided how she felt about it. She didn't know what others would think about her interest in it. She suddenly realized that she didn't want to face their disapproval. That Aunt Tara didn't think it was dangerous reassured her considerably. She decided then and there that she would go with Lugh and see what happened. She immediately felt something within her freed from some previously hidden constraint. The joy of the moment spread across her face.

Tara noticed. She also felt pleased and aware of something she could not describe. An energy filled the room that felt very familiar. Tara paused in wonderment.

In what seemed like a response to her aunt's unspoken query, Promise exclaimed, "Oh, Aunt Tara, I almost forgot! I wanted to tell you a dream I had the other night. Do you remember when I had the one about the huge crystal a few years ago?"

Tara nodded, eager to hear more. "I do!"

"Well, I saw it again in another dream." Promise continued, "It was huge! The sparkles of color and the rays of light that diffused through its prism were breathtaking. This time, I saw it while sitting with a group of young women all dressed in white. The setting felt very sacred. One of the women really drew my attention. The more I gazed at her, I realized that she felt like you! How weird is that?! Do you think it was real? Could she have been you?" Promise asked.

Tara sat stunned by her godchild's dream. Once again, she reflected on the vague sense of familiarity she experienced with Promise from her earliest childhood. Who was she?! Tara could only respond, "It may well have been! I have had dreams of living a lifetime as a priestess in a setting very much like that. Do you know who you were in the dream?"

Promise shook her head. "No, I don't. I only experienced myself as an observing consciousness. The feeling was really warm, though. Full of respect and a kind of love. In many ways, it reminded me of how I feel towards you now. You didn't look the same, but how I felt told me it was you!"

Tara sighed. "So many mysteries! Whoever you were, I am glad to know you again in this lifetime, that is for sure. You have always felt familiar to me in an indescribable way. Perhaps we will eventually discover our mutual past. In any case, I am honored to have you in my life again!"

Promise beamed. She didn't know what all this meant, but it felt right. She hoped for its revelation in time.

25

SATURDAY, THE FIRST DAY OF AUGUST, dawned sunny and hot. Brittany and Peter planned to spend the day at the beach with Tara and Alex. Lizzie had to work at the pool. As Brittany and Peter gathered their chairs and umbrellas, blankets, snacks, and other needed possessions, Promise collected her own items according to the list recommended by Lugh. He told her to bring a seat cushion and yoga mat, a blanket for her body and a covering for her eyes, water, food for lunch and dinner, a notebook and pen, and a drum and/or rattle if she had them. Anything she couldn't provide, he would.

Peter and Brittany had taken their daughter's explanation of her day's event in stride, neither one experienced with the shamanic tradition. Promise felt a little nervous about the potential introduction of Lugh to her parents, but she accepted this tension as part of her makeup. In truth, she looked forward to her Saturday's unfolding.

Just as Peter and Brittany were sharing their own affectionate goodbyes with Promise and Lizzie, Lugh arrived. Sporting a tank top and shorts, his tanned, muscular frame and carefree, respectful manner immediately impressed Peter and Brittany with a sense of ease. Brittany, in particular, felt comfortable in his presence. Peter experienced an odd feeling of disjointed familiarity. Lugh shook hands with everyone, including Lizzie, which she enjoyed thoroughly. After their initial greetings, Lugh couldn't take his eyes off Peter's spiral-marked jaw.

Peter noticed and made a quizzical facial expression. Lugh responded immediately with an apology. "I'm sorry, sir, but I'm curious about your birthmark. It seems I have the same one."

Lugh briefly turned his back to them; the ancient insignia clearly manifested behind his left shoulder. Promise had never seen it. Standing behind Lugh at this point, her surprise registered on her face. Peter recognized her emotional shift and quick headshake, silently indicating that Lugh had no idea that she also bore the mark. She purposely wore a sleeveless top whose V-neck did not expose the spiral over her heart. Peter's returned glance toward her wordlessly conveyed that he would not betray her confidence. Lizzie, too, remained discreet in this regard.

In the momentary pause that followed, both Brittany and Peter privately wondered if Lugh might have any relationship to Mark Roland. Lugh's energy did not feel the same, however – to their considerable relief. Their observations of Lugh and his solicitous relationship with Promise gave them no cause for immediate concern. They all parted company, wishing one another a good day. Even so, the whole experience triggered many questions and unsettled feelings, which Brittany and Peter discussed at length with Tara and Alex as they drove to the shore.

Meanwhile, Promise and Lugh's travel to the Lughnasadh celebration site required almost one hour's drive. During that time, they shared what personal life happenings had occurred since their last exchange. They had communicated numerous times by phone as the summer months passed by. Usually, those conversations included their ongoing discussions about shamanism, anthropology, and psychology as well as increasingly more personal reflections. Promise looked forward to their connections very much.

As he drove, Lugh eventually confessed to his deeper feelings about having the spiral on his shoulder. "I've always thought it interesting, like it might mean something, but I've never been able to figure it out. No one else in my family has it. To see the exact same mark on your father's jaw unnerved me, I must admit. I hope I did not offend him."

Promise replied, "I don't think you did. I think he was just as mystified as you were. He always told me that the spiral indicated some ancient lineage of leadership. He experienced that during a past-life regression long ago. He has never really told me much more about it, though. I am suddenly wishing he had!"

"Maybe you can ask him sometime – when it feels right, of course. By the way, I like your family. Your sister has the family sparkle. I hope it's not too forward of me to say that I like yours the best." He offered his last comment with a glance at Promise that included a twinkle in his eyes. He also needed reassurance that she did not find his comment disconcerting.

Promise simply smiled, blushed a little, and mumbled, "Thank you!"

They drove in silence for a brief time before arriving at their destination, a rustic center in the middle of farmland, cornstalks, and fallow fields. The property included a spacious, outdoor meadow of rolling hills. Lugh explained that a Native American medicine wheel had been placed in the far corner of the estate. A fire pit marked a more central location. Upon entering an octagonal-shaped building, Lugh guided Promise to remove her shoes. He then showed her where to put her things, where to set up her seat cushion, mat, and blanket, and where to keep any food that required a colder temperature. They claimed a space wide enough for two at the perimeter of the circle gradually forming as other participants arrived.

Lugh then greeted Dylan warmly and introduced Promise with

enthusiasm. Promise sensed a delightful, yet provocative quality in the man who stood before her, wearing colorful clothes and tattoos to match. He actually had an Irish accent, which not only surprised her but added more authenticity to the mix. Promise shook hands with him, gratefully sensing that he and the space around her felt safe and welcoming.

Before they officially began, Dylan attended to the last-minute touches needed on the altar at the center of their circle. At the heart of the altar stood a foot-tall quartz crystal that supported a lit candle. Its shimmering effect highlighted the beauty of Sovereignty, Promise would soon learn, while anchoring the strategically placed crystal-held flames, one for each of the four directions surrounding it. A bowl of holy water from a sacred well in Ireland, a vase of flowers, a bowl of fruit, feathers from an eagle, and a rock from Iona occupied the spaces between the four directions and the central fire. A beautiful tapestry provided the base upon which the entire altar rested.

The participants' mats, set back from the altar, extended outward from the center like rays of the sun. Promise observed all this while also being introduced or introducing herself to the other members of the group. It seemed like a warm, pleasant gathering of seekers, each person ready to engage the ritual with serious commitment.

Dylan prepared everyone for the day's celebration by reminding them that the work of a shaman is to set an intention, attend to it, and trust. He invited them to silently formulate their personal aspirations while, as a group, they would focus on Lughnasadh, welcoming in the Celtic season of autumn by honoring the ancestors and any visionary experiences that might come forth. Promise could not deny her own excitement. She turned to Lugh and smiled; he grinned and winked in return.

As they called in the directions and honored Sovereignty as a group, they sealed their circle for the sacred work that would follow. The participants introduced themselves and mentioned their previous experience with such rituals. Promise felt relieved to learn that she was not the only novice in their midst. In response, Dylan provided a more detailed overview of his plans for their gathering that day. He also gave elaborate instructions preceding each of the steps they would accomplish together. The first item on their agenda involved determining each person's power animal, or spirit guide, for the day.

Dylan explained that one's power animal provides support, protection, and guidance in the context of journey work. Traveling in an altered state of consciousness, especially if one hopes to do it meaningfully, requires that the shaman demonstrate respect for the spirit world and gather one's allies to negotiate its mysteries. He suggested that each participant identify a partner for whom he or she would act as shaman to determine the other's power animal. He gave the group a few minutes to make their selections for pairing.

Lugh turned to Promise and said, "I would be happy to partner with you, but I don't want you to feel any obligation to agree. You may feel more comfortable with someone else you've met here. I would totally understand."

Promise appreciated his sincere offer. She spontaneously replied, "That is thoughtful of you, Lugh, but I'd be happy to pair up with you." As she said this, she had an odd sense of having said something similar long ago. To Lugh? To someone else? In any case, how strange. She kept this part of her experience to herself.

Lugh smiled and said, "We're partners for the day, then!"

Promise smiled in response.

Dylan then told them that they would take turns. One partner would lie passively on the mat while his or her companion drummed and journeyed to the spirit world to be granted a vision of the other's power animal. Dylan cautioned them to not let the intellect discredit their otherworldly perceptions. They must trust whatever presented itself. After sharing with their companions what had come to them in their visions, the partners would switch roles. Dylan would lead the drumming. Everyone agreed and took their positions. Lugh drummed first for Promise.

At the end of the sequence, Lugh and Promise sat together, as did all the paired couples, to share what they had experienced. Promise admitted that she felt lulled into the rhythm of the drum and had a vague sense of stomping feet. Lugh, who actually did the journeying, told her that her power animal was a lion. He saw his massive, maned, muscular form swiftly running through the desert. He amicably joked, "I know not to mess with you!"

Promise laughed. She took a quiet moment to see if she could sense a lion at her side. She couldn't tell if she had made it up, but that doubt likely came from her mind. Experientially, she truly perceived his powerful presence. She even thought she detected a roar.

They switched roles. Promise took Lugh's drum in hand and sat next to him as he lay on his mat. The drumming began. Promise joined the others in pulsing the rhythmic beat while her consciousness took flight. She saw men in a forest, working as a carefully trained unit. Their leader had long, dark hair, wore animal skins, and held a knife in one hand, whereas his other arm bore a shield with a carved animal upon it. His facial expression reflected his fierce commitment to the task at hand: they were hunting a wild boar. She saw the sharp, pointed tusks as the beast rushed toward the leader. Suddenly, the boar halted and stared at the man. The leader courageously faced his assailant in return. The boar turned into shimmering light and merged with the animal on his shield. The man stood taller then. Promise felt certain that she knew him.

Dylan brought the drumming to conclusion and suggested that the partners share once again what they had discovered. Lugh sat up cheerfully and quickly noticed that Promise had a confused look on her face. He incorrectly assumed that she had difficulty with the process of journeying. He tried to comfort her. She tuned in to his words as she returned to ordinary time. She took a deep breath and quickly decided to limit her description of her experience to the animal itself. If it felt right, she would share the rest with him later.

"No, Lugh, it's okay. I did see your power animal. It's a wild boar. Does that mean anything to you?" Promise asked.

"No, not really. Should it?" he responded now with his own confusion. Something within him recognized the correctness of her naming that animal for him, but he couldn't explain why. They both shrugged their shoulders and agreed to let the rest of the day's adventure unfold.

Dylan explained that they would now break for a late lunch and follow this with a journey to a wise guide who would assist them in pursuing their intentions for the day. Promise and Lugh welcomed the pause in such intense work. They gathered their food and decided to sit under a tree outdoors. A gentle, though hot breeze intermittently wound its way past them, but they hardly noticed. The pleasure of sharing this unusual experience together gave them much to discuss and to ponder.

26

JUST BEFORE THEY RETURNED to the circle for the next phase of their shamanic journeying, Promise thought to ask Lugh, "So, what did it feel like to have a vision of my power animal? Was it okay for you?"

Lugh paused, surprised by the question. He responded honestly, "I guess it was okay. I'm really thinking that I might have made it up – a thought I'd prefer to ignore – but I suppose it made the whole thing easier for me, so I could cautiously proceed." He hesitated, gazing more directly at Promise before he continued, "I suspect that's not the answer you wanted to hear?"

"No, it was fine, Lugh. Actually, I think you identified my power animal quite well. What your experience may suggest, though, is that significant emotions and/or physical sensations were not associated with your visualization. Still, that doesn't necessarily mean you made it up. It takes time to learn how to interpret such things."

Promise suddenly wondered if she had shared too much. Lugh

looked at her with greater respect, however. "It seems like you've had lots of practice with understanding your visions. Am I right?"

Promise replied, "Let's just say that I've had several opportunities, and they have confused me over the years. My aunt has helped me considerably in my attempts to make sense of them. If my telling you such things makes things worse for you, please let me know."

"Honestly, Promise, I hope you will continue to share with me the wisdom you've worked so hard to acquire. It may make me uncomfortable at times, but that's my problem, my growing edge, as they say. I hope to figure this out, and I won't if you keep silent. Just please let me know if I hurt your feelings. That is not my intention whatsoever! Okay?"

"Okay!" Promise asserted with a smile.

Dylan called them back to the group. They reentered their gathering place for the afternoon and prepared themselves for their next journey into another dimension. Promise intuited that she would soon experience a very meaningful encounter. She let her excitement have its place in her being without any expectation of a particular outcome.

Dylan explained that their next shamanic engagement with the spirit realm would involve a journey to the lower world. The three worlds – upper, middle, and lower – each had their associated gods and goddesses, gifts, and challenges. At this point, he told the story of Lugh, much as his namesake had related the tale to her more than six months ago on the track. Dylan then described how the god Lugh, as part of his ritual dying, descended to the lower world before his eventual rebirth. Each participant would also make this descent to identify and release any doubts, fears, or limiting beliefs that prevented him or her from being reborn as a true self.

Dylan continued to delineate their process: as the drumming began, they would first thank their power animal for accompanying them on the journey. Then they would imagine themselves and their protective companion running through the forest. At some point, they would descend through a hole in the ground, or slide down the roots of a tree, and enter the netherworld, where they would meet Lugh or another wise guide who would answer their questions and address their intentions. Again, Dylan cautioned them not to critique, edit, or doubt their experience. This part of the journey required their trust.

Everyone lay down on their mats and blankets, covered their eyes, and let the steady rhythm of Dylan's drumming lull them into an altered state. Promise greeted her lion who roared his welcome to her. She approached him respectfully and acknowledged her gratitude for his protection during this journey. Together, they took off at a run. Promise tuned in to the sounds of her feet and his pads on the ground beneath them. The familiar experience of runner's high pulsed through her until it transformed into a reliable sense of floating in whatever direction she chose.

She and her lion effortlessly descended down a hole in the forest floor. Leaving the trees of the woods behind them, they slid along the path of a very long root, further and further down into the earth. They eventually landed gently in a smoothly carved-out cave filled with the shadows cast by a small central fire delimited by a circle of stones.

Promise appreciatively noted how her lion stood resolute at her side. She glanced around her, observing the rocks and boulders as they shapeshifted in the fire's glow. She also noted the sound of water dripping somewhere in the distance. She waited.

Moments later, a robed, female figure appeared from behind one of the boulders. Her long, white hair draped her shoulders, shimmering in the fire's reflection. She smiled warmly and extended her hand, suggesting that Promise might like to sit with her on a large, flattened rock nearby.

Promise took her seat next to the elder woman and looked into her eyes expectantly. The gaze returned to her surprised her deeply. She felt truly seen in a way that she had not ever experienced before. Again, she waited.

The woman spoke these words to her: "Promise, I have looked forward to this day for a very, very long time. Thank you for making the effort to visit this realm so that we might meet. This encounter between us is very important. But first, I'm sure you have many questions. Please ask me whatever you like."

Promise found words difficult, but she soon realized that they weren't absolutely necessary. Still, she tried to put language to her experience so that she might remember it more easily later. She began, "Thank you for appearing to me. We were told that we would meet Lugh or a wise guide and that we could ask about our intentions for this journey. I am assuming you are that guide? Do you have a name?"

"Yes, my dear, to both questions. Your Aunt Tara knew me as Alethea. Your Uncle Alex and your father called me Alicia. I have lived many lifetimes. You may call me whatever you like."

Promise experienced surprise that the beloved adults in her life had never mentioned meeting such an amazing woman. She didn't know what to make of their reticence, but she decided she would explore that with them later. She would use this time for her own benefit.

Promise replied, "I would like to call you Alethea. For some reason, that feels right to me. We were asked to formulate our questions and intentions before making this journey. Mine relate to my ability to foresee or see things that other people don't. Why was I given this gift? What purpose does it serve?"

Alethea smiled wistfully. "You ask two very important questions. You likely do not realize that this is not the first lifetime during which you have had the second sight. You have known it more than once, and it has wounded you. The wound was not your fault, but it must be healed."

Tears sprung to Promise's eyes with this confirmation. She had sensed this in some wordless way many times during her young life.

Alethea prompted her, saying, "Please tell me about your experience of your gift thus far."

Even as Promise continued to lie still and silent in the octagonal room of Dylan's drumming, in the cave she passionately exclaimed to Alethea, "It hurts! It always hurts. I try to help people with it, but most of the time they don't want to listen. I feel ignored or ridiculed, and the terrible thing happens anyway. What good is it if no one will listen?!"

"That is exactly what wounded you in the past, Promise. I, too, know the pain of this, as does your father from the lifetime we shared together as elders. That wound needs to be healed."

"But how does one heal such a wound, Alethea?"

Alethea nodded with compassion as she replied, "There are two primary ways. One is that someone important actually listens to you, takes you seriously. But you also have to let their trusting response consciously penetrate your wound for the healing to be successful. The second way is to develop a greater wisdom regarding the knowing available from higher realms – while also not letting the relative ignorance of this world define you. Either of these paths means nothing without experiencing one or both of them directly. You have to live into it, into them. You have come to earth in this lifetime to do just that."

Promise looked to her teacher with marked confusion written all over her face. She asked, "But how do I go about pursuing either path? The first one feels especially beyond my control – the second one not far behind it!"

Alethea replied, "You are correct in the obvious ways, but the truth is that you are already on the right path. You have mostly completed the part of your earth journey that had to remind your consciousness of its mission here. Now, it is time to acquire the tools for the healing. You have actually been doing this as well. I am here to tell you that you are being steadily guided and held in love, and that you have responded well to that guidance. Don't lose faith. As you pursue your own healing, others may also reap some benefit. Your own healing is primary, however. Remember that."

"I will, Alethea. Thank you. May I mention you to Aunt Tara, Uncle Alex, and my parents?" Promise asked.

"Please do, my dear. And know that if you so choose, you and I will meet again!"

Alethea rose from her seat and disappeared behind the boulder just as Dylan's drumbeat shifted, pulsing the prearranged call to return to ordinary consciousness. Promise would have liked to converse with this wise woman for hours. Alethea's departure left her feeling amazed, grateful, and a little sad. Promise consoled herself with the thought that they might one day reconnect. In the meantime, she pledged to do her best to make sense of her elder's wisdom.

Promise and her lion retraced their ascent along the root of the immense tree that would take them back to the forest. They returned to their starting place just as the drumming came to an end. Dylan suggested that they lie quietly for a few minutes to ground themselves in the here and now before committing their experience to words in their journals. Promise discreetly wiped the tears that had wet her face and hair, hoping to escape everyone's notice as they individually recovered from their own trance state.

Eventually, Promise shifted to a seated position and retrieved her journal and pen. She tried not to glance at Lugh for fear the sight of him would distract her. She did manage one glimpse and was relieved to note that he, too, seemed immersed in the process of recording his own journey.

After several minutes of silence, Dylan suggested that the participants might wish to share something about their experience with their partner, and/or to take a needed break. They would regroup for discussion and an explanation of the evening's activities before taking some time for dinner.

Lugh remained preoccupied by his inner experience and politely indicated that he planned to take a brief walk alone outdoors to "let the dust settle." Promise appreciated the opportunity to be still, without social involvement, as she worked to better understand and integrate the gift she had just received.

When the participants gathered once more, some members shared the contents of their journeys; some asked questions. Several remained silent while continuing to reflect on their private experience, Lugh and Promise among them.

Dylan then explained that all the Celtic seasons were celebrated with a fire ceremony. Tonight, they would burn the Wicker Man, an ancient ritual that dated back to a time of human sacrifice. In the more modern version, they would load a man's clothing with straw along with the handwritten notes of what each participant hoped to release to the fire. Separately, they would also include their written intentions for what qualities they would like to develop in place of those relinquished. Once the Wicker Man had burned completely, they would celebrate with more feasting and bring their ceremony to a close.

All this transpired just as Dylan had described it. Promise and Lugh remained socially cordial to each other and the members of their group as the evening progressed, but each clearly felt something deep within that they had yet to understand. Their drive home that night began a process of discovery and healing that would last well into the season of Celtic autumn and the next.

27

AFTER THEY BADE THEIR FAREWELLS and gathered their things, Lugh and Promise walked in silence under the stars to the car. Without light pollution, the Milky Way paved its glorious, twinkling road in the sky, leaving Promise in awe of its splendor. Lugh explained that many ancient cultures believed that the Milky Way guided people to the afterworld. His comment further heightened Promise's sense of wonder. She recognized Orion the Hunter overhead. She immediately thought of Lugh and his power animal. She gazed at him more thoughtfully.

Lugh felt her attention in the dark of the evening. He unlocked his car, and they packed most of their possessions into his trunk. As he closed that compartment, he turned to her and said with great tenderness, "Promise, I really appreciate that you came with me today. Your company has made this whole adventure easier and more meaningful for me. Thank you."

He gently touched her cheek. When she didn't pull away, he kissed her. She returned his kiss with her own. She then added, "Lugh, today has been magical in so many ways. It will take me a while to understand them all. Your invitation has made all this possible; without it, I would never have experienced this. I don't know anyone else who participates in shamanic rituals!"

They both laughed. Suddenly, an automobile's headlights flashed in their direction, and they immediately realized that Lugh would need to move his car. They glanced at each other with a smile, then quickly seated themselves in his vehicle for departure. They rode for several minutes before Lugh spoke.

"Promise, do you think there are such things as past lives?"

She replied simply, "I certainly can't prove that there are, but the idea resonates strongly with me. Why do you ask?"

"Well, the journey I took to the underworld unnerved me a bit. Do you mind if I share it with you?"

Promise thought she detected Lugh's earlier preoccupation with his journey flash once more across his face. She quickly responded, "I'd be honored. Can you drive and describe it at the same time?"

Lugh replied, "I'm going to try. I don't want your parents to worry that I've abducted their precious daughter!"

Promise laughed. "I'm sure they would appreciate your thoughtfulness, but do be safe! Okay?"

Lugh nodded his agreement, then he proceeded to tell his tale. "My perception of meeting the god Lugh seemed very vague to me, but I did ask him to show me why I have such difficulty with visionary experiences. I detected a smile before he directed me to a scene in which I led men through a forest. They were all wearing animal skins. Some of their faces were painted or otherwise vague. I didn't recognize anyone as familiar. They took orders from me, clearly. We were hunting a wild boar.

"Suddenly, one of the men made a misstep. The boar turned to attack that man. I felt a terrible sense of potential loss and rushed to save him. The boar gored me instead. That's all I remember. I asked Lugh, my namesake, about it. He said, 'Understanding your difficulty with visions will involve facing some painful memories. You have a choice to make.' And then the journey concluded. Dylan called us back."

Lugh added, "I'm sorry to burden you with this, but there aren't many people who would understand it. Thanks for listening, at the very least."

Promise sat in silence for a few moments before she decisively replied, "Lugh, it makes sense why that journey unnerved you. You were left with a difficult choice to consider, and you don't even know how painful those memories will be.

"If it helps to know this," Promise continued, "I do believe in past lives, even more so now. When I journeyed to discover your power animal, I saw a man leading a band of hunters. He was tall, dark-haired, dressed in animal skins, and very brave. A boar chased him in my vision. The man turned to face the beast, then stood quite still. Instead of being gored, as I expected, the boar fixed his eyes on the man with respect, then turned into a shimmering light and merged with the animal figure carved on the man's shield. The man stood taller. That's how I knew it was your power animal."

Lugh had to pull the car to the side of the road at this point. Fortunately, there was little traffic. He flashed his emergency lights just in case. He turned to Promise, awestruck.

"Really?! You really saw all that?" This time, Lugh believed that she could. He even wanted her to confirm the reality of her vision. He needed the strength of it. He did not want to fail – again – whatever that meant.

Promise hoped that she accurately perceived the feelings beneath his words, but she couldn't be sure. Perhaps this might lead to one of those healing experiences Alethea had mentioned to her. She decided to take the risk. She affirmed her knowing. "Yes, Lugh, I did. It felt very real to me. I have no doubt that it was."

Lugh sat back and stared straight ahead, letting these possibilities work their way past his long-held resistance. He wanted to believe her. He needed to believe her. He wanted to heal whatever this was. How bad could it be? What did he have to face? Did he have the courage? Promise seemed to imply that he did.

Lugh turned back toward Promise and humbly said, "You have just given me a huge gift. I don't know what all this means, but I sense it is really important. Thank you. Given my previous reaction to you on the track last winter, I appreciate your willingness to tell me this. Again, thank you."

A tear escaped and rolled down Promise's cheek. She gestured to brush it away, but Lugh got there first. He kissed her cheek, then her lips, and once more said, "Thank you, Promise."

She responded with her own more passionate gratitude. A truck's headlights soon beamed on them from the other side of the highway, returning them both to this world. They chuckled before Lugh restarted his car; they proceeded on their way. Lugh finally returned Promise to her family's sanctuary. He still had another hour's drive before he arrived at his own.

Lugh helped Promise carry all her things from the trunk to their porch. As they parted, he said, "I am really looking forward to our next semester together. By the way, Dylan will celebrate the next Celtic holiday at Samhain closer to campus. If you would like to join me again, I would love it!"

Promise glowed, detectable even in the dark. "I would too! Thank you again for a wonderful day and some amazing journeys!" She reached up and kissed him good night.

He replied, "One more for the road?"

They laughed. They kissed. He left. Both smiled into the next several days.

28

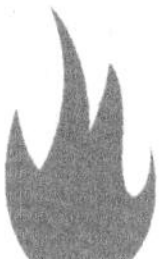

SUNDAY MORNING SUNSHINE eventually woke Promise from a very deep sleep. The shift in her consciousness immediately brought the magic of the previous day and evening to her attention. She smiled. She had no idea what might unfold during the next semester, but she looked forward to it now more than ever.

She eventually made her way to the kitchen, where her parents had already convened for breakfast. She casually asked them about their time at the beach.

Peter responded, "It was quite nice, actually. Not as hot as here and, of course, it's the beach! We had a good time."

Brittany asked, "How about you, Promise? How was your day? Lugh seems very nice, by the way."

Promise knew they would ask about her experience. She decided to be honest and to ask the questions that would confirm or deny the validity of her journey. She began, "Well, it was very interesting – really surprising, in fact. It seems that shamanic journeying is a more intentional way of accessing the kinds of perceptions I have received unpredictably through dreams and visions. A woman appeared to me. She called herself Alethea. Dad, she said that you knew her as Alicia. Does this make any sense to you?"

One look at Peter's stunned face and Promise knew that it did. She couldn't help it. She blurted out, "She was real?"

"Yes, Promise, she was very real," Peter replied and then added, "Your Aunt Tara knew her as Alethea. Uncle Alex and I met her at St. Raphael's and knew her as Alicia."

Brittany asked, "Did she communicate with you?"

Promise nodded and said, "She did. She told me that I have had the second sight in past lifetimes. She said that I am here to heal a wound related to those experiences. She said that you, Dad, and she were elders together during one of her own lifetimes and that you both foresaw difficulties, but no one would listen. Is that true?"

Peter's raised eyebrows accompanied his momentary speechlessness. Finally, he found some words: "Actually, I was never absolutely certain of Alethea's presence during that lifetime. I was an elder of an ancient community that had established itself around a huge obelisk. Omens and other indicators suggested that a great cataclysm would soon occur. The elder woman in our leadership community never spoke with me directly. Her facial expressions communicated volumes, however. That you now confirm her identity as Alethea feels right to me, especially after listening to your Aunt Tara's description of her. In anticipation of the impending disaster, Alethea and I wanted everyone to evacuate. Instead, they opted to stay. Most died, and our civilization was destroyed."

At the mention of the huge obelisk, Promise's own jaw dropped. She finally admitted to her parents that she had seen that same obelisk in two dreams. The convergence of all this information astounded her. It especially confirmed that her vision of Alethea during her shamanic journey offered serious encouragement and important advice for her during this lifetime. That this wise guide had played a role in the lives of her loved ones suggested a huge web of even greater mystery.

Peter, Brittany, and Promise sat together, stunned and silent, for several minutes. In the context of all this, Promise couldn't even imagine where her anticipated conversation with Aunt Tara might lead. Before she met with her dear mentor, however, she had a few more questions to ask her parents.

Returning to her curiosity of the previous day, Promise asked Peter, "Can you tell me more about the spiral, Dad?"

This question startled Peter back to the present moment. Promise could not mistake her father's confusion on this issue. He hesitantly replied, "I've had this on my face my whole life. As a child I felt really embarrassed about it. As soon as I could grow a beard, I covered it. When Mom and I met, she had no idea that I had this mark on my jaw. I didn't shave my beard until I experienced another past life during which I learned that the spiral conferred the role of leader upon select members of the tribe. It seems that in the ancient past my father, his father, and my grandfather's mother all bore the mark. In that lifetime, I did as well, along with my older brother."

Promise mused, "So, why do you think you also have it in this lifetime? Why do I have it? Why not Lizzie? And what about Lugh?!"

Brittany interjected, "Actually, Promise, that's what we were trying to figure out for most of our time at the beach. We found the part about Lugh especially mystifying."

Peter inquired, "Do you happen to know if anyone in his family also has the mark?"

Promise shook her head. "No, he spontaneously said that no one did. He has wondered about it all of his life. He also admitted that he, too, was shocked to see it on you, Dad. He still doesn't know that I have it as well. I don't know why I didn't tell him, but it didn't feel right just yet. Thanks for not saying anything about that yesterday."

"It sounds like there are more questions here than answers!" Brittany exclaimed.

Peter quipped, "Well, it's not like we haven't experienced *that* before!" More seriously, he added, "We can only keep asking the right questions and let the answers unfold in time. Hopefully, we'll figure it out!"

Promise smiled. "Aunt Tara once commented that whenever you say that, you are usually right!"

29

THE FOLLOWING SUNDAY, Promise rang the doorbell to Aunt Tara's home. Uncle Alex responded with a cheery greeting. They warmly embraced as he said, "So, how's my favorite shaman?!"

Promise laughed and joked back, "I have no idea! I will need a few more journeys to figure that out. Any traveling plans for yourselves yet?"

Tara came from the living room just then. Having heard the question, she replied with a wink, "We're working on that!"

Alex tilted his head and smiled, gratefully adding, "We are, indeed!"

Promise hugged her aunt, then they proceeded toward her healing room to meet for the last time before Promise returned to campus for her sophomore year. Tara knew about the dilemma of the spiral. She had not yet heard the details of Promise's journey. Even so, she knew they would have much to discuss.

Promise took her usual seat, smiled as she reached for the rose quartz orb, then launched into her adventure from the previous week.

She described the ritual in more detail than she had shared with her parents, including the more specific aspects of her journey. When she got to the part in the cave where she met Alethea, she paused.

"Aunt Tara, the wise guide that I met there was an elderly woman with long, white hair. She smiled at me warmly and invited me to sit by her side. She told me her name was Alethea and that she knew you."

Promise again paused to appreciate her aunt's reaction. The startled look on her face soon gave way to a broad smile. "I suspected that she was involved somehow! Please tell me more."

Now Promise felt surprised. "How did you guess that?"

"My first clue came from your dreams of the obelisk," Tara confessed. "When you dreamed of the priestess gathering and recognized me, I knew she had to be present. She was our teacher. Still, I am in awe that she appeared to you. I am also very happy for you. You could not have a better guide!"

Promise felt a deep sense of peace in response to her aunt's revelation. She then proceeded to tell Tara what Alethea had told her about her second sight and the wound she needed to heal. "Alethea told me that I've already had the necessary experiences to remind me of that wound. She also said that I've taken the right steps to develop some tools to deal with it. I immediately thought of you when she said that, Aunt Tara! You've been teaching me all along!"

Tara's momentary bewilderment again spread into a broad smile. Her dream of Alethea long ago, before Peter and Brittany had even married, when her beloved mentor asked her to facilitate a greater awareness of time – the impact of sudden surprises on the trajectory of past into present into future so that something crucially different might unfold – now made extraordinary sense to her. That very important something involved the birth of Promise and her journey to heal. Tara's assistance to Brittany and Peter with past-life regressions and points of clarification had supported their discernment process and the deepening of their relationship. Alethea had certainly guided Tara as priestess in a similar way. Why not Promise as well?

Tara felt like one mystery had been solved. Still, many more awaited her discovery. Tara replied to her godchild, "Promise, it has been an honor and a pleasure to mentor you in this part of your becoming. Bits of confusion from the past have suddenly morphed into a better understanding for me, that what I have done over the years involved exactly what was needed. It is very gratifying to finally realize this. I am grateful to you!"

Promise sighed. "It sounds like both of us have had to live our lives not knowing if we were on the right track. I, too, really appreciated Alethea's confirmation that I am following my path. Why is it like that, do you think? Why do we have to live life with so much uncertainty?"

Tara thoughtfully responded, "I don't know for sure – which only proves the point – but I do know that when certainty eludes us, dealing with the unknown requires that we notice our instincts and intuitions and decide whether we will pay attention to them. It becomes a particularly difficult choice when social expectations run counter to this inner wisdom. Do we sacrifice our inner guidance to belong to the group? Or do we stand true to our nature and risk ostracism? Ideally, we honor our true selves and hope to find the right community to welcome us. But that part, too, is filled with unknowns. Consequently, the ego is at a loss. This aspect of psychology leads to the spiritual path."

"Aunt Tara, I really appreciate how wise you are! What you tell me is difficult, but at least it makes sense. I hear you constantly telling me that there are no easy or absolutely right answers, only the challenge of living the life I was born for, making the choices that open the necessary doors, and having the courage to see what unfolds. Do I have that right?"

"Promise, I couldn't have summarized it better myself! You learn well!!"

Promise blushed and beamed simultaneously. She then turned her attention to the more delicate topic on her heart and mind that day.

"Aunt Tara, do you mind if I ask you a few questions about Lugh and the spiral? I don't want to talk behind his back. I can only speak about my experiences of him – in this lifetime and in the past, or so it seems. Is that possible? Have I shared a past life with him?"

Tara tilted her head as a quizzical look also crossed her face. "It is possible. What makes you ask?"

"Well, I've had a few flashes of feeling something oddly familiar when I'm with him, but I can't say what it is. I also had a vision of his power animal that, it turns out, may have involved his experience in a past life. I personally wasn't in either scene, mine or his, and didn't detect anything recognizable in my vision or in his telling. Consequently, I have no idea if I knew him in that lifetime or not. It's just weird.

"Added to that, my visions freak him out – at least, they did last winter. He essentially disappeared for the rest of the semester and didn't reappear until the end when he sent me a bouquet of a dozen multicolored roses to apologize. From our talks together, it seems like we have different aspects of the same wound to heal: he struggles with my having visions, and I hurt when mine are not taken seriously. It feels like we have work to do together, but I have no clue if I'm right, or what that work might be. It's just weird!"

Tara nodded her understanding, which she followed with some reflection: "Promise, you may be right about all this, but it's impossible to know for sure at this point. You can only put one foot in front of the other and decide: Will you follow your nature's instincts and intuitions? Or will you resign yourself to our culturally defined, should-oriented perspective regarding other people's expectations and needs. That challenge may even involve your relationship with Lugh: your nature versus his needs. You will always have a choice, no matter how challenging that choice may present itself to you at times. No one can make it for you. It is the essence of freedom."

Promise looked deeply into her aunt's wise eyes. Her instincts told her she had to go forward. Her intuition flashed the knowing of difficult times ahead. She suddenly remembered the equally difficult invitation Lugh received from his namesake during his journey. They each had choices to make. She hoped that her lion and his boar would help to carry them through.

30

PROMISE PLANNED TO RETURN to campus a week early, hoping to apply for a part-time job to support her new chariot. She laughed at the thought. How anthropological! She and Lugh had also decided to meet for dinner at the local diner to share their ongoing reflections about their Lughnasadh experience as well as their schedules for the new semester. Excitement permeated her being. Still, leaving home once again proved bittersweet.

Fortunately, this parting seemed easier for Lizzie, which also made it easier for Promise. Peter and Brittany felt the loss keenly, however, along with their significant, unspoken concerns, yet they also wanted to support their daughter's budding independence. Promise sensed this, appreciated them all the more for it, and assured them that she would call them upon her arrival on campus.

Fortunately, the dorms had opened to accommodate the pre-semester activities of the sports teams and incoming first-year students. Mel and Promise had already, gladly arranged to room together for their sophomore year. Mel would arrive the following day. Promise knew exactly where to place her things. Friends assisted her by unloading and carrying her heavier objects. Familiarity had its perks!

Early the next morning, before Mel arrived, Promise kept the appointment she had made at the local medical center that had posted a part-time position for an evening and weekend receptionist. She found its location easily; the neighboring strip mall along the main road provided a helpful landmark. After the interview, she returned to her dorm to discover that Mel had already settled in and left her a note. They would reconvene later that evening. In the meantime, Promise looked forward to having dinner with Lugh. She arrived at the diner with good news.

"Lugh, I got a job!"

"Really? Congratulations! Where is it? Doing what, if I may ask?" Lugh privately hoped it would not interfere too much with their ability to spend time together.

Promise responded, "It's at the Dunkirk Hollow Medical Center, a mile down the road. They need a receptionist for the building two nights a week and Saturday mornings. It's very similar to the job I had this summer. I should be able to do some homework during the slow times while I'm there. My boss is a very nice woman, but she also strikes me as shrewd. I suspect she runs a very tight ship."

With relief Lugh replied, "That's great! When do you start?"

"Next week. She has already given me the tour and introduced me to some of the doctors and staff. Of course, I met the day people. The evening crew will likely be different. I'm excited!" Promise exclaimed.

They shifted their conversation to the topic of their classes. Promise planned to take the next level of psychology courses along with a class in the myths of Sumer and ancient Egypt. She dreaded the required statistics course, which had earned a daunting reputation. Lugh assured her that it was truly quite manageable. He would help her should she run into any problems. This time, Promise felt the relief. She also had another required biology course on her roster. She capped it off with a class in music.

Lugh indicated that his own schedule was equally hefty. He had three anthropology classes: Human Paleontology and Prehistoric Archeology, Anthropological Linguistics, and Medical Anthropology. He tagged on an elective in music as well; he needed only a few more credits to graduate. He apprehensively added that the instructor for the Medical Anthropology course suddenly resigned her position for some unknown reason. He truly hoped they would not cancel the class.

Promise empathized with his concern, then mused, "It sounds like the content in some of our classes may interweave once again."

In response to her comment, Lugh smiled broadly. "It does. Your biology course and my fossils. Your myths and my sojourn into the land of ancient linguistics. It should be fun! I expect it will make our runs on the track very interesting this year!"

Their conversation about the ancient past naturally segued into their more personal reflections about Lughnasadh. Lugh spontaneously noted, "I've given the feelings stirred by my past-life vision deeper consideration. It seems to me that the person I tried to save from the boar's attack may have been my son. I could be totally wrong, of course. I can only say it based on my realization that it *felt* that way. Do you have any thoughts about this?"

Promise honestly admitted that her own sense of his experience did not offer her any relevant information. She could only encourage him to stay with his feelings and see where they might take him over time.

Lugh appreciated her suggestion. He then added, "Promise, we spent most of that evening talking about my journey. During our few phone calls since then, I never did ask you about yours. You haven't mentioned it either, so I don't want to pry. I only want to express interest if you care to share."

Promise suspected that Lugh might ask her about this at some point, and she hadn't yet decided how to respond. In that moment, she remembered her Aunt Tara's advice; she chose to honor her instincts. She replied, "Well, it was strange really. An elder woman appeared to me as my guide and told me that she knew my aunt, my uncle, and my father in past lives. She told me that I've had the second sight in other lifetimes and that I experienced a wound related to that gift in some way. She told me I am here now to heal that wound."

Noticing that he didn't seem to emotionally retreat, she added, "The really weird thing about that, Lugh, is that my father and my aunt both confirmed that they knew the elder woman. She had guided them as well. It blew me away!"

Promise didn't know if she had shared too much. She tentatively awaited his response.

Lugh seemed pensive. After a very long pause, he responded, "That really *is* strange. With what I'm about to say, Promise, I want to be very clear that I believe you one hundred percent. Honestly, though, I am having trouble with the concept that the timelines and our consciousness are so fluid."

Seeing that he had not offended her, he continued, "I realize this has something to do with how my brain is wired, or maybe with how it has been conditioned. Yet, here I am studying the ancient past as if it matters. I guess the difference is that I can study the past and not have to relive it. It is separate from me. Your suggestion implies that it is not so separate. Maybe that's what Lugh, the god, was trying to tell me during the journey. To heal those wounds, I have to re-experience the painful feelings. That's like living the past in the present but without all the physical contributors and consequences."

Lugh quickly added, "And please forgive me. I don't mean to make this all about me. It must be amazing to have the experiences you have!"

Promise responded, "Amazing, yes, and hard. I appreciate what you said about the blurring of time and consciousness. It would seem that it's the emotions, the feelings, that truly have to heal. But to do that we have to feel them all over again. I respect the courage it takes to face them for the purpose of healing."

Lugh sighed. "It seems like we both have our work cut out for us."

Promise smiled wistfully. "I suspect we do. Thanks for staying with me regarding this conversation. It matters and means a lot to me."

"You are most welcome," Lugh replied. "I appreciate your listening to me as well." Taking a moment to survey the diner, Lugh added, "Given that our waitstaff would likely welcome a new set of customers now that we've finished our meal, might I interest you in some coffee or tea, either one hot or iced, at my apartment? We walk by it on the way to your dorm. My roommate may still be there. He's a good friend, and I'd like for you to meet him."

"That would be great!" Promise responded.

They left the diner and casually walked in the direction of Lugh's senior-year residence. He had a second-floor walkup. Promise commented, "I guess this keeps your running legs in shape!"

They laughed as he opened the front door and invited her to enter first. His roommate, Brad, lounged on the sofa watching a sports show broadcast on their wall-mounted, flat-screen television. He quickly sat upright and smiled toward Promise as Lugh introduced them to each other. Brad's slender form stood to medium height, noticeably shorter than both Promise and Lugh. His long, curly, black hair playfully accented his animated, friendly demeanor as he turned off the show, assuring them that he had to leave for a meeting soon anyway. He and Promise shared some superficial details about their majors before he left. On his way out, he added that he would be gone for the next several hours.

Lugh shrugged and smiled, then invited Promise to pick her beverage. She selected iced tea. As he prepared the brew, she noted her surroundings. The partially shaded, large windows allowed a fair amount of light into the open living room and kitchen area of darker woods and furniture. Paintings and posters included an eclectic collection of impressionistic art and modern jazz. The space had a comfortable, yet decidedly masculine feel to it. Promise reflected this to Lugh with respect for his role in the arrangement.

Lugh took that as a compliment and thanked her as he handed her a glass of iced tea. She thanked him as they positioned themselves together on the sofa recently vacated by Brad. Promise suddenly sensed an uneasy space between them. Her desires wanted to bridge the gap, while her instincts warned her to wait.

Lugh sensed it too, but with no such reservations. He faced Promise directly and said, "Promise, I don't want to make you uncomfortable here. I won't lie. I'm very attracted to you. I told you the day I met you that I think you are very beautiful. Still, I value our friendship and don't want to lose that. We can watch TV, play a board game, or talk about fossils. Whatever you like."

Promise couldn't help herself. She gazed into his eyes with the longing she felt in her heart. It surprised her. She had no clue as to whether this new feeling reflected her instincts, her intuition, or something completely different. Lugh saw it and read it well. He gently reached across the space between them and stroked the soft skin of her cheek. Again, she couldn't help herself; she leaned into his touch. His whole hand held her face now as he drew her toward him. She dissolved into the moment as they kissed more deeply and passionately than ever before. The moment lasted into eternity. His hand gently slid down her neck and under the opening in her blouse. She suddenly thought of the spiral birthmark over her heart and instinctively pulled away.

Promise immediately wanted to cry. She could explain none of this to herself. Lugh did not let go of her hand even as he let her separate from him. He wanted to stay connected, even if it had to include her pain. He couldn't comprehend why he felt this so insistently. He just knew he had to stay true to her in that moment. A grief threatened to explode within him if she disengaged from him entirely. They stared into each other's wound without fully recognizing it. It rendered them speechless for several minutes.

Promise finally found some words for her inner experience. "Lugh, I'm sorry. I'm just not ready, I guess. It's not you at all. It's me. I don't know what it is, but I'm just not ready. I'm sorry."

Lugh quickly responded, "Promise, no need to apologize. I meant what I said earlier. Your friendship matters to me beyond measure. I'm hoping you realize that you can say no to this moment and not lose me as a friend. If anyone should apologize, it would be me."

A tear rolled down Promise's cheek. "Something is going on inside me, Lugh; something I don't understand. I need to understand it first. I can't be with you like this until I do."

"I'm with you on this, Promise. Honestly, something is pulling at me as well. Maybe we can both take a little time to figure ourselves out and still run on the track together?" Lugh hoped with all his heart and breath that she would say yes.

"That would be perfect. Again, I'm sorry, for me as much as you. Thank you for understanding and for acknowledging your own confusion. Maybe we've just tapped into our work together?!" With irony she added, "Oh, happy day..."

Lugh chuckled, grateful for a shift in their mood. "I suspect you are right about that. All the more reason for us to each figure out our part in it. I would personally prefer that our heroic efforts not go on one minute longer than necessary!"

Promise laughed as well. She felt a measure of relief that their bond had not been broken. They agreed to call it an evening. Lugh walked her to her dorm and lightly kissed her goodnight. She smiled at him appreciatively. They parted.

Promise managed to collect herself before she reconnected with Mel. Fortunately, her roommate was exhausted. They agreed to have breakfast together in the morning when they could more coherently engage in meaningful conversation. Mel quickly fell fast asleep.

Promise lay in the dark of their room for almost an hour, thinking about her evening with Lugh. She recalled her Aunt Tara's wisdom about honoring her instincts and the risks that those choices might entail. She had come face to face with that reality this evening. To her great relief, Lugh responded well to her choice. It seemed to trigger something uncomfortable in him as well, but he did not run away from it. Maybe this was exactly the path they needed to travel after all?

On that brief note of inner peace, Promise finally surrendered to sleep.

31

LUGH AND PROMISE MET on the track the following Wednesday. They had not seen each other since their evening at the diner, soon followed by the uncomfortable confusion that had settled between them in Lugh's apartment. Promise felt awkward though eager to see him. Lugh eased their transition with his warm greeting, "How's my friend?!"

Promise smiled with relief and appreciation. She replied, "Well, thank you. How's *my* friend?!"

He beamed in return. They set their pace and related the details of their lives over the past several days. Classes had begun and Promise had completed her first evening's employment at Dunkirk Hollow Medical Center. They had much to share.

Promise described how her psychology class this semester focused on child development. The instructor engaged her class with a reflective, youthful lightheartedness. He shared stories from his many years of experience that included hilarious encounters and moments of deep gratification as well as humanly induced heartaches and unavoidable tragedies. Promise acknowledged her appreciation for his sensitivity and teaching style. She then characterized her statistics professor as stodgy, but she indicated with relief that the assignments thus far seemed manageable. She found her mythology class fascinating once again. Biology was biology. Her music class promised to be fun.

Lugh listened with genuine interest. Before he launched into his own class experiences, he wanted to know more about her new, part-time job. Promise smiled as she recalled the evening. She reported, "The place is busy. They give me lists of who is scheduled for each department. My job is to note their arrival and send them to the right place. Some of the doctors have a private entrance, but all of their patients have to come past me. The receptionist for the family physician is a hoot! She privately confessed that she loves astrology. She even offered to teach me a thing or two!!"

Lugh laughed. "I know nothing about astrology, but it does interest me. The ancients were accurate observers of the stars, you know. Does she teach the subject on the side?"

Now Promise laughed. "I don't know, but I'll find out!"

Promise then asked Lugh to describe his classes. He portrayed his Human Paleontology and Prehistoric Archeology professor as having much in common with Indiana Jones – seemingly very professional in his suit and tie, but able to tell tales that only the brave adventurer would dare to experience repeatedly. Promise thought she detected a gleam in Lugh's eye; he obviously liked the man and respected him. She found herself wondering if he might like to live such a life. In that moment, she didn't have the courage to contend with his answer. Instead, she asked about his other classes.

Lugh readily expressed how his Anthropological Linguistics professor obviously loved her work. While it seemed fairly tedious and challenging in many ways, she clearly possessed the passion to hunt for clues about meaning. It required getting into the mindset of an ancient people. He expected to enjoy the course thoroughly. He thought his music class would be quite easy in comparison, for which he felt considerable relief.

Promise then asked him about the Medical Anthropology course: "Was it cancelled? Did they find someone?"

Lugh's facial expression brightened considerably. "They *did* find someone! As it turns out, a physician from the local hospital offered to teach a class. They asked him if he knew anything about ancient medical practices. He described himself as an expert in the field, and they hired him on the spot! That's the story he tells, anyway. I'm not sure how expert he really is, but when I challenged him on a particular issue, he accepted my point of view. I suspect we will have many lively discussions. I like him!"

"That's great!" Promise exclaimed. "You need that class to graduate, don't you?"

"I do," Lugh confirmed. "His experience as a surgeon will have much to offer us, even if he doesn't know much about ancient techniques."

"A surgeon?" Promise suddenly felt overcome by a very uncomfortable feeling. "Lugh, what is his name?"

Lugh noticed the shift in her mood and demeanor. He replied, "Mark Roland. Why?"

Promise stopped running and stood quite still. She found herself wondering why that surgeon would want to teach a class at Stella Maris. He certainly knew that Mel was a student at the university... and that likely she was too? A chill ran up her spine and suddenly made her shudder.

Lugh stopped just as abruptly and faced her, feeling very concerned. He asked, "Are you having another vision?"

She looked directly into his eyes now and said, "No, Lugh. Just an intuition. My parents have a painful history with him. He and I met when I went to visit Mel after her appendectomy. He was her surgeon. He gave me the creeps. I look like my mother. I am wondering why he is here."

Lugh once again had to confront his own inner conflict. He liked the man, and he wanted this course to run to completion. Yet here was his "friend" telling him that she felt very uncomfortable in this surgeon's presence. He checked his impulse to minimize her feelings. Still, he didn't want to indulge them either.

Lugh finally responded, "Promise, I want to be sensitive to your feelings. You don't have to meet him, you know. Maybe it's all just one grand coincidence. I'm sure he's so busy that he will not spend much extra time on campus. My class meets weekly on Wednesday mornings in the Honors Center. You can hopefully avoid him without any trouble. Does that help?"

Promise recognized Lugh's clumsy attempt to comfort himself by trying to alleviate her concerns. Her intuition was too strong, however. She decided not to press the issue, given that she had no justification for doing so and no overt reason to worry. Lugh was correct: she could avoid contact with the surgeon. In fact, what a gift to have Lugh give her this advanced warning. That thought did bring her some relief.

She replied honestly, "A little. I am grateful for the information regarding his presence on campus. I will avoid the Honors Center on Wednesday mornings. I hope you will let me know if you notice any changes in his schedule or whereabouts?"

"Of course, if you want me to. You really are concerned! I'm sorry about that, but I truly do hope it proves to be nothing. I will keep an eye out for you, okay?"

"Okay. Thanks!" Promise perceived the need to let this part of their conversation come to its conclusion. As a result, however, her ambivalence about resuming Aikido classes also came to an end. She firmly decided to enroll in a weekly class, no matter how much strain it added to her busy schedule. Doing something proactive felt better to her than waiting passively for her intuition's warning to unfold.

They finished their run and parted company with plans to meet again in a few days. Lugh sensed that the mention of Mark Roland had inserted another small wedge between them. It disturbed him greatly for reasons he could not explain. He returned to his apartment knowing that he had yet one more mystery added to his lengthening list of growing edges. He resolved to face them in their turn. He hoped he would handle them well.

32

AS THE WEEKS PASSED, Promise's hypervigilance about running into Dr. Roland gradually abated. She had enrolled in a weekly Aikido class. Her academic courses progressively required more of her attention. She also found herself enjoying her employment at the medical center very much. Meeting new people, some of them fellow students scheduled for sports physicals, enlivened her evenings and Saturday mornings while also allowing her to complete some of her class assignments. Having her own car made the commute easy. She also enjoyed learning a little astrology from Kay, the family doctor's receptionist, when time allowed.

Promise and Lugh maintained their contacts on the track at least twice each week, often more. They also had dinner together on the weekends, having agreed to keep things light between them. These casual contacts only fueled their inner fires of attraction, but each of them recognized that something lay buried deep within. It nudged at their consciousness, especially in each other's company, but neither discussed it with the other. Pounding the earth with their feet and talking about what interested their minds allowed them to keep the deeper tensions building within and between them at a manageable level. Promise knew it couldn't last much longer. Once again, her intuition proved itself correct.

In early October, Promise arrived at the medical center on Tuesday evening, accompanied by an uncharacteristic, vague sense of unease. She readied her lists and settled her reading materials discreetly at her desk. Kay arrived and they chatted briefly. Kay had her own preparations to make for the family doctor and his patients before their office hours began. Various people came and went, registering with Promise as they did so.

Strangely, Lydia Keegan, the owner of the medical center and Promise's boss, also made an appearance that evening. Lydia explained that as a consequence of their contract with Dunkirk Hollow General Hospital, new physicians occasionally replaced others at the medical center when their professional responsibilities took them elsewhere. A new doctor would arrive this evening. She would be giving him a tour. Promise would have his patients on her list once he officially began his work at the center later that week.

Not minutes after Lydia offered her explanation, a tall man emerged out of the shadows of the entrance's walkway. Lydia greeted him cordially, shaking his hand and welcoming him to the medical center. She then turned to introduce him to Promise. Promise sat at her desk, stunned. Before her stood Mark Roland.

Lydia made the introductions without noticing Promise's reaction at first. Lost for words, Promise nodded briefly and said little. He extended his hand. She did not take it. Her own hands remained planted on the desk. Struck by her receptionist's sudden shift in mood and behavior, Lydia finally sensed Promise's discomfort. Lydia decided to deflect Dr. Roland's attention with casual conversation related to his work there. She would ask Promise about her behavior later.

"Dr. Roland, Promise is our receptionist on Tuesday and Thursday evenings, the two nights you will be working. All of your patients will sign in with her. She will then direct them to your office. It is my understanding that you have agreed to complete many of the sports physicals for the university. Let me show you around the medical center now. You will likely enter and exit through the door closer to your suite. There are a few parking spaces near that area for your convenience. You and Promise will likely not see each other much, so I am glad for the opportunity to introduce you to each other now."

Mark Roland's eyes lingered in Promise's direction before he turned to Lydia and thanked her for the opportunity to know more about the process for his patients' arrivals and departures from the medical center. He turned back to Promise and icily stated, "It has been a pleasure to meet you again. I look forward to future encounters."

Promise sat at her desk, immobilized. Her facial expression remained flat. She said nothing. Again, Lydia silently noticed, then ushered Dr. Roland to another section of the building. Once they left her, Promise still could not move. She struggled to keep her mind out of panic mode.

Promise suddenly thought of her father and his insistence that she learn self-defense. Now, she fully understood why. He had also suggested that it would help her to think on her feet. Spontaneously, she stood. Somehow, that made a difference. Her body memory for Aikido came alive and gave her a greater sense of strength. She took a deep breath, then reseated herself. Lydia would ask her about her behavior, she had no doubt. She needed to consider her options and have her response ready.

Other patients arrived, gave their names, and proceeded to the correct offices for their appointments. In between these duties, Promise's mind reeled. Why was he here? She held no confusion on that point: he clearly wanted to frighten her. He had done this to her mother long ago. She would not let him succeed. That meant that she would not quit her job, but she could ask if she might work different evenings. If that proved unfeasible, she needed to be very careful in the parking lot, especially when she left for the evening. Hopefully, on this particular night, he would have his tour and depart well before she did. She would need a strategy for all the nights thereafter.

Lydia completed her meeting with Dr. Roland after providing all the necessary details that would affect his work at the medical center. Having concluded, they stood once again at the front door near Promise's desk. Promise picked up the phone and pretended to engage in a work-related conversation with a patient on the other end of the line. She hadn't realized how creative she could be for the length of time required to maintain it. Dr. Roland seemed to linger, intentionally prolonging his departure, hoping to speak to Promise once again. Promise outlasted him, however. He finally gave up and left.

Lydia then turned to engage Promise, who decided to end "the call." Seeing that her receptionist was now available for a discussion, Lydia joined Promise at her desk and pulled up a chair. She wanted to speak discreetly without taking Promise away from her duties. Promise graciously made room for her employer near her seat.

Lydia inquired, "Do you know Dr. Roland, Promise?"

Promise replied, "We met when my roommate had an emergency appendectomy. He was her surgeon. We did not exchange names or any conversation at that time."

"I sense there is something awkward or uncomfortable between you. Am I right?" Lydia asked.

"He makes me very uncomfortable, yes." Promise tried to honestly respond without appearing upset. It required enormous effort, but she succeeded.

Lydia asked her directly, "Is working on the evenings he is here going to be a problem for you?"

Promise spoke her truth: "I do not want to give up this job. If I can work different evenings, that would be great. If not, I will manage."

Lydia appreciated her employee's commitment and honesty. She replied, "Unfortunately, the woman who works the other evenings for me has no flexibility to switch. The office can only accommodate Dr. Roland on Tuesdays and Thursdays. I regret that I cannot offer you another option. I appreciate having you work here. The choice to stay or go is yours. Of course, I hope you will stay."

Promise firmly stated, "Then I'm staying. I'll continue to work my scheduled hours. Thank you for considering my request."

They nodded their agreement to each other. Lydia rose from her chair, placed it back where she had found it, and left. Promise sighed deeply. Now, she would clearly need her strategies.

The evening ended. The parking lot sprawled before her, empty except for her vehicle, which she had fortunately parked under a very bright, overhead light. Promise gathered her things, secured the exit to the building, and walked as fast as she could without running. She got into her car and quickly locked the doors. She had never felt so vulnerable in her life. She reminded herself that she knew Aikido, had friends, and could strategize with them about how to deal with this. She had two days before she had to confront this situation again. She would dare to hope for the best.

Upon returning to her dorm, Promise promptly told Mel of her encounter with Dr. Roland. Mel empathized completely. They began to envision survival tactics that quickly degenerated from the practical to the absurd. The blessing of their laughter helped Promise considerably. Promise discovered that perspective responds beautifully once the most ridiculous alternative has had its voice in the discussion. Promise had resources and she would use them!

The next day, she and Lugh met for their run together. Not long into their conversation, Lugh spontaneously remarked about another encounter he had with Dr. Roland in class. He described how his instructor glibly discoursed about prehistoric societies and their utilization of surgical procedures to drill holes in human skulls and treat wounds without any anesthesia. Lugh felt the need to point out how painful that must have been. He also wondered how that kind of experience impacted the consciousness of those ancient cultures. He noted how the good doctor had no comeback in reply, but the class became engrossed in a fascinating exchange of ideas thereafter.

Lugh clearly enjoyed these power games with Mark Roland. Promise observed that Lugh didn't seem to engage this way with anyone else. She thought to comment on this, but she felt a more urgent need to relate her own experience with the infamous surgeon. She shared with Lugh how Dr. Roland had appeared at Dunkirk Hollow Medical Center the previous evening and that he would be working the same evenings she did. Lugh's pleasure with his own interactions in class quickly shifted as he noticed Promise's concern. The more he gazed at her, he decided that "concern" clearly understated her feelings on the matter.

He sensitively responded, "How are you with this?"

"Scared," she emphatically replied. "He has ill intentions toward me, Lugh. I leave the building last each night. He will be in the same parking lot, potentially at the same time. I refuse to quit, but I don't feel good about this at all."

"Promise, what makes you so sure he has nefarious intentions toward you?" Lugh asked.

"I just know, Lugh. I just know." Lugh could not mistake the seriousness of her distress. He didn't want to believe it, however. They ran in silence for a few minutes before Promise elaborated upon her apprehensions and suspicions.

"Lugh, the man is clearly insensitive if you have to point out how surgery without anesthesia is extremely painful. You have expressed your doubts about his competence to teach your class. I'm glad that makes it possible for you to show him up periodically. You are very bright, and he is a cad! Can't you see that?" With each point, the intensity in her voice escalated. She suddenly realized that she had probably overstepped her bounds.

Lugh continued in silence. Finally, he said, "While I don't see him as a 'cad,' to use your word, I do see you as very frightened at the prospect of having to leave work alone. I am your friend. Why don't I plan to be in the parking lot before you leave the building. That way you won't have to be alone. I don't want you to be scared."

Promise stopped running, then stood and faced Lugh directly. "You would do that for me?"

"Absolutely, I would. You are my friend…and more. I don't want you to be scared."

Promise sighed deeply. "Thank you, Lugh. I gratefully accept your offer."

33

NEXT THURSDAY EVENING, Lugh and Promise agreed that she would text him thirty minutes in advance of her anticipated departure from the medical building. Lugh planned to jog to her parking lot. She would drive them both back to campus, where she would park her car, then he would walk her to her dorm. Promise felt enormous relief with this arrangement. She expressed her gratitude profusely.

The evening itself passed smoothly enough until a fellow student, Alice Danvers, a member of the university's swim team, came for her required sports physical. Approaching the reception desk, Alice recognized Promise from campus. They engaged in a lively, though brief, conversation before Alice proceeded onward to her appointed destination. Promise settled into the mythology assignment for her class the next day while she continued to respond to the occasional phone call or patient signing in.

One hour later, Alice left the building. She had to walk past Promise, but she made no eye contact. Her face was flushed. Something within Promise went on high alert. She specifically called out to Alice to say goodbye. Alice pretended she heard nothing and left quickly. Promise suddenly felt a wave of nausea. It passed, but not fast enough to ignore. Promise then felt like she needed to cry. She wondered if the stress of the week had overloaded her circuits. She took a deep breath and tried to relax.

The evening ended around nine thirty. Promise had texted Lugh at nine. She proceeded to secure the doorways upon her exit. She left the building to find Lugh waiting for her as agreed. The parking lot was otherwise empty. She felt a little sheepish but mostly relieved. Lugh greeted her with his familiar, warm smile. He graciously made no mention of the good doctor's absence. He simply welcomed the opportunity to see Promise once again.

Promise's gratitude only deepened. Lugh spontaneously stated, "You know, this was really a great thing to do. I enjoyed the run, and I get to see you again! Can I do this next Tuesday as well?"

She spontaneously hugged him and kissed him on the cheek. "You absolutely can, thank you! I can't tell you how much better I felt all evening knowing you would be here. If it's really not a bother, Tuesday evening would be wonderful."

"Tuesday evening it is! And maybe this weekend for dinner as well?"

"Of course, my friend. My treat!"

Lugh looked at her with more than gratitude. Promise couldn't stop herself. She hugged him, tighter this time. She almost started to cry. Oddly, Lugh seemed to be near tears as well. When they leaned back from each other and gazed into each other's eyes, they recognized the pain in the other once again. Promise felt it keenly. She poignantly wondered aloud, "Lugh, what is going on with us?"

Lugh shook his head and honestly stated, "I have no idea! Something is, though. I'm both sorry and glad you feel it too."

They both sighed, then laughed at themselves.

As he chuckled, Lugh suggested, "Let's get out of this parking lot, shall we?"

"Great idea!" Promise ushered in the transition with the customary beep. They got into her car, and she drove them to her campus parking space. They exited her vehicle.

While she beeped the doors locked again, Lugh came to her side of the car and gently asked, "Promise, may I kiss you just once before we walk to your dorm?"

Promise looked into his eyes and melted. "Only if you make it a very long kiss..."

"That's easy!" Lugh made good on his offer, then they walked to her dorm. She hugged him good night at the entranceway. The complexity of the evening lingered between them and within each of them. They smiled to each other as they parted, planning to run together the next day and have dinner together on Saturday. They lived into their confusion while hoping for clarity. They each understood that they walked a challenging path.

The following days passed well in the absence of unpredictable stressors and complications. Promise arrived at the medical center on Tuesday feeling much better in response to Lugh's attentiveness and life's fullness. She settled in and recorded the arrivals of all the patients. She noticed that Dr. Roland had five students on his schedule – three men and two women. She also observed that the three men and the first woman each remained in his office suite for no more than thirty minutes. The last young woman, Viola Rhodes, did not leave until an hour had passed. She, like Alice, seemed noticeably distraught upon her departure.

Promise again felt that same wave of nausea and a tearful reaction that proved impossible to ignore and more difficult to explain. Both sensations eased after a few minutes. She decided to pay more attention to the departure times and emotional states of Dr. Roland's patients.

On a hunch, she copied the logs from that evening and the previous Thursday, then made notes regarding what she remembered of their exits from the building. She decided that, from now on, she would make sure that her observations of time and demeanor were more accurate.

Yet again, on Thursday evening, Promise observed a similar pattern of events. This time, three women and two men had appointments with Dr. Roland for physicals. Again, the men and the first two women left after thirty minutes. Most of them interacted with Promise without any sign of emotional disturbance. Oddly, the last young woman's appointment took one hour. Promise made special note of her name, Kassi Jones. This athlete seemed particularly distraught and left the building in a hurry. The wave of nausea and urge to cry overtook Promise once more. She could no longer mistake the association of her personal reactions to these three women. She copied the logs and made her notes. If it happened again, she would tell Lydia.

Lugh came as promised both evenings that week. On both occasions, they found no sign of Mark Roland in the parking lot. In celebration, they indulged in one, then two kisses before parting company at Promise's dorm. Their runs together continued to elicit lively discussions between them. They shared a pleasant weekend that not only included dinner, but collusion in the library as well. Their friendship deepened for all the constraints they otherwise tried to maintain.

Promise chose not to share her suspicions with Lugh about Dr. Roland's involvement with select female students just yet. These disturbing intuitions did weigh heavily on her heart, however. Lugh mentioned his esteemed instructor less often in their conversations together, having tuned in to her ongoing, though vague, discomfort. As October made its gradual passage toward November, he continued to offer his accompaniment for Promise's departure from work.

On the following Tuesday, Promise noticed that all Dr. Roland's sports physicals involved male students. Every one of them left after twenty or thirty minutes. One of them even asked her for a date, which she politely declined. She experienced no sensations of nausea or tearfulness. Promise made her copies and her notes, feeling all the more concerned.

Thirty minutes before her expected departure, Promise texted Lugh as had become their custom, but he did not respond. Promise felt her tensions mounting as the evening would soon come to a close. Dr. Roland's last patient had left more than an hour ago. She dared to hope for the best.

Promise texted Lugh once again. Still, no response. Having no other options, she locked the building's doors behind her and headed toward her car. Unfortunately, she had not been able to park in the well-lit spot that evening. Expecting Lugh to join her, she had not processed much concern about that – until now. As she quickly approached her vehicle, she felt before she heard a shuffling sound behind her. She turned. Mark Roland stepped forward, tall and hovering, looming out of the darkness and trapping her between himself and her car. Promise quickly remembered her Aikido training. She stood firm in her stance and prepared to drop her things to do whatever might be needed.

His visage bore a menacing glare, like a hungry tiger desperate for his next meal. The fact that there were no female students on his schedule that night suddenly registered in her brain. Promise knew she had to get away.

He hissed, "Promise Holmes-Thomas… You look just like your mother. You both are quite attractive, I must say. I am very glad to see you in my neck of the woods!"

Raw fear pulsed through her being. Promise did her best to hold her ground, however. She found her voice and replied, "Get away from me! You're a predator! Get away!"

Mark Roland laughed. He more quietly stated, "I don't think so, my dear!"

Just then, Promise heard what had become the familiar tramp of Lugh's running feet. She dared to hope for safety. Before she could repeat her demand that Roland leave her alone, Lugh arrived, surprised to find his instructor speaking with Promise in the parking lot. Lugh had heard the doctor's laughter. He wanted to assume that they were engaging in casual conversation. The look on Promise's face told him otherwise, however. In an instant, Mark Roland worked to deflect the tension of the moment. He turned toward Lugh and quickly shifted his tone and facial expression to promote a collegial encounter with his student.

"Ah, my star anthropologist! What brings you to this forsaken parking lot in the dark of night?"

Lugh felt caught in an insidious bind. He decided to try protecting Promise while not alienating his instructor. He replied, "I'm here to escort my girlfriend home. How about you, Dr. Roland?"

Mark Roland chuckled. "Girlfriend, huh? How nice. How do you find time to challenge me in class the way you do and have a girlfriend besides? Good work, in any case!"

Promise felt horrified, especially when Lugh made a lighthearted response. "Maybe I'm a well-rounded student!"

The surgeon snorted while his face contorted in reaction to Lugh's attempt at humor. He icily replied, "Well, I'll leave you both to your romantic encounter then. I'll see you in class tomorrow, Mr. Anthropologist. Have a good evening." He then abruptly turned and left them in the shadows.

Promise could not stop shaking. Fear overwhelmed her, with anger not far behind. Lugh just stared at her, still trying to understand what had just happened. She attempted to push past him to get into her car and as far away from both of them as she could. Lugh placed his hands on her upper arms and held her tightly in place. She wanted to yell, but she did not want to draw that hateful man back into their sphere. She tried to break free, but Lugh would not let her go.

He quietly said, "Promise, I don't know what happened here, but I can see that you are really upset. You don't have to talk to me tonight, but you can't drive right now. I will drive you to your parking space, make sure you get to your dorm safely, and leave if you want me to. I hope we can talk about this soon, though. You just can't drive right now."

Lugh felt her shoulders slump in silent acknowledgment of his words to her. He guided her toward the passenger side of her car, took the keys from her hand, opened her door, and closed it behind her once she had settled into her seat. They rode back to the campus parking lot in silence. Promise spoke not one word as they walked back to her residence hall. Once they reached the security office, she stared at Lugh before she turned and walked away.

Lugh felt like someone had died. He watched her through the entranceway to her dorm, working hard to hold back his tears. She had been gone for more than several minutes before he, too, turned and left.

34

PROMISE RETURNED TO HER DORM ROOM, relieved to find Mel's note explaining that she would not return for another hour or more. Promise sat on her bed and stared at nothing. Even her thoughts deserted her for an insensible period of time. When word consciousness finally returned to her mind, she tried to slowly process what had occurred that night. It was all too much. She had to break it down into small bits. Slowly, her reasoning returned.

Her observations led to questions. Tonight, only men came for physicals. All of them took thirty minutes or less. Why, on previous evenings, did the last athlete on Dr. Roland's list – when female – consistently require twice as much time, or more, for the same physical? Why did that student leave the building distressed when none of the others seemed similarly affected? Why did Promise's experiences of nausea and the urge to cry occur only with these women? She could not deny what all her instincts, intuitions, and evidence gathering told her. She felt sick to her stomach once again.

It suddenly became very clear to Promise that Mark Roland had left her alone on those evenings after he molested the other young women. This evening, he had no prey to satisfy his obvious hunger, so he turned on Promise instead. Did he plan such behaviors, or did he have no control? She couldn't know for sure, but his tactics seemed to lack forethought. He would have tried to rape her in the parking lot. She had no doubt.

For the first time in hours, she sighed a deeper breath. She focused on the word "tried." She would not have made it easy for him. She suddenly wondered how her mother had fared under similar circumstances. With sensitivity to her mother's feelings, Promise knew she would choose the timing of her question carefully. For now, she had to process this shrewdly on her own and carefully calculate her next steps.

Then there was Lugh. Why didn't he answer her texts to him tonight of all nights?! She checked her initial temptation to be angry with him about that, knowing that technology isn't perfect and that people get distracted by other people. In any case, he still came. She had to appreciate that. If it weren't for his presence, the night would have ended very, very badly. Some of her anger began to ease.

Still, he had engaged his instructor with camaraderie. Roland's slick switch to friendly teacher mode more than disgusted her. That Lugh allowed it to pass for normal social exchange did nothing to lessen her nausea. Did he not see how distraught she felt? Of course he did! He wouldn't let her drive home, after all. And why did he refer to her as his "girlfriend"? Was that his own possessiveness in action, or did he want to give the predator a message? If the latter, Lugh may have risked his academic success in that class. Roland certainly expressed his displeasure toward Lugh with a menacing tone as he departed the scene. If, instead, Lugh felt possessive, how dare he!

Promise suddenly realized that she didn't know what to think about Lugh's behavior. Mark Roland had surely threatened her and violated her. Lugh did not acknowledge that even though he did try to help her avoid a reckless drive back to the dorm. If she still wanted to call him friend, they would have to discuss this. The tears began to roll down her cheeks.

Promise let herself cry for as long as she needed. As her sobs subsided, she sighed as she recalled the Greek myth of Persephone. Zeus and Hades had bargained over her fate without asking her preferences or permission. Promise resonated with Persephone's experience during those moments in the parking lot. Hades then abducted Persephone and took her to the Underworld as his prize. The surgeon tried to do this to Promise and would have succeeded if it weren't for Lugh. When Demeter, Persephone's mother, discovered the plot, she raged above ground so that no grains or fruits grew on earth until her daughter was returned to her. Promise had no trouble seeing her own mother in that role. Even so, Persephone remained in the darkened misery of Hades' terrain, passive and helpless to do anything but appreciate the caverns of depression and grief. Sadly, Promise resonated with this experience as well.

Remembering how deeply she connected with the myth of Cassandra last spring, Promise could not help but compare the two. Cassandra had experienced the same miserable, bargained victimization. She foresaw her own death and ran toward it without any hesitation. She had given up all hope. In contrast, Persephone lived in the realm of the dead as a living, breathing consciousness. She waited patiently, not giving in to despair. Eventually, others arranged her release, at least for part of the year. When Persephone returned to the Underworld every six months, as required by the updated version of the bargain, she did so as queen of its domain.

Promise decided that the chances of feeling good about the outcome of her current circumstances were slim to none, especially on the short term. If she had to dwell in grief for a time, better to do so as Persephone than as Cassandra. She would confront Lugh and ask him about his behavior. She would not retreat from his answers. She would remain true to herself. If she had to bear more sorrow, she already knew how to do this. She would trust and try to patiently wait for her heart's healing and their relationship's evolution in time.

Having given this all the thought she could muster that evening, Promise took a shower and finally fell asleep. She did not see Lugh on the track the next day. Tears escaped from her heart-aching eyes as she walked back to her dorm. She told herself, no matter. She would continue to live her life and hope for the best.

Lugh finally approached her in the library early Thursday afternoon. He quickly noticed that Promise greeted him with less anger and more uncertainty. He suggested that they take a walk. She agreed to his invitation.

They bundled up in the late October wind as they walked the streets of the residential neighborhood nearby. They said little to each other until Lugh offered his apology. "Promise, I'm sorry I missed your texts. I had turned my phone off because a stupid group text was blowing it up. I had fully planned to turn it back on in time for your contact, but when Brad came back to the apartment and asked me about a situation that troubled him, I got distracted. I am really sorry about that."

Promise accepted his apology before she initiated the conversation that played over and over in her mind. "Lugh, even though you didn't respond to the texts, I would like to thank you for showing up the other night. If you hadn't, Mark Roland would have tried to rape me."

"What!" Lugh exclaimed. "I knew you were upset, but I never considered that. I heard him laughing. I thought you both were engaged in a social conversation. What happened?"

"I know you wanted us to be engaged in a social conversation. You haven't wanted to believe that your instructor might be capable of sexually assaultive behavior. I understand that for you as his student, acknowledging this ugly fact would place you in a considerable bind.

But this is happening to me and other women on campus. When does anyone begin to listen?!" Tears threatened to spill from her eyes.

Lugh stopped abruptly and turned to face Promise directly. "Please tell me what happened."

Promise's anger flared. All her suspicions, observations, and disgust flooded forth and filled the space between them. She concluded her story with her personal experience in the parking lot. "He had no female students to assault that night! He came for me! He said my full name, commented on how I look like my mother, and how glad he was that he had such access to me. I told him to get away from me. I called him a predator. *That's* when he laughed. *That's* what you heard! He more quietly told me he had no intention of stepping out of my way. I felt trapped in the shadows between him and my car. If you hadn't come just then, I hate to think what would have happened...."

The tears of trauma finally poured down her face. Lugh drew her to him and felt her shaking in his arms. He stood there stunned, still not wanting to face what this really meant to her and to his grade in the course.

As Promise continued to cry and the minutes passed on, Lugh could not deny that his instructor had given him a more difficult time in class the next day. Roland directed several insidious, insulting comments specifically in Lugh's direction. Still, Lugh outwitted him. The thinly veiled hostility on Mark Roland's face thereafter did not escape Lugh's notice, nor that of his classmates. The impact of Roland's wrath on Lugh's final grade did concern him, but the depth of the man's treachery had not fully penetrated his awareness until now.

Lugh could not yet identify the best approach for handling this situation in all its ugly ramifications. He did know that Promise's anger and the possibility of separation from her felt unbearable. He would not risk losing her. He would try to bridge this painful gap between them.

He gently stroked her hair while still holding her tight in the cold wind. As her tears began to abate, he gently said, "Promise, I am so sorry. I will come this evening to be there for you if you will let me."

Promise felt the sincerity of his offer, but she had one more question to ask. "Lugh, what did you mean by calling me your girlfriend?"

This took Lugh by surprise. He spontaneously responded, "I wanted him to know that you matter to me. I know we never really discussed the nature of our relationship in that kind of detail. I didn't want to presume. I just wanted him to know that I play a role in your life. Why do you ask?"

"I didn't know if you were claiming territory or protecting me. Your comment about being a 'well-rounded student' seemed too collegial to me. It didn't sit well with me in the context of what had just happened." A residual nausea threatened to surface. Promise did her best to wait for his reply.

"Oh my God, Promise. Now, I can understand why you were so angry with me that night. It looked like I was trying to save my grade at your expense. I am so sorry. This whole situation really baffles me, I must admit, but of one thing I am certain. You matter to me more than any of it. When you left me in anger that night, I felt horrible, like a precious part of my existence had just left me. I will do whatever it takes to make this right with you." Lugh begged, "Promise, please give me the chance."

Promise began to cry again, this time with relief. Her intuition told her that they still had more to resolve about all of this, but their talk had offered a good beginning for the process. This time, when he drew her close, she hugged him back.

Lugh rubbed her back as he held her. They sighed simultaneously, then smiled at their reconnection.

As they disengaged, Lugh added, "I had planned to remind you about the Samhain celebration this weekend. It will take place all day Saturday at a retreat center not too far from here. I am hoping you still want to go with me. I suspect we really need it."

Promise nodded. "I do want to go. I suspect we need it as well. And thank you for offering to come to the medical center tonight. I appreciate that now more than ever."

Lugh brushed away Promise's residual tears and gently kissed her lips. He then added, "My phone and I will be ready and waiting for you. I promise."

She smiled. They walked back to the library arm in arm, binding themselves together against the bracing autumn wind.

35

THURSDAY EVENING at Dunkirk Hollow Medical Center passed uneventfully. Promise noticed that once again there were no women on Dr. Roland's schedule. Lydia also did not appear during Promise's scheduled hours that night, although she did leave a note granting Promise time off that Saturday. Promise experienced all of these factors with tentative relief.

Promise knew she had to do something to address her horrendous suspicions; unfortunately, she didn't feel confident about Lydia's response. Her boss hadn't seemed overly concerned when Promise first expressed her discomfort with Mark Roland. Lydia clearly prioritized the functioning of the medical center over her employee's apprehensions. Promise wanted to take a stand on this issue, but it also felt imperative to her that it be effective as well. She dared to hope that her time at the Celtic ceremony would offer her the needed inspiration.

Lugh arrived at the medical center a few minutes early and actually came into the building. Promise smiled at him upon his arrival. Lugh could not mistake her gratitude; it warmed his heart. They left together without any sign of the surgeon's presence. Promise sighed deeply once they seated themselves in her car. Lugh reached for her hand and said, "I hope you know how very brave you are. I am in awe of you."

Promise squeezed his hand in return. "I think I'm not the only one taking risks here. I am really grateful to you."

They lingered over their goodbye in the campus lot before Lugh walked Promise back to her dorm. He reminded her about the Samhain celebration. They made their plans.

They departed early Saturday morning. Lugh drove to the gathering after they had loaded his car with the necessary equipment for their journey work. They experienced more frequent periods of silence between them during their trip, but neither one felt particularly concerned about that. They arrived with plenty of time to set up their mats and greet Dylan once again.

This time, they met in a converted old barn set in the woods, a mile down the road from the local highway. The barn's exterior had recently received a fresh coat of paint to coax visitors into its modernized interior, which actually offered fully functioning restrooms and a separate kitchen. Their group had full use of the building that day. A few participants had even taken advantage of the overnight lodgings available on the remodeled second floor.

They met in the large community room at the far end of the barn. Others soon joined them. Promise recognized many faces from their Lughnasadh gathering. Their familiarity felt comforting to her. Reconnecting with these acquaintances filled her heart with warmth and moments of peace.

Dylan opened their circle once again by calling in the four directions around the altar centered by Sovereignty. This time they would celebrate the North and the season of winter, which, according to the Celtic tradition, begins each year on the first day of November. This feast of Samhain also marked their New Year. Dylan explained how during this time, the Veil to the Otherworld is very thin. Souls that had already crossed over in death might be more accessible to the living. Souls requiring assistance in completing their transition to the Other Side would benefit from the efforts of the group to support them.

Dylan mapped out their journeys for the day. They would first meet a spirit guide with whom they could clarify their personal intentions for the Samhain circle and for the New Year, asking any questions that concerned them. During the second journey, they would explore what might interfere with living fully into those newly set intentions. Before the conclusion of their time together, they would share the healing that they had received with those in need beyond the Veil. Their power animals would accompany them on their otherworldly sojourns once again.

Everyone lay down, covered their eyes, made themselves comfortable, and prepared to enter an altered state of consciousness. Dylan commenced the process with his rhythmic beating of the drum. Promise began as before, greeting her lion and thanking him for his protection. Together, they ran through the forest, picking up the pace until she felt herself carried with her lion on a journey through time and space. She rose high into the sky and flew over the trees, across flat lands, then past a deserted beach. Across the water they soared like birds in flight. She and her lion noticed a craggy coastline in the distance. She somehow recognized this as her destination.

Promise and her power animal landed softly on a flattened segment of the rocky terrain. She stood quietly, patiently waiting for whatever or whoever might appear. From behind a tall boulder, Alethea slowly came forward. Promise delighted in their reunion.

Alethea greeted Promise warmly and invited her once again to sit at her side. Promise did so willingly as her lion lay down nearby, attentively keeping watch. Strands of Alethea's white hair floated in the breeze, but they never seemed to distract her. Alethea focused completely on Promise.

Alethea began, "Promise, it is good to see you again. Thank you for coming to visit with me."

Promise replied, "I am grateful to see you as well. I have much to ask you. There is much on my mind." When Alethea nodded her understanding, Promise continued, "Something is happening between Lugh and me that I don't understand. I also have to make big decisions about how to handle Mark Roland. I assume you know who these two people are?"

Alethea nodded once again and said, "I do."

Promise then asked, "Why is all this happening? It feels bigger to me than just coincidence."

Alethea responded, "Your intuitions are correct on every count. You likely recall that I told you about the wounds you are here to heal. These experiences that concern you are part of that wounding and healing. The injury happened long ago, but some form of it must be repeated so that you remember to attend to it during this lifetime. I suspect both Lugh and Mark Roland feel at least a little familiar to you?"

"They do!" Promise exclaimed. "I knew them in a past life?"

"Yes, you did," Alethea replied. "You three have work to do together. It is best for you to remember through experience rather than my just telling you, however. Are you willing to let yourself go more deeply into the past, to have a vision within a vision so that you can know this for yourself in your current awareness?"

"I am willing. I trust you will guide me?" Promise asked.

"Of course, my dear, but I suspect you will have no trouble accomplishing this on your own. All you need to do is close your eyes and imagine yourself taking a walk down that path over there. It leads to the shore below. There you will encounter your distant past."

Promise quickly released her concern about failing at this and let herself relax into her imagination. She closed her eyes and saw herself rising from her seated position, walking toward the path, then making her way down the narrow, stony trail. As she descended, she discovered that she wore animal skins. She also felt progressively more encumbered by a weight in her abdomen. Upon reaching the bottom of the incline, she realized that she was very pregnant – and very anxious. Soon, another woman appeared, also wearing animal skins. She felt an immediate, very strong bond with the woman – the warm intensity of the feeling reminded Promise of her relationship with Lizzie.

The woman called her Glenna. She found herself calling the woman Fiona. Fiona, too, was very pregnant. They embraced like sisters. Together, they made their way to the boggy woods nearby while deftly avoiding the stinging nettles that grew abundantly all around them.

It became clear that Glenna and Fiona had agreed to pick berries for their tribe, but Glenna's anxiety required their prioritized attention. Fiona noticed her dear friend's distress and asked her about it. Glenna replied by describing the dream that had startled her from her morning's sleep.

"A pregnant doe is grazing in a field with her young buck not far away. She falls to the ground to give birth. There is trouble. She bleeds and bleeds, growing weaker as the minutes pass. It seems that she will die.

"In the next part of the dream, a young woman steps onto the beach and walks toward the approaching sunrise. An orange glow fills the sky, and she glides with outstretched arms as if calling forth the light. The horizon comes alive with a bright fire in the shape of a spiral, our tribal sign of leadership. She calls the fiery figure to her. It settles on her palms as she turns on her heels and retreats.

"Then the young woman comes to the doe in the field. She places the spiraling fire on the doe's belly, and a buck is born with the spiral birthmark on his forehead. The doe sees her newborn marked with succession. She lays back, satisfied, and takes her last breath."

After Glenna told Fiona her dream, Fiona empathically trembled with her own resonating anxiety. Both of them felt overwhelmed. Not knowing what else to do, they picked their berries, then trekked back toward their respective dwellings in the rocks.

Before they reached their destination, Glenna started to bleed from her womb. After trying to make Glenna as comfortable as possible, Fiona ran for help. Glenna lay there alone and scared. Fiona returned with a tall man, also clad in animal skins; he had a spiral birthmark on his shoulder. This man obviously loved her. He felt like a mate to Glenna; Fiona called him Alasdair.

Glenna begged Alasdair to carve a spiral on the wall of a cave on the shoreline, hoping it would signal the woman with the spiral light to come to her aid. Glenna recognized the imperative to safely birth her baby. Then, the scene suddenly ended. There was nothing more that followed.

Promise's eyes shot wide open. She immediately asked Alethea, "Did I die?"

Alethea nodded. "Yes, you did. Tell me how you felt in that moment before your death."

Promise paused as she let the feelings wash over her once again. "I felt desperate. Frantically hopeful. Sad to leave Alasdair and Fiona behind. Worried for them. Unsure if they would follow through with my request to carve the spiral. Helpless. They hadn't had the dreams and visions. They didn't know how important my baby's birth would be. I could only trust them. They seemed more consumed with grief at losing me than committed to the importance of the mission. I had anguishing doubts about how it would all unfold. Then, nothing."

Again, Alethea nodded. "Promise, these are the very feelings that need healing in this lifetime. Do you have any reservations about accepting your role as Glenna in the past?"

Promise pondered this question before she confidently replied, "No. It felt too real. The feelings were very intense – and familiar to me in this life as well. Wow!" After a brief pause, Promise asked her guide, "Why did I feel so desperate for that child to be born? Of course, I wouldn't want anything bad to happen to my baby, but this went beyond that. I had a deep sense of foreboding should he die along with me. Why?"

Alethea wisely replied, "That, too, would be better for you to experience directly. You and I will meet again this day. You will discover the answer to your question then."

Promise abruptly tuned in to the shift in the drum beat. Dylan had initiated the rhythmic call back to current reality with the agreed upon pattern of pulses. Responding to the cue, Promise bowed to her mentor, then took flight with her lion once again, retracing her path to the forest and back into the room.

When she finally opened her eyes, she was surprised to discover that Lugh had left his mat and was nowhere to be seen. Alarm permeated her being. Dylan calmly came to her side and reassured her that Lugh simply needed some private time. She would do well to journal her own experience and remember to trust.

Promise sensed Dylan's care for Lugh, which helped her relax. She took his suggestion and recorded her own experience. It left her feeling mystified and confused. Trust proved to be quite the challenge under such circumstances. Perhaps experiences such as these defined its very nature and necessity. In any case, she vowed to do her best.

36

DYLAN INVITED HIS SAMHAIN participants to take a break for lunch. Lugh's continued absence puzzled Promise, but she decided to cope and trust. She joined three other members of their circle for the meal, then spent some time alone to journal and reflect.

Lugh did not return until the beginning of the next journey. They had little time to talk. Promise could only ask, "Are you okay?" to which he replied, "I think so. I will definitely fill you in later." They nodded and prepared for their next otherworldly adventure.

Dylan reminded them that their focus this time involved an exploration of what interferes with the pursuit of their intentions. Still confused by her first journey, Promise did not know what to expect this go-round. More trust seemed required of her. She lay on her mat, covered her eyes, and relaxed into the sounds of the drumming.

As before, she and her lion soared to the mount where Alethea greeted them once again. She reminded Promise of her question: Why did Glenna feel so desperate to have her baby born even if she herself might not live? The feeling of that desperation had troubled Promise since the completion of the last journey. She hoped for an understanding that might bring some relief.

Once more, in response to Alethea's suggestion, Promise closed her eyes and imagined herself walking toward the path, then down through the crags. This time she was still pregnant but not as far along. At the bottom of her descent, she met Fiona, who also evidenced an earlier stage of pregnancy. A terrible sense of foreboding overcame her, as Glenna, yet again.

She and Fiona walked to the ocean this time. Not quite midway through their pregnancies, they were both more limber and better able to negotiate the rocky terrain. On this occasion, they shared the task of watching the children while the men disappeared into the woods to hunt wild boar. Glenna already had a young son; she thought of her firstborn and shuddered.

The other children joyfully, boisterously played with one another, but Glenna's son – seemingly four years old – stood aside, swinging a very large stick while he carefully scrutinized his peers. From their vantage point on the rocks, she and Fiona were engaged in an intense conversation about Glenna's specific concerns regarding the lad. In a moment of distraction, she had not noticed how her son targeted a younger child and began taunting him with his stick. The little one ran as fast as he could to get away, but not fast enough. Glenna's son poked the boy with his weapon, knocking the young child off balance; he fell forward, cutting his knees and face on the rocky, shelled, and sandy beach. His wail of pain commanded the attention of Glenna, Fiona, and the other mothers, all of whom swiftly ran to his aid.

Glenna grabbed the stick from her son. Fiona led the other children away as the younger one's mother tried to comfort her yowling little boy. Glenna's four-year-old just stared at her, furious, without any trace of remorse. Glenna felt something in her heart turn cold, not from lack of care for him but from the alarming confirmation of her previous concerns. How could her own child be so callous? She had tried to talk to his father about her disquieting premonitions, but Alasdair would not listen. He chose to explain their son's fierceness as the sign of a warrior and a leader. He assured her that their young boy would mature and develop more skillfulness in managing his aggression as he grew.

In the midst of the stalemate instigated by her son's defiance, Glenna felt a rumble in her womb. She immediately recognized that the child she carried within her would bring balance to the devastation her older son would unleash upon their people. *This child had to be born.*

When nothing else manifested in Promise's vision, she opened her eyes to find Alethea supportively sitting by her side. Promise involuntarily shuddered. Not only did she intellectually understand her desperation, but she also felt her nauseated reaction to her past-life son's behavior: his thorny capacity for icy aloofness and heated violence unnerved her. What distressed her all the more involved her recognition that her current life had presented her with the same horrifying challenge. She could not deny it: her contacts with Mark Roland felt too much like this past-life experience with her own young son.

Promise almost didn't want to ask her question, but she knew she had to do so while she had the chance. She inhaled deeply, then asked Alethea directly, "Is Mark Roland a reincarnation of my son from that past life?"

Somberly, Alethea nodded her yes.

Promise could only shudder once again. "Ugh!" she cried. "How am I going to manage this?! He is older than me, taller than me, more prestigious, and disgusting! He will deny any accusation I make, no matter how valid. No one will believe me!" Tears spilled forth and trailed down her cheeks.

Alethea nodded her understanding. She opted to respond to Promise's question with the wisdom she had accumulated over many centuries. "Promise, I can assure you that I do understand how overwhelming this must feel to you. Hopefully, you can see that your intentions to understand the complexities you have experienced with Lugh and Mark Roland have been fulfilled?"

Promise wiped her eyes and arched her eyebrows in response. "Mark Roland, yes. But Lugh?"

Alethea gently inquired, "What does your heart tell you?"

In the silence that followed, Promise searched her depths, then sighed. "Lugh is Alasdair. Of course he is! Loving me. Not believing my intuitions and premonitions. The bond between us that neither of us has been able to explain...and my reluctance to allow our bond to deepen. I need to know he won't abandon me. Oh my God!"

Oddly, a wave of sadness passed across Alethea's countenance, then just as suddenly it disappeared. Alethea continued, "Mark Roland has wreaked havoc across lifetimes, both before he was your son and since then. I cannot tell you what to do. You also have the right to do nothing. This segment of your journey work today is about identifying your fears. First, however, you need to formulate your intentions. You have come to this lifetime with unresolved, very old wounds. You have the opportunity to decide if you want to address them during this incarnation and if so, how. No one can make that decision for you. Either way, I assure you that I will remain available to you. Your soul has brought with you everything you need. Still, the choice is yours."

Promise could not mistake the commitment with which Alethea offered her support. She sensed her wise guide's warrior spirit and found an inkling of it resonating in her own heart. She sighed.

Promise knew that she could not let Mark Roland continue to harm other women. She had no idea where Lugh would land regarding his own sense of resolve. While she had doubted her true alignment with the qualities of Prometheus, she suddenly felt her own capacity for shrewdness and forethought rising from her depths. She would have to find a way. She would have to face her fears. What were they? That no one would believe her? That she didn't have the power to affect this situation? Glenna had done her best with great courage. Promise had access to even more resources. She would have to reflect on all of this more deeply, but she came to her decision then and there.

"Alethea, I will deal with this. I don't have a clue as to how I will manage it, but I will deal with this. Please help me?" Promise begged.

"I promise, my dear. I promise."

Dylan called them back with the changing beat of his drum. Promise returned her consciousness to the room and lay still for a very long time. When she finally sat up, she discovered once again that Lugh had disappeared.

37

MIDWAY THROUGH THE DINNER HOUR, Lugh returned to the kitchen area where Promise had propped herself on one of the cushioned stools set around the breakfast bar. He spied the empty seat next to her and asked if she might like company.

With genuine invitation, Promise replied, "You know I would!"

He smiled wanly. He retrieved his food from the refrigerator, heated some of it, and brought all of it to his place at her side. Before he took the first bite, he said to her, "I'm sorry I've been unavailable. It's been quite a lot to process."

She replied, "No problem, Lugh. We came here to figure things out. I trust you are doing what works best for you."

He looked at her more directly. "I really don't deserve you, Promise. Thanks."

Promise's face registered her puzzlement before she realized that Lugh might have had another past-life journey. If he remembered his life as Alasdair, he might be feeling a complexity of emotions. Did he realize that she had lived with him as Glenna? She decided to wait for him to tell his own tale and his interpretation of it. She felt very clear that she could not be the one to hold all the deeper information in their relationship any more.

They sat in silence for some time. Lugh finally acknowledged that he wanted to share his experience with her, perhaps on the way back to campus if that felt right. Promise expressed her interest and suggested that they stop at a local highway diner on their return trip. With an attempt at humor, she reminded him that her parents were not waiting up for her. More to the point, she felt concerned for the depth of whatever had apparently overwhelmed him. He welcomed her suggestion as a great idea.

The last segment of their Samhain celebration involved a group discussion of their journeys and a ceremony of commitment to their intentions for the New Year. Promise and Lugh shared little with the others about the specifics of what weighed heavily upon their hearts. Instead, Promise declared that in the New Year she hoped to have more courage. Lugh talked about facing his feelings and also needing courage to do it. As a group, they keened for those souls who required assistance to cross the Veil. The evening ended with a Samhain blessing and warm partings until they met again for the next Celtic festival at Imbolc in February. Lugh and Promise packed their things in Lugh's car and headed back to campus by way of the diner.

They said little in the car. Promise felt strangely comfortable in the silence. Having named her fears, she at least knew what likely lay ahead for her. In contrast, what she and Lugh might discuss filled her with curiosity. She decided to be patient and let him take the lead. Once they were seated in a fairly private booth at the diner, he did not disappoint her.

"Promise, I need help making sense of what I experienced. The part I do understand fills me with sadness and remorse for how I likely behaved in a past life. If I can figure the rest out, maybe I can also determine how to right some wrongs that I think I may have committed. I don't want to burden you with this. If you don't want to listen, please tell me. I will sincerely respect your wishes."

"Lugh, we came here to have a better understanding of what seems to happen between us on some mysterious, deeper level. I want to hear what you have to say. It may help me understand my own experience as well. Please share."

Lugh sighed. "Okay, here's the first journey. I am a leader in a tribe that lives near the ocean. I have the spiral, a mark of leadership, on my shoulder – not exactly where it is now, but I still found that very strange. We all wear animal skins, so it must be a fairly primitive society. I am wedded to the village seer. She has had dreams warning me that our son is too aggressive. She is pregnant with another son, or so she tells me. She fears she will die, based on the dreams she is having. I don't want to believe her. Sadly, I come to realize that she was right all along. She does die and our second child is never born. I grieve terribly. I feel horrible guilt."

Lugh quickly covered his eyes with his palms. Promise could not mistake the tears that flowed beneath them. She instinctively wanted to comfort him, but she simultaneously realized that he grieved because he hadn't wanted to believe *her*. He hadn't been able to face the reality of her fears. He didn't take her seriously in the distant past. What did that mean going forward?

Lugh continued speaking although his eyes remained closed and covered. "I didn't want to believe you on the track last winter. I didn't want to take you seriously about Mark Roland either." At this point, he lowered his hands and gazed at Promise directly. "You were right, just as my mate also knew what would befall her in the past. I've been reacting to you in a way that stupidly tried to spare me the memory of the guilt I felt then. I haven't wanted to feel the loss and the terrible remorse I have carried ever since, if that makes any sense at all."

"It makes sense, Lugh. Thank you for telling me."

He nodded appreciatively and then said, "There's more. In the second journey, I led the men on a boar hunt once again, only this time there were two men who stood out. Maybe you recall that I thought one of them felt like my son?"

Promise nodded and said, "I do."

Lugh continued, "Strangely, in this journey I had two sons. Both had the birthmark, one on his calf, the other on his forehead."

Hearing this, Promise arched her own eyebrows in wonderment. "Really?"

"Yes. The one who made the misstep in the Lughnasadh journey did it again in today's vision. I made the same move to rescue him as I had in the past, which at that time had caused me to be gored by the boar. This time, however, the younger son quickly climbed a tree and pulled his brother to safety. Because of his bravery, my life was spared as well.

"As we transported the boar back to the village, the men cheered the bravery of the younger boy, while the older one seethed in resentment. I had never wanted them to fight; I had always wanted them to rule together. The older son never wanted that, however. Despite what I professed all along, I myself had blamed the younger one for the death of my mate in childbirth – which makes no sense because she died before she could give birth to him in the first journey today.

"It just became very clear to me that I had misjudged my firstborn from the very start. My mate had described to me numerous times how he hurt other children. Villagers expressed their concerns for how badly he treated his younger brother in my absence – until I made it very clear that I would not listen to such reports. All the signs of his viciousness and cruelty had escaped no one's notice – except mine. I died realizing that my sons would never co-rule; one of them would have to kill the other someday. I couldn't bear it. I recognized that I had betrayed my mate once again, and my younger son as well." Lugh slumped in his seat. Again, he drew his palms to cover his face in shame.

Promise sat quite still. Lugh had yet to realize that they had shared this lifetime together in the distant past. She wanted to tell him, but Alethea's wisdom flashed through her mind and heart. Alethea had invited her to make her own associations to people from her former lifetime. Promise directly experienced how the process of discerning the past for herself made a huge difference in terms of her ability to own it and its consequences. Perhaps Promise could do the same for Lugh? She would try.

She invited his attention: "Lugh?" He lowered his hands and gazed directly into her eyes.

Having received it, she inquired, "Did your older son from the past feel like anyone you know in this lifetime?"

Lugh carefully considered her query. After a few moments, he responded, "My Medical Anthropology instructor? Ugh! Yes!! That leering look on his face that escapes his limited control in class. I saw it in the past-life scenes: when he tried to lure that boar in the woods long ago; at other times when he goaded his brother – even though I tried hard not to notice. That's really weird. Do you think the two are the same?"

"I can't know for certain. I can only ask you if you find yourself relating to Mark Roland the same way you did with your son."

Another pause before Lugh's palms slid to his forehead as if trying to hold some measure of self-respect alongside his dawning realization. "I put him in his place whenever he says something arrogantly ignorant. He used to put up with it, at least superficially, until that evening when I came upon you both in the parking lot. I wanted him to be better than he is. I needed him to be better than he is. If they aren't the same person, I certainly am. Ugh! I feel even worse about this than I already did."

Promise then dared to ask, "Does your mate from the past feel at all like anyone you know in this lifetime?"

Lugh startled at her question. He paused and seemed to go inward.

He blinked a few times as if trying to connect the two worlds converging within him. He looked at her with poignant focus as he replied, "I've treated you the same way I treated my mate. I care about you with the same depth. You have the same gifts as seer.... Please don't tell me I abandoned you like that?"

Promise smiled but with obvious sadness. "Lugh, these are our wounds. I did not feel believed. You did not want to face the truth revealed through the painful visions I had. Yes, I was your mate. My name was Glenna. Yours was Alasdair. You were in my journey today as well.

"If it helps to know it, I had a vision of a woman who would come to help me birth my second son. He would have the spiral mark on his forehead. I asked you to carve the symbol on the wall of a cave to guide her arrival from a place out of time. It all sounds really strange, I know, but my point is, you likely did that for me. You must have gone to carve the spiral in the cave as I had begged you to do. I died not knowing if you actually did it; nor did I know what happened after that. But it seems that somehow the second son was born!"

Lugh just stared at her. Something in his brain froze. He desperately wanted it to thaw so that he would not abandon her again. Things were just not making any sense. He reached for her hand, hoping to come back to reality. At the instant of her touch, a flood of feelings, mostly love and regret, overwhelmed him. Tears welled up in his eyes as he said, "How can you sit here with me?"

Promise smiled more fully now. "If you can believe me and feel what you feel, it makes all the difference. It would seem that the love between us hasn't diminished one bit. We have found each other again, and we did not run from each other when things got awkward or downright hard between us. Maybe we can figure this out? Maybe we can heal?"

"How can we possibly figure this out?" Lugh mumbled aloud.

After a momentary pause, Promise grimaced as she replied, "I haven't a clue. We also have a past-life son who needs some serious parenting. The weird thing is, he's older, more experienced, and more powerful than we are now. It feels both bizarre and very real at the same time."

Lugh nodded his own despondent recognition of the reality currently facing them.

Promise sighed, thought of Alethea, then said, "Something has guided us this far. I suspect we will continue to receive all the help we need. We just have to decide if we want it."

Lugh witnessed the determination in her eyes. He smiled for the first time in hours. "All right, then. Let's ask for help. We have spirit guides and power animals. We also have each other. I do hope you will forgive me. I will find a way to make this up to you. I promise!"

38

LUGH AND PROMISE RETURNED to campus with a new resolve that prevailed over their fear and confusion, at least on the shorter term. They lingered in the parking lot, enjoying the peace of knowing that their long history together might now also have a more positive future. Eventually, Lugh escorted Promise to her dorm, both of them laden with the day's equipment and other necessities. The security guard, quite used to the comings and goings of college students well past the midnight hour, just waved them onward.

Lugh quietly deposited Promise's belongings in a corner of her currently vacated room. Mel's absence suggested that she had her own commitments to keep elsewhere. Their eyes met for one long, wordless communication before Lugh kissed her lightly, gently caressed her cheek with a smile, then left her to sort out all the paraphernalia, events, and feelings of the day. The reality of their situation would confront them soon enough.

They continued their runs and dinners together. With genuine devotedness, Lugh met Promise at the end of her two evening shifts at the medical center each week. Their reliable reunions supported each of them as they dealt with the dilemmas confronting them.

Lugh understood that his academic standing in the Medical Anthropology course would likely require an appeal to higher officials after Dr. Roland punished him with a failing grade. Consequently, Lugh worked diligently to ensure that his papers and class participation met the highest standards of excellence. He would need them and potential witnesses as evidence if his suspicions and sense of foreboding proved correct.

Meanwhile, Promise spent long hours concocting methods to keep the young women on Dr. Mark Roland's patient registers safe. On the following Tuesday evening, Promise actually detained a male athlete in the main waiting room near her desk, hoping that the woman last on the list might come early. She did. Promise sent her down to Dr. Roland's office suite first, which further irritated the young man. In response, Promise maintained her calm and apologized for her "mistake."

Once Promise felt certain that enough time had passed for the female student to have settled into the office's medical routine, she notified Dr. Roland's nurse, Christina, that the male student expected to be seen as soon as possible. Promise apologetically admitted to her error once again and explained that this none-too-pleased patient had another commitment that would benefit from Dr. Roland's efficiency and customary speed. Christina indicated that she would alert the doctor; she directed Promise to send the young man to their office suite immediately.

Promise felt totally relieved when Dr. Roland's last female patient for the evening departed the building not long after her call to Christina. The young woman seemed calm and in the same apparently good mood that she brought with her that evening. Regrettably, Promise also realized that she could not use the same tactic repeatedly. More creativity would be required of her with each successive evening.

On the following Thursday, only men were scheduled for physicals. Promise breathed a sigh of relief. Unfortunately, the patient list for the following Tuesday cited women's names only. Promise reluctantly decided that her only hope was to alert Christina to maintain careful watch on her patients.

Uncharacteristically, Promise called to announce the arrival of the fourth student scheduled. She then dared to ask Dr. Roland's nurse, "Christina, while I have you on the phone, I have a question that's been on my mind for several weeks now. Do you happen to know why Dr. Roland's last physical of the evening takes longer than the four preceding it?"

The line went silent on the other end. Promise thought that very strange. She asked again, "Christina, are you there? Did you hear my question?"

Christina began to mumble. Finally, she decided to be honest with the college student who only worked part-time. She replied, "Dr. Roland has offered that I can leave before the last student is finished if I've attended to all my duties. He always asks the student's permission for my departure, of course. They always give it once he explains that I have an elderly mother home alone, waiting for my return. She gets really frightened in the dark when I'm not there. I didn't realize that the last physical takes longer. Maybe he really needs me to be here, after all."

Promise felt her stomach turn. She felt compelled to be honest. "Christina, he doesn't take that long when a male patient concludes the evening. They leave in the usual twenty or thirty minutes. It's the women, if they are last on the list, that take an hour or more. I was wondering why."

Again, silence on the other end of the phone. "Promise, I don't know what you're talking about. You need to be careful about the implications of what you are suggesting."

Promise responded, "Christina, I know that. I have to tell you, though, that the women who have had the last, longer appointments always leave here quite obviously upset. Can you please stay in the room with them from now on? Or work to have men's appointments end the evening?"

Again, a long pause. Christina finally responded, "I will see what I can do."

"Thank you, Christina. The last appointment will be here soon. Please don't leave her alone." Promise heard the click as Christina abruptly hung up.

Promise inhaled deeply. She struggled with whether she should say something to the young woman before her appointment. She had learned in her young life that such statements carried huge consequences. She would trust Christina this night, keep her eyes open, and if the student didn't return within the usual half-hour, she would go to the office suite herself. What she would do once there, she had no idea. Her mind raced. She did her best to think as clearly as she could. She prayed for an inspiration.

Christina must have taken her seriously. The young woman left within the thirty-minute window and did not seem upset. Promise sighed with relief and thanked the heavens for answering her prayer.

Lugh arrived a few minutes early once again. Having entered the building, he could immediately discern that something unusual had occurred that evening. Promise decided not to tell him until they left for the evening. She had not yet spoken to Lydia about her concerns, in part because she had not crossed paths with her employer since her suspicions had taken on some clarity. Promise dared to hope that Christina's awareness might eliminate further incidents. Still, the women who had already been hurt nagged at her consciousness. Their distraught faces haunted her day and night.

Something had to be done, but what? Promise still had no idea. Again, she prayed for an inspired flash of wisdom. She deeply sensed that Alethea also wanted to right this egregious wrong. Promise quietly and specifically asked her wise guide for assistance. She intuited that what was needed would unfold in its proper time. For once, she hoped her intuition would prove correct.

39

LUGH AND PROMISE HAD DEVELOPED a ritual of running on the outdoor track every Wednesday afternoon, weather permitting. The last full week of classes before their Thanksgiving break included the stress of academic projects soon due as the end of the semester quickly approached. Even so, they kept to their routine for various reasons, the greatest being their deepening fondness for each other.

Mid-November brought with it an unusually windy, colder blast, which only made them run all the faster. They saved most of their conversation for the cool-down phase of their workout. This gave each of them the opportunity to more deeply ponder their personal concerns and how they might impact the other. Promise had already shared the events of the previous evening with Lugh during their ride back to campus together. Still, she had yet to formulate a plan of action.

Lugh, on the other hand, had new happenings to report. In his Medical Anthropology course, the number of intense interactions with Mark Roland had progressively increased. Lugh had also applied for graduate programs in his field. They would take him away from Stella Maris – both during the interviews and after graduation. He struggled with how to tell Promise. In truth, he also felt torn within himself. Would she be safe in his absence? Would their relationship survive a potential separation? So many unknowns, not to mention the possibility that Mark Roland might give him an F in his class. He would fight it, he knew, but how long would that take, and how might that impact his status with graduate schools? So many unknowns...

They had warmed up considerably as they ran so that when it came time to slow their pace, they could converse easily despite the wind and cold. Promise spoke first.

"Lugh, you seem concerned about something. Am I right?"

"As usual, my friend, you are. Several things, really. Roland's attempts to attack me in class are increasing steadily. I counter well, I think, but I'm surprised by my own level of frustration. Sometimes, I truly feel like his father, wanting him to just give up the nonsense and settle down, behave himself, and get on with living like a mature human being. He is angry, however. He knows we are on to him. His anger is escalating."

Promise sighed. "Do you think he will try to negatively affect your grade?"

"I do. I'm preparing for that by working extra hard to write high quality papers and to do my research before each class so that he can't shame me. My efforts may not save my grade, but I do hope they will provide good evidence if I have to appeal the injustice of his vengeful behavior."

"It sounds like a lot of work for you...and stress." Promise resonated strongly with his situation. She also struggled not to feel responsible for it.

"I'll manage that all right. Honestly, what also concerns me is the impact it might have on my applications for graduate programs. This might get messy. I don't know how long it will take to clean up, but resolve it I will! These difficulties are not a given, though. Consequently, I must proceed to apply and have interviews."

Promise recognized this as the conversation she had avoided two months ago. Lugh had to follow his heart. She knew this. How her heart would respond could only reveal itself in time. That time had come, or at least had begun. She drew in a deep breath and asked her questions: "Where are you applying? What do you hope to study in a graduate program?"

Lugh glanced at Promise, trying to seriously assess her readiness for his answer. He recognized the present moment for the truth it demanded of him. "There are three programs – none of them close by, unfortunately – that specialize in the area that interests me most: civilizations that existed before the flooding events of the last Ice Age. I am feeling really torn. I already don't want to be apart from you, but these mysteries have haunted me my whole life. I don't have the right to ask you this, especially now, but I am wondering if someday you might want to join me wherever life may take me."

Promise stopped running. She turned to him and thoughtfully responded, "Thank you for inviting me to do that. Life feels like a huge muddle right now, but it's something I would seriously consider, Lugh. I'm not sure I want to part from you either."

"Really?" Lugh's relief and shock simultaneously overpowered his facial expression as he stood facing her. Promise smiled at the transformation in his eyes and realized that on some level she felt relieved as well.

"Really," she candidly affirmed. "I know we have work to do here. Yet my sense of my own future still mystifies me. I can only trust that I will receive the signs I need going forward. Still, I have spoken the truth of my heart in this moment."

Lugh could not doubt the sincerity in Promise's words. He pulled her toward him and kissed her.

He had one more piece of news to share with her. His earlier conversation with Brad made this one a bit easier. Lugh sighed, then straightforwardly stated, "And there's one more thing I need to tell you today. I have received a call for an interview to the program that interests me most."

Promise spontaneously exclaimed, "Lugh, that's wonderful! Where is it? When?"

"It's in Arizona on the Thursday after Thanksgiving. One nice feature is that the weather will be considerably more comfortable there at that point in time. The bad news is that I'll need to leave on Wednesday morning, missing my Medical Anthropology class – a plus – but also our run together that afternoon – a serious loss. What has especially concerned me, however, is that I'll be gone that Thursday evening. I don't want you to leave the medical building alone. Especially now. Roland may suspect I'm gone when I'm not in class on Wednesday. I'm not sure what he will do as a result. If you will accept this, I've asked Brad to meet you that night before you leave work. He is more than willing to do this and to escort you back to the dorm."

Promise couldn't respond immediately. She realized with surprise how much his absence sparked deep feelings of fear. She inhaled deeply. The memory of her past life as Glenna, left to parent their son alone when Alasdair led the men on a hunt, overwhelmed her momentarily. Remembering this helped her understand that her present reaction carried within it a significant past-life component. She need not be that afraid. That Lugh had thought to ask Brad to provide an escort and that Brad had agreed could finally bring her comfort. Promise sighed, then she thanked Lugh for his care.

Lugh acknowledged her gratitude, but in the several moments of silence preceding it, he had looked at her quizzically. She readily explained the deeper processing of her past-life associations, then once again expressed her appreciation. He nodded his understanding just as the images of a dream returned to his consciousness.

"Promise, I know you're the one to have big dreams. I hardly ever remember any of mine. I even almost forgot to tell you this one, but your mention of our shared past life jogged my memory. I had it last night; it really unnerved me."

"Please tell it to me," Promise invited.

Lugh shared it with her gladly: "I am in a cave, again wearing the animal skins of that time long ago. I'm very sad – I might have even been crying. I'm carving a spiral shape into the stone wall inside the cave. All of a sudden, a woman appears. Strangely, she's wearing modern-day clothing. She asks me why I'm upset. I tell her my mate is dying. She says, 'Take me to her.' ... What's really weird is that the woman looked exactly like your mother!"

Promise's eyebrows shot upward on her forehead. "My mother?!" she echoed.

"Yes, I'm sure of it. What do you make of that?"

Promise suddenly remembered how her parents had spoken of past-life experiences with Mark Roland. "Lugh," she said, "do you have plans for Thanksgiving? I think my parents may be able to fill in our blanks!"

40

PROMISE WORKED HER USUAL HOURS at the medical center the following Tuesday. Its relative lack of drama helped her relax to some degree. The next morning, she and Lugh set out for the trek home to be with her family for the Thanksgiving holiday. She always looked forward to these reunions. This one would be decidedly different, however. Not only would Aunt Tara and Uncle Alex not join them – they had traveled to be with Karli in her new home with her new family now living at a distance – but Promise had also invited a guest. She had already arranged for Lugh to sleep in her bedroom during their stay. Lizzie eagerly anticipated sisterly sleepovers, four in a row, before Promise returned to campus on Sunday.

Their arrival at the Holmes-Thomas residence sparked the predictable round of excitement, not the least of which involved Quirkie's adjustment to the relatively new presence of Lugh. Promise and Lizzie engaged in their typical, long, reconnection embrace. Peter and Brittany thrilled at the return of their oldest, who looked more mature and more beautiful with each reunion. Peter shook hands warmly with Lugh and welcomed him to their home. Brittany gave him a welcome hug and offered the travelers something to eat after their long trip.

The evening passed with food preparations and movies, brief updates, and pizza. Later that night, when the sisters huddled in Lizzie's bed, Lizzie shared her latest news regarding classes, sports, and romantic interests. She asked if Promise and Lugh were dating. Promise hadn't thought of it that way, but given the frequency of their contacts and the depth of her feelings, she had to say yes. Lizzie expressed her happiness for Promise, stating that she liked Lugh very much.

Peter's parents and other extended family members joined them for the holiday meal the next day. Well before their arrival, the lower level of household activity accommodated a run shared by Brittany, Lizzie, Lugh, and Promise. Peter contented himself with creativity in the kitchen. The joggers helped set the table upon their return. Showers, the donning of appropriate attire, the arrival of guests, and much laughter preceded the Thanksgiving feast.

Lugh enjoyed meeting Peter's parents. He specifically noticed that no one had a spiral birthmark in any observable location. Peter paid special attention to Lugh, wondering why he felt so familiar. He clearly discerned that the feeling of familiarity had nothing to do with Lugh's demeanor or relational style. It seemed more related to his bearing – some hidden aspect of leadership still masked by youthful confusion. He hoped for the chance to better understand his intuition once the holiday hubbub had passed.

On Friday, Peter went to the gym. Brittany took Promise and Lizzie shopping as part of their longstanding Thanksgiving tradition. Lugh used the time to jog a longer distance than was his custom, hoping to work out his inner restlessness as he ran.

Lugh did his best to appreciate the welcome and warmth of Promise's turf, but he felt a need for deeper grounding. He had many challenges and projects awaiting him upon his return to campus. He had hoped this interlude would provide additional clarity regarding his strange dream, but each passing day seemed to take him farther from both agendas. Still, Lugh also recognized that Promise needed to enjoy these rituals with those she loved. She had as much to deal with as he did, perhaps more, depending upon one's perspective. He decided that he would be patient and vigilant for inquiring opportunities.

Lugh returned to their home just as Peter pulled into the driveway. They greeted each other, sweating and feeling much better following their recent exertions. Peter invited Lugh to join him for a beer. Lugh gratefully accepted, hoping it might provide the chance to explore his deeper questions.

Lugh opted to get right to his point. "Peter, do you mind if I ask you a personal question?"

Peter smiled. "You took the words right out of my mouth. No, not at all. I'll ask mine later, assuming it isn't the same one as yours!"

Lugh laughed and appreciated the encouragement. "Great! Please tell me about the spiral birthmark. Promise suggested that it has ancient roots as a sign of leadership. What can you tell me about it?"

"It seems that our minds are running along the same track. I learned about it during a past-life regression." Peter hesitated to continue without asking, "Does that strike you as strange?"

"No. I've been having my own past-life intimations during the shamanic workshops I've attended with Promise, which is why I'm really curious about this. No one in my family has this mark. But it seems I did in the past." Lugh had to add, "Does this strike *you* as strange?"

Peter really laughed now. "Yes and no!! This life gets weirder all the time. But one can't have a daughter like Promise and call too much strange anymore."

Lugh also chuckled. "I know what you mean! Please tell me about your past life, Peter. I am really interested."

Just as Peter prepared to share his experience, Brittany and his daughters returned. Lugh nodded his agreement in response to Peter's unspoken question. Promise would benefit from hearing her father's story as well.

Now that they had all convened in the living room with no significant social interruptions or commitments to distract them, Peter updated the women on his and Lugh's conversation. Lizzie had never really heard about her parents' prior lifetimes, but she and Promise had shared enough for her to know what past lives are and why they matter. Lizzie joined the group with ears eager to learn more.

Peter turned to Brittany and said, "Actually, you may wish to start this story with your own experience because it leads into mine. It will make less sense if I go first."

Brittany nodded. Promise and Lugh glanced quickly in each other's direction, aware that their questions might soon be answered.

Brittany began, "More than twenty years ago, I first met Mark Roland at work. After my initial, appalling contact with him, followed by a few more equally unpleasant encounters, I had strange dreams, which led me to have my own past-life regression. That former life took place on a rocky coastline during a time long, long ago. I and my fellow villagers wore animal skins." She stopped abruptly when she noticed the looks on Lugh's and Promise's faces. "You knew this?"

Promise replied, "We didn't know that was your experience, Mom. It's just that we've had similar experiences ourselves, separately, on more than one occasion. Please go on!"

Brittany's facial expression registered her own curiosity, but she honored Promise's request and continued. "Okay. My mother, Fiona, lost a dear friend and cousin named Glenna before I was born. Glenna, who felt like a sister to her, had died in the process of giving birth to her second child. Sadly, that child also died with her. Losing Glenna broke Fiona's heart.

"The backstory is also important. Fiona's dear cousin had mated with the leader of our village, Alasdair, who bore the spiral birthmark of leadership. He grieved his mate's loss terribly. Glenna and Alasdair had a son, four years older than I, whose behavior and reputation stirred fear in the hearts of all his peers as well as the women who had to watch over him in his father's absence. When I was six years old, I challenged him when he hurt my younger brother. He had it in for me thereafter.

"When I was ten years old, my mother died while begging me to 'remember the mark' and pass it on to my descendants. Glenna made Fiona promise to do this so that someone from the future would be able to travel back in time to help Glenna give birth to her second child. The spiral had been carved on the wall of a cave nearby to guide the future assistant."

Promise and Lugh listened attentively, astounded to hear their experiences confirmed.

Brittany continued, "During that lifetime, Drust, Glenna's first son, grew into a truly wicked human being. When he came of age, he joined the men for a boar hunt during which he carelessly provoked the boar. He inherited the leadership role after his father died from being gored by that same boar in an attempt to save his son. The boar would have otherwise killed Drust."

Again, Brittany paused her narration when she observed the shocked look on Lugh's face. She quickly asked, "Lugh, are you okay?"

Lugh sat speechless for a few moments before he could respond. "Yeah. I'm just overwhelmed by the similarities between your story and the experiences I've had. I'll tell you about that after I've heard both of yours, if that's okay."

Brittany's brow conveyed her own puzzlement, but she nodded, opting to continue as requested. "Drust tried to physically and sexually attack me during that past life, just as he tried in this current lifetime."

Now, both Promise and Lizzie gasped with horror in response to their mother's report. Noticing this, Brittany quickly responded, "He did not succeed in either lifetime. But he was furious. In that past life, I had to leave the village in order to survive."

Brittany consciously decided that her daughters didn't need to hear the details about Dierdre and how Drust had abused his bride on their wedding night. Peter noticed her omission and silently agreed. Promise and Lizzie had enough to process. He would omit that part as well.

Brittany concluded, "That's all I remember from that lifetime. Your dad's part of the story takes over from here."

Peter interrupted, "Not quite, Brittany. Remember the part about the cave?"

"Oh my gosh, yes! You're right. That's really important. In this lifetime, Peter and I took a trip to Iona and Mull, where we actually found a cave with the spiral carved on the wall."

Lugh's eyes almost popped out of his head. Both Peter and Brittany noticed. Promise looked shocked as well. Promise had intuited some of this, but the actuality of hearing her mother's words surprised her nonetheless. "Please go on, Mom!"

"Well, your dad and I both made counterclockwise circles over that spiral and left the cave in a funky mood that lasted for weeks. I finally consulted with your Aunt Tara who helped me journey back to the cave. There I met a man in animal skins, tearfully telling me that his mate was about to die. I said to him, 'Take me to her.' He did, and there I met my mother, Fiona, who was pregnant with me in that lifetime. She was trying to help her dear friend that I now know was Glenna.

"Glenna was obviously bleeding to death. Somehow, I managed to help Glenna give birth to her baby. It felt like something beyond me aided the process because I certainly didn't know what I was doing. As a result, her second son was born. He had the spiral birthmark on his forehead. He didn't die, unlike the outcome in *my* past life regression. This is where your dad's story begins."

Astonished, Lugh could only listen, overwhelmed as he was by Brittany's story and how it supported the accuracy of his dream. Even his shamanic journey at Samhain had revealed a second son with a birthmark on his forehead. He couldn't make sense of all these correspondences, other than to accept them all as told to him. Because he had not yet shared his own experiences with Brittany or Peter – and Promise had assured him that she hadn't either – the confluence of these stories literally blew his mind wide open. Reality would never be the same.

Lugh couldn't speak. Promise noticed this and reached for his hand. Turning to her father, she said, "Dad, we need to hear your story too."

41

PETER NOTICED several things at once: Lugh's shock, Promise's genuine affection for this young man, Brittany's concern for everyone seated in their living room, and Lizzie's puzzlement. Peter had his own confusion to manage as well. He fully recognized that something related to the ancient past stirred in the steaming stewpot of this current situation. His own story, he suspected, would add the needed dash of seasoning.

Before he launched into his tale, Peter decided to check in with Lizzie. He turned to her and specifically asked, "Lizzie, how are you doing with all of this so far?"

"I'm fine, Dad. This is really interesting! I can't wait to hear the rest."

Peter's eyebrows did a quick rise and fall as he decided to continue. "Okay, then. Well, my past life began with the memory of being raised as the son of Fiona alongside your Mom, whose name was Màiri in that lifetime. When I reached the age of four, Fiona told me that I was really Glenna and Alasdair's son. I had to live with Alasdair then… and Drust, who hated me.

"I spent most of my young life under threat from my older brother's physical, emotional, and mental abuse – or so we would label it in this lifetime. In sharp contrast, our father wanted us to grow up with 'brotherly love' so that we would rule well together when the time came for our succession. Unfortunately, Drust had no such intentions. As we grew, it became clear to me that Drust wanted me dead."

Lugh sat transfixed, struggling to appreciate that this man who sat before him, the father of the woman he was growing to love more by the day, had been his son in a past life, the one that he, Lugh, had treated unfairly. Through his own past-life journey, Lugh already had acknowledged his own tragic, unjust behavior. He braced himself to hear Peter's version of that experience from the receiving end.

Peter continued, "When Drust came of age, our father appointed Darran, the best warrior of our tribe, to train Drust in the arts of combat and hunting for wild boar. Drust had other intentions, however; he used his training to threaten me. Consequently, I privately begged Darran to teach me as well – even though I was still four years too young – so that I could properly defend myself. Bravely, without my father's permission, Darran agreed. We made a secret pact. He instructed and drilled me before the sun rose each dawn. Drust had never applied himself well to Darran's lessons, but I did. Practicing in the shadows of moonlight gave me an edge that Drust would never have.

"That same scene described by Brittany, where Drust provoked the boar, happened in my lifetime as well, except I recognized the danger to our father, who made moves to rescue Drust. Instead, I climbed a tree and pulled my brother to safety. Drust seethed in rage and jealousy when I earned the respect of the men. Our father witnessed this. I sensed that he finally realized and began to accept that his sons would never rule together. Alasdair foresaw, just as I had, that eventually Drust would provoke the clash: one of us would have to kill the other."

Peter paused, again taking in the reactions around him. Lizzie continued to calmly take in the story, like a plot from a novel unfolding with the good part not many pages away. Promise's facial expression suggested that numerous questions had found some answers. Lugh, on the other hand, seemed overwhelmed with emotions. Peter found himself wondering, for reasons he could not yet explain, if guilt surpassed them all. Brittany held no such confusion; she recognized that feeling and suddenly suspected that Alasdair sat before her. She said nothing, however. She respectfully left that for Lugh to share.

Lugh finally asked, "What happened? Did one son have to kill the other?"

Peter's own face darkened. "Sadly, yes. After our father died, Drust threatened Màiri. He had continued to torment the villagers. He commanded that Darran, my trusted friend and teacher, be beheaded. Not yet of age to rule myself, I challenged Drust to a duel for rulership. In his drunken stupor, he accepted. My skills far outranked his. Two days later we faced each other before the whole village. Eventually, I disarmed him and held my knife to his throat. I gave him the option to surrender. Instead, he threatened to harm Màiri. I'm not proud of this, but I killed him."

Lizzie gaped at her father in shock. Brittany gently touched Peter's back with comfort. Promise and Lugh both felt near tears as they now realized that Peter had suffered greatly in response to the events of that lifetime. As his parents they felt responsible. The realization that Drust and Mark Roland shared the same soul did nothing to comfort them.

Peter noticed all these reactions once he recovered from his own, which didn't take long, given his twenty years of reflection and practice. He began to suspect that Promise and Lugh played some role in his story, and Brittany's as well, but the full clarity eluded him. He had to ask, "Promise, Lugh, you seem to resonate with all of this in a deep way. Would you care to share your experiences with us?"

Lugh turned to Promise and said, "Would you please go first?"

She understood immediately and agreed, "No problem."

Promise turned toward her parents and began her own version of the tale. "During our shamanic Samhain celebration, I journeyed again to Alethea. She invited me to walk a path down the sides of a rocky cliff toward the shore as a way to experience my past life. I had two experiences like this. Chronologically, the second vision happened first, so I'll begin with that one.

"At the bottom of the cliff, I discovered I was wearing animal skins and I was pregnant. My dearest friend and cousin, Fiona, also with child, joined me. We were to watch the children playing near a cave on the shoreline while the men went hunting.

"Fiona and I sat on the rocks above the children. I shared with her my ongoing concerns about my four-year-old son's aggressive behavior. In an instant of distraction, we heard a cry and discovered that he had chased, then poked a small child with his large stick. The child lay there hurt, but my son didn't care at all. I grabbed the stick from his hand while the other mothers comforted their children. My son just glared at me. In that moment, a rumble in my womb told me that the child within me would bring balance to my older son's aggression. My child needed to be born!"

Peter's eyes just stared at Promise as she told her tale. He quickly realized that she had been his mother in that lifetime, the mother he had never had the chance to know. He had never appreciated how the grief of her loss weighed heavily in his being. How amazing that she would come to him in this lifetime as his daughter.

Brittany sighed. She had only to wait a few minutes more to hear what Promise had experienced related to the birth of her second child, Micheil.

Promise sensed that both her parents were amazed by her story. It suddenly dawned on her that neither of them would have experienced the scene she had just described because they were both still in the womb. She said aloud, "I guess neither of you had yet been born when I as Glenna had that experience on the rocks with my older son."

Peter and Brittany nodded their agreement with their daughter's assessment. They couldn't manage any other response in that moment. Brittany finally found words and asked, "Promise, you said you had another journey?"

"Yes, Mom, I did. In this one, I was still very pregnant, likely close to my due date. I shared a dream with Fiona about a doe giving birth to a fawn in a pool of blood. In the next part of the dream, a woman appeared on the beach. She called a spiral of light to herself and carried it to the doe who was bleeding profusely from her birthing process. The woman placed the spiraling light on the doe's belly. A fawn was born with the spiral mark on his forehead. The doe saw the sign of succession and died in peace.

"After Glenna shared this upsetting dream with Fiona, they picked their berries, then they made their way through the bog back to their caves. Before they reached their destination, Glenna started to bleed. Fiona ran for help, found Alasdair, and brought him back to be with her. Glenna felt desperate to have her child born. She begged Alasdair to go to the cave and carve the spiral into its wall so that when the woman in her dream came from the future, she would know how to find Glenna and help her. I as Glenna died without knowing if my second son was ever born."

Brittany exclaimed, "So, that's how it happened! I had always wondered how there could be two parallel lifetimes and why that spiral drew me to itself in the cave! Promise, it seems that in this particular version of that lifetime, you as Glenna didn't know about the part where I came to you before you died.... How hard that must have been for you."

Promise gazed at her mother with new eyes. Some of the feelings from her Samhain journeys had not yet found the words needed to accurately describe them to Promise's consciousness. For the first time since the Celtic New Year, Promise felt seen in her grief. She responded,

"Thank you for naming that for me, Mom. I am so glad to hear that my second son lived – even though I'm also shocked to realize that he was you, Dad."

Peter smiled. "No more shocked than I am to learn that you were the mother I never got to know." Peter shook his head.

Lizzie spoke spontaneously for the first time. "Am I in this story at all?"

Promise looked to Brittany only to find her reciprocating her gaze. Simultaneously, they each turned toward Lizzie and said, "You were Fiona!"

Peter sighed and smiled with recognition. "Of course she was! Lizzie, you mothered us both!"

"You mean I was *your* parent?!" When they both nodded, Lizzie gazed at Peter and Brittany triumphantly and exclaimed, "That means *I* get to tell *you* what to do!"

Peter chuckled. "That's history, my dear Elizabeth. This go-round, it's our turn!!"

Lizzie suspected as much, but that didn't prohibit her from making a dramatic gesture of surrender. Everyone laughed.

Still facing Lizzie, Promise said with great seriousness, "In that lifetime, Lizzie, you were like a sister to me!"

Brittany suddenly, more deeply understood her daughters' struggles with separation from each other. She specifically directed her reflections to both of them: "After Glenna died, I remembered my mother, Fiona, as very sad most of the time. She really missed her dear friend Glenna. The two of you have had trouble parting from each other as if that lifetime might repeat itself. You've done an admirable job of working it through, though. It's just that now we can understand the root of it."

Promise and Lizzie gratefully held each other's gaze for several moments. They had so much to process already, but Lugh had yet to share his journeys. He realized his time had come. All eyes converged on him. He sighed and said, "I guess it's my turn."

42

LUGH SIGHED AGAIN. He gathered his courage and straightforwardly said to Peter, "I was Alasdair, and I sincerely apologize to you for how I treated you in that lifetime. I don't remember all the details, but you have filled in the blanks and explained the reason for the intensity of my feelings. I died feeling incredibly guilty for misjudging you and your brother. I left you in an impossible, horrible situation because I couldn't face it myself. I doubt that I can ever make it up to you, but I am really sorry."

Stunned by this confession and the strangeness of such direct conversation with the man who had fathered him so very long ago, Peter sat speechless for several minutes. He never disconnected from Lugh's gaze, however. He held no animosity toward Alasdair from the past, having felt compassion for him even during their past life together. But to actually receive his spoken apology took him completely by surprise.

Having anticipated this, Brittany witnessed Peter's reaction and knew he needed time to process it all before he might make a meaningful response. She decided to indulge her curiosity in the meantime by asking Lugh to share his journeying experiences. Lugh readily complied.

"I've had three past-life memories and a dream. Not until listening to your stories today, have they made sense to me. In the first, I was a leader of men on a boar hunt. I was wearing animal skins and had a spiral birthmark on my shoulder. One of the men – who, I later realized, felt like a son to me – carelessly provoked the boar to attack him. I tried to save my son; in the process, the boar gored me.

"In the second memory, I was that same leader, wedded to the village seer. We had a young son whose aggressive behavior concerned her. She was pregnant and having dreams that she would die giving birth to our second child." Lugh gazed directly at Promise as he said, "I didn't want to believe her." He regretfully continued, "Sadly, she did die. She had been correct about everything. Our second son was never born. I grieved her loss terribly and felt unforgivable guilt."

Lugh paused at this point. Promise smiled to give him reassurance. He sighed and smiled wanly in return.

Lugh continued, "This is where I'm still confused, because in the third journey, I had two sons. We were on a boar hunt; my older son still provoked the boar, only this time my younger son climbed a tree and pulled his brother to safety. As we made the return trip to the village, I realized that they would never rule together. I had made a huge mistake by assuming that the older one would share the leadership role. All along, I had blamed my younger son for my mate's death. I never saw him for the true leader he had become. My oldest would set the stage for the tragedy: one would have to kill the other to assume the leadership of our village. I couldn't bear it. I wanted to die and did so before I had to witness the outcome."

Lugh paused. Only Quirkie's rhythmic breathing, as he lay curled up in the corner, interrupted the silence. Lugh considered that he deserved no more than this, so he decided to continue. "I couldn't make sense for how in two of my experiences I had only one son, and in the last one I had two. In my dream, I carved that spiral into the cave wall as Glenna lay dying, and you suddenly appeared, Brittany. That's what prompted Promise to invite me here for Thanksgiving. We had no idea how this would turn out. I don't know how to do it at this moment, but I want to make this right."

More silence. Promise squeezed Lugh's hand once again. She also nodded her encouragement, sensing that he had a question to ask. He took comfort from her understanding and wondered aloud, "Your lifetimes impressed me as the same yet different, almost like parallel universes. If I may presume to ask, would you be willing to help me understand that?"

Brittany chose to respond. "We have puzzled over that mystery these many years. The best we can offer you is our sense that there were two worlds: one filled with violence and ruled by Drust, the other eventually ruled by his brother, Micheil. Glenna's intuition involved a deep knowing for how to mend the split between these worlds. She prayed for that mending. Perhaps, Lugh, as Alasdair you wanted that mending as well. It's just that Drust had other ideas."

Lugh felt touched by the kindness of her insight. An aspect of the gripping tension inside him eased. Brittany sensed this with compassion for his struggle. She continued to share her reflections.

"During my past-life regression, I remembered the world ruled by Drust. Through dreams about Fiona, I pursued the path that helped me to relive this and to honor her call to 'remember the mark.' In an attempt to understand all this more fully, Peter and I found our way back to that cave and entered the spiraling vortex of the past – an alternative past. In that past, Micheil was born even though Glenna still died.

"In this lifetime, Peter has worked hard to orchestrate a more peaceful solution to this ancient conflict. In response to Mark Roland's aggressive acts, we opted to use the legal system this go-round to ensure a safe distance between him and us, rather than brute force and violence. Our plan worked fairly well, or so we thought, until the paths of Promise and Mark Roland converged in Dunkirk Hollow."

Daring to pose the question pressing on her heart, Brittany braced herself in anticipation of hearing their answers: "I have to ask you both what role Mark Roland has played in your lives."

Lugh and Promise looked directly to each other for guidance about how much to reveal. Promise led the way. She replied, "He took a job at the same medical center where I work. Our schedules overlap two nights each week. He knows I am your daughter. His threats have not materialized into anything physical thus far. Lugh has made a point of accompanying me to the parking lot and back to campus as I close the building each evening. I don't see Mark Roland at any other time."

Brittany's hand came to her mouth to cover the expression of her horror as she remembered what it felt like to live in such fear of the man. Promise witnessed this and understood. She added, "Mom, I didn't have the same past life with him as you had. I was his mother. Knowing that going forward gives me an edge you didn't have. Thanks to Dad's insistence, I've learned Aikido and I still participate in those classes every week. With Lugh's help as well, I will be okay."

This did little to comfort Brittany's mother-heart. Before she could respond, Lugh spoke to his experiences as well. "It turns out that Mark Roland signed up to teach one of my courses after the professor suddenly had to resign. I need this class to graduate in the spring. Roland's stance toward me changed after he realized that I am protecting Promise. As a result, I anticipate some difficulties with him over my grade, but I am prepared to deal with that. Now knowing that I was his father also gives me the understanding I have needed and an advantage going forward. I will continue to meet Promise when she leaves work every evening, and I'll find someone to take my place when I can't. She won't face him alone."

Peter listened to all of this with a father's ear. Finally, he spoke: "I have two very important points to make; the first leads into the second. Lugh, I want to begin with your apology to me related to the past life encounters we shared.

"During my past-life regression, I experienced Alasdair as a man of integrity and ideals, even if he lacked the capacity for fatherly warmth. I see now that this was likely impacted by his grief and guilt. Even before he died, I felt compassion for the man as I realized that his dream of his sons co-ruling their village would end in the death of one of us. I knew that he would opt to die before he had to witness it himself. I hold no animosity toward Alasdair, but I never once imagined I would ever hear a spoken apology from him. Your words have touched me deeply."

Lugh couldn't believe what he heard. Tears welled up but he kept them under control.

Peter continued, "As for your current contacts and conflicts with Mark Roland, I know from experience that he is cunning but impulsive, and consequently stupid, but that doesn't change the fact that he is still very dangerous. I don't want you in his field, Promise. I say that as a father. But I've learned that these things are bigger than what I want. That you would wind up in the same locale and remember your past lives with him speak to higher intentions.

"Lugh, you were a leader with high values and tremendous courage in a fight. I can only hope that you have brought those skills with you into this lifetime. Promise, you were a visionary and still are. Please honor your intuitions and dreams. I don't want to let either of you return to Stella Maris, but that's like saying I don't want you to live your lives. I can only ask that you promise me you will call upon me and ask for my aid if you need it. You kept that promise long ago, my dear daughter…and mother. I hope you will make it and keep it again."

Peter's reference to Promise's experience of tragedy during her sophomore year elicited a painful memory that required no further elaboration. His daughter understood.

"I will, Dad. I promise. Thank you for trusting me."

Lugh had never met a man with such wisdom and integrity. He gazed directly at Peter with profound respect and vowed, "I appreciate the healing you have granted me this day. Mark Roland was never yours to battle. Dealing with him was, and continues to be, my responsibility. I will protect your daughter with my life. And I will definitely call upon you if we need you. I promise."

Peter stood and so did Lugh. They shook hands, then Peter gently pulled Lugh toward him. They embraced each other with respect and forgiveness. The tears finally escaped the hold of their respective eyelids. They let their mutual healing permeate the room.

Brittany and Promise both understood what this meant for the men they loved. Lizzie couldn't escape the poignancy of the moment, resonating on some unconscious level with the profound reconciliation that they had all just experienced. Brittany patted both sides of the couch where she sat, inviting Promise and Lizzie to join her. She placed her arms around her daughters and held them close. Together, they gathered their courage for whatever lay ahead.

Part Three

43

HOURS LATER on that mind-boggling Friday afternoon, after the men had showered and everyone had enjoyed Thanksgiving leftovers for lunch, Peter sat pensively in his study. Alone in the silence, he absent-mindedly gazed out the window, barely noticing what few leaves remained on trees as they fluttered in the wind. Promise had gone for a run with Brittany and Quirkie. Lugh went for a walk. Peter had no doubt that Lugh welcomed the time to process his reactions to their conversation, just as Peter also needed this pause to comprehend his own. Lizzie had a commitment with friends.

Peter leaned forward, resting his elbows on his desk, holding his face in his hands. He suddenly remembered that his palms covered the spiral that seemed not only to mark his face, but to portray the markings of time. The threads of at least six souls had bobbed and weaved in and out of one another's lives across lifetimes. That count didn't include Tara and whoever else he forgot to consider. What could all this possibly mean? He immediately realized that he had asked too broad a question in his desperate effort to make some sense of those earlier, mind-bending revelations. Instead, he had to start with what he knew: his own experience. That, too, seemed rather overwhelming at the moment.

His birth as Micheil in the past had resulted from Glenna's prayer to mend a split – as best as he could determine, that is. Peter now realized that Alasdair's dream for his sons to co-rule reflected a similar, ancient longing for that same mending. That Alasdair's sons would be as opposite as night and day, or good and evil, challenged all of them, past and present. Peter had learned years ago that the reconciliation of opposing forces required no small measure of work on this earth plane. That effort also offered no timely guarantee of success.

Conceptually, Peter had no problem reflecting on his experience in these archetypal terms. The emotional implications triggered an entirely different, more difficult struggle, however. His intense anger toward Mark Roland erupted from a reactivated wound that Peter had once thought healed and buried. That the surgeon would now threaten his daughter sparked even greater surges of fierce protectiveness than what he had felt when Brittany had to undergo the same ordeal.

Even then, Peter had grappled intensely with how to manage the barrage of his conflicted feelings while trying to honor the wishes of the woman he had come to love. Brittany's autonomy and her decision to fulfill the duties of her employment steadily risked further contact with their nemesis and challenged Peter's endurance considerably. In contrast, Peter had spent twenty years carefully guiding and safeguarding his daughter. That he could not do so now felt untenable. A battle raged inside him.

As Peter contemplated the dovetailing details that emerged from their shared past-life experiences, he couldn't deny how strange it felt to meet his parents from that previous lifetime. That they remembered their roles and confessed their feelings about how it had all unfolded did heal something within him that he hadn't realized needed the healing.

He admired how Promise and Lugh committed themselves to righting the wrong from long ago. Still, they were young now and their ancient souls were relatively inexperienced in the ways of this modern world. Mark Roland had professional clout, financial backing, and years of practiced cunning, not to mention physical stature and decades, even lifetimes, of anger that could easily overwhelm and disable any efforts his young idealists might hope to make. Peter also realized that Promise and Lugh were smart enough to know this already. He truly admired their courage.

None of these considerations provided the clarity he needed to handle this horrendous situation, however. He sat back in his desk chair, overcome with emotion and paralyzed with indecision. Once again, he remembered Brittany's wisdom from long ago; faith, the only way to deal with such overwhelming unknowns, had guided him well since then. Nonetheless, Peter had never experienced a test like this before. He sighed and sat still in the silence.

Meanwhile, Brittany and Promise went for a long run on a local school track vacated for the holiday. As they neared their cooldown stretch, Brittany broke the silence between them. "Promise, I can't lie. I'm afraid for you."

"Please tell me what it was like for you when you knew Mark Roland, Mom."

Brittany met her daughter's gaze, hoping to read her intentions. Sensing the seriousness of Promise's request, Brittany slowed her pace accordingly. She decided to be honest.

"I was really scared, Promise. He was taller than me, held a higher rank in the hospital, and leered at me in a way that made my skin crawl and my stomach turn. That I might see him at some unpredictable moment in the hospital made it hard to go to work every day. Your dad really struggled not to interfere on my behalf, but I had asked him not to. He did finally make his presence and protectiveness known, only to suffer a flimsy but financially demanding, time-consuming lawsuit over the Rainbow Center in retaliation. It was a very difficult time for us, Promise, and it lasted for more than two years. I don't want you to have to go through that."

Promise felt her own anxiety level rise in response to her mother's words. She tried to swallow it down before she replied, "I don't know how you can spare me, Mom. I can't leave this alone. He has hurt some people, and I won't be able to live with myself if I just walk away. Did you walk away?"

Brittany stopped and turned toward her daughter with tears in her eyes. "No, I didn't. I'm crying because I know you well enough to recognize that you won't either."

"Then share your hard-earned wisdom with me, Mom. I need it."

Brittany reached for Promise and held her in a tight embrace. When she finally released her, she said, "I hate saying this, but you need to know: he likes to go for the throat with his right hand. If you know any Aikido moves to protect yourself from that thrust, practice them. He also doesn't expect his advances will be met with any kind of powerful resistance. That takes him off-guard momentarily. You have to capitalize on that vulnerability because he rallies quickly. He is also very protective of his hands, as you can imagine."

Promise absorbed her mother's advice like a notebook draws in the ink of the writer's pen. The images conveyed by her mother's words penetrated her mind's eye, stimulated bodily perceptions and responses, and awakened the warrior within her. She would not forget.

To comfort her mother, Promise said, "Come for my throat like he would, Mom."

Brittany looked horrified until she realized what Promise intended. She then did as her daughter requested. Promise deftly demonstrated an Aikido move while also catching Brittany before she fell in response to it.

Promise then said, "I promise you, Mom, I will practice this and several other techniques. I don't want to hurt him, necessarily. That is not the way of Aikido. But I want you to know that I will be able to protect myself. Okay?"

Brittany just shook her head in amazement. "Okay!" She added, "I can see Glenna's strength in you, not just physically, but spiritually and emotionally. Still, I hope you will ask me for help if you need it?"

"Mom, you know I will. I did in the distant past and you saved my son's life. I can't know what lies ahead. But I do know I love you. You are an amazing mother. Thank you!"

Again, Brittany held Promise close to her. "I love you too, my precious daughter. Please take good care of yourself."

"I will, Mom. I promise." They exchanged appreciative smiles, called Quirkie to join them, and then went home.

Upon their return, Promise headed for the shower. Quirkie sniffed his way to Peter, and Brittany followed their capable retriever. She found Peter staring at the air, looking fairly distraught.

Peter responded to her arrival with a glance in her direction. Her radiance never failed to momentarily capture his breath. He couldn't help but sigh. He invited her to join him. She walked toward his desk and sat in his lap. Quirkie curled himself at their feet.

Brittany smoothed the furrows in his brow and held his head to her heart. She recognized his struggle and suspected that its intensity far outweighed what they had shared together long ago. Their daughter's life bound them and involved them in a way that partnering as independent, relational adults cannot touch. They just held each other. Peter let the tears of his overwhelming confusion flow forth.

Brittany did as well. After several moments of needed release, she shared with him her conversation with Promise on the track. She added, "We will need to deal with this in a way that honors her path and helps us stay sane. Once again, we may need to consult with Tara and Alex. We will get through this, Peter. We will."

She kissed his head. He kissed her heart. They carefully rose from his chair to avoid stepping on Quirkie. Together they left his study. They went on with life.

44

LUGH SAT QUIETLY in the passenger seat as Promise drove the three-hour route back to campus. They had had little time alone together to process their experiences of the weekend. Promise sensed something deep and troubling churning within Lugh. She didn't want to pry, hoping instead that he would spontaneously share with her what concerned him. They traveled for more than thirty minutes in relative silence before he finally spoke.

"Promise, I'm sorry I've been so quiet. It's been a true gift to spend so much time with your family, and I don't want you to think me ungrateful. Your father just blew me away."

Promise chuckled. "He has a way of doing that. Even so, it was all pretty intense. I honestly had no idea it would turn out the way it did. Personally, I am glad to now know those past-life details that eluded us."

When Lugh didn't respond, she asked, "Are you okay?"

Lugh looked directly at Promise and caught her gaze as she glanced in his direction while driving. She deserved his honesty. He finally found the words that had escaped him until now. "I feel horrible about the way I acted in that lifetime. Nothing your father did as my son in the past warranted the way I treated him. You as Glenna knew what was needed. You were the village seer, after all, and I did not listen to you. Tragedy followed tragedy, and here we are again, only now you are more at risk than ever. I won't let him hurt you, Promise. I will do everything I can to keep you safe."

Lugh had tears in his eyes – as best as Promise could tell for the tears in her own. She spotted a rest stop ahead and pulled into it. After parking the car, she turned to face Lugh directly.

"Lugh, we have all done things in the past that we regret. Life is about having experiences, which include trial and error. As a culture, we never talk about trial and success because our brains are so riveted on avoiding the mistakes that lead to disaster. Yet we all make those mistakes at some point, often while trying our best to succeed. It's not about the errors. It's about what they teach us, how we learn from them, the new things we try as a result, and the courage to risk trial and success or error all over again. It's just the nature of life.

"That's what forgiveness is for, by the way. Without it, we just wallow in guilt and keep making the same mistakes over and over again – like traversing a circle, always on the same plane. With forgiveness, we can begin anew, hopefully with more wisdom, but still, we must go forward with humility, knowing that we risk making more mistakes. It's like traversing a spiral: we meet the same challenge again but, hopefully, from a higher plane of consciousness. Ultimately, we have the opportunity to choose: Will we allow ourselves to be forgiven? That's the crux of the matter."

Lugh sighed. "You truly are your parents' daughter. Does wisdom grow wild at your house?"

Promise laughed. "I am honored. Thank you." She felt compelled to add, "Lugh, you were a strong, capable leader in that lifetime. Our son – *our* son – didn't wreak his worst havoc until you died. We both could rein him in then, at least somewhat. Admittedly, I don't know if I would have been able to do that once he grew, but you would not have allowed him to hurt me then either. We both wanted the same things: balance, unity, and peace. It seems we've been given another chance."

Lugh just shook his head in amazement. "I appreciate what you are saying, but I also meant what I said about keeping you safe. This is my responsibility now."

Promise sighed, then smiled. "I am truly in awe of you, Lugh. Your integrity clearly has spanned lifetimes. I suspect my father learned quite a lot about integrity from you as his father – how circuitous this all is! Still, this responsibility does not belong to you alone. I have always had it as well. Glenna felt a deep sense of mission. I know that for certain. It helps me understand why I also have the mark."

"What?!" Lugh exclaimed. "You have a spiral birthmark too?"

Promise hadn't planned to tell him this way. Actually, she hadn't considered how or when she might confess her truth. Speaking of Glenna and remembering how she felt in that lifetime emboldened her to be honest. Lugh's remorse and care for her had dissolved her last reservation about sharing this with him. She nodded, then discreetly unzipped her coat and the top button of her blouse to show him the spiral over her heart. She then said, "We must deal with this together."

Overcome with surprise, Lugh's eyes shifted from the spiral to her face and back again multiple times. He had no words to offer in response.

Promise reflected further, "I don't think Glenna had the spiral. I share her soul though, and I am meant to be a leader in this lifetime's drama as are you. Our spirals tell us that our consciousness must rise. We must let the past be the past, learn from it, deal with this now, and make a better future. We are meant to do this together, Lugh. I feel certain."

Lugh just shook his head. "Promise, will you ever stop amazing me?"

"I hope not!" she spontaneously exclaimed. They both laughed.

Promise added, "I also do appreciate your wanting to keep me safe. I really do!"

Lugh smiled for the first time since they departed her parents' home. Then with utter sincerity he said, "Promise, I still feel for you the way I did in that lifetime, only more so. Your courage is astounding. Losing you then seriously challenged my ability to go on. I'm not sure I can bear it again. I will do whatever it takes to protect you. Leaving for my interview later this week really concerns me...."

Promise inhaled deeply. "Lugh, I won't lie. I am really glad that you asked Brad to be with me this coming Thursday evening. That will help with my own situation. The real problem for me involves how to handle what I've witnessed and what I suspect. He hurts people. He is also hurting you. I have to figure out a way to call him to task and, in the meantime, to keep the women safe who are scheduled for appointments with him at the medical center. My suspicions will not suffice to make a difference on the longer term. I need proof."

"That part is very risky, Promise. How can you ever get proof unless the women come forward about their experiences with him. If you have to witness what he is doing directly, he will certainly know, and you will be even more vulnerable. Please don't do anything rash on your own!"

Promise swallowed hard to subdue the anxiety that periodically threatened to overwhelm her. Then she responded to his caution: "I'm not planning anything crazy, and I hope there are no surprises. If Christina does her job, I won't need to intervene with any urgency. I've often wondered how at risk she might be professionally if others realized she has been leaving early. If maintaining her license depends upon it, she may fulfill her duties more responsibly now that she knows I'm paying attention."

"That's a good thought...." Lugh's voice drifted into his unspoken, ongoing worry.

Promise surmised his apprehension and decided to change the subject, "What about you? Have you thought more about how you will handle whatever grade he gives you?"

"I'll have to see what it is first. If he's smart, he'll make it less than what I deserve but not too much less. That way, he might assume that he won't have to deal with my contesting it, that I won't go to all that trouble for something that makes me look petty and egotistical."

Together they chimed, "He's not that smart!" Their brief laughter quickly led to Lugh's mention of his anticipated next step: appealing the grade. He had already researched the requirements. He was gathering what evidence he could in advance.

Lugh then stated, "That was a slick change of subject, my dear. I'm still concerned for your safety, however."

Promise replied, "I am not defenseless, you know. Let me practice some Aikido with you. Hopefully, it will help me and reassure you."

"Excellent idea! But I don't know anything about Aikido."

"Actually, that's good because neither does he, I would imagine. You will offer me some practical experience for what may be needed, although I truly hope it won't be. In any case, I would really appreciate your doing that with me."

"Okay, we'll do it!"

She kissed him. He added another one to hers. A nearby honking horn and the warmth of the midafternoon sun in the car reminded them of their location and visibility. They reluctantly decided to continue on their way. The remainder of their trip included lively conversation about all the many aspects of life they enjoyed.

45

TUESDAY EVENING ARRIVED all too quickly. Even though Lugh had to leave early the next morning for his interview, he still insisted upon meeting Promise after work and riding back to campus with her. She deeply appreciated his care. With ongoing concern for what challenges might arise during her working hours, she arrived at the medical center a few minutes early for her shift.

To her surprise, Lydia greeted her at the reception desk. Promise had the sense that Lydia had planted herself there, wanting to speak to Promise about some issue. Her misgivings were soon confirmed.

Lydia introduced her agenda by saying, "Promise, I appreciate that you came in a few minutes early this evening. Would you please join me in the backroom where we can speak more privately?"

"Of course," Promise replied. She anticipated trouble while she also simultaneously wondered whether she might talk to Lydia about her concerns regarding Mark Roland. Once they were seated in a more secluded setting, Lydia made her point.

"Promise, it has come to my attention that you have been interfering with the efficient flow of patients to Dr. Roland's office. He has lodged a formal complaint, but he also specifically stated that he didn't want you to lose your job. He hoped our discussion of the matter would put an end to your "meddlesome interventions" – those are his words. Are you aware of what he is reporting?"

Stunned, Promise did not know how to respond. Lydia clearly had already taken his side. Because Promise had only very strong suspicions and no evidence to support her suppositions about the surgeon's behavior toward women athletes, she doubted that Lydia would take her seriously. Christina's professional status would also come into question. Would Christina tell the truth? Would she lie? Promise recognized the risk: everybody's word against her own lone voice. This kind of situation had become all too familiar. She decided to trust her intuition: the time for complete honesty had not yet arrived.

Promise replied with a half-truth: "I did make an error one evening, sending the last patient to his office before the young man who preceded her. I apologized. Otherwise, I don't know what he is talking about. Do you?"

Lydia paused. "Honestly, he didn't give me more details than what you just described. He just seemed very angry about the whole situation, implying there was more to it than that. It is now clear to me that you two do have a problematic relationship with each other. I don't want to fire you, Promise. Can you assure me that there will be no further incidents?"

Promise nodded and said, "I will do my best to follow the order of the patients on the list."

Having accomplished her mission, Lydia simply replied, "Good. Thank you. By the way, we haven't discussed how to handle your hours here during your semester break and the holidays. I assume you will be absent between Christmas and New Year, but I will otherwise need you to keep to your schedule. Will that be a problem?"

Promise had anticipated this question and had not yet figured out a solution. With the dorms closed during the break, she needed an alternative place to stay. She simply could not afford to live in a hotel for several weeks. The long commute to and from home multiple days also seemed prohibitive. She thought of asking to camp out at Lugh's apartment, but that felt much too forward and complicated. She stalled. "I don't think so, Lydia, but I'll get back to you with confirmation once I set that up."

"Thank you, Promise. I look forward to hearing from you about this. If we don't cross paths, you can leave a note in my mailbox."

"Will do."

Their meeting concluded. Promise assumed her position at the front desk and completed her tasks with her usual efficiency. With relief she noticed that the one woman on Mark Roland's roster that evening had two men scheduled to follow her.

In the pauses between her responsibilities, Promise attempted to process the audacity of Mark Roland's accusations. He obviously suspected that she had intervened with Christina, but he disguised this with bluster. Lydia succumbed to his authoritarian pressure like a plastic bottle flattened by the tires of a car. The sad part, Promise reflected, was that Lydia didn't even realize it. Her employer's lack of consciousness would not bode well for a more honest conversation about young women's lives ruined by "the doctor."

Promise's plans to complete some of her class assignments while working that evening fell completely to the wayside. Between bouts of unexpressed anger at Mark Roland's insidious, damaging tactics, she wondered if he might be capable of more cunning than what she had previously considered. He had clearly altered Lydia's opinion of her. If his attempts to discredit Promise continued, the situation could turn even more ugly quite quickly.

Promise also struggled with whether to share the surgeon's formal complaint with Lugh that evening. He already worried about her a great deal. She had no doubt that if he knew about this, it would make leaving for his interview even more difficult for him. As Promise deliberated, she recognized that increasing Lugh's worry would solve nothing. She decided to tell him upon his return.

The evening concluded without further drama. The young woman on Dr. Roland's schedule departed after the typical thirty minutes. Christina made no attempt to contact Promise. Lugh arrived a few minutes early, entering the building consistently now to provide a visible, protective presence. Promise immediately detected the apprehension in his brow. His travel plans would challenge what little peace he could muster. Promise did her best not to add to his stress.

They left the building together, then Promise locked the doors behind them. They made their way to campus and lingered in the parking lot. Promise wanted to ease his mind, relieve him of his tension and doubts, and bolster his confidence. He wanted to know that she would feel safe enough in his absence. Promise sensed this and hoped to satisfy both their needs.

She said, "Lugh, I am going to be fine. I will miss you like crazy. I do hope you will let me know how your interview goes? Please don't worry about me. Just focus on your purpose for being there. I know you will do well! During your absence, I have lots of classwork to complete. I will lay low. I will try not to stare at my phone too much, waiting for you to call me!"

Lugh laughed. "Okay to all of that! I will do my best with the interview and call you when it is over. I will text you periodically too! I'll be back Friday, late afternoon if all goes well. Can we have dinner together that night?"

"Yes, please!"

"Great! By the way, I've confirmed it with Brad. He will drive to the medical center Thursday evening as soon as you text him. Here's his phone number to contact him for that and any other reason. He will come into the building, see you to your car, and follow you back to the lot. He will make sure you get to your dorm safely.

"Promise, I've also been thinking about the holiday semester break. If you have to work and need a place to stay, Brad will be gone the whole time and has welcomed you to use his room. I'll be honorable and not take advantage of the situation. Just in case you need this. Okay?"

"Lydia asked me about those hours just this evening. I really appreciate the offer. Let's talk more about it when you get back, okay? And thanks to you both!"

They lingered more. No further words were needed. Instead, they shared their hearts in the tender touch of love. Eventually, Lugh walked Promise to her dorm. One last kiss goodnight sent them both on their separate paths.

46

WEDNESDAY FELT EMPTY with Lugh gone, but Promise did her best to fulfill her commitments without constantly checking her phone. She marveled at how one person could make her world feel so alive, how his absence filled the day with loss. She ran the track without him, thinking of him often while also wondering how to manage the intensifying dilemma at the medical center. She needed proof! How would she ever find it?

Thursday afternoon, Promise went to the library, aware from Lugh's earlier text to her that he had arrived safely and that his interview would take place very soon. She sent him loving, Reiki energy, intending that it somehow convey whatever he needed across the distance. She found her favorite cubicle on the second floor and settled herself into the space. Today she needed to research the topic for her final mythology paper, the goddess Inanna of Sumer.

Promise learned that six thousand years ago, the Sumerians worshipped Inanna as Goddess of Heaven, Earth, and Underworld.

Initially, they honored her for her attributes of love, sexuality, fertility, and procreation. Over time, as neighboring cultures threatened Sumer's independence, she also became known as a goddess of war. Her depictions usually portrayed a lion by her side. At this revelation, Promise smiled and remembered to acknowledge her own lion, invisible to everyone but known well to her own heart.

Promise also discovered that Inanna had many lovers, the most famous being Dumuzi, a shepherd god. Their union nourished the earth and promoted the seasonal changes as celebrated in various versions of the myths about her. Complications arose from their mating, however; their tales often included themes of death and descent to the Underworld.

Perhaps two thousand years later, Inanna's rule continued to comprise Heaven and Earth, but her sister Ereshkigal, a corn goddess, took over the dominion of the netherworld. Inanna's choice to descend to those depths to resurrect her lover – the timing often associated with the dark phases of the moon – involved that she be stripped of all her power and that her skeletal form hang lifeless unless and until Ereshkigal chose to release her. With forethought, Inanna had arranged for another agent of rescue to ensure her return to life above ground. Promise marveled at how a goddess would choose to be powerless in the name of love.

As centuries passed, a priestess took on the role of Inanna. Her sacred consort, with whom she usually had a child, would be ritually killed at the harvest. Especially in the context of her current emotional state, Promise wondered how a mortal woman might ever manage such an anticipated loss. Assuming that the priestess loved her consort, how might she ever experience joy during her season of love with him while knowing her partner's death lay on the imminent horizon?

This myth reminded Promise of a conversation she had shared with Kay just weeks ago. Kay described the astrological birth chart as divided into twelve houses, each one representing a phase of development as well as a particular facet of life experience. The eighth house symbolized love and death, otherwise known as intimacy. Transformation and rebirth also resided within its domain.

Promise questioned the association of love and death initially, but now she understood. To love someone on the earth plane encompasses myriad opportunities for loss. The only true consolation for loss is love. Love and death, partners in the deepening process of consciousness, which leads all its travelers to the One – if they dare to undergo the journey, that is.

Inanna dared. She chose to descend to her death for love, unlike Persephone whose uncle abducted her, negating any opportunity for choice as he forcefully took her captive to his realm below. Promise considered her own situation more deeply. What would she choose?

Her mythic heroines offered a broader perspective. Cassandra received a gift that she didn't want; when no one believed her predictions, she ran to her death in desperation. Persephone's journey to the Underworld resulted from her uncle and father's collusion, but, despite their treachery, she chose to accept her fate and master her underground terrain. Unlike her Greek sisters, Inanna battled, protected, and chose her path, above ground and below.

As a goddess of love, Inanna had many lovers; consequently, her journey took her to dark places. Still, she executed her choices consciously and made them meaningful. In anticipation of Ereshkigal's demands, Inanna wittingly secured her own escape from the Underworld in advance. She would not dwell in darkness forever. Promise decided that, at least in some aspects, she would choose to live like Inanna.

Yet, how might that inform her path now? She had to admit it: she had fallen in love with Lugh. Each of them had to face their own descent into the dark world of their own fears – regarding their relationship to each other, the potential repetition of the past, and Mark Roland's role as Ereshkigal wanting to doom them eternally to the world below. Promise really didn't want to travel to the netherworld at all, but with self-awareness she could not deny that she felt herself already spiraling downward. To secure her release in advance of the ultimate plunge, she needed to use cunning and forethought. She smiled as she recognized these as the strengths of Prometheus.

Promise also suddenly realized that Inanna consciously utilized these very gifts as well. This goddess was no stranger to war. Promise had to muster her own courage and begin to think like a warrior in battle. She could still harness the philosophy of Aikido while doing it, however. She did not want to annihilate her opponent. She actually hoped to engage him for his greater good. With foresight, she knew he would make a fight of it, however. She had to be ready.

With these realizations, a force flowed through her that she had rarely felt before. It calmed her nerves and filled her with resolve. She looked up in that moment to observe Alice Danvers entering a private sound booth on the other side of the library floor. Promise asked herself, Do I dare? Without further thought, she rose from her seat and followed her classmate into the booth.

Alice looked up in surprise, which a moment later turned into shock. She blushed bright red and turned to look away. Promise's heart broke for this woman who had obviously met with trauma during her contact with Dr. Roland. Promise wanted to proceed as gently as possible.

"Alice, I'm sorry to disturb you. May I please talk to you for a few minutes?"

"Really, Promise, I'm very busy. I don't have time to talk right now."

"Alice, I understand. I just need to say one thing. I have strong suspicions about what Dr. Roland did to you and to other women at the medical center. It's horribly wrong. My suspicions alone won't stop him. I need help to keep this from happening to others."

Alice shot Promise a glance filled with fury and hatred. "Promise, you *don't* understand! If you did, you would never have let this happen!

I work night and day trying to forget it. Don't ask me to dredge this up just to help you feel better. You will have to find another way!"

"Alice, I didn't know! You were my first clue, and even then, I didn't know how to interpret your behavior or my emotional response to it. But it has continued. A pattern has emerged. He even threatened me in the parking lot. He is a lecherous man who has professional power and clout. No one will believe me without proof. I want to ask all the distraught women I've witnessed leaving his appointments to speak to their experiences. My job there is already under scrutiny over this. If I'm not there, there will be no one to ensure that at least some of the women are spared. If we don't band together, women will just continue to be hurt!"

At this point, Promise couldn't hold back her own tears. Alice softened as she witnessed the strain Promise bore as a result of suspecting the abuse and having little means to address it. Still, the idea of confronting that doctor filled her with fear. She felt paralyzed. Promise sensed Alice's inner shift as well as her struggle. She understood.

Just then Promise's phone rang. She desperately wanted the caller to be Lugh, but she dared not look in that moment. Promise sighed instead. She gently affirmed, "Alice, I would never ask you to take him on alone. I have names. I have what I witnessed. I can't take him on alone either. I am simply asking you to help me – and hopefully also to heal something for yourself. Please think about it. Here is my number. You can call me anytime."

Promise reached across the table and handed Alice a piece of paper containing her name, phone number, and dorm room. She consciously connected with her eyes, sending compassion and courage to the wounded woman before her. She concluded by saying, "No matter what happens, thank you so much for listening to me."

Promise turned and left the room. She discreetly wiped her face and headed for the restroom. When she had reclaimed her social demeanor and voice, she returned to her cubicle, gathered her things, and left the library. She brought her phone to her ear and returned the call.

With the love she felt for him, she enthusiastically inquired, "Lugh! How are you? How did it go?!"

47

AS SHE DROVE TO WORK that evening, Promise smiled as she recalled how Lugh excitedly described his interviews with the chair of the anthropology department and another prestigious professor. Not only did Lugh feel gratified by the latter professor's response to his interests and questions, but he thoroughly enjoyed their ensuing discussion of possibilities for Lugh's future research. Lugh seemed equally impressed by the sunny, Arizona campus and hoped he might show it to Promise someday. Intuitively, Promise sensed that she would not only visit that university, but that perhaps she might be attending it as a student one day as well.

Of course, Lugh also asked about her day. Promise tried to keep it light, making no mention of her conversation with Alice. Promise could not trust her own capacity to describe their exchange with an even emotional tone. The encounter had truly upset her, but she didn't want to worry Lugh when he could do so little about it. She planned to tell him everything when they reunited upon his return.

Promise pulled into Dunkirk Hollow Medical Center's parking lot, only to discover that her favorite space had an occupant. The only other spot available offered the shade provided by beautiful trees on sunny, hot days, but not the kind of lighting Promise would prefer, especially that evening. She had no choice, however, so she opted to make the best of it and to trust that Brad's company would compensate for her departure in the dark.

Once at her desk, Promise reviewed the schedules for the various doctors' offices. Dr. Roland had all women on his list for the evening. Promise felt her stomach turn. Would Christina stay the entire time? Promise would have to vigilantly persevere through the evening hours before she had her answer.

Fortunately, the evening flowed without incident. When the last student arrived for Dr. Roland's office, Promise made special note of the time and the young woman's demeanor. She also said a prayer for all concerned and tried to remember to breathe. When the female athlete left the center in a timely manner, Promise could finally relax. She wondered how much longer she might have to work like this. She knew she wouldn't deliberately leave her position until she had resolved this situation. She hoped no one would force her to do otherwise.

Toward the end of the evening, Promise texted Brad, and he responded immediately. He would arrive in fifteen minutes. The last patient left, soon followed by the remaining staff members who used the main entrance for their comings and goings. Promise began to turn out some of the lights while waiting for Brad's arrival.

She watched as he drove his car into the otherwise empty lot, her own car now hidden in the shadows. Brad parked his vehicle in such a way that his headlights beamed on her sedan for a minute or two. He finally entered the building, looking more concerned than she had ever seen him. He made his point immediately.

"Hi, Promise. I'm sorry to say this, but I think I saw a tall dude standing in the bushes near your car. He didn't make any movement.

Still, I'm pretty sure I'm right about that. Could that be the guy you're worried about?"

Promise momentarily froze. Brad noticed her distress and tried to say something reassuring. "You know I have a black belt in karate, right?"

Promise regained some composure in response to his statement. "No, I didn't know that. Really?"

"Actually, not really. I just wanted to reassure you somehow. I would have done my best to pretend, though!" Brad peered into the darkness now that his headlights were off. He asked, "Do you want to call the police?"

Promise waffled initially, then she remembered her desire to think like Inanna. She could call the police and be honest. A record of this might prove helpful. She replied, "Good idea!"

She made the call, described her situation, and stated her concern. The respondent on the other end replied, "You know we're not an escort service, but an officer happens to be cruising a few blocks from your location. I'll ask him to drive through your parking lot."

Promise decided to ignore the sarcasm and express her gratitude. Within minutes, a police car arrived. The officer apparently detected a man standing near her car when he flashed his headlights in that direction. Promise and Brad witnessed the officer gesturing to the man to step forward. When Mark Roland strode into the light, Promise quietly gasped. Brad gently touched her arm for reassurance.

Together they continued to watch as the policeman obviously requested identification. With the vehicle's light shining on Mark Roland's face, they observed his haughty compliance with the officer's request. After another few minutes, the surgeon walked past the main entrance, glaring into the interior to convey his wrath for the way Promise had foiled his attempt to frighten or harm her. Once he drove away, the officer entered the building.

Officer Robertson immediately introduced himself and asked, "Are you Promise Holmes-Thomas? Did you make the call?"

"Yes, Officer, I did. Thank you for coming."

He then turned toward Brad and queried, "And you are...?"

Brad responded immediately, "Brad Schultz. A friend. I came to escort Promise back to campus. I spied him in the bushes when I pulled into the lot. I was told he did this once before. I was concerned."

Officer Robertson raised his eyebrows. "I must say, it did look very suspicious, but since he is a doctor who works here and nothing happened – I am correct about that?"

"Yes, Officer, you are," Promise replied.

"Then, I had no cause to detain him. If he has done anything to harm you or has made credible threats, you can petition the court for a protection from abuse order. Is there anything else you need from me this evening?"

"No, Officer, but I do have a question. Will you be making an official report about this?"

He considered her intent, then asked, "Do you have reason to need one?"

Promise allowed her vulnerable feelings to show as she responded, "I may down the road. If you have that option, I would appreciate it very much."

Officer Robertson nodded his understanding. Promise responded with her thanks.

Everyone went to their respective automobiles. Brad followed Promise to the campus lot, then drove her to the front of her dorm.

While still seated in his car, Promise turned toward him before she parted company to say, "Brad, if you hadn't come this evening, I don't know what would have happened. I am forever grateful to you."

Brad returned her gaze with concern. "Promise, I am happy to have been of some help. I will retrieve Lugh from the airport tomorrow. I'm sure you both will have much to discuss!"

Promise gave him a grateful hug, then returned to the safety of her dorm.

48

MEL GREETED PROMISE upon her arrival to their dorm room. When Promise shared what had happened that evening, Mel's response offered Promise some validation. "How creepy! I'm glad you called the police on that guy. Are you okay?"

Promise admitted to her frazzled nerves. Mel immediately added some lavender essential oil to her aromatic diffuser. The scent filled their room with soothing and calm. Promise appreciated her friend's thoughtfulness immensely. Even so, falling asleep that night proved quite difficult. Promise comforted herself with knowing she would see Lugh the next day.

The following morning, Promise awoke from a very strange dream. In it, she stood on the shore, gazing up at the sun. A dark spherical body rose from the east, temporarily cloaking the sun's light as it journeyed across the sky. Its interference darkened all the land. Despite the glimmer of light that embraced its perimeter, the orb held onto its darkness. The sun's full brightness returned once the black sphere moved on.

Next, another distinct orb rose from the east; only this time when it passed in front of the sun, it welcomed the sun's rays, which embraced it in a spiraling flash. This globe grew in brightness, then it, too, moved onward across the sky.

Finally, the two spherical bodies converged in the heavens. The dark orb continued to refuse the light of its companion. The brighter one persisted, however, until finally the radiant sun joined them both. Ultimately, the brightness of the two outshone the darkness of the one. They all set together on the western horizon.

Promise awoke from her dream, feeling very confused. Even more strangely, she sensed that she had dreamed this dream before. She could not remember having done so in this lifetime, however. It simply mystified her. She would hope to share this with Aunt Tara when they met during her Christmas vacation.

Promise attended her classes, then went for a run on the track. The outdoor chilliness did not deprive those with unwavering determination the opportunity to enjoy the fresh air. As she completed her first loop and made the turn toward the athletic building, she thrilled to see Lugh waiting for her at the far end. She ran all the faster. She witnessed his responsive grin, followed by his own sprint toward her, counter to everyone else's direction. She couldn't help herself. She leapt into his arms. He swung her around as they laughed. All fell silent; the cold all around them transmuted into warmth as they kissed their greeting. Then they laughed once more. Lugh's consciousness returned to reality as he spied several runners about to overtake them. He gestured and she responded; they resumed their jog in the proper direction, maintaining a discreet distance from everyone else.

As they ran, Lugh told her all about his interview and Arizona's campus, how she might really like it, how he hoped to share it with her someday. Promise listened with rapt attention. Her intuition about attending that university only intensified.

Lugh already knew about the drama of the previous evening because

Brad could not wait to tell him as he drove his friend home from the airport. Lugh wanted to hear how Promise felt about all of it as soon as they could be together somewhere private without environmental distractions. He sensed her tension. He also witnessed her genuine interest in his experience. He had done little but think of her and his interview since he left. He hated their separation. Despite all the complexities, their reunion felt joyfully sweet.

They decided to do takeout for dinner. Brad would be gone until later in the evening. Lugh's apartment offered the privacy they needed for the conversation each anticipated would unfold between them. After showering, Lugh met Promise outside her dorm. They picked up their meal and walked to his building. Once inside, Lugh placed the food on the counter, took Promise's coat, and put it and his jacket on the chair nearby. He then turned to Promise with outstretched arms; she instinctively folded into his embrace. Without warning, the tears came in a flood that lasted several minutes. As she sensed her deluge near its end, she thought to herself, So much for living like Inanna the warrior!

Lugh had never experienced Promise this way. He suddenly realized that she had more to share than what had occurred in the parking lot the night before. He held her tight until her tears subsided. He offered her a cloth to wipe her face. Then Lugh gently guided her to the sofa and beckoned her to sit next to him and give voice to all that had happened. Promise felt embarrassed by her outburst while also grateful for his care.

Promise related the admonition she had received from Lydia along with her suspicions that Mark Roland hoped to diminish her credibility at the medical center. She also shared her conversation with Alice and how upsetting that had been for both of them. Finally, she described her feelings about having to contact the police because Mark Roland had clearly planted himself near her car, obviously intending some kind of threatening encounter. When she finally finished, Lugh sat speechless.

Promise held the sides of her face in her palms for grounding. Lugh finally uttered, "Oh my God! ... I hate saying this, but I bet he's even angrier now. I respect your commitment to keep your job so that you can try to prevent his disgusting behavior from harming more women. Still, if Lydia fires you for some improbable cause, you have to know that whatever happens thereafter won't be your fault." Lugh shook his head as he continued to process the depth of it all. He then added, "On top of all that, it must have been really difficult to speak with Alice. Promise, I'm sorry I wasn't here. You have to know that I am genuinely in awe of you!"

While on some level Promise appreciated his praise and support, the situation's bleakness threatened to overwhelm her once again. She struggled to keep her tears in check as she replied, "Lugh, I'm feeling caught in a horrible bind with no vision for how to rise above it. Your experience in Arizona gives me hope, but I feel sick at the thought that he might try to deprive you of that wonderful opportunity. I don't know how to stop him! We have to stop him!"

Hearing the intensity in her voice, Lugh immediately responded, "I'm glad you said 'we.' I can only imagine how difficult it was to witness Alice hurting so much. We need a plan with or without her assistance. You said you have the names of the women you think he may have harmed. Maybe we can track them down and see if they might be willing to come forward. I hate to think what painful work that will be, having to repeat your conversation with Alice over and over again. Maybe there's a way around that?"

"How can we ever find them? I only have names and appointment dates and times. The rest of their information is confidential...."

"Ah, but they had appointments with him because they play a sport at SMU, correct?" When Promise nodded, he continued, "Maybe we can use the time between semesters to research the members of all the sports teams that compete during the fall and winter seasons. You may recognize faces if we have photos. There may be lists somewhere

– the campus paper, for example. Maybe there is info online."

Promise gazed at him with hope and tenderness. He gently stroked her cheek. "We're being guided, remember?"

Promise smiled. "Thank you for reminding me!"

"No problem. By the way, when I invited you to stay here during the break, I meant it – not only the invitation, but that I would be on my best behavior. I would also feel better knowing firsthand that you are safe."

Promise felt both comforted and disappointed, not wanting his behavior to be all that "best." After a momentary pause during which she worked to sort out her conflicting feelings, she simply wrapped her arms around his neck, once again saying, "Thank you."

He hugged her in return, then with stalwart determination he kept true to his word. He intentionally shifted the energy to ask, "Are you hungry?"

Promise immediately felt the many layers of her response, all of which cried, "Yes!"

Lugh heated up their food, produced a beer for each of them, and set plates on the counter of the breakfast bar. With a half-serious apology, he proclaimed, "It's not the most deluxe ambiance, but at least we don't have to worry about prying ears. After all the chaos of the airport, I am happy to have you all to myself in the quiet. I hope this suits you."

"Lugh, this is perfect. And thank you for understanding the intensity of what I'm feeling. I truly appreciate your help with all this. I can't imagine how hard this would be if I had to handle it alone."

"Ah, but you don't. I may have set that up in the distant past, but I won't do that to you anymore. We both clearly have our roles in this drama, but we will manage them together. Deal?"

Promise smiled, raised her beer with the gesture of a toast, and said, "Deal!"

49

DECEMBER ROLLED IN with its customary colder temperatures. In his study, Peter sat at his desk and stared out the window, marveling at how the trees, plants, birds, and animals gracefully accommodated Nature's changes year after year. On this particular Saturday morning, just one week after the Thanksgiving holiday's astounding revelations, Peter continued to process the nauseating worry that disturbed his inner peace all week, now intensified in the absence of distractions from work. A letter lay open before him. Its contents would need a response.

A national organization of holistic healers had voted to recognize the Rainbow Healing Arts Center as a major contribution to its community, along with Peter's role in its founding. If he accepted their nomination, he would need to attend a formal dinner and presentation in the late spring. They invited him to include up to ten guests at their expense. He truly felt gratified that the Rainbow Center's success had attracted so much positive attention, especially in light of all the challenges that had confronted him during its gestation, birth, and infancy. Fortunately, the Center functioned quite smoothly now with the right people at the helm. Peter sighed.

Perhaps it was no accident that he would receive these accolades at this time when his current emotions recaptured those of that initial, sometimes agonizing process. Admittedly, he experienced those feelings even more intensely now that his daughter also had to face their old nemesis. Peter appreciated that she called them every few days to reassure them of her safety. Still, he hadn't heard from her since Tuesday afternoon. It felt like a very, very long week.

Peter tried to focus on what he might learn from these recurrent circumstances. He could not deny that he felt vulnerable in a way that he had not ever personally experienced – except perhaps when that tractor trailer barreled down the road toward him ten years ago. Why so much more defenseless now? Because this involved Promise. She did not have his muscular bulk – nor the learning opportunities and consequent wisdom afforded by a longer life – to help her deal with the likes of Mark Roland. And, most importantly, she carried a part of Peter's heart. She was very vulnerable now, thus so was he.

Unable to do anything to improve the situation, he had to sit with this feeling every day. He wanted it gone. He wanted her safe. He wanted this conflict to resolve itself without her having to intervene in any way. He felt like he wanted the moon.

Brief periods of distraction did nothing to comfort him. He soon realized that the torment would continue and recur until some unpredictable moment in time when it might then be over in one way or another. Those possible "ways" of resolution did nothing to console him, however.

His imagination took a nasty turn too many times. The power of the mind. He would choose not to give the horrific alternatives too much attention. He suddenly understood more viscerally than ever what Promise had to bear throughout her life.

The next onslaught of anxiety would come, guaranteed. Peter felt like Prometheus waiting for the vulture to return and tear his liver apart day after day. Chiron's pain differed in that it never physically subsided. Prometheus had brief periods of respite from bodily torture, but his mind probably terrorized him in the interim. Who suffered more? Peter really couldn't say. While he had always thought they had two very distinct roles to play in that ancient myth, maybe they weren't so different, after all.

The melancholy of these reflections lingered into the afternoon and evening. Brittany and Peter planned to join Tara and Alex for dinner. Peter dared to hope that perhaps Tara had some of her amazing wisdom to share that might ease his internal distress.

The foursome convened in the Haskins-Lakelyn kitchen and sipped their wine as they caught up on more recent events. Tara had finally decided to retire at the end of February. Alex had already booked a trip for them to the Caribbean to enjoy the warmth of March in a southern climate. Brittany announced Peter's nomination for the holistic organization's award. Their friends joyfully congratulated him, knowing how hard he had worked for the Rainbow Center throughout its history, from initial concept to vibrant reality. Peter invited them to be two of his guests. They gratefully accepted.

Tara sensed that something troubled Peter. He and Brittany had not yet shared the revelations of the previous weekend. They did so now. Alex found the interweaving of their lifetimes fascinating. Tara perceived a deeper, enigmatic layer of trouble, particularly as it involved Promise. She now more fully appreciated the source of Peter's and Brittany's concerns.

Peter confessed, "I feel so helpless. Today I found myself thinking of Prometheus chained to the rock, unable to do anything about the vulture's next feeding. The suffering pervaded both his body and his mind. My mind, and the fear it generates, threaten to spin out of control. As Micheil, I could ask Darran to train me. As partner to

Brittany, I could lift weights and share self-defense maneuvers to prepare us both to deal with him, as equals in age at least. Now, Promise lives a three-hour's drive away, and I have no idea what's happening with her. She is young and relatively inexperienced. I suspect she has tried to spare us the worst of what's been going on, which doesn't comfort me at all. And we haven't heard from her since Tuesday."

Peter tried valiantly to remain calm. He massaged his face with his palms. Brittany lay her hand gently on his arm. She quietly said, "We can call her, you know."

Tara replied, "Peter, why don't you? Call her now if you like."

Peter sighed. "Because I think if she doesn't answer, I'll go mad."

"If she can't answer, she will call us back, Peter. You know she will." Brittany offered this from her own inner anxiety that also wished for some relief. If Promise didn't return the call by tomorrow, they would go to campus. Brittany knew that. She respected Peter's attempt to give their daughter the independence she requested, but as a mother Brittany also recognized that too much time had elapsed, given the current circumstances. As parents, they had their needs as well.

Peter looked to Tara and Alex and said, "You really don't mind?"

They both shook their heads and fully supported his making this contact. Peter dialed the phone and placed it on speaker.

A few rings later, Promise answered, obviously laughing and out of breath. Immediately, Peter and Brittany relaxed. Promise also connected the speaker phone so that they could hear Lugh in the background. After their initial greetings, Promise more fully explained: "Lugh and I are in the gym. I am showing him some Aikido moves."

Lugh interjected, "Yeah! She told me to grab her throat – hard for me to even consider, I must admit – but when I realized why, I complied as quickly and stealthily as I could. Before I knew it, I was on the floor. You called just as we were laughing about my shock! I still don't know how she did it, but I am very glad that she did!"

Peter and Brittany could sense Promise's feeling of accomplishment even if invisible to them on a phone. They both looked at each other with raised eyebrows and sighed.

Promise then said, "Mom and Dad, I'm sorry I haven't been in touch since Tuesday. It's been a challenging week, but we're on the other side of it now. It's obviously not the best time to talk. Are you okay, though?"

Brittany responded, "We're fine, Promise!"

"Good! Can I call you tomorrow?"

Peter replied, "That would be great! Lugh, thanks for the reassurance. I hope she didn't hurt you too much!"

Everyone laughed. Lugh replied, "She intentionally went easy on me. I'll make sure she doesn't make that a habit."

Peter smiled. "Good man! Thank you."

They bid their farewells and concluded the call. Peter and Brittany sat back in their chairs, more relaxed than they had felt in days. Tara smiled with empathy. Alex just shook his head. He knew from his own experience that the unknowns of parenting had challenged him more than his professional dilemmas as a physician ever could.

With greater peace, they proceeded to enjoy the fruits of Alex's delectable cuisine. Over their meal they discussed a variety of topics, which eventually returned to the myth of Prometheus. Peter shared his earlier reflections about the similarities between Chiron and Prometheus. He realized that both were helpless; neither one could make himself feel better.

Peter wondered aloud, "What does that say about the human condition?"

Alex responded with the wisdom acquired from his decades of practicing medicine. "We humans need each other. It is as simple as that, really. Medicine is founded upon that principle. Of course, so is the work of the auto mechanic, the plumber, and the farmer. Especially in our times, when everyone is so specialized, we cannot survive on our own."

Peter nodded and reflected further, "Still, in those moments when no one showed up, when they were suffering alone, before Hercules talked Zeus into making the trade, was there some meaning in their experience? Were they only meant to helplessly wait until some miracle occurred?"

Tara thoughtfully replied, "Peter, your question marks the path of the spiritual seeker. What depth and understanding, what meaning can be given to the profoundly painful pause between the initial injury or need and its healing or resolution? The deepening qualities of patience, trust, faith, and compassion are all tested. The longer the ordeal, the more challenging the test, the more profound the resolution. Chiron and Prometheus were gods. To respond as they did is sacred work."

Peter sighed. Brittany smiled. "Tara, you always know what to say. Not that your perspective was incorrect or inadequate in any way, Alex. It seems that the timing of those helping interventions usually follows a pause, though. It's the pause that leads to growth. The healing or helpful response then reaffirms and deepens one's faith. The timing of the aid may make all the difference. Even providing it, at its best, is an act of faith and trust."

They sat in a momentary silence filled with the blessing of consciousness and some degree of comfort. Peter and Brittany returned home that evening filled with the gifts of insight and friendship, and gratitude on every level. Before they drifted into sleep, they held each other close as they reflected on their shared challenges: mysteries slowly revealing their secrets; worries transforming into trust; patience allowing for a gestation invisible to the eye.... Such is the journey of life.

50

FOR PROMISE AND LUGH, end-of-term papers, finals, and Christmas shopping filled the days and weeks that followed. Promise made more effort to call her parents on a regular basis, hoping to minimize the escalation of their concerns. She and Lugh applied themselves to their course requirements. Lugh had his last class with Mark Roland during which his scurrilous instructor took every opportunity to criticize and humiliate his best student. Lugh weathered that storm with the help of Promise's perspective. Still, the experience did not bode well for his grade.

Promise struggled with how to tell her parents that she intended to stay at Lugh's apartment during the Christmas break so that she might maintain her hours at the medical center. They had never really discussed this kind of issue in the past. Promise could only remember how her father had reacted to the arrival of her companions that night before the junior dance. Yes, she had introduced her parents to other young men over the years, but her relationship with none of them had been serious. Her feelings for Lugh were decidedly different, and they knew it.

When Peter broached the subject of her holiday schedule, Promise took a deep breath and simply told him the truth: she planned to stay at Lugh's apartment until the day before Christmas Eve. She would spend the following week at home with them, then have to return January third. Peter responded with silence, initially. His father instincts were clashing with his life-learned wisdom and his trust in his daughter. He waited until the latter finally won out.

Peter finally replied, "I understand, Promise. I trust you have given this careful thought. Just please be careful. I appreciate your commitment to the job, but don't forget that other things are also important, if not more so."

Promise heard her father's unspoken thoughts and felt the feelings conveyed beneath his words. She replied, "Dad, thank you for your trust in me. Thank you for not making this difficult. I really appreciate you!"

Peter sighed. "Let's both do our best to be happy about this decision in the end, okay?"

Promise smiled and said, "I will do my part, Dad. Thanks!"

When exams concluded, Lugh helped Promise move what things she needed into his apartment. Brad would be leaving a few days later. In the meantime, Promise slept on the sofa. Brad graciously accommodated her presence. In fact, the three of them enjoyed their time together enormously. This helped Lugh and Promise adjust to the change in their proximity to each other, which would have stirred considerable tension otherwise. When Brad left, Lugh suggested that they go for a run. The energetic release relieved them both – at least for a while.

They had one week remaining before they parted company for the Christmas holiday. Each had invited the other to their family's gathering, but they both realized that they needed to be with their respective loved ones for various reasons. Lugh had not seen his parents for the entire semester. Promise knew her parents would feel relieved with her company. She also wanted to meet with Aunt Tara and hoped their schedules would make that possible. Promise and Lugh planned a small Christmas celebration together before they departed for their family festivities. Promise already looked forward to their reunion.

Fortunately, nothing problematic occurred at the medical center during that last week. Christina had confirmed in advance that they would have no sports physicals or office hours during the semester break. Consequently, Promise felt safe enough to let down her guard temporarily. Lugh continued to come for her each of those evenings, however. He didn't trust Mark Roland at all.

Days before Lugh and Promise would part company for the holidays, they received their final grades. Promise did very well, even in her statistics class! Lugh also experienced success with all of his courses – except Medical Anthropology. The villainous Dr. Roland had given him a D.

Because Lugh had already researched the protocol, he knew he had to contact his professor directly before he might take any other official action. He sent Mark Roland an email immediately, working hard to be respectful but direct. Lugh included a summary of his grades for each assignment, along with a reference to his active participation in class. He requested an explanation: How did his final grade merit a D? He offered to meet with Dr. Roland directly to discuss the matter. Days passed with no response. Lugh tried not to let his anger ruin his time with Promise.

On their last evening together, they arranged a special dinner and exchanged gifts. They laughed when they realized how their thoughts had converged. Promise gave Lugh a sculpted miniature of a wild boar. Lugh found a stuffed lion that looked more cuddly than fierce, but he trusted it would suit his purpose. The intensity of their love and desire for each other stretched their self-restraint almost beyond endurance. Lugh had made a commitment, however. He would honor it.

They made their respective drives homeward lost in thoughts about each other. When Promise arrived at her front porch, Quirkie's barking and pawing for attention quickly reoriented her to the here and now. Lizzie soon followed after him, immediately embracing Promise with their traditional, warm, prolonged hug while Quirkie continued to dance at their feet. Peter and Brittany appeared moments later to share and enjoy more hugs and laughter. This reunion felt especially sweet.

They readily settled into their family rituals for celebrating the holidays. Tara and Alex would join them this year for Christmas dinner. Promise would meet with her aunt one evening midweek. Lizzie requested that Promise have a sleepover with her at least twice during their time together. Promise eagerly agreed.

Lugh and Promise had planned to check in with each other, even if briefly, at some point that evening. Lugh called just after Promise finished dinner with her family. She detected a strain in his voice and asked him about it. He confessed that he had just received Mark Roland's terse response.

Lugh tried to speak in a matter-of-fact tone of voice: "He stated that my final paper deserved an F because it did not meet the criteria he had in mind. He could not see how the Ice Age had any relevance to medical anthropology. He specifically indicated that my 'extracurricular involvements' must have interfered with my attention to the assignment. He even questioned whether I had plagiarized the content in some way. He refused to meet with me, claiming that his busy schedule in the operating room would not accommodate my request." Lugh worked hard to manage his fury. He only partially succeeded.

Promise sensed the intensity of emotion raging within him; it sparked her own as well. She tried to reassure him. She reminded him that they would face this together. Lugh expressed his appreciation for her support, but Promise recognized that her efforts had limited effect. As they made their goodbyes, she encouraged him to not let the surgeon's malice ruin the joy of spending time with his family. Mark Roland did not deserve that triumph. Lugh laughed and acknowledged the wisdom of her words. "Okay, wise woman, I won't!"

Promise confirmed, "We'll deal with it, Lugh, in the New Year!"

When Promise rejoined her family, they noticed her change in mood immediately. Promise shared Lugh's disappointing news. Peter and Brittany simply exhaled deeply. They weren't surprised, but the news clearly put a damper on their previous merriment. Promise decided to take the advice she had just given Lugh. She shared it with her family as well. They all agreed, at least in theory.

Peter and Brittany each privately planned to have a conversation with Promise at some point during the week. They looked to each other and silently agreed between them to make the most of their family time together while they had it.

51

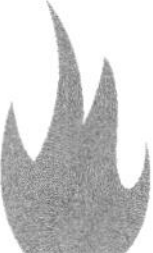

PROMISE AND LIZZIE had their first sleepover that very night. Lizzie had much to share about her friends, her recent dating interest, and her hopes for the future now that as a junior she had to think about college. Promise did not elaborate much about her own worries, instead focusing on her classes, how much she enjoyed mythology, how little she appreciated statistics. When Promise spoke of Lugh, Lizzie detected an intensifying spark of love that had not manifested as fully at Thanksgiving. She asked Promise about it.

Promise replied, "Lizzie, I do love him. I can't imagine living the rest of my life without him. We have to deal with Mark Roland first, but I hope it all works out."

Lizzie supportively hugged her sister. She whispered, "I hope it does too!"

That night, Promise awoke from another dream of the orbs. It unfolded just as before. She could not help but wonder: Why have it again, and why now? It clearly did not want her to forget something important. Did the news about Lugh's grade have something to do with its reemergence? Somehow, Promise sensed that it did.

When Promise awakened from her dream, so did Lizzie. Lizzie recognized the look on her sister's face from years of experience. She asked her to tell her the dream. After Promise finished describing the images, Lizzie said something startling to both of them. "Promise, I've heard this dream before. I know I have. Is my brain out of phase? Is it déjà vu?"

"I've never told you this dream in this lifetime, Lizzie. I dreamt it for the first time a few weeks ago." When Promise remembered the circumstances – that she had called the police about Mark Roland that evening – she felt certain that Lugh's grade played into this repetition. "I didn't tell you about it then, so I don't know when you could have heard it…unless it was during our past lifetime together…."

Lizzie's eyes opened wide. "Wow! Maybe I really did live in another lifetime!"

Promise smiled. She had no doubt of it. She would definitely have to share this dream with Aunt Tara. Before too long, Promise and Lizzie fell fast asleep.

The joy of Christmas came and lingered. Promise and Tara confirmed their meeting for Wednesday evening. In the meantime, with the weather's cooperation, Brittany and Promise went for a long run on Tuesday. As they slowed for their cooldown, Brittany took the opportunity to express her concerns.

She gently asked, "Promise, you and Lugh seem to be very fond of each other. Am I right?"

Promise looked into her mother's eyes and smiled. "You have always been very perceptive, Mom. You are right, of course. I haven't felt this way about anyone I've ever dated. And my feelings just keep getting stronger and deeper."

Brittany nodded knowingly. "He is a good man. That's been very obvious."

Promise sensed that her mother had something she wanted to ask, perhaps some advice she wanted to give. But she also didn't want to be intrusive. Promise opted to cut the tension by sharing these perceptions.

Brittany sighed. "Okay, I am simply hoping that you have thought through – as best as any of us can – what you are wanting from your relationship with Lugh, and what you are choosing as you deal with Mark Roland. These are both huge decisions with profound long-term impacts. I love you. I just want you to be safe and happy."

Promise smiled as she said, "Thanks, Mom. I guess it's obvious that I am falling in love with Lugh. Maybe the past is repeating itself in some ways. But he also really is different, even from when we first met last year. He doesn't shy away from my intuitions, dreams, or visions anymore. He keeps the promises he makes. He meets me after work every evening that I'm there. I'm feeling loved by him, especially when the promises he makes and keeps are so difficult. If he decides to attend the graduate program in Arizona, I might like to transfer. How would you feel about that?"

Brittany paused before she thoughtfully responded, "Promise, if that university's curriculum supports your future goals for yourself, I'm all for it. I just don't want you to surrender your future to another person, *any* other person. You were born for a particular reason, which a partner can support but cannot define. Do you understand what I'm saying?"

"I do, Mom. I need to be who I am at all times, or else I'm not an equal partner to anyone."

"Exactly!" Brittany exclaimed.

Promise decided to ask a more delicate question that she hoped her mother would answer honestly: "Mom, if you don't mind my asking, did you and Dad live together before you got married?"

Startled by her daughter's directness, Brittany needed a few moments to consider a meaningful response. She honestly replied, "Yes, we did.

I won't judge you for a similar decision, but I have to add that both your dad and I had finished our educational programs before we moved in together. We didn't have you until after we had officially pledged ourselves to each other. By then, the ordeal with Mark Roland was also behind us, or so we thought.

"Having children is a blessing and a wonder best appreciated without the complications of academic challenges or the hazards of dealing with someone so dangerous. If you were to choose to live together before those issues are resolved, I would simply caution you to be very careful. I know you to be responsible and thoughtful about what you do. Please know that I will love you no matter what you decide or what happens. I just hope for you to feel fulfilled and happy."

Promise felt a weight lifting from her shoulders. Her mother had just given her the freedom to make her own choices without having to risk losing her mother's love. She stopped in her tracks, turned toward Brittany, and simply said, "Mom, you are amazing. You have always been amazing. If I ever get to be a mother, I hope I will be just like you!"

Brittany smiled. "No, Promise. You will be just like you. That's what this is all about. I have been blessed to have you for my daughter. Just please always remember you can call upon me if you need me."

"I will, Mom. Thank you!"

With that burden lifted from both their shoulders, they returned home. Promise now looked forward to her conversation with Aunt Tara. She also had no doubt that her father would make his thoughts known as well. She opted to focus on their love for her. Their wisdom would follow; she would tend it mindfully.

52

PROMISE CURLED HERSELF into her aunt's cozy armchair while holding the rose quartz orb in her hand. She consciously appreciated its silent, mysterious resonance with the love in her heart. Tara joined her moments later, after quickly attending to a small chore that needed a finishing touch. They each beamed in the presence of the other. They reveled in a bond that seemed to transcend time and place.

Tara admitted to her awareness of the revelations shared between Promise, Lugh, Peter, and Brittany during the Thanksgiving holiday. Promise expressed her appreciation for that knowledge, glad that she did not have to recapitulate their stories in all their complexity. She welcomed her aunt's perspective on the matter, however. She also wanted to recount her dream, having had it twice just a few weeks apart. Tara suggested that Promise tell her the dream first, as it might meaningfully help her to expand upon her reflections. Promise gratefully complied.

At the conclusion of her narration, she noticed an odd look on her aunt's face, almost one of wonder and utter confusion. Promise speculated aloud, "I suspect this dream has made things harder to understand instead of easier?"

Tara simply shook her head at first. She finally shared the reason for her bewilderment. "Promise, I've heard this dream before. I know I have."

Promise now felt equally astounded. She replied, "Lizzie said the same thing when I woke up with it the other night! I can tell you, as I told her, that it's not possible because I only first dreamed it in this lifetime a few weeks ago. Both times, Mark Roland had done something threatening to me or Lugh. What do you think is going on?!"

Tara shook her head once again. "I'm not certain, really, but it is very interesting. Assuming it's true that Lizzie shared that past lifetime with you as Fiona, she would have known you in a way that your mom and your dad never could have – since they both were born after you died. You might have told it to Fiona. Would you have also told it to me? Perhaps…although I can't say what role I would have played in your life back then. Still, even though we may never know the answer to that mystery, we can try to understand the dream."

"That would be great, Aunt Tara. To have it twice strikes me as very important. It's like it wants, maybe *needs*, me to understand."

This time Tara nodded. "Agreed," she replied. "What we can safely assume, given our hints about its connection to a past life, is that you initially had this dream as Glenna. Because the characters that were important to you in that ancient time had not yet been born – except Alasdair and perhaps the young soul of Mark Roland – we can wonder if the dream offered a prediction or some kind of guidance. You as Glenna were a seer even then."

Promise replied, "This all makes sense. Please go on."

Tara responded, "A dark orb that stays dark and refuses light… Does that sound like anyone you know?"

Promise laughed. "Mark Roland, of course!"

"I would agree with you there. How about the other mysterious orb that allows itself to be embraced by spiraling light... Who might that be?"

Promise paused. "Well, it could be my dad...."

"Yes, it could. It could also be Lugh, don't you think?" Tara asked.

"It could. Does it matter that we figure out who that orb belongs to?" Promise wondered.

Tara shook her head. "Not necessarily. Besides, dream symbols can be very comprehensive. It may apply to each of them under different circumstances. Let's keep going. That may help us figure this out."

Tara continued, "The enlightened orb tries to embrace the darkened orb, but the darkened orb refuses the light. That was your dad's experience in both his past and current lifetimes."

Promise spontaneously added, "Lugh isn't getting anywhere either, and I daresay he won't, given the intensity of Mark Roland's anger when I called the police on his menacing behavior."

"You what?! What happened?" Tara asked aghast. She suspected that Peter and Brittany did not yet know of this.

Promise immediately realized that she hadn't shared this with her family. She looked to her aunt for assurance that she would keep Promise's concerns confidential. Tara recognized the issue and renewed her pledge to honor Promise's decision about what to reveal to her parents and when.

Feeling reassured, Promise responded, "Lugh has been meeting me at the medical center at the end of my evening shifts since Mark Roland started working there. After that lecher threatened me in the parking lot in October, Lugh has even come into the building to walk me to my car. When, as Lugh's instructor, Roland knew that Lugh had traveled out of town for a graduate school interview, he hid in the shadows near my car, probably thinking I would leave work alone that night. But Lugh had arranged for his roommate to meet me after work instead. Brad saw a tall man skulking near my car when he parked his own. He came into the building to tell me. That's when I called the police.

"Mark Roland was furious about having to show his identification to the police officer. We saw that clearly when he glared in the window at the two of us on his way to his own vehicle on the other side of the lot. Lugh received a D for the course taught by the nefarious Dr. Roland not long after that. I know it's because he's furious; he wanted to retaliate for the humiliation we caused him."

Promise had not yet shared this information with anyone but Lugh, Brad, and Mel. Doing so now brought very raw, vulnerable feelings to the surface. She tried to keep them in check so as not to further alarm her aunt. It didn't really work, however. Tara recognized the danger immediately, and Promise knew it.

Tara focused on practical matters first. "Promise, how can you keep safe while you're on campus?"

Promise responded with more confidence than she actually felt. "Mark Roland hasn't pursued me anywhere other than at the medical center. We don't cross paths there unless he intends it, but, as I mentioned, Lugh meets me after work. He has never approached me in Lugh's presence.

"I know Mark Roland took that job because I work there. No other surgeon would content himself with routine physicals for healthy athletes. Unfortunately, he has opted to use his position to molest young women on occasion. I have tried to minimize his opportunities, but I need proof to make him stop. Lugh and I will tackle that when we return to SMU after the New Year. Mark Roland won't return to the medical center until the next semester begins. Lugh continues to meet me after work anyway. I've been practicing my Aikido as well. I'm pretty sure I will be okay."

Promise hoped she hadn't shared too much, but she also felt released from the burden of carrying this alone for so long. She paused and prayed that her aunt would have something supportive to say.

Tara simply looked aghast. After a few moments, she gathered her wits and tried to offer what she could to her precious goddaughter, who had already endured so much. She carefully responded, "Promise, I think your parents will want to know. But I will not interfere. It is up to you when and how to tell them. Please know that they can be helpful to you. They have had lots of experience with him – across lifetimes, in fact. Please don't forget that."

Promise nodded her agreement.

Tara continued, "As for your dream, the sun finally joins forces with the enlightened orb. Who might the sun be?"

Promise shifted her mental gears and considered her aunt's question. "If the enlightened orb is my dad, the sun could be Lugh."

Tara agreed, then added, "And if the enlightened orb is Lugh, the sun could be you. It could also be a higher power, a power that can override the horrific darkness which Mark Roland seems to have attracted to his soul. Light overcomes darkness. Your dream suggests that those forces of light, whomever they symbolize, are gathering. Light will prevail in the end – or so your dream suggests."

Promise sighed with a relief she hadn't felt for a long while. "Aunt Tara, that feels right to me, and it comforts me more than you can know. Thank you."

Tara added, "Promise, your dream wants to give you hope. That is clear. Please maintain a proper perspective, though. The sun is a celestial body of light. Its symbolism suggests that it is not under your control even though you may reliably track its path across the heavens. You must stay attuned to your spiritual guides, your intuition, and your instincts. Nothing else will serve you now."

Promise felt something settle deep within her. She knew exactly what her aunt meant, and she would honor it. When they finally parted company for the evening, they embraced each other tenderly. Promise pledged to keep her aunt posted. Tara would welcome the updates.

Promise returned home feeling much lighter. She hadn't decided when to tell her parents, however. The next afternoon, when only Peter and Promise were home together, Peter relieved her of that indecision by asking her directly. They sat in his study. Promise couldn't keep her eyes off the obelisk on his shelf. The feeling it engendered grounded her, supporting her through the difficulties she would have to describe. She suddenly felt an even deeper trust that her father would hear them well.

Peter began with his honest confession: "Promise, I sense that you have been trying to spare your mom and me excessive worry by avoiding or minimizing the full details of what has been happening to you. I want to respect your privacy and independence – as difficult as that has been numerous times. As far as I know, you've never lied to me. I really need to hear what you are dealing with. My imagination, I suspect, is far worse than the truth. Either way, however, I'd rather we deal with this together. I hope you will tell me now, face to face."

Promise sighed deeply, then she told him everything about her experiences at the medical center: her observations and intuitions about the young women athletes, how Mark Roland approached her in the parking lot months ago, the way Lugh protected her after his initial struggle to accept that his instructor might have such dastardly intentions, the difficulty sharing her suspicions with her boss, Alice's reluctance to come forward, and Promise's need to call the police during Lugh's absence when Brad discovered the surgeon in the parking lot skulking near her car.

Peter just listened, discretely pulling on his fingers, which were positioned on his lap and hidden by the desk in front of him. Promise detected his effort not to bite his lip. She felt horrible for inflicting such pain upon him in the telling of her tale.

Peter sensed this as he witnessed the look on her face. He replied, "Promise, you know this is hard to hear, but I want you to recognize that it is not your fault for having to share this with me. You didn't make this pain. You have courageously borne it alone long enough."

He rose from his chair and approached her with his arms outstretched. She fell into his embrace. They both cried.

Feeling enormous relief, Promise hugged him especially tight before she released him to say, "Dad, thank you."

Peter just shook his head and sighed deeply. He queried, "I trust you have a plan for how to deal with this?"

Promise smiled. "You know I have! Lugh and I are going to try tracking down the women I suspect may have been molested. I am hoping at least some of them will find the courage, strength, and endurance to come forward. Only then, can we press charges. Through all this, Lugh will continue to meet me after work. He will contest his grade. I suspect he has a few strategies in mind that he hasn't shared with me yet. We are both practicing Aikido. We can only work toward and hope for the best."

Peter nodded. "Your plan makes sense. Consider asking your mother if you have problems tracking down your witnesses. She has a knack for finding people, which amazes me every time! We also have access to a lawyer, a friend of mine, who can help you with any legalities that may arise. Fortunately, your campus is in the same state jurisdiction, so she will be familiar with the laws. If you give me permission, I will also speak with her in advance to see if there's anything you can do now."

"That would be great, Dad!"

Peter then added with great seriousness, "And, Promise, you must swear to call me if you feel threatened in any way."

Promise couldn't believe how well this conversation had gone. She gazed into her father's eyes and saw something ancient and familiar in them. He trusted her. That gift in itself felt huge. She would honor it. She responded, "I will, Dad. You know I will!"

53

AS SHE DROVE THE THREE-HOUR TREK back to Stella Maris, Promise found herself more deeply pondering her conversations with each of her parents and her Aunt Tara. If her aunt's hypothesis had merit, Promise's dream suggested that she may have been conscious of this challenge with Mark Roland across at least two lifetimes and that potential resolution might be possible in this one. Promise still could not answer her own pressing question, however: How might that occur? At least she no longer had to keep secrets from her loved ones. Her Aunt Tara had also offered her good advice: her parents did have plenty of wisdom and experience to share.

Having finally arrived at Lugh's apartment, Promise parked her car in Brad's spot and carried what she could up the stairs to their second-floor walkup. Once inside, she noticed that Lugh had already arrived, but he was nowhere to be found. Somewhat disappointed, she returned to her car, gathered what remained, then made the last climb up the steps to put her things in a manageable location. She appreciated these accommodations, but she couldn't help but feel that she had invaded someone else's space.

Two hours later, Lugh returned in a more buoyant mood than Promise had anticipated, given the discouraging news about his grade and Mark Roland's response to his email. To her delighted surprise, his eyes sparkled at the sight of her. He swooped her into his arms and kissed her passionately. Promise reciprocated, of course, then hoped to query him regarding the source of his lightheartedness.

Lugh didn't wait for her question. Instead, he immediately reported his amazing news.

"Promise, you won't believe what happened!! When I went for my interview in Arizona, I took along a copy of my final paper. I had worked really hard to make it the best presentation of my interests and research on the topic of the last Ice Age, the Younger Dryas. Coincidentally, the professor they selected to interview me has achieved a significant reputation on the subject. I had even cited his work in my review. As we got to discussing my hopes for graduate pursuits, our mutual interest quickly came to the fore. We had a great discussion, and I left a copy of my paper with him.

"Would you believe that he not only actually read it, but he emailed me about it just this morning?!"

"Wow! What did he say? Did he like it?" Promise excitedly asked.

"Yes!! He thought it a 'commendable undergraduate effort to explore a very complicated and controversial topic.' He hoped I might choose to attend the university. He expressed his interest in future conversations down the road!"

"Lugh, that's wonderful!!!" Promise exclaimed. "This is the same paper that Mark Roland graded with an F? The one that took your A average down to a D because he decided to weight the final assignment so heavily?"

"The very same! Not one change did I make after giving it to the graduate professor, anticipating it might come to this. I did not expect him to send me this email, though. I would need to have his permission to share his comments in my appeal process, of course, but either way, it helps me feel vindicated. I can now more confidently promote my stance in my petition."

Promise hugged him warmly. "I am so glad! How brilliant of you to share your paper with your interviewer. We need lots of good surprises like this! While we can't count on them, it seems important not to write them off as impossible – note to self!" She made this last comment while tapping on the side of her head.

They laughed. Lugh added, "Agreed! Speaking of which, how are you? Any good surprises from your holiday at home?"

Promise described her dream and the content of her conversations with each of her loved ones. Lugh asked about her interpretation of the dream; Promise shared what she could. She also expressed her need to stretch her limbs after her long ride. Lugh offered to accompany her for a run on the athletic field's track, where they began to plan. They spent the rest of the day strategizing their individual and joint approaches to the challenges that lay ahead.

Lugh had already begun to draft his formal appeal, which he would first direct to the department chair. He anticipated that the process would move along fairly quickly, given his senior year status and the impact of the final grade on his future academic pursuits. He had an appointment with the chair of the anthropology department on Wednesday of the following week.

While Lugh focused on his appeal, Promise planned to explore ways to connect with the women on her list. The library and its campus newspapers would offer a good starting place. The cold of winter would make running outdoors more challenging, but Lugh and Promise planned to do so together the following day as well.

The next morning, Promise began her search at the library, where she was able to identify two of the young women on her list. Newspaper articles and accompanying photos of the aquatic and soccer

teams helped her associate athletes' names with facial recognition: she already knew that Alice Danvers swam for the former; she discovered that Kassi Jones competed for the latter. Photos of the third woman would likely involve a winter sport. Promise explored more recent editions of their campus paper and finally found the needed information. Viola Rhodes played basketball. Promise suddenly found herself wondering if Mel might have to face Dr. Roland for her hockey team physical as well. She shuddered in response to these thoughts.

When Promise then directed her quest to include social media, looking for clues that might help her contact Kassi and Viola directly, she felt dismally overwhelmed. Taking a break from the intensity of her mission, she suddenly remembered her father's suggestion to seek assistance from her mother. Promise decided to call her that evening. She anticipated that her mom would welcome the opportunity to do something more constructive than sit idly by, feeling helpless.

That afternoon, Promise and Lugh went for their run on the outdoor track. Lugh reported that he had left a message with his graduate interviewer, asking if he might share his comments about his final paper with his department chair, Professor Abrams. Unfortunately, Lugh had not yet received his reply. Promise sensed Lugh's anxiety about the entire situation in general, along with his urgent hope that he might use the Arizona professor's review to bolster his appeal. She wanted to encourage him in every way she could.

"It's so hard to wait!" she began. "You had to wait for Mark Roland's email, then for the appointment with your chair, now for your interviewer's reply. Thousands of seconds fill a day. Multiplied by the number of days it takes for something to unfold, that can add up to millions of seconds. And any one of them could be the moment when the answer comes, or the surprise happens. We have no idea when it's coming, but the more we look for it, the more it seems to elude us. Like 'the watched pot that never boils,' we know it will begin to boil eventually, just not while we're looking. This will work out, Lugh. It has to!"

Lugh smiled. "Thanks, Promise. I appreciate your perspective on things. I especially appreciate your willingness to support me through this. The consequences feel like a very big deal."

"They are, Lugh! If it would help, I would be happy to accompany you to your meeting next week. I can hang out in the waiting room and send you good energy, maybe even put a respectful face on your 'extracurricular activities'!"

Lugh laughed. "Promise, that would be great! Thank you."

54

AS THE HOUR for his meeting with Dr. Abrams approached, Lugh could not dispel his inner tension. He still awaited permission from his graduate school interviewer to share his emailed compliments regarding Lugh's final paper. Promise sensed his despondency about this, recognizing that his gloomy mood would not bode well for the successful outcome of his appeal. She encouraged him to appreciate his intended argument on its own merit, describing the graduate professor's opinion as dessert for an already delicious meal. Lugh laughed. His energy shifted. They proceeded to his appointed destination hand in hand.

Upon their arrival, Ms. Dobson – secretary for the anthropology department's chair, Russell Abrams, Ph.D. – greeted them and invited them to have a seat. Professor Abrams had intentionally left his office door ajar. When he overheard Ms. Dobson's professional, conversational tone, he personally entered the waiting area to acknowledge his senior student. Lugh and his department chair shook hands, then Lugh introduced Promise as his girlfriend, in keeping with their earlier agreement. Professor Abrams extended his hand in warm welcome. Promise appreciatively reciprocated his graciousness.

Professor Abrams then explained, "Lugh, I didn't have the opportunity to inform you of this, but I have invited Dr. Roland to join us. I did receive your documentation about his refusal to discuss the grade with you. Nevertheless, it felt unfair to me to make this decision in the absence of his input. He kindly agreed to meet with us. I expect he will be here very soon."

Lugh and Promise did their best to respond to this notice with respect for the difficult and delicate situation this appeal presented to Dr. Abrams. Still, Lugh's heart skipped a beat, and Promise sensed the tension in every muscle of her body as if she were preparing for battle. They each did their best to breathe deeply.

Professor Abrams noticed their reactions. Lugh's did not surprise him, but Promise's did. His confusion came to clarity when Dr. Roland made his characteristically haughty entrance into the chair's office waiting room. Upon seeing Promise, the surgeon scowled at her. She maintained a steady demeanor, but her eyes glared at him in return. Professor Abrams witnessed it all. He said nothing, however, other than to welcome Dr. Roland to the meeting before he gestured to usher his newest adjunct instructor and Lugh into his office.

Before Lugh left her side, he quickly turned to Promise and handed her his cell phone. He straightforwardly asked, "Promise, would you mind keeping an eye out for that email? Perhaps Professor Abrams won't mind if you have to knock on the door if it arrives and supports my case?" Lugh made his last comment while looking directly at his department chairman.

Professor Abrams responded, "I don't know what you're expecting, Lugh, but if it is relevant, I won't mind at all."

Promise nodded, then quietly took her seat, staring at Mark Roland as he departed. Lugh did not look back, but their nemesis did. He found Promise glowering at him with defiance.

Once the office door closed, Promise sat patiently – as patiently as she could under the circumstances. Her fingers betrayed her attempts to mask her anxiety as she nervously checked Lugh's cell phone every two minutes. Ms. Dobson kindly offered Promise a cup of coffee, but Promise politely declined. She smiled to herself, thinking that her father would never say no to coffee. She had not yet acquired a taste for the beverage, but thinking of her father did bring her a measure of comfort.

Promise began to contemplate the thousands of seconds she had mentioned to Lugh while they ran on the track. The wait seemed endless, empty, filled with longing. For some reason, she thought of Dylan in that moment and his description of "holding space" for his group participants while they journeyed to one of the three shamanic worlds. The thought that Promise might now hold space for Lugh gave her waiting a purpose. She decided to focus on that intention while extending her email checks to every five minutes. She chuckled at the realization that this might considerably improve the phone's battery life during this trying time, maybe her own inner "battery" as well.

Near the thirty-minute mark, Promise heard Mark Roland raise his voice, although she could not quite make out his words. She did not hear Lugh's intonation rise in kind, which she hoped boded well for his command of the situation. Distracted by the intensity of the discussion and Ms. Dobson's obvious concern, Promise absentmindedly checked Lugh's email once again. There it was! She dared to read it: "Yes, Lugh, by all means feel free to share my email with whomever you like. I wish you the best with your appeal."

Promise abruptly stood and gestured to Ms. Dobson with Lugh's cell phone. Having heard Lugh's request and Professor Abrams' approval, Ms. Dobson simply nodded. Promise proceeded to knock on the chair's office door.

Dr. Abrams quickly appeared, seeming to welcome the break in their obviously heated discussion. Promise simply stated that Lugh had received the email he needed. She extended her hand, offering the phone. Professor Abrams gestured for Lugh to receive it, which he gladly did with a broad smile.

Once again, the office door closed before her. She resumed her seat, smiling as well. Ms. Dobson took the cue and noticeably relaxed. Another twenty minutes passed before the door opened once again. This time, Dr. Mark Roland appeared, barely restraining his outrage. He briefly glowered toward Promise, then ignored her and Ms. Dobson altogether as he hastily exited the office suite.

The door closed once again. Promise sighed heavily as she and Ms. Dobson exchanged knowing glances. It seemed clear that Lugh had succeeded in his mission. Promise noticed how much easier the waiting felt now. Even so, she continued to hold space for the man she loved.

Another ten minutes passed before the door opened for the final time of their meeting. Lugh exited, beaming, quickly followed by Dr. Abrams, who seemed relieved by the clarity that had apparently unfolded. Lugh turned to Dr. Abrams to shake his hand with sincere gratitude.

Dr. Abrams replied, "Congratulations, Lugh. You deserve every success. I am glad this situation has come to a clear resolution." He then turned to Promise and said, "Ms. Holmes-Thomas, it has been a pleasure to meet you." He shook her hand once again before they parted company. Promise and Lugh also bade Ms. Dobson a grateful farewell.

They discreetly made their way out of the building before Lugh turned to Promise and embraced her with great excitement and thankfulness. Promise couldn't help but let the tears of tension fall from her eyes, soon replaced by tears of joy. She promptly said, "Lugh, you have to tell me all about it!"

Lugh immediately and enthusiastically complied. He described how he had presented his appeal based on the grades he earned for all of his assignments throughout the semester, his participation in class, and the quality of his final paper. He then challenged Dr. Roland's points of criticism one by one. Regarding the doctor's reference to his "extracurricular activities," Lugh specifically pointed out that what students did outside of class was none of his instructor's business. Lugh countered the charge of plagiarism with a credible discussion of his paper. Mark Roland belittled those facts, and Lugh knowledgeably responded with counterarguments. This led to the surgeon's elevated vocal volume – and Lugh's calm rebuttal.

Promise smiled broadly at this point. She shared how she had imagined Lugh taking this in stride.

Lugh responded, "It was strange, but I actually felt like a father dealing with his son's temper tantrum – or what I think that would be like, at any rate. I felt very practiced at it, though! Maybe a past-life remnant?" Lugh shrugged, then continued with his tale.

After observing the dynamics between Mark Roland and Lugh, Dr. Abrams asked his adjunct instructor if Lugh's discourse in the office paralleled his responses in class. His department chair later confided to Lugh that when Mark Roland said yes, Dr. Abrams made his determination. When Promise offered the email confirmation for the quality of Lugh's paper, it sealed the outcome.

Dr. Abrams then diplomatically thanked Mark Roland for assisting their department's adjustment to the abrupt departure of a faculty member. He also firmly indicated that Dr. Roland's service would no longer be needed. At that point, Mark Roland abruptly stood, obviously intending to leave their meeting. Noticeably angry, he worked to maintain his pride by arrogantly claiming that this adjunct faculty position at Stella Maris fell below his pay grade. He had already decided that he would no longer teach at the university in any ongoing capacity. Having made his statement, he left.

Lugh then added, "In his final comments to me, Dr. Abrams stated that he would have my final grade changed to the A I deserve!" Lugh was ecstatic. Upon hearing this, Promise was too.

She spontaneously said, "Lugh, we have to celebrate! And we have to tell our parents!"

"Agreed!" he replied before he kissed her once again.

55

IN THE MIDST OF THEIR EXHILARATION that Wednesday afternoon, Promise and Lugh opted to make their phone calls at the same time. When Promise called Peter, anticipating that his work schedule might accommodate her call better than her mom's, he answered immediately. He could hear the excitement and relief in her voice, which eased his own elevated level of concern. He offered to share the good news with Brittany, who also hoped to connect with Promise later for several reasons. She had a few questions and some potentially useful information for Promise in her search for the whereabouts of the three young women on her list. Promise expressed her sincere gratitude for how her parents always supported her throughout her life. Peter gladly concluded their call on this happier note.

Lugh's conversation took a bit longer, but both of his parents were thrilled. Of course, they wanted the best for their son, even if the fulfillment of his dream might take him over two thousand miles away. It suddenly dawned on Promise that if she accompanied him, that distance from loved ones would apply to her as well. It gave her pause – enough to realize how she felt about Lugh and that she would want to go anyway. She decided to begin exploring academic programs in Arizona, just in case.

Next on Lugh's agenda, he wanted to send a grateful acknowledgment to his graduate interviewer and share the good news. He did so immediately by email while also wanting to more tangibly complement his written appreciation. With this aim in mind, Promise and Lugh joyfully considered some creative options throughout the remainder of the day. They went for a run and planned to have dinner at a nearby restaurant, fancier than the local diner but still within their budget. They would celebrate with some champagne upon their return to the apartment. Other concerns would require their attention soon enough.

During dinner, as they reveled in Lugh's success earlier that day, they could not help but share their sense of gratification in defeating Mark Roland's devious intentions. In the midst of their merriment, Promise's inner eye suddenly flashed to a scene from her past life: she grabbed the stick from her four-year-old son, who had just used it to torment a smaller child. Her feelings from that ancient time welled up within her.

Promise looked at Lugh pensively. He immediately noticed and asked her about it. She replied, "You know, Lugh, there was a time when we loved him, or his soul at least. Didn't we? He was our child, after all. Assuming we did love him, does that have any influence upon us and our feelings toward him now?"

Lugh's brow furrowed briefly in response. He then replied, "What a concept to contemplate! I sense that it has merit, though.... In our past life, I worked hard to acknowledge and shape the good in him, hoping he would eventually learn to control his more aggressive urges. You had the clearer perspective about him all along. Even so, you tried to help me see what he really needed. I had more time with him than you did, but much hurt and destruction resulted from my blindness. Still, I agree. I did love him. I know you did too."

Promise nodded. She then stated, "I did. I only knew him until he was four years old, yet my past-life memories suggest that my interactions with him, especially when he hurt others, made me shudder. They still do. Given all his belligerent comments and actions toward us and others in this lifetime, do we still love him?"

Lugh raised an eyebrow. "That invites the question: What does love mean in a situation such as this?"

Promise shook her head and sighed. "I'm not sure. I'm okay with the idea that I want the best for his soul. But I don't love his ideologies, his verbal expressions, his arrogance, or his actions. Is that enough to call it love?"

Lugh grumbled, "In this case, it's all we've got!"

Promise smiled. "I guess so. Then what is best for his soul? Can we ever know that? Is that even up to us?"

Lugh's raised eyebrows minimized the breadth of his forehead considerably. "You ask difficult questions, my dear!"

Promise chuckled. "What fun would it be to do otherwise, *my dear*!"

Lugh laughed too. "Okay, if we seriously consider your question, ultimately, I don't think we can know. What seems obvious to me is that it's *not* good for his soul to get away with hurting others. So, what we did today was good for him even if he didn't like it. Let's face it: to like it, or at least to appreciate it, his personality consciousness would have needed to align with his soul."

Promise added, "That obviously didn't happen! He seemed seriously enraged as he left Dr. Abrams' office."

Lugh responded, "Don't think that doesn't concern me. You are his next target. I don't want to alarm you, but I think I'm not saying anything you haven't already considered. My primary desire is to keep you safe. Ensuring the integrity of his soul is purely secondary."

Promise winced. "I appreciate that, Lugh. I really do. Maybe we can aim for a both/and result? I know we can't measure our success by what happens, but we can at least hold the best for his soul as our intention. I don't want to decimate him. I just want his despicable behavior to stop. I would love it if he saw the light, if he realized what havoc and destruction his approach to life has caused. I don't know that we will ever witness that transformation in him, however. It doesn't even matter, really. He just needs to be stopped, at least at the medical center. Better yet, let's include his professional and personal circles. Perhaps having him arrested is a good start!"

Lugh sat speechless. They hadn't yet discussed this aspect of what would follow in any detail. He recognized immediately the danger involved. He gazed at Promise with deep love and fierce protectiveness in his eyes. She felt it penetrate her soul; even deeper healing for her ancient wound had arrived.

They concluded their meal on this somber note and walked arm in arm back to Lugh's apartment. Upon their arrival there, Lugh took Promise's coat and placed it and his own on the armchair nearby. She waited, her eyes on his every move, beholding the man she had known across centuries with deep love.

Their eyes met in one long moment that communicated everything they truly felt. Lugh touched her cheek gently before pulling her to him. She folded into his embrace with deep longing. One kiss led to another. Lugh's best behavior transcended to another level, taking Promise along with him. No regrets. They were bonded – past, present, and future.

56

JUST AS THE SUN'S FIRST RAYS streamed through Lugh's blinded window, he awoke to the sound of moaning. Disoriented at first, he soon realized that Promise lay next to him. In sleep something seemed to upset her. Moments later, she cried out in desperation, "Please listen! Please listen!" His heart ached for her. He could not deny that he had likely stirred similar, grief-stricken feelings for her during their past and present lives.

Just as he reached to gently awaken her, she sat up on her own, trying to get her bearings. She recognized Lugh's bedroom and soon felt his hand softly stroking the side of her arm. She turned toward him and realized that she had just had a dream, really more a nightmare. She tried to hold the tears of sleep's desolation from spilling into her day without success. Lugh embraced her and tried to comfort her as her tears slid down her cheeks. Her intense confusion initially provoked her to resist, but Lugh gently persisted. Not wanting to repeat his past mistakes, he quietly said, "Promise, please tell me your dream."

Promise wiped her eyes. She gazed directly into his and could not mistake his sincerity. She felt the tension mount again as she recalled the images. "I'm in a gray place with no walls or windows. The three women whom Mark Roland molested are standing before me but far apart from each other. Oddly, there seems to be a fourth vague person in the background. I am asking them to come with me to tell the police. Each one looks distraught. They begin to cry. They tell me they can't. They won't. I am begging them. They don't want to listen to me. I feel utterly helpless to make them see."

She started to cry again. This time, she accepted Lugh's tender embrace. He gently stroked her hair, empathizing even more deeply with what it must be like for her to have such disturbing visions.

He asked her, "Can you tell the difference between a personal fear and a likely occurrence? Please know, I'm not doubting you. It would just help me to comfort you better."

Promise sighed, then said, "Not with one hundred percent accuracy, unfortunately. Yes, I am afraid the others will respond the way Alice did. But when a dream is this intense and the figures seem real, not symbolic, it does suggest this may likely happen. And what was that fourth figure about? Is he going to do it again?! I guess I want some resolution to this whole mess even more than I already realized. I don't know what I will do if they refuse to come forward."

Lugh held her in the silence that followed. Finally, he replied, "We have to take this one step at a time. Remember those thousands of seconds you told me about, and how any one of them can hold the key to a positive surprise? We may have to hope for this and patiently wait. You helped me wait for my interviewer's email. I will help you with this. One step at a time, okay?"

Promise nodded. Lugh kissed her forehead, then focused on the day before them. Promise had to work that Thursday evening. Brad would return on Saturday. The dorms would reopen on Saturday as well, and the semester would begin on Monday.

Lugh asked for her confirmation: "You have to work this evening and Saturday morning, right?"

"Oh my gosh, yes! I completely forgot!" More sheepishly, she added, "I guess my mind has been elsewhere...." Then she smiled at him.

He smiled in return. "Are you okay with what happened last night?" he asked her.

Again, she gazed into his eyes. She replied, "Lugh, I don't know how we managed to wait so long, but I feel like I am 'home' with you. I am more than okay."

Lugh stroked her cheek and beamed. "Good! Me too. We have a lot happening in the next several days. Shall we have breakfast and get out bearings? Brad returns on Saturday. We need to figure a few things out!"

Promise laughed. "Okay, then. Let's get on with it, shall we?!"

Despite her obvious shift in mood, they both recognized that nothing would ever be the same. What anchored them in the present had little to do with what had supported them in the past. That lay all askew now. Mark Roland's fury and need for revenge presented a wild card in the midst of a new semester, new schedules, Lugh's decisions about his future, and Promise's as well. The three student athletes still beckoned her attention, unbeknownst to those women themselves, which only made the situation more difficult. Promise would return to her dorm, changed in many important ways. It all felt raw and fresh, both frightening and exciting. Yes, she felt bonded to Lugh, but she needed and hoped to find a new grounding within herself as well. She prayed for it to come.

Promise did not anticipate any difficulties at work that evening. Mark Roland would not reappear for more sports physicals until the following week when the second semester began. For the time being, in anticipation of Brad's return, she focused on collecting some of her things, now strewn around the apartment. Mid-morning, Brittany called during a break in the action at work, hoping to ask Promise for some needed information. Still feeling unnerved by her dream, Promise responded with a tone that alerted her mother to her level of distress.

Brittany asked, "Promise, are you all right?"

"Yeah, Mom, I am. I just had a nightmare this morning about the three women not wanting to listen to me, that's all."

Sensing the dilemma this caused her daughter, Brittany sighed. She replied, "Oh Promise, that must have been very upsetting. I can appreciate how much this means to you, considering all that you've witnessed and experienced, and what he tried to do to Lugh. Still, you don't have to go through with this. What does your heart say?"

"You know it says that I have to pursue this and do what I can. I really appreciate your efforts to help me, Mom. I'll find a way to make them listen. At least, I will try very hard. I do realize that in the end it's not up to me. I can only do my best."

"That's right, honey. This whole thing is bigger than you are. Please be careful."

"I will, Mom. What is it you wanted to ask me, by the way?"

Brittany shifted gears to respond. "Do the names Anne, Joachim, and Joseph – all either plural, or possessive with an apostrophe 's' – mean anything to you?"

Promise paused, feeling their familiarity, then instantly replied, "They are the names of dorms here!"

"Perfect!" Brittany replied. "Then Viola Rhodes lives in Anne's; Kassi Jones lives in Joachim's; and Alice Danvers lives in Joseph's."

Promise jotted this down as her mother shared her discoveries. "Mom, how did you ever figure this out?"

Brittany laughed. "It's a long story. Let's just say I have experience in snooping online. It's why I've always stressed that you and Lizzie need to be careful about what you post on social media. Actually, your restraint has probably saved you from having Mark Roland know more than he does. Your peers are obviously not so careful."

Promise's jaw dropped. Lugh, who had busied himself with a project at the breakfast bar, noticed her reaction. He heard Promise thank her mother profusely and give her word to stay in touch before she concluded her call.

Promise answered Lugh's inquiring gaze, saying, "She figured out which dorms they live in!"

Lugh exclaimed, "Really?!"

Promise sighed. "Yep, really. Now it gets serious. Next week, I have a mission."

57

PROMISE AND LUGH CONTINUED to run together on Wednesday afternoons, relieved to discover that their class schedules for the new semester easily accommodated what had become a welcomed weekly event. On her way to the indoor track, Promise found herself reflecting on key events from the previous few days.

Promise had left Brad's room completely restored to its original condition before she left for work Saturday morning. When she returned that afternoon, Brad had already arrived. He and Lugh were conversing at the breakfast bar; they welcomed her immediately. Promise felt a momentary awkwardness, but Brad quickly put her at ease with his joke and broad smile: "I was wondering how long it would take you two to find each other in the night! I'm happy for you both." Promise blushed. She and Lugh smiled at each other. The camaraderie of their threesome resumed.

On Monday, the second term began. Promise enjoyed her new classes. Some of them naturally followed the courses she had taken during the previous semester. She also elected to take another mythology class as well as an introduction to anthropology. Lugh's discussions had sparked her interest, so she decided to experience the topic for herself. The required psychology course in research methods and data analysis impressed her as fairly dry, similar to statistics. The developmental psychology class on adulthood and aging seemed relatively more interesting.

Immersing herself in these diverse subjects helped her appreciate how much she preferred to use her brain's creative right hemisphere rather than her logical left half. She hoped that the dutiful exercise of her weaker side with topics like statistics and data analysis might provide some balance and serve her well in the end. Still, it required much effort, more so than running on the track!

As Promise continued to reflect on the events of her week, she remembered how she had anticipated her Tuesday evening at the medical center with trepidation. This only heightened upon her arrival when she noticed that there were three women on Dr. Roland's schedule, all of them toward the end of the evening. Because Promise and Christina never crossed paths, Promise had no idea what to expect. Fortunately, all the female athletes left before the allotted thirty-minutes had passed.

Lugh came to meet her, having jogged the route now well-known to his sneakers. Promise felt and expressed her gratitude in the ways love affords. Lugh tenderly reciprocated before they made their way to Promise's dorm. She longed to sleep with him again, but she didn't want to make that a habit so early in this new phase of their relationship. Lugh understood, which mattered a great deal.

Her reverie came to its natural conclusion once she arrived at the indoor track. Promise spotted Lugh near the far bleachers. They ran together and shared reflections on their new semester. Lugh had elected to supplement his two anthropology courses – Environmental Archeology and Researching of Environment and Culture – with a history course on ancient societies in the Middle East. They both recognized that this would be his last semester at Stella Maris. Everything would change thereafter.

Once they parted company, Promise ventured toward St. Anne's Residence Hall to see if she might somehow encounter Viola Rhodes. She stood outside in the icy wind, waiting and hoping to find Viola leaving or entering her dorm. Promise didn't want to violate Viola's safe space by entering the building only to approach her with a potentially intrusive and unsettling request. Unsuccessful in her efforts after having tolerated as much cold as she could, Promise decided to leave and to formulate a more practical strategy. As she turned to depart, she spotted Viola walking toward the dorm with a young woman. Promise inhaled deeply and stepped forward.

"Viola?" she hesitantly began. When Viola stopped and looked at Promise, unsure of who approached her, Promise continued, "Viola, I'm Promise Holmes-Thomas. I am a student here at Stella Maris, just like you, but I also work at the medical center down the road. We met on the evening you were scheduled for your sports physical."

Viola acknowledged her parting with her friend before she fully turned her attention to Promise. Viola's facial expression, initially open to Promise's introduction, suddenly became aloof and dismissive. She replied, "I don't know what you want, but I am busy. I have to go."

Momentarily disheartened but bolstered by empathy and courage, Promise pressed on. "Viola, I understand why you don't want to speak with me. Dr. Roland is insidiously dangerous. You are not the only one. I want to stop him from doing to anyone else what he did to you. I can't, though, without your help."

Viola just stared at her. Promise could feel the emotional torment stirred by her words. She wanted more than anything to take Viola's pain away. Promise couldn't, however, and she knew it. She could only try to spare others the same heartache.

Remembering her commitment, Promise continued, "I am asking

everyone who I suspect may have experienced what happened to you to help me. I have tried to keep the women listed on his schedule safe, but I have limited control, and if I leave that job, he has free rein. He has threatened me in the parking lot as well. I am truly sorry to upset you with this request, Viola. There's just no other way around it."

Viola just continued to stare at nothing, her eyes glazed over as if having a flashback. Promise felt horrible. She decided that she had said enough. She handed her a paper with her name, dorm, and phone number on it. She asked Viola to contact her, especially if they might help each other in any way. Viola took the paper and silently walked away.

Promise returned to her dorm and sobbed. Mel entered their room in the midst of Promise's meltdown and assumed that she and Lugh had had an argument. Mel hugged her roommate and let her cry it out before she inquired about the reason for her tears. Promise appreciated Mel very much in that moment. Promise's empathic resonance with Viola's torment had overwhelmed her. Promise needed Mel's warmth to counter the cold emptiness bequeathed to Viola by Mark Roland.

Silence permeated the room for several minutes after Promise explained what had happened. Mel then confessed that she, too, had an appointment scheduled with her former, infamous surgeon for a hockey physical. She didn't want to keep it, but she didn't know what alternatives she had. She wanted to play her sport. Mel more deeply appreciated the necessity of Promise's mission – and the difficulty of it. She offered to help in any way she could. Promise sincerely thanked her for her friendship and for listening. They decided to comfort themselves with dinner in the cafeteria followed by a typically off-limits dessert.

Later that night, as Promise tried to fall asleep, her dream of the three or four women came to mind. Her tears from the dream merged with her lingering tears from her encounter with Viola. Slumber would elude her unless she found a way to cope with this ongoing trauma.

Suddenly, she remembered that Alethea had pledged to help her. She silently prayed for her wise mentor's assistance. Oddly, she felt a peace come over her. She understood that she did not have to face this alone. She finally drifted off to sleep.

On Thursday evening, Promise returned to the medical center and fretted once again when she noticed that four men were scheduled to see Dr. Roland before a woman concluded the evening. She sensed trouble and carefully noted her name, Marcia Evans, along with the time she arrived for her appointment. After thirty minutes, Marcia had not returned to Promise's receptionist desk. After forty minutes, Promise couldn't wait any longer. She called Christina's line. Appalled that Christina actually answered the phone, Promise asked her directly, "Christina, the last young woman hasn't left yet. Are you aware of what may be happening to her?"

Christina gasped. "I'll go check...."

Minutes passed. More minutes passed. Promise felt her inner alarms screaming at her. She left her post and ran down the long hallway to Dr. Roland's office, only to meet Marcia hurriedly coming the other way. Once again, Promise felt the wave of nausea and the urge to cry. She quickly retraced her steps to accompany Marcia back to the front desk.

Trying to be discreet and gentle, Promise said, "Marcia, if anything happened to you, if Dr. Roland did anything to you, I want you to know that I am trying to stop it."

Marcia just glared at her and ran out the door.

Promise stood there, frozen, anguished, wishing she had worded her statement better, not knowing what to do. Why was Christina not in the examining room with Marcia?! Christina now had to realize that Promise knew enough to implicate her in a horrible nightmare. Still, Promise recognized that she had no proof that would suffice for the police. She tried very hard not to cry.

Lugh arrived thirty minutes later and sensed immediately that something was terribly wrong. He maintained discretion but glanced at Promise in a way that communicated his limited understanding. Patients were leaving at this point. There were many moments of enough privacy that Promise could convey the gist of what had happened. Lugh's nostrils flared. Oddly, he also felt some measure of the same paralysis that Promise struggled to override.

That night Promise stayed with Lugh after notifying Mel not to worry about her absence. They agreed that both Marcia and Kassi would need to be contacted, the sooner the better. Promise planned to call her mother to see if she might help her identify Marcia's dorm. Lugh offered to be available to Promise immediately after each contact. Her gut remained twisted in a knot for hours. Sleep came very slowly that night. Lugh's comforting embrace helped eventually.

Unexpectedly encountering Kassi in the library over the weekend, Promise approached her as she had the others, telling her story and making her request. Kassi seemed more willing to engage with Promise, but she confessed that she hesitated to come forward because she worried that her jealous boyfriend might abandon her if he knew. Promise empathized with Kassi's concern while also gently pointing out that she needed and deserved some support for her ordeal. Promise presented the necessary contact information and expressed her hope that Kassi would consider being in touch with her soon.

Finally, with Brittany's help, Promise stood outside Marcia's dorm on the following cold Wednesday afternoon after her run with Lugh. She waited for over an hour before she spotted Marcia exiting the building. Marcia remembered what Promise had said on that harrowing evening and tried her best to avoid her. Promise persisted, however, while also not wanting to traumatize her further. She just needed Marcia to listen. Promise felt determined to try. She could only hope for the best.

When Promise said, "I've been trying to make him stop, but it didn't work. You are the latest casualty. Without proof, I can't notify the police or even my boss. I have contacted three other women who experienced the same as you, maybe worse because no one intervened. Please help me, Marcia!"

Marcia turned and glared at her. "How can you even stand there and say that?! How can you even work there?!"

Promise retorted out of her own pain, "If I quit, there's no one to stand in his way!! But I can't keep doing this, and I can't stop him alone. I need you and the three other women to come forward. At least, please think about it? I have already called the police on him once for stalking me in the parking lot. It went nowhere. Please think about it, Marcia. That's all I ask. Here is my contact information. You can call me anytime."

Marcia inhaled deeply. She took the paper Promise held out to her, then turned and walked away.

Promise stood there alone, feeling the cold emptiness that had nothing to do with the weather. Lugh tried to comfort her later that evening with limited success. He did remember to mention the next Celtic gathering scheduled for that Saturday at the same location where Samhain had taken place. They would celebrate Imbolc, the beginning of spring. Lugh described how the Celts always celebrate their seasons when they begin to stir under the ground, or in the unconscious, weeks before they actually manifest on earth. He hoped they might find some wisdom in their shamanic journeying to help them negotiate the difficult days ahead.

Oddly, Promise found this very comforting. She wanted to see Alethea again. Dylan's guided explorations seemed to help her do so with greater clarity. She needed her wise guide now more than ever.

58

LUGH DROVE THE NOW FAMILIAR ROUTE to their Imbolc celebration as he and Promise speculated further on the events of the past week. On Tuesday night, five male athletes filled Dr. Roland's schedule. The evening passed without incident even though Christina had called the office stating that she could not work her shift. On Thursday, when Promise had arrived at work a few minutes early, she found Lydia waiting for her but obviously in a hurry to leave. Lydia quickly informed her that Christina still felt ill; unfortunately, she had provided less than two hours' notice. In the absence of a nurse that evening, there would be no one to assist Dr. Roland. With four young women scheduled for physicals, Lydia made the executive decision to cancel their hours.

Lydia asked Promise to please make the calls; their phone numbers had been added to her list. As she prepared to leave, Lydia also remembered to mention that she received Promise's request to have Saturday off. Lydia told her that would not be a problem.

The intensity and suffering caused by Mark Roland's destructive actions weighed heavily upon Promise's shoulders and on her heart. Her empathic sensitivities even included Christina despite the nurse's negligence.

As Lugh continued to drive and listen, Promise conjectured, "I suspect Christina feels awful about what's been happening. She has likely felt caught in an impossible bind – caring for her mother while trying to fulfill her professional responsibilities – but she opted to deal with it by denying the problem altogether. Last Thursday evening's experience with Marcia put it right in her face, however. And she can no longer pretend that I am unaware of her role in the tragedies that have occurred. I'm sure she feels sick – and not from a virus! I just keep asking myself: What can I do about it?"

Lugh responded, "That's a hard one, Promise. You still have no specific proof other than what others would call a 'suspicion' that she wasn't in the examining room when she was supposed to be. We both know that you feel sick about this too – and you didn't even do anything wrong!"

They exchanged quick glances of acknowledgment before Lugh returned his attention to the road. Their painful quandary sat like an unwelcomed guest in the back seat of their vehicle for the remainder of the trip.

They arrived at the gathering site midmorning and quickly noticed that the falling leaves of Samhain now lay crackling and frozen on the cold earth at their feet. The unadorned limbs of trees waved and splintered in the blasts of wind that had just begun to swirl around them. They bundled themselves more tightly in their coats and scarves, then carried their blankets and other items into the barn.

Once in the meeting room, they quickly recognized and greeted many of their fellow participants. They found two spaces near the heater, which Promise greatly appreciated. Dylan came to welcome them; they each hugged him warmly. Dylan immediately noticed the growing bond between Promise and Lugh, rightly surmising that they were a couple now. He winked at them before he moved on to acknowledge others as they arrived.

After Dylan lit the altar candles and solemnized the circle by calling in the directions, he explained that Imbolc not only celebrates the onset of spring, when the seeds first release their roots downward into the earth. It also commemorates the return of the old hag of winter to the Isle of Eternal Youth. Rejuvenated there, the goddess Brigid emerges as the maiden of spring.

In this context, Dylan invited each member of the group to consider three questions: What had come to its natural conclusion in their lives? What needed to be released so that it might seek renewal in its proper place? What needed to come into being, perhaps young like a seedling that would grow over the coming year? Their journeys would help them explore these questions. Their power animals would accompany them.

Everyone settled themselves on their mats and covered their eyes as Dylan began to drum the rhythm of transport to another world. In her mind's eye, Promise stood at the edge of the forest where she greeted her lion and thanked him once again for his faithful accompaniment and protection. They ran together through the woods as before, but this time they came upon a cabin in a clearing of trees. Promise found Alethea standing in the doorway of the dwelling, waiting for her.

They embraced each other with great affection, welcoming their reconnection. Then Alethea invited Promise into her sheltering abode to sit by her side at the hearth. Promise's lion settled himself as sentinel at the door.

This time, Promise spoke first. "I am so glad to see you, Alethea. I really need your advice."

"I know, my dear. These have been difficult days for you. Please put your question into words for both of us to hear."

Promise readily complied: "Mark Roland has hurt four women and tried to hurt me. I must make him stop, but I can't do it alone. I have asked the four women he has victimized to help me, but my request simply causes them to relive their trauma. I truly understand that and feel awful about it. I hate hurting them all over again. I just don't know any other way. Is there another way? What can I do?!"

Alethea's gaze held the utmost compassion. She replied, "Healing sometimes requires great effort from us. It becomes especially difficult when the wound has already sapped our energy reserves dry. Trauma does that. It depletes the system entirely. Only then, however, can we discover that another Energy Source exists, and that It steadfastly invites us to use It and rely upon It for our restoration and greater good.

"You and the four women are in the midst of a great healing. They have their separate paths, of course. We can only attend to yours. To the degree that you all dwell within the same web, your healing may impact theirs as well. That becomes a matter of faith and trust.

"You have come to me asking for advice. Perhaps you are also seeking a renewal of the energy you need to honor your commitment to stop Mark Roland. You have carried this intention across lifetimes. It is an intention that I have lived as well."

Promise looked at Alethea with even greater curiosity now. "You did mention that his despicable behavior predated his birth as my son in that ancient lifetime, but have you also known the soul of Mark Roland personally?"

Alethea sighed sorrowfully for one brief moment before she responded, "Yes, my dear, I have. It is a sad story of long, long ago, even earlier than when you knew him as Glenna. I was his mother then. I also had the second sight, but the gift was new to me, and I hadn't yet learned to trust it. I foresaw that a murderous gang of outlaws wanted to hurt my family. I told my mate, who didn't believe me – like your Alasdair from the past and, initially, your Lugh in the present. Consequently, I told myself I was wrong. I tried to ignore my inner knowing.

But the thugs came just as I had predicted. They killed my mate and me, and all but one of our children.

"Mark Roland, who had then incarnated as my child, somehow physically survived that horrendous tragedy. What happened to his soul, however, became a tragedy of its own. He turned to hatred; he lusted for power. He despised weakness in any form, vowing never to let anyone hurt him like that again. Abusing women satisfied these monstrous needs and gave him not only pleasure but comfort, all very temporary, of course – so short-lived that he had to repeat his crimes over and over until his cruelty became a sick habit.

"I had dared to hope that in future lives, if he were to experience enough love, he might heal from the tragedy that had befallen him. I blamed myself because I had failed to honor my vision. Despite my many attempts, his soul's transformation has not yet occurred, as you well know. He came to you, as Glenna, already seriously wounded and progressively inured to his darkening path."

Promise truly felt compassion for her wise mentor. "Alethea, I am so sorry. I know from my own experience that coming to trust our visions takes a lot of training, effort, and practice. I hope you still don't fault yourself for what occurred so long ago."

"No, my dear, I have learned to forgive myself. I have truly appreciated witnessing your growth in those ways as well. You must give yourself credit for that."

"Actually, Alethea, I give the credit to my parents and my Aunt Tara. Without them I would still be struggling as you struggled in the distant past. But here we are, still having to deal with the soul of Mark Roland. I appreciate that you are helping me. What am I to do?"

"Promise, you are already setting a proper intention: to stop him without annihilating him, assuming that option presents itself to you. There are great forces at work here, forces stronger than his evil or your desire for good. There are also great lessons to learn, both for you and for me."

"For you, Alethea? I had assumed that you have already mastered all that can be known. Isn't that true?" Promise asked.

Alethea smiled ruefully and replied, "My dear, I have definitely grown in wisdom through my many lifetimes, but I have more healing to do. That is why I wanted to incarnate in this lifetime as you."

"*What?!*" Promise's head spun.

"Yes, you heard me. I am your higher self. Through your soul, you and I have shared several lifetimes as the mother of Mark Roland's soul. It only matters that you remember the one as Glenna because by then we had grown sufficiently to honor our visionary gifts and to possibly make a difference. We actually did heal a huge fracture in the rift of worlds created by that first horrendous tragedy. Mark Roland is the last remnant of what has needed healing across all those lifetimes. Fortunately, I think I now understand what our remaining lesson is. But Dylan is calling you back now. I will tell you during the next journey."

Promise could not believe what she had just experienced. Still, Alethea's parting words did help her reorient to the sound of Dylan's drum and the need to return her consciousness to her fourth-dimensional world. Promise called her lion to her, and together they ran through the forest, parting company just in time for her to lay dazed on her mat for several minutes.

When she finally removed her eye cover, she found Lugh gazing at her intently. She quietly said, "Lugh, this time I'm the one who needs to take a walk. I'll be back for the next round."

59

PROMISE RETURNED to their gathering room just as Dylan began the introduction to the next journey. His words escaped Promise's attention, however. She still struggled to understand what Alethea actually meant. Alethea was her higher self? Her mind could not grasp the implications of this. Promise quickly offered some reassurance to Lugh, then prepared herself to journey once again.

Dylan began the pulse of transport. Promise and her lion ran through the woods as before and found Alethea eagerly awaiting them. Promise entered the cabin with her wise mentor. Her lion assumed his post as sentry. Alethea and Promise returned to their seats by the hearth's fire and resumed their conversation as if nothing had ever interfered with it.

Promise stuttered her confusion and asked for deeper understanding. Alethea gladly complied. "You are a promise, my dear. A promise I made long ago to set my mistake right. Your parents do not give themselves enough credit for their gifts of intuition. They use them well, however, especially together, and that is all that matters. When they named you, they tuned in to the core of your soul...our soul. We made that promise to heal the past. We have one last thing to learn from it."

"What is that, Alethea?" Promise asked.

"Simply, to let him go."

"I don't understand. Please help me understand," Promise begged.

Alethea sighed with tenderness for her human incarnation. She truly appreciated that her human self had learned to listen to the soulful level of her being. How many painful lifetimes had elapsed to develop this precious gift. She would make the most of it and hope to communicate in a way that might help her human self more deeply connect with the wise soul within her.

Alethea began, "The soul serves as a bridge between our human sense of self and the Spirit, which enlivens us. Our soul lives beyond physical death and incarnates many times – in different bodies, sometimes in different genders – to experience this earth plane and to know love in relationship, which the One can only share through Creation. In the course of our incarnational undertakings, however, the human side of the soul bridge often gets damaged. These wounds interfere with knowing and experiencing the flow of love between human consciousness and divinity. These wounds need to be healed.

"Our soul was deeply wounded by the tragedy of long ago, but we healed because we were able to know love over many lifetimes. We grew in wisdom. We knew your father as an elder and mentored your Aunt Tara as a priestess when, as Alethea, we served as woman elder on the council. We and your Aunt Tara have helped each other often across lifetimes. She was the village seer when we lived as Glenna. She taught us then how to interpret our dreams, just as she has helped you remember how to do that in this lifetime. We have shared many lifetimes with your father as well, your mother not as often, but she did help us birth your father as Micheil when the time fracture needed to be healed. We even knew of your Uncle Alex in our lifetime as an elder. As Dorian, he sailed the seas. He loved your Aunt Tara even then."

Promise listened intently. She noticed that something settled within her, like a knowing that she didn't know she knew. Of course! That's why everyone felt so familiar in an odd sort of way. She had taken it all for granted, but this detailed awareness made much deeper sense to her.

Alethea had paused to give Promise the needed time for integration. Promise then asked, "Alethea, this helps me understand my current life, but what is it about Mark Roland that we are to learn. You said something about letting him go?"

"Yes, my dear. We have tried and tried to keep that promise we made long ago to assist his soul's return to Love. We had assumed we had that power. We don't. Love is greater than us, even as a soul. It holds us, surely, but it is much more encompassing than we can ever be. It is for Love to affect him, to change him, not us. And he can still refuse. We can stop him from being more destructive if we so choose – and if we are blessed with the assistance of the One moving through the Web – but we must make it a humble effort. Given that Mark Roland cannot rest until he hurts us – and perhaps not even then – ignoring him is not an option. We must do our best to stop him.

"If we are successful in your mission to have him arrested and sent to prison, he will suffer there, no doubt. Evil has a way of destroying itself over time. How much time will it take for him? Will he experience a transformation? We cannot know, so we obviously cannot control it. This is where we have to let him go. We cannot undo the wrong that transpired so very long ago. We can only dwell in the Love that breathes through the core of our soul. We have to let him go. We have to release ourselves from that promise. You can make a new one for us. That is the beauty of Imbolc's preparation for spring."

Promise suddenly felt at peace. She smiled at her soul. She and Alethea would live as one hereafter.

Promise suddenly thought to ask, "Alethea, how has Lugh figured into our lifetimes?"

Alethea smiled broadly, "Oh, my dear, we have loved him more than twice!"

Promise laughed, not only in her journey but in the gathering room. Just then, Dylan's drum sounded their return to consciousness in the fourth dimension. Promise hugged her soul, called her lion, and ran through the forest, eager to return with her heart full of gratitude, wanting to share it with the man she loved.

60

AFTER CONCLUDING the Imbolc celebration, Lugh and Promise stopped once again at the highway diner on their return trip to campus. They sat in a private booth where Promise tried to give words to her journey's mind-bending experience. Lugh listened with fascination. He described how ancient civilizations, especially in their mystical sects, would likely understand what Promise described. Lugh wondered if this might be an aspect of what the Mystery Schools were all about. This only added to her sense of awe; something so profound had occurred, not only that evening but since antiquity as well. As a result, Promise found herself reflecting on her anthropology class with even greater interest.

While their mutual amazement continued to dominate their conversation, Promise also took the opportunity to ask Lugh about his journeys. He responded eagerly, "They were so uplifting, unlike my previous experiences.

"I know we were supposed to meet Brigid, but Lugh showed up

again for me. He invited me to see that how I handled the appeal process marked a turn in my soul's journey. That I could remain calm in the midst of Roland's verbal assault, and that I continued to hold my position without blaming anyone or destroying him, has shown that I am ready to progress onward to the next phase of my growth. I asked him what that might look like. He told me that was entirely up to me."

Promise smiled and shook her head. "Isn't it just like these higher powers or higher selves to leave everything up to us in our ignorance?! I do appreciate that they help us when we make a wrong turn, but it would be so nice to avoid making that mistake in the first place!"

Lugh laughed. "Agreed! Although I have to add that I did get some assistance in my decision-making from the second journey." In response to an enthusiastically curious nod from Promise, he continued, "It seems that anthropology and the search for pre-Younger Dryas civilizations suit my soul's quest perfectly. With my namesake's acknowledgement and support, my passion for the subject increased exponentially! I feel like I'm on fire with a mission. I don't know where it will take me. I just know I have to follow it."

He paused and gazed more deeply into Promise's eyes, hoping to peer into her heart and soul's reaction to his words. He tentatively asked, "Of course, I am hoping you may want to accompany me?"

Promise smiled broadly. "I am thinking I might. How would you feel about two anthropologists in the family? These shamanic journeys – and mythology in general – have sparked a curiosity within me that I'd like to explore further. Maybe we can complement each other's work?"

"Are you serious?!" Lugh exclaimed.

Promise honestly replied, "I need time to explore this further, of course, and time to think about it and feel into it. Maybe I shouldn't have said anything yet. In any case, I already have. I just want to feel the same fire you do, Lugh, but for myself. Your flame is wonderful, but I can't derive my own energy supply from it. It will strangle you and leave me feeling desperately dependent upon you. I want and need to find my own fire!"

Now Lugh's smile lit up the diner. "Promise, those are wise words. Absolutely, I will make space for you to find your own passion. I want you to. We've both known for a while that it really isn't psychology. I look forward to witnessing your journey!"

On that more deeply bonding note, they concluded their meal and returned to Lugh's apartment. They had agreed at the diner that Promise would spend the night with him. Brad seemed very comfortable with this arrangement. Mel knew to anticipate that her roommate might not return that night as well. Promise felt herself settling in to a new sense of herself. Still, she recognized this as a work in progress.

On Monday, Promise planned to spend an hour at the library researching a topic for her anthropology course related to ancient Sumer. There, she found numerous references to one of her favorite goddesses, Inanna. As she reflected on Inanna's journey to the Underworld, Promise suddenly thought of Alethea's story about the wounding of Mark Roland's soul. Somehow, these narratives seemed related.

Upon first learning the myth, Promise understood that Inanna had chosen to descend to the dark, life-stripping depths to release her lover from Ereshkigal's imprisonment. Alethea – and Promise's own soul, it would seem – had also traveled to these depths of tragedy and probable despair multiple times before finding a way to rise and heal. They had plunged themselves into the bone-chilling darkness to redeem a child, their child, over and over again. Lifetime after lifetime, they had tried to save him, descending with a cyclical frequency reminiscent of each month's new moon.

Promise now comprehended that Cassandra's desperation and Persephone's abduction had really offered them no choice at all. Inanna, on the other hand, had chosen her path carefully, even establishing a plan of assisted exit from the realm below should she need it. It suddenly occurred to Promise that Inanna's descent to the Underworld truly was a choice because it's alternative, not to descend, was equally an option that required her discernment. Overwhelming compulsion or abduction would not have offered her that choice.

During Imbolc, Alethea, the hard-won wisdom of Promise's soul, had spoken: they would no longer subject themselves to the ravages of hell to try saving a soul that by all indications did not want to be saved. Promise sat staring at nothing in particular as the full implications of this decision penetrated the depths of her heart. Was this abandonment? Was it a self-serving desertion to ensure her own survival? Was it simply a statement of truth?

Mark Roland hadn't asked for help of any kind. He hadn't even realized he had a problem, other than that Promise and Lugh kept thwarting him, as had Peter and Brittany twenty years ago, as had Micheil and Màiri in the more distant past. Alethea and Promise's soul had clearly endured countless painful lifetimes in their efforts to redeem him. Alethea had healed herself enough in the process to finally surrender the hubris of that mission. Promise also remembered her own father's discourse on the fated outcome for the compulsive rescuer: becoming the victim, then feeling or acting out one's own anger or destructive rage for being victimized. Conscious or not, Rescuer – Victim – Persecutor usually kept company together.

Promise sighed. She decided for herself that Alethea's wisdom had merit. From a soulful perspective, Promise would not abandon her past-life son, but she could not help someone who had abandoned himself. Her own survival did matter. Only a Greater Love might impact Mark Roland now.

Promise suddenly returned her attention to her environment and the clock on the wall nearby. Her next class would begin in twenty minutes. Just as she prepared to read a few more paragraphs before concluding her time at the library, she spotted Alice not twenty feet away. Alice stopped abruptly when she recognized Promise. She almost turned away, but Promise could sense a rise of will in Alice, who tentatively resumed her steps and came directly toward Promise's carrel.

Promise detected a pronounced anxiety within the young woman standing before her, but Alice's bravery prevailed. She said, "Promise, I've been thinking a lot about what you said several weeks ago. I can't go on living like this. I am willing to help you. If you will go with me, I will tell the police what he did."

Promise's jaw dropped, but she quickly recovered from her shock. She immediately gathered her own courage, recognized the incredible importance of the moment, and replied, "I will go with you, Alice. Shall we go now?"

Alice responded in the only way she could. She nodded.

Promise reached for Alice's hand and squeezed it with reassurance. She then collected her books and walked with Alice to her car. Together they rode to the police station in silence.

61

BEFORE PROMISE AND ALICE exited the car, Promise turned to her companion and said, "I just want you to know, Alice, I deeply respect your courage."

Alice smiled wanly as she replied, "I think you've got a whopping dose of it yourself!"

They chuckled, more to relieve their tension than in response to anything else.

Once inside the station, Promise approached the woman at the receiving desk and stated that they had come to report a sexual assault. The female officer at the counter abruptly shifted her attention from her mindless paperwork to their needs. She asked their names, then ushered them into a stark but private room and said a detective would be with them soon.

They both looked around and observed a long table and four chairs surrounded by nothing other than space and walls. Even the colors of this environment were somber, reflecting the nature of the many accusations and confessions released into its domain. The minutes ticked by, fifteen into twenty. Promise worried that Alice might change her mind. Instead, in that moment, Promise detected a deepening determination in the woman sitting next to her. A female detective entered the room moments later.

The officer, dressed in professional attire but not the typical uniform, introduced herself as Detective Julia McPhearson. Promise immediately noticed this policewoman's no-nonsense attitude; Promise also intuited the kindness she masked with a practiced professionalism. Detective McPhearson began by directly asking about the nature of their complaint.

Promise summarized their intention to report Dr. Mark Roland as a sexual predator, noting that his actions specifically occurred at the Dunkirk Hollow Medical Center over the past several months. She briefly explained Alice's and her own respective roles and how, to date, they had limited knowledge regarding the other's personal experience. Promise only knew that others had also been affected and that Dr. Roland must be stopped.

The detective listened with her painfully earned expertise in such matters. She proposed that she speak with each of them separately: Alice first, then Promise. The young women agreed. Promise left the room.

Promise found a quiet area across the hall, starkly furnished with folding chairs and a rack hosting the usual office magazines. A plain black and white clock ticked on the wall nearby. She prepared herself for a not-so-comfortable waiting period, vastly different from her vigil for Lugh during his appeal. That association reminded her that once again she could hold space for Alice. Surely, Alice needed all the support available to her.

An hour later, Alice joined Promise briefly before they traded places. Alice had obviously cried during her part of the interview; she seemed weary but resolute. Promise hugged her. Alice returned Promise's embrace and whispered, "It's going to be okay."

Promise felt surprised to hear Alice say this, and also encouraged. She then joined the detective in the interview room. They sat facing each other in the room's stark stillness while life went on beyond its walls. In response to the detective's questions, Promise shared what she knew, what she suspected, and what she had personally experienced regarding the doctor's stalking behavior in the parking lot on two occasions. She mentioned that she had called the police the second time; she hoped Officer Robertson had filed the report that she requested.

Detective McPhearson maintained an impartial affect while she listened to Promise's narrative. She then asked for further clarification regarding Promise's position at the medical center, her observations regarding Dr. Roland's patients, and the cause for her suspicions. The detective rightly questioned how these offenses could have occurred in the presence of a nurse whose duty included being in the examining room with each woman during her physical. Promise paused, caught between her empathic awareness that Christina would suffer serious consequences from a truthful response to this question, and her realistic recognition that anything less than the truth would place this case in jeopardy. If Promise waffled on this point, Alice might have come forward to provide her courageous statement in vain.

Promise took a deep breath, then she told the officer what she knew. Detective McPhearson questioned Promise about her reluctance to share this information. Promise honestly responded, "Detective, I feel for Christina's struggle to care for her mother while also having to work. I know that telling you what I have already shared will likely create grave consequences for her. Her choices gave Dr. Roland free rein to hurt young women, however. I have had to make my own difficult choice. Even though I do regret having to cause her pain, I can't see any other way around it."

Promise felt the tears she had long suppressed coming to the surface. Detective McPhearson responded with the kindness and compassion

Promise not only needed in that moment, but that she had also intuited in this officer. Perhaps this explained why Alice felt it would all work out. Promise dried her eyes and prepared herself for further questioning.

The detective had only one more inquiry. She asked for the names of the other victims. Again, Promise paused. This time she chose not to comply, stating, "Detective, I can appreciate why you want to know, and, frankly, I would love to tell you. But when I approached these women to ask them for their help, I could see in their eyes that my request had traumatized them all over again. I would really prefer that they opt to meet with you on their own initiative, not because I betrayed their confidence. Can we give them a little more time to come to their own decisions about this?"

Now Detective McPhearson sighed. She replied, "I understand your feelings, Promise. Input from the others would strengthen a case against him, of course. Nonetheless, I would like to bring him and Christina in for questioning. I'll know better what position to take about the other women after that. Given that he has stalked you twice, you will need to be careful. He does not know how to contact the others, does he?"

Promise responded, "I don't think so. I only know their dorms because my mother used to work for a detective; she helped me find them. Our specific dorm is not usually listed on our mailing address at Stella Maris. Based on that, I don't know how he would find out. At least, I hope he doesn't."

Promise felt markedly anxious at this point. Detective McPhearson observed this and sensed that these two young women had spoken the truth. She wanted to offer some measure of comfort and support. She replied, "I think I can arrange for our patrol cars to make more of a presence around the Dunkirk Hollow Medical Center on Tuesday and Thursday evenings. Would that help?"

"Enormously!" Promise exclaimed. "Thank you!"

The detective nodded and concluded their time together, stating, "I'll be in touch. Call me if anything, *anything*, of concern arises, okay?" She handed Promise her contact card.

"I will. Thank you again."

Promise reunited with Alice in the waiting area and together they returned to Promise's car. They shared their impressions regarding the detective and their respective interviews during the ride back to campus. They also exchanged phone numbers, expressing their commitment to give each other ongoing support. Promise left Alice near her dorm, then parked her car in its spot in the lot. She quickly texted Lugh.

Shocked at this turn of events, he immediately responded and suggested that they have takeout for dinner in his apartment. Promise felt comforted by his suggestion and agreed to his plan with sincere appreciation. Lugh managed the food so that when Promise arrived, she need do nothing but share the details of her day. They sat at the breakfast bar while Promise did so, factually at first. Her feelings about it all threatened to surface at any moment, however.

Lugh listened attentively, very much aware of the upset underlying her words. He gently asked her about how she felt. Promise held her face in her hands, then dragging them down her cheeks, she admitted to her fright about what Mark Roland might do. She had no idea when the police might question him or how he might respond. She anticipated more rage, but she could not predict the form it might take. She also felt conflicted about having divulged Christina's role in the matter. She prayed the other women would come forward on their own. Promise really did not want to reveal their names.

Lugh sensed the internal storm brewing within the heart of his beloved. He rose from his seat and came to her with open arms. She folded into them and cried. He held her close until her tears subsided. He fully recognized that his confrontation with Mark Roland during the appeal process hardly compared to this.

Lugh invited Promise to stay with him that night. She declined but hoped he might be open to tomorrow evening instead. He gracefully accepted the alternative. He also insisted that she call him at any time, day or night, if she needed his listening ear or the support of his presence for any reason. She gave her word.

Lugh walked Promise to her dorm and kissed her tenderly before they parted. He added, "Promise, you are the bravest woman I know."

Promise smiled, then replied, "You don't know my mother very well. I'm betting she's got me beat!"

62

THAT NIGHT, PROMISE SLEPT FITFULLY, tossing and turning from dreams filled with scenes of herself being chased, interspersed with the leer on Mark Roland's face. In moments of fuller awakening, she regretted not staying with Lugh, then thought that at least he might sleep more peacefully as a result.

Tuesday dawned gray and misty as the winter temperatures shifted from cold to slightly warmer. She had two classes that day, one in the early morning, the other after lunch. Work at five o'clock hovered in her awareness despite her determined attempts to refocus her attention on the here and now. She decided to simply break her day into tiny bites and to concentrate on those segments one at a time.

After her shower and a light breakfast, Promise gathered the necessary notebooks and texts and proceeded to her research methods and data analysis class. She wryly wondered why anyone would think it a good idea to schedule such a course so early in the morning. Especially after her poor night's sleep, staying awake would prove to be a major challenge.

Her professor called on her just as her chin fell off her palm, waking her from her doze. He made a comment about too many extracurricular activities, which made those of her classmates who happened to be awake snicker and giggle. Their laughter woke up the others. Promise sighed and tried to smile. The best she accomplished was a smirk. She could not help but think, If you only knew the half of it…!

Promise then went to the library where she received a text from Lugh asking, among other things, how well she slept the night before. She responded with emojis, not wanting to complain or alarm him. She asked how he had managed the same challenge. His emojis suggested similar difficulties. She concluded their exchange with the hope that they might have better success together that night. He sent a smiley face in return. Promise smiled to herself. She felt grateful for his presence in her life. She intended to tell him so that evening.

She tried to resume her research on Sumer for her anthropology course, but she fell asleep instead. A friend passing by wakened her, suspecting that she would want to attend the class they had in common. Promise thanked her friend profusely as they walked together to the lecture hall. She had slept through lunch but, fortunately, she wasn't hungry. Having had a nap, Promise managed to stay alert. She found the anthropological topic for the day fascinating, which helped in no small measure.

After class, Promise went to the cafeteria, realizing she needed to eat something before having to work that evening. After her meal, she returned to her dorm, where she received a phone call from a vaguely familiar number. She decided to answer. Detective McPhearson's voice immediately sent her entire inner system on alert.

The detective addressed the purpose of her call directly: "Promise, I want to let you know that I met with Christina this morning. She confessed to her absences from the last appointments of the evening, then she came to the station with me and provided a statement. She also gave me the name of the fourth young woman. I have not contacted her yet. We do have enough for a warrant, however. Dr. Roland will be arrested this afternoon, taken to the station, interviewed, and likely charged. I don't think you will see him at work this evening. I thought you might like to know."

Promise sat speechless; her jaw dropped and froze in place for several moments. Detective McPhearson asked, "Promise, are you there? Are you all right?"

Promise shook her head, trying to relieve her shock. She then replied, "Yes, Detective, I'm here. I'm fine. I'm just surprised, that's all. I hadn't expected this to move so quickly. All morning and afternoon, I've been dreading going to work this evening. Thank you so much for letting me know!"

"You're welcome, Promise. I'll be in touch about the next phase of this investigation within the next few days. Thank you for your help with this."

"My turn to say 'You're welcome.' I'll let Alice know."

"That would be great. Thank you." Detective McPhearson concluded the call.

Promise stared at the wall for another few moments, then immediately called Alice. Alice, too, seemed shocked. Both of them realized, undoubtedly, that the next stages in these developments would present their own grueling aspects, but at least no other women would be harmed. They decided to focus on what peace might come to them in the interim.

Next, Promise wanted to notify her parents. She knew they worried about her, especially in the context of her proximity to Mark Roland. They deserved some relief as well. Again, suspecting that her mother might be busy in the emergency room, Promise opted to call her father. Peter answered immediately.

Promise shared all that had happened in the previous twenty-four hours. He could hear a returning lightness in her voice that he had missed for quite some time. He felt himself relaxing as well. He assured her that he would inform Brittany of this good news. Peter also reminded his daughter of her pledge to inform him if she needed any help whatsoever. Promise agreed. They concluded their call on this uplifting note.

Finally, Promise called Lugh. She wanted to tell him about all her contacts, so she saved his call for last. He, too, answered immediately. Thrilled to hear about this turn of events, Lugh also spontaneously stated, "I'll still come for you this evening, okay?"

Promise smiled, which he couldn't see, while gratefully responding, "Lugh, you know you don't have to, but I have to also admit that I would love it if you did. It's going to take a while getting used to these dramatic changes. Besides, I love your company."

Lugh's smile came through the phone. "That's what I like to hear! I'll be there. Just text me as usual."

"Will do!"

Tuesday evening passed uneventfully, other than Lydia greeting Promise at the reception desk once again to inform her that Dr. Roland's hours were indeed cancelled. Lydia seemed unaware of the reason, or at least she gave no hint of it. She simply requested that Promise notify the athletes affected by this scheduling change. Newly released from her previous strain, Promise happily made the calls; she tried to adopt an apologetic tone for any consequent inconvenience.

Promise and Lugh slept well that night, enfolded in each other's arms. Wednesday and Thursday followed peacefully, except for the news of Mark Roland's arrest. The local newspapers commented on the shock of it as well as the distress that his absence from the hospital would cause for his patients awaiting surgery. Students in various settings spoke of it. Promise made no comments to anyone other than Lugh, Brad, Mel, and Alice. The five of them simply appreciated their temporary relief.

Promise actually looked forward to working Thursday evening. She had her homework assignments planned, hoping to complete them during the quieter times. Now that Dr. Roland no longer had office hours, she anticipated more periods of calm, or so she hoped.

Thursday afternoon, Lugh offered to come for her at the end of her work shift, as usual. Promise looked forward to seeing him, as always.

63

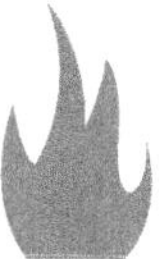

AS FEBRUARY'S COLD WIND SEEPED through his windows on Thursday afternoon, Peter sat at his desk, gazing at the weather station's unannounced snow flurries. He chuckled while thinking, Just like Mother Nature to remind us that we only know so much. He noted how, in so many ways, She really does impact the course of earthly affairs. He also wryly reflected, We keep forgetting that we are Her welcomed, and sometimes not so welcomed, guests.

Peter had just contacted Brittany who would arrive home within the hour. He decided to use this time to reflect on his acceptance speech for the award, which would be presented to him by the holistic organization mid-May. With a few months at his disposal to formulate his response, he reminisced about his early inspiration for starting the Rainbow Healing Arts Center. His appreciation for the sacrifices of Chiron and Prometheus had only heightened over the years. Peter acknowledged that he, too, had made his offerings, sometimes at great price.

Peter's thoughts immediately diverted to Promise: Had he committed his daughter to a lifetime of similar sacrifices by naming her after his hero? Had he influenced her recent decisions to take on their ancient and ongoing adversary? Their Thanksgiving holiday conversation about the distant past quickly refuted that last consideration. Promise had her own stake in dealing with Mark Roland. Peter simply wished it could have been easier for her – and safer.

Having to accept once again his limited control over this situation, he returned his attention to his speech. What message did he want his comments to convey? That healing is a complicated as well as spiritual affair? That cure and healing are not the same? That everyone deserves the opportunity to heal? That traditional medicine has much to offer, but it has its limits, and there is so much more? Yes, yes, and more yeses. He decided to begin by listing his priorities.

Brittany arrived home just before five o'clock and came directly into his office. She had spoken briefly with Promise that day. Their conversation had helped her feel more hopeful that Promise might soon be safe on a longer-term basis.

Peter and Brittany both realized that the next phase of Promise's journey would involve some stressful interactions with lawyers. Long ago, Brittany had personally experienced the harrowing inquisition staged by the type of individuals most likely to defend Mark Roland. She cringed at the thought that Promise might have to deal with them as well. Fortunately, attorneys like Angela Rilken also existed on the planet. Brittany tried to console herself by remembering this and knowing that she herself had wisdom in the matter. She would share it with Promise, along with her love and support.

Peter and Brittany had continued their conversation for almost an hour when Peter's cell phone rang. Surprisingly, Lugh's name appeared on his caller ID. Peter immediately answered and heard the distress in Lugh's voice.

"Peter, you know that Mark Roland was charged with sexual assault on Tuesday. This afternoon he had his bail hearing. He posted the huge amount required by the judge and is now out of jail. It's all over the news here. But Promise hasn't heard. I'm heading over to the medical center now. I thought you might want to know."

"I absolutely do! Thank you for going to be with her. I'm on my way, but it will take me three hours, or less if I'm lucky. Let's keep each other posted." Peter hung up.

Despite Peter's relatively calm demeanor, Brittany empathically tuned in to his sudden burst of inner turmoil. She looked at Peter with horror in her eyes. All she could say was "What?!"

Peter shared Lugh's message. Brittany insisted that she accompany Peter, but he calmly stated – in as calm a voice as he could manage, that is – "Sweetheart, you need to stay here for Lizzie. I also need you to get the full name and address of the medical center so that I can plug it into my GPS. Please call Lugh in thirty minutes to make sure he is with her. I will stay in touch with you. I promise."

Peter left immediately and drove as fast as safety and police-dodging would allow.

64

THURSDAY EVENING, Promise arrived at Dunkirk Hollow Medical Center, this time to find a note from Lydia requesting that she cancel Dr. Roland's patients – no explanation given. Lydia had handwritten the phone numbers next to each student's name. To her surprise, Promise once again felt relieved. These cancellations reinforced the welcomed, though not yet fully assimilated rearrangement of previously traumatic circumstances. She smiled and set about her assigned task.

Thirty minutes later, Promise's cell phone rang. Promise now recognized the number as belonging to Detective McPhearson. Promise had an unusual, intense sense of foreboding as she answered the call.

True to form, the detective quickly made her point: "Promise, despite the District Attorney's best efforts, the judge saw fit to gratify Mark Roland's slick lawyers. He is now out on bail. I want you to know so that you will be careful. I have asked our patrols to make additional circuits around the medical center this evening. Will your on Tuesday. This afternoon he had his bail hearing. He posted the huge amount required by the judge and is now out of jail. It's all over the news here. But Promise hasn't heard. I'm heading over to the medical center now. I thought you might want to know."

"I absolutely do! Thank you for going to be with her. I'm on my way, but it will take me three hours, or less if I'm lucky. Let's keep each other posted." Peter hung up.

Despite Peter's relatively calm demeanor, Brittany empathically tuned in to his sudden burst of inner turmoil. She looked at Peter with horror in her eyes. All she could say was "What?!"

Peter shared Lugh's message. Brittany insisted that she accompany Peter, but he calmly stated – in as calm a voice as he could manage, that is – "Sweetheart, you need to stay here for Lizzie. I also need you to get the full name and address of the medical center so that I can plug it into my GPS. Please call Lugh in thirty minutes to make sure he is with her. I will stay in touch with you. I promise."

Peter left immediately and drove as fast as safety and police-dodging would allow.

64

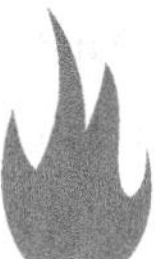

THURSDAY EVENING, Promise arrived at Dunkirk Hollow Medical Center, this time to find a note from Lydia requesting that she cancel Dr. Roland's patients – no explanation given. Lydia had handwritten the phone numbers next to each student's name. To her surprise, Promise once again felt relieved. These cancellations reinforced the welcomed, though not yet fully assimilated rearrangement of previously traumatic circumstances. She smiled and set about her assigned task.

Thirty minutes later, Promise's cell phone rang. Promise now recognized the number as belonging to Detective McPhearson. Promise had an unusual, intense sense of foreboding as she answered the call.

True to form, the detective quickly made her point: "Promise, despite the District Attorney's best efforts, the judge saw fit to gratify Mark Roland's slick lawyers. He is now out on bail. I want you to know so that you will be careful. I have asked our patrols to make additional circuits around the medical center this evening. Will your young man come to accompany you back to campus when you leave at the end of your shift?"

Promise gulped. Her stomach turned with fear. She managed to respond, "Yes, he will come."

Detective McPhearson simply said, "Good. You have my number if you need me, okay?"

"Yes. I have it with me. I will enter it into my contact list. Thank you for letting me know." The call ended, but the fear and anxiety within Promise mounted. She gripped the edge of her desk and forced herself to concentrate on trying to relax. She remembered a tapping technique that her aunt and her mother had taught her long ago. She might not do it perfectly, but she would use it nonetheless.

Thirty minutes later, Lugh ran into the center, attracting the attention of those sitting in the nearby waiting room. He immediately resumed a more normal pace as he also sighed with relief to find Promise sitting behind her desk. Their eyes met; they both realized that the other knew. Promise invited Lugh to come into her reception area and sit by her side.

Promise quietly described the detective's call to her, mentioning the facts first. She couldn't help but express her greater concern about the investigator's deliberated request for an increased police presence that evening. Although Promise did appreciate Detective McPhearson's care for her safety, this plan only reinforced both Promise's and Lugh's anticipation of Mark Roland's unrestrained need to retaliate. Lugh's mention that he had contacted Peter, who departed immediately, only confirmed the reason for her dread. Suddenly, Promise remembered her dream of being chased. She dared to hope that it had simply portrayed Monday night's impression of her fear.

Minutes later, Brittany called Lugh. He resolutely assured her that Promise had his dedicated presence and support during her working hours and that she would not leave the building alone. Promise told her mom not to worry. Of course, everyone recognized that as an impossibility, but Brittany appreciated her daughter's kind attempt at reassurance all the same. The rest of the evening passed smoothly enough, except that Promise couldn't concentrate on any of her assignments. People arrived and departed, mostly preoccupied with their own lives and completely unaware of the potential danger hidden in the darker places.

After everyone left, Promise gathered her books and possessions, then placed them in her bag. She turned out all the lights before she and Lugh proceeded to the front door. The outdoor lighting made their forms quite distinguishable in the night. If Mark Roland lurked in the distance, he would see them, no doubt.

Lugh firmly placed his hand on Promise's shoulder and said, "We are going to be okay. We are going to walk quickly to your car and get into it as fast as we can."

Promise responded, "Got it!"

They closed the door behind them. She locked it, then they stepped into the parking lot. As they hurried toward her vehicle, Lugh spotted the sudden glare of headlights in the distance. The double beams, accompanied by shrieking tires, barreled toward them at tremendous speed. Promise and Lugh stood in the middle of the lot, stunned momentarily, before Lugh yelled, "Promise, we have to run!"

She instinctively threw down her bags, and together they did what they did well, only faster. They strategically stayed close to the trees that lined the lot until their border disappeared into another vast parking area for the neighboring shopping center whose stores had already closed. As they ran through that lot, Mark Roland's car closed in on them. Promise spied two narrow alleyways between three of the buildings. The surgeon's encroaching proximity negated the possibility that either Promise or Lugh might cross midline to join the other. She screamed, "Lugh, we have to split up!"

The speeding vehicle would overtake them in moments. No time to think. Only instincts prevailed. Lugh yelled back to her, "I will find you!" They each ran to the alley closest to them.

Suddenly facing nothing but brick, Mark Roland screeched his car to a halt, took stock of his options, then sped around the strip mall to intercept Promise on the other side.

Lugh's ears recognized immediately what had happened. He ran faster than he ever thought he could, thinking only of Promise and how to reconnect with her as quickly as possible. His vantage point on foot did not afford him a perspective that might offer a plan. He just ran and prayed for her safety.

The alley came to an end, finally; Lugh realized that he now stood in front of the shopping center. He stopped in his tracks. Seeing no sign of Promise, he listened intently. He heard the revved motor and the shrill of skidding tires far to his right. He headed in that direction.

Meanwhile, Promise ran, thinking of Lizzie, trying to match her sister's speed. When she made it to the sidewalk of storefronts, she stopped to get her bearings. Roland's speeding headlights turned the corner and beamed on her presence. With no place to hide, she continued to run straight ahead toward the highway. A trash dumpster offered her a tangible barrier, at least for a few moments. Perhaps one of those patrol cars would come soon. Her phone had gone down with her books.

As Promise ran toward the dumpster, she heard the engine's roar fast approaching from behind her. Did she also hear Lugh calling her father's name? No time to look, just run. She circled behind the huge metal cube brimming with rubbish just as Mark Roland's tires squealed to full stop. He could not proceed further without ramming himself and his vehicle into the dumpster. He leapt out of the car and ran toward her. With her back to the refuse bin, they stood facing each other amidst the smell of trash.

Mark Roland raged, "How dare you!! How dare you have me arrested! Put in jail!! You will pay for this. I will not have it. Your mother got away too easily, but you won't!!"

Promise stood still, her chest heaving but her mind very still and clear. She knew Aikido. This despicable perpetrator had long ago been her son. She would give him one more chance to redeem himself, then let him meet his fate without any guilt whatsoever. She calmly stated, "Mark Roland, you have harmed too many people. You will do so no longer. Stop this now before you have even more to regret."

Promise thought she heard footsteps running toward her, but she dared not take her eyes off her opponent. He snorted like a bull. He callously responded, "It is not I who will have regrets, my dear. But you will!"

With no other warning, he made the move her mother had predicted and demonstrated, the move Promise had anticipated in her practice with Lugh. Mark Roland lunged to grab her throat, leering at her as he had in her dream. Because she had foreseen his menacing glare, it did not disturb her focus. He extended his arm. She quickly deflected it with her own, then stepped out of the way. His vengeful thrust carried him forward on his own momentum. He crashed forcefully into the dumpster, hands first in his attempt to brace himself from the impact. The delicate bones of his professional career fractured into shards of memory. He lay on the ground, howling and venomous. He looked up to find Lugh and Peter now standing at Promise's side.

Lugh gazed down at the man who had once been his son and simply shook his head. "It's over for you now. You can rot in prison or use the time to evolve your soul. Your choice – the only one you'll be allowed to make now. All the rest is over."

Peter smiled. Mark Roland glared at Peter. "You again! What are you doing here?!"

Peter chuckled. "Just witnessing the excellent work our parents just accomplished."

"*What?!!!*" Mark Roland snapped.

Peter shook his head in wonderment. His only response: "You heard what I said. Think about it! You will have plenty of time to do so."

Several police cars, sirens blaring and lights flashing, suddenly arrived on the scene. An ambulance appeared soon afterward. Promise assured everyone that she felt quite fine. The police escorted Mark Roland's transport to the emergency room. They assured Promise that he would remain in custody thereafter.

Promise reached up to hug her father, appreciating his love more than ever. He kissed her forehead with tears in his eyes. He said, "Not in a million years would I have ever wanted this for you. Still, you handled it amazingly well. And I saw that Aikido move. Nice work!"

Promise laughed. She quickly responded, "We can thank my loving sidekick for his willingness to meet the floor over and over again while I practiced!" Promise went to Lugh and kissed him tenderly.

Lugh caressed her face and replied, "When we split up back there, I thought my life would end if I didn't find you on the other side of that building. Please don't ever do that to me again! ... And your dad is right. That Aikido move did the job! You are so brave."

Lugh turned to Peter. "Sir, would you like to stay at my apartment tonight? I'm sure it's been quite a day for you, and it's a long drive home."

Promise glanced toward Lugh before she turned to her father to add, "I'll be staying there tonight, Dad. We can make it a party...." She looked to Peter with hope for his understanding.

Lugh placed his arms around Promise's shoulders. He could feel her tremors from the night's perils demanding their release. He held her close with obvious love.

Peter readily appreciated the situation. He had prepared himself for this weeks ago. He took it in stride as he responded, "Thanks, but not without your mother, who will need her own comforting this evening, I'm sure. The police will want a statement from us – tomorrow, I'm told. I trust you both will be safe now. Let's plan that Brittany and I will return tomorrow and be with you both when you meet with the police."

Promise reached to hug Peter again. She asked, "Will you be okay to drive all the way home tonight, Dad?"

As he embraced his daughter, he, too, felt her trembling. Peter assured her, "I will be fine. The drive will give me a chance to unwind. Don't worry, just sleep. I trust you are in good hands." He made this last comment while looking directly at Lugh.

"I will take good care of her, Peter. I promise you."

Peter shook Lugh's hand with both of his own. He gently caressed Promise's cheek, then wearily returned to his car. The police escorted Promise and Lugh back to her vehicle, where she also retrieved her bag and keys. Peter spoke with Brittany for most of his trip home. Promise and Lugh returned to his apartment, showered, soothed each other with tenderness, and fell fast asleep.

65

THE SUN STREAKED THROUGH Lugh's bedroom blinds and shone brilliantly in Promise's eyes, awakening her from a dream. Alethea had come to her and smiled with approval and gratitude. Promise let herself come to consciousness gradually, soon realizing that Lugh had already risen. The smell of breakfast permeated the airspace. She readily acknowledged her hunger.

She dressed and greeted Lugh at the breakfast bar with a grateful caress. Brad soon appeared, clearly having just awoken and still working to fully focus on the day. He hadn't heard about the events of the previous evening. Lugh poured him a cup of coffee and invited him to share the meal with them while they told him all about it. By the end of breakfast, Brad just stared at them, wide-eyed and amazed that they seemed so calm.

Promise sat with her chin in her palm and just smiled. She peacefully responded to Brad's reaction by saying, "The worst is over now. Roland's lawyers will offer their challenges, but nothing can top last night. The worst is definitely over."

Brad mused aloud, "I wonder if it made the news?" He turned on their television and found the proper station.

Within minutes, the news host described the hospitalization and re-arrest of "Dr. Mark Roland, a noted surgeon at Dunkirk Hollow General Hospital, who had been released on bail Thursday afternoon for charges related to sexual assault. Only hours later, he tried to run down one of his alleged victims with his car. In the altercation that followed, his hands were severely injured. He will remain under police custody while he is being treated for his injuries. We will have more on this story when that information becomes available."

Lugh glanced toward Promise to find her looking at him with surprise. "I know I said the worst is over just minutes ago," she reflected, "but hearing this adds nerve-racking publicity to the whole scenario. It occurs to me that some listeners will enjoy the melodrama, some will feel betrayed, and some will feel frightened and maybe then relieved to realize he can't hurt them anymore. I really do want to avoid the thrill-seekers. They only traumatize people all over again."

Lugh nodded. "Let's try to keep a very low profile on this whole thing, okay?" He said this while gazing directly at Brad.

Brad responded, "You can count on me to keep a lid on it. The announcer's energy alone felt wicked. I don't want either of you to have to face that."

Promise replied, "Thanks, Brad. Thanks for your help and your friendship all along the way." Brad just smiled and gestured with his upward-directed thumb.

Promise helped Lugh restore the kitchen to order while Brad showered. In the midst of these activities, Brittany called and felt immediate relief to hear Promise's voice sounding fairly calm and stable. Brittany's own memories of the morning after Mark Roland had assaulted her – and how vulnerable she felt afterward – had risen to the surface of her consciousness. Promise sensed this and said, "Mom, maybe we both need to do some tapping to get past this. You can refresh my memory for how to do it when you come today!"

"Good idea!" Brittany replied. She also confirmed that they hoped to arrive by one o'clock. Detective McPhearson had already contacted them, wanting to take Peter's statement at two. After Brittany and Promise completed their call, the detective called Promise as well. They would all meet together at the police station at two o'clock.

Promise and Lugh abandoned all intentions of attending classes that day. Instead, they went for a run, showered, and walked to Promise's dorm where she could change her clothes and explain all that had happened to Mel, who listened with rapt attention. At the conclusion of the narrative, Mel breathed a sigh of relief; she would no longer have to keep her scheduled appointment with Dr. Mark Roland.

Peter and Brittany arrived at Lugh's apartment as the one o'clock hour approached. With hugs all around, everyone tried to valiantly engage with superficial conversation. Brittany finally stopped them, saying, "Last night, Mark Roland tried to kill you both. There is nothing normal about today whatsoever! We don't have to pretend. I'm just glad you three are safe!"

Peter reached for Brittany's hand. While she had not been physically present for the traumatic events, they had impacted her profoundly nonetheless. Lugh sensitively reached for her arm and stroked it for comfort. He understood, now more than ever, what it feels like to watch and wait.

Lugh had purchased lunch items for all of them based on Promise's suggestions. They sat together for a quick meal before heading to the police station. Upon their arrival there, the officer at the desk ushered them to the quieter waiting area where Promise had once held space for Alice. They each took a seat on the not-so-comfortable folding chairs.

Not minutes later, the door to an interviewing room opened and Viola exited, discreetly wiping residual tears from her eyes. Promise rose immediately and approached her.

"Viola...," she gently murmured.

Viola saw Promise and approached her with a hug. Tears again poured down her cheeks as she quietly said, "Promise, I'm so sorry I didn't come forward sooner. Maybe if I had, he wouldn't have been released on bail. I know you were the one he tried to run over with his car. I am so sorry. I'm so glad to see that you are mostly all right. Are you okay?"

As they separated from their embrace, Promise kept her hands on Viola's arms while saying, "Viola, I am fine. I so appreciate your courage to come here. I assume you just made a statement to the police?" When Viola nodded her yes, Promise continued, "All of us together will put him away for a very long time. Thank you so much."

They exchanged phone numbers with their phones in hand. Viola departed as Detective McPhearson appeared from behind the same door. She invited them all into the room and apologized for the starkness of their gathering place. She dryly noted, "My office is the size of a shoebox."

Promise made the introductions, then they all took a seat. Detective McPhearson first directed her comments to Promise. "Are you all right? Were you hurt in any way by what happened last evening?"

Promise reassured her, "I'm fine. I really only have one sore spot on my arm that will probably turn black and blue, but I'm sure it will fade with time."

Brittany looked alarmed. Peter remembered the bruise Roland had given her many years ago. Clearly, what happened to Promise had reactivated that former assault even more acutely than Peter already realized. He would make special effort to help Brittany through this when their interview ended. In the meantime, he fully expected her to produce a tube of arnica cream for Promise's use.

The detective asked Promise to show her the injured area. Brittany's alarm only intensified when Promise reluctantly lifted her sleeve to reveal the six-by-three-inch display of red and blue discoloration along the outer edge of her left forearm. In keeping with Peter's prediction, the arnica cream appeared. Detective McPhearson suggested that they take certified photographs of the contusion on Promise's arm as evidence of Mark Roland's aggression. She also asked Promise to explain exactly how the bruising occurred.

Promise looked to Lugh, who stood in response to Promise's wordless communication. Promise also stood, smiled at him, then, turning to the detective, said, "This is exactly how it happened. Lugh will stand in for Mark Roland."

Peter smiled and spontaneously offered, "And I'll catch him before he hits the floor!"

Lugh winked at Peter and said, "Good man! Thank you."

With that, Lugh slowly gestured to grab Promise's throat as they had practiced numerous times. Promise described how she responded while she also physically demonstrated her actions. She raised her left forearm to deflect Lugh's/Mark Roland's right-handed lunge toward her neck, but this time she made no physical contact – her arm really hurt too much for that. Her movements flowed like a martial arts master; she explained them in the language of Aikido. Lugh dutifully let his slow-motion thrust propel him forward, trusting that Peter would, in fact, catch him.

Peter did so with a grin. He said, "You took the floor for her all those times. It saved her life. *Thank you!*"

Lugh smiled broadly. Detective McPhearson was obviously impressed. Promise then also described how Mark Roland fell into the trash dumpster on his own momentum. She surmised, "That's why he probably fractured some bones in his hands, while I only have this one bruise."

The detective smiled wryly and simply exclaimed, "Well, then!" She added that Mark Roland had sustained significant injuries to his fingers and wrists, likely jeopardizing any hope for his future surgical career. She also added that with two claims of sexual assault, Promise's allegations that he stalked her and made verbal threats of harm, followed by last night's attempt to run her and Lugh down with his vehicle, while out on bail no less, he would certainly not be granted bail this time. He would also likely spend the rest of his life in prison.

Promise, Lugh, Peter, and Brittany all heaved a simultaneous sigh of relief. Detective McPhearson witnessed this and at first assumed that these parents were simply grateful for their daughter's future safety. She soon discovered the backstory when Brittany produced her document.

"Detective, I don't know if you realize that Mark Roland has a long history of sexual assault, physical aggression, and verbal threats." Peter, Lugh, and Promise exchanged glances, wondering how far back she planned to describe.

Brittany continued, "He threatened me and tried to assault me before Promise was born. I planned to press charges then, but we agreed that if he left his position at the hospital immediately – where I also worked – and avoided all contact with me, did not work within a one-hundred-mile radius of my current or future employment, and did nothing to harm Peter or myself, we would drop the charges. We insisted that he sign a document admitting that he had assaulted me, and that I might produce it if he violated any of those conditions."

Detective McPhearson reviewed the document, then said, "Technically, he hasn't violated the conditions noted here, assuming you haven't changed your work location or residence. How might this be applicable?"

"Detective," Brittany retorted, "I don't know if you have children, but if you violate my daughter in any way, you violate me. My submission of this document stands. He has a history of assault that dates way back."

Peter, Promise, and Lugh caught the *double entendre* and discreetly masked their smiles. Lugh glanced toward Promise. She tilted her head in a gesture that implied: See, I told you my mother had warrior blood in her! Lugh wordlessly acknowledged her intimation with a smile.

Detective McPhearson replied, "Point taken!"

They concluded the afternoon with formal statements taken from each of them. Just before they planned to part company, the detective received notice of another complaint related to sexual assault that would require her attention. Appreciative for the timing, they left the room together. Promise glanced into the waiting area across the hall and received one more surprise.

Kassi saw Promise and immediately rose from her seat and approached her. The bruise around her eye sparked Promise's noticeable alarm. Promise stepped away from her loved ones to speak more personally to Kassi, who shyly realized that her mark of liberation had stirred Promise's care and concern.

Promise quickly asked, "Kassi, are you all right?"

Kassi responded, "I am now. I was a fool to think that a jealous boyfriend was worth my suffering in silence. He hit me for other reasons, but no matter. I saw the light. We aren't together anymore, and I am free to do what I should have done when you first contacted me. I saw in the news what Mark Roland did last night. I knew you had to be on the receiving end. You were right all along. We have to stick together. I'm here to give my statement and add to the length of his sentence. He can't be set free to roam the streets ever again."

Promise reached forward to hug Kassi. They resolutely held each other before they exchanged their phone numbers. Kassi then entered the interview room, soon to be joined by Detective McPhearson.

In the momentary interim, Promise glanced toward the reception area to witness Marcia talking to the officer behind the desk. Promise quietly noted to the detective, "She will make the fourth. I have no other names for you!"

Detective McPhearson smiled. She excused herself briefly to Kassi, then walked with Promise and her loved ones toward Marcia. Promise intuitively, correctly assessed that Marcia needed a hug. They embraced; Promise thanked her for her courage. She introduced Marcia to their detective, who immediately did her best to set Marcia at ease with the process that would follow. She invited her to have a seat in the waiting area. She would be with her as soon as she could.

After the detective returned to the interview room, Promise explained that there were now five brave women willing to testify against Mark Roland, ensuring that he would remain in prison for a very, very long time. Promise then asked Marcia if she needed someone to be with her. Marcia declined that offer, stating that a friend would soon join her. They exchanged phone numbers before parting company, both committed to the path ahead.

That evening, Peter and Brittany enjoyed having dinner with Promise and Lugh, Peter's treat. During a quieter moment in the midst of their meal, Peter wondered aloud, "So, do you think life will be normal now?"

They all looked at him quizzically. Brittany shook her head and asked, "Peter, what does that even mean?"

They all laughed. They really didn't know!

66

AS FEBRUARY'S COLD WINDS blew into March, Promise and Lugh finally settled into a welcomed rhythm for their last semester together at Stella Maris University. They continued to meet for a run on the indoor track whenever they could; Wednesday afternoons had become a reliable ritual. They immersed themselves in their classwork and shared lively discussions regarding their discoveries, especially when the material either one learned complemented the other's. Most weeks, they also spent two nights together in Lugh's apartment. Mel adjusted nicely, having developed a relationship of her own.

Meanwhile, Lugh received official notice of his acceptance to the graduate program of his choice in Arizona. He immediately sent word to the professor who had interviewed him months ago, thanking him again for the use of his complimentary email. Lugh also respectfully expressed his interest in furthering their connection once he moved closer to campus. His professor responded with enthusiasm, eagerly looking forward to more stimulating discussions with Lugh.

Consequently, Promise also researched academic programs in Arizona, having made the decision to accompany Lugh there. She also considered an alternative major. She appreciated learning about how human beings think, feel, and act, as discussed in her psychology classes. She sensed an unacknowledged bias that pegged these parameters to a particular societal upbringing and the collective sense of normality, however. Her intuition suggested that she might like to explore what lay beyond the "standard" definitions of normal.

Through her extensive discussions with Lugh, Promise recognized that cultural differences might affect one's psychology, as would an individual's relative capacity for insight. Lugh frequently hypothesized that *Homo sapiens* have cyclically advanced and regressed in their development of consciousness, as reflected in the progress and destruction of their successive civilizations across the centuries. He and Promise both suspected that, relatively speaking, the ancients may have possessed more knowledge and ingenuity than currently recognized by modern theories.

Additionally, Promise often wondered how shamans and those with extrasensory perceptiveness, such as herself, might expand psychology's understanding of what it means to be human. That expansion would need to include an exploration of the unconscious. Aunt Tara had mentioned the work of Carl Jung several times. Promise wanted to sort this out more carefully. She hoped her aunt would have wisdom to share when they met during Promise's spring break.

The frequency of Promise's contacts with Detective McPhearson had decreased considerably. During their last call, the detective requested Promise's logs and notes. They agreed that Promise might redact the names of patients not related to their case. The investigation was proceeding smoothly, given that all those involved, except for Mark Roland, cooperated with the necessary interviews and the production of what evidence they had to offer. Detective McPhearson stated that she would forward these documents to the district attorney within a few weeks. The legal process would likely drag on in response to the obstructions posed by the doctor's lawyers. No matter. The case would make it to trial within a year or two. If Promise moved out of state, she should simply plan to return when the court required her testimony.

Promise admittedly didn't appreciate having this hang over her head for two years, but with perspective she realized that it proved infinitely better than having to be vigilant about Mark Roland's whereabouts and his impulsive, destructive actions. Others would now also be safe. She decided to make some notes for herself so that her memory would be accurate for her eventual role as a witness.

Promise also continued to work at Dunkirk Hollow Medical Center, where a physician's assistant took over the responsibility for completing sports physicals for SMU. Christina no longer worked at the center. The new nurse presented as a very responsible professional. Promise observed no further oddities in the scheduling and provision of athlete physicals thereafter.

Strangely, Lydia never said anything about what had happened that night to Promise. Consequently, Promise felt no loyalty to the job, and no concern regarding her decision to take vacation time during the week of spring break and to leave her position altogether by the end of April. Anticipating a move to Arizona in the fall, she wanted to spend the summer with her family. She would enjoy hearing more about Lizzie's college plans as they evolved as well.

During spring break, Promise and Lugh parted company, both realizing that they needed to spend time with their other loved ones. They connected by phone at least once every day during that time. Being apart helped each of them realize how much they truly appreciated being together.

Promise and Lizzie enjoyed two sleepovers that week. Brittany and her daughters also went for a run as the weather shifted to warmer temperatures. Peter found himself relaxing into the relative peace even as he continued to contemplate what thoughts he might share when he accepted the Rainbow Center's award. No longer having to worry about Promise did free his consciousness for inspiration. He simply needed to wait for its arrival.

On Tuesday afternoon, while Lizzie attended her high school classes followed by track practice, and her mother was still at work, Promise found Peter sitting at his desk, staring out the window. Quirkie lay at his feet, simply lifting his head in response to her appearance at the door. Promise smiled, remembering Fonzy with great fondness. Peter noticed her presence and welcomed her to join him.

Promise picked a comfy armchair positioned close to his and settled in. Peter smiled with his own memories of her sitting on his lap as a three-year-old. How things had changed! At least she could pronounce Prometheus' name correctly now. He told her that story about "Pemus" and Promise laughed.

Promise finally asked the question that had come and gone in her mind throughout her life: "Dad, why did you name me Promise, really?"

Peter chuckled as he replied, "I really wanted to name you Prometheus, but your mother wouldn't have it. She suggested Promise, so we made the compromise. When you were three and could only say 'Pemus,' your mother had some good 'I told you so' moments. In retrospect, I truly think Promise has suited you much better."

Promise smiled. "During one of my shamanic journeys, Alethea said that you and mom haven't given yourselves enough credit for your intuitions. She said it with praise, noting how you have let them guide you nonetheless. It seems my interactions with Mark Roland were related to a promise, after all. You named me well."

Peter's facial expression registered his simultaneous surprise and pleasure.

Promise asked, "What were you working on when I interrupted you?"

Peter tapped the eraser end of his pencil on the papers before him, suddenly looking more concerned. "A holistic organization has decided to recognize the Rainbow Healing Arts Center with an award. You and Lugh are invited to be my guests, by the way. It's set for mid-May, after your semester concludes, I think."

"That's great, Dad! Congratulations! We'd love to come. But, why do you look so concerned?"

"I have to give an acceptance speech, and I'm not sure what to say. I know the myths of Chiron and Prometheus played a huge role in my decision to take on the project in the first place, but I'm at a loss for the overall message. I have several ideas that are logical, but nothing stirs my soul. I'd like this to be meaningful. I'm just a little stuck. Any thoughts, my dear mythology wizard?"

Promise laughed. After a few moments of deeper reflection, she replied, "Dad, maybe your interest in Chiron and Prometheus can provide the deeper meaning you seek. They both suffered. They both had to wait and endure while in pain. They did so with a very particular attitude toward their process. They both issued forth some form of light in the end. You had to stand by and wait while I worked it out with Mark Roland – maybe also long ago while Mom did too, I'm guessing. You may be able to draw upon your own experience."

Peter nodded his agreement in response to that painful recognition.

Promise continued, "Maybe between the two of us, you are the real Prometheus. I'm thinking that I resonate with Inanna better anyway. You really have lived his story, especially while working to establish the Rainbow Center. Maybe Prometheus can guide you to help us all understand more about the healing process?"

Peter's eyebrows furrowed in deeper thought. Moments later, he said, "Promise, my dear, I think you have suggested exactly what I need! I can see my way through this now. Thank you!"

"Anytime, Dad! Glad to be of help."

They smiled at each other. Peter rose to give Promise a huge hug. He added, "You are an amazing young woman. I like your Lugh too.

I'm appreciating our much healthier and happier family reunion." He winked. Promise laughed.

She replied, "Me too, Dad! Me too!"

67

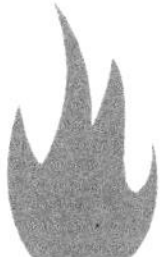

AT THEIR APPOINTED TIME on Wednesday afternoon, Promise rang the bell to her aunt and uncle's residence. Tara opened the door, beaming at the sight of her beloved protégé. They hugged with warm affection, then went to the kitchen to prepare a refreshment for their time together. Alex had to attend a professional meeting, but he hoped to return before Promise departed. Quick updates included that Tara had retired at the end of February. To her surprise, she enjoyed her newfound freedom and looked forward to experiencing the Caribbean with Alex the following week.

Once they settled themselves in Tara's healing room and Promise had reached for the rose quartz orb, they smiled in recognition of their ritual and launched into their discussion. Promise shared the most recent news regarding the police investigation of Mark Roland's criminal actions. She also reflected on her classes, and, of course, her relationship with Lugh. Tara witnessed the joy this relationship brought to her cherished goddaughter's life. She rejoiced in her happiness.

A pause arose in their conversation during which Promise considered once again how she might tell her aunt about her shamanic experience at the Imbolc gathering. Tara sensed Promise's inner flummox and waited with great curiosity. Promise sighed, not knowing how this might sound to her aunt's ears. Would it even make sense to her? Promise decided to simply state the truth.

"Aunt Tara, I'm wanting to tell you about the shamanic journeys I had during the Imbolc celebration in early February. There's no easy way to say this. Alethea came to me again, both times. She told me that she is my higher self. We have shared the same soul across lifetimes. It also seems that you and I have been traveling together and helping each other for a very long time."

Tara's eyes almost popped out of her head. She sat speechless for several minutes as her mind wordlessly processed her many memories: all the strange feelings of familiarity that she had experienced throughout Promise's life; her goddaughter's dreams about the obelisk as well as seeing Tara as a priestess during that same ancient lifetime; and the odd sense that Tara had heard the dream about the orbs before – even though she didn't understand it so fully until recently. As her shock receded, she smiled.

Tara simply said, "Of course you are!"

Promise laughed. She had never imagined this response. Once again, it helped reinforce her own deeper knowing. Promise added, "Alethea told me that you were the village seer during my lifetime as Glenna. You were teaching me how to interpret my dreams even then!"

Tara just shook her head in amazement. Her aunt then confessed, "Promise, before you were born, I had a dream in which Alethea – your soul – came to me, asking that I guide others through an experience of time. I now realize that you as Alethea were hoping to ensure your own birth. You needed to deal with Mark Roland, I guess? To meet Lugh again? To finally meet your father, who was your just-born son in that ancient lifetime? Does all this make sense to you?"

"It does, Aunt Tara, and I can make even more sense of it for you. It seems my soul, which I can call Alethea for clarity, had experienced a tragedy of huge proportions many lifetimes ago. Her mate and all her children were killed, except for the soul of Mark Roland, who survived in a traumatized state of hate and vengeance. Because Alethea had the second sight even then, she had predicted it, but when her mate didn't want to believe her, she tried to ignore the warning. Sadly, the onslaught happened just as she had foreseen it. She blamed herself.

"Since then, Alethea's and my soul incarnated many times as the mother of Mark Roland's soul, trying to heal the tragic damage to his psyche with no success. She finally realized that she needed to release the promise she had made long ago to save him. My incarnation was to accomplish that very deed. The night he chased Lugh and me with his car, I did give our former son one last chance to change his ways. He refused and tried to physically attack me instead. I simply stepped aside, and he fell to his own ruin.... In hindsight, it seems my parents named me well, but it really had little to do with Prometheus."

Tara nodded her understanding. "Prometheus always spoke to your dad's soul, really. But you have lived well into your name, after all."

"Thank you for all your help with that, Aunt Tara. I could not have done so without you. I do have a question, though."

"Please ask whatever you like," Tara replied.

"Well, I've been studying mythology, and I especially resonate with the story of Inanna. She descended to the Underworld, which the earliest myths described as a place of regeneration for the next growing season. Later in the development of the human psyche, that lower realm became associated with a hellish place. The first description sounds like healing, the second more like punishment and destruction. Why that difference? What is the Underworld, really? And how can we relate to it?"

"Good questions! I suspect your experience with Mark Roland has prompted some of this?" Tara asked.

"Actually, yes. Alethea's and my soul made a promise to reincarnate many times, hoping to rekindle in him the experience of what love feels like. He rejected that love over and over. If my experience as Glenna reveals anything at all, it highlights the price she paid, the suffering she endured in her efforts to further that aim. Our society supports our collective agenda to suffer on behalf of others. Religions encourage it, in fact. Are they actually asking us to go to a hellish place in an attempt to have another soul released? Does that really work? It didn't for Mark Roland. Alethea's intention for this lifetime, now my new mission, has been to finally let him go.

"Oddly, I have no guilt about what happened to him after he chased Lugh and me with his car that night. He will never work again as a surgeon, and he will never get out of prison, hopefully. I feel no need to save him. I have surrendered him to a Higher Power, a power greater than anything I might ever have. But that doesn't accord with what religions tell us to do. Can you help me make sense of all this, Aunt Tara?"

Tara sighed. "I want you to know that I just love your soul, Promise. Such deep, profound questions! I also think your thoughts are dancing around something very important.

"It would seem that the Underworld has layers. Souls in the darkness who have not forgotten the light, who hold it in their hearts and long for it to return to their lives – they do suffer but not needlessly or without meaning. Your goddess Inanna descended to the Underworld to release her lover, if I recall correctly. She trusted and did what she could to ensure that the light would find and revive her. It did. This was a meaningful and purposeful descent. It changed her, and she insisted that it do so for her betterment. This has been your soul's journey as well.

"In contrast, when a soul dwells in darkness and cares nothing for the light, when all it can call to itself is more darkness, that would be hell. Evil heaped upon evil until it destroys itself. That's what happened to Mark Roland. It sounds like your soul finally realized that it does not belong in Hell. His continuing refusal to seek the Light has rendered all your efforts to release him from that infernal state ineffective and meaningless. He made his choice. So did you. You refused to give up the Light. You can't dwell in Light and reside in Hell for more than a very brief visit. Hell will not want you within its domain!"

Promise laughed with deep recognition. Alethea had offered similar reflections. Promise mentioned this to Tara, who laughed in turn. Tara added, "Alethea once told me that we have lived many lifetimes together, alternating roles as to who taught whom. I guess we have rubbed off on each other significantly!"

Promise smiled. "Yep! You have certainly rubbed off on me!"

When this topic seemed finished, Promise shifted their focus onto her more pressing thoughts about her future. She shared that she very much wanted to join Lugh in Arizona. Tara simply nodded knowingly. Promise also questioned her pursuit of a psychology degree in the context of her more current interests.

Promise summarized all this by saying, "I realize that I am profoundly fascinated by mythology, shamanism, and the human experience of what lies on the other side of this reality's consciousness. I truly suspect that these areas of exploration have informed what Lugh describes as a prior human civilization that had much more wisdom and functionality than we do now.

"It seems to me that empires and societies reach the limit of their productivity when some form of human hubris takes over. Their consequent decline leaves an enormous amount of destruction in its wake. In many ways, this reminds me of Mark Roland's trajectory as an individual, but I am now also considering a grander, collective scale.

"Our world situation seems to be in a similar state of peril. How can I use my gifts to improve our odds? Is it best to sit with individuals in a counseling session, one after the other, to accomplish this mission? Are there ways to communicate deeper, broader understandings that might help a larger number of people? Which academic course of study will guide me to make the most of my life?"

Tara smiled once again. "As I said a few minutes ago, 'such deep, profound questions!' Let's tease these apart one by one.

"Psychology will give you a wonderful understanding of the human ego, how it is formed, what injures its development, and how it malfunctions when things go wrong. We need a healthy ego if we are to function well in the day-to-day, conscious world. With this in mind, the study of psychology also offers an exposure to numerous kinds of therapy for how to address dysfunctional egos.

"But there is also an unconscious realm that the ego cannot know. In its never-ending pursuit of wholeness, the mysterious unknown steadily reveals itself to egos willing to see it. Generally speaking, wounded or vulnerable egos may try to block access to the unconscious as a method of self-protection, but in such cases, the hidden realms slip through those defenses willy-nilly. People with such wounds and defenses may blurt things out or act impulsively, for example. In contrast, those with healthy egos can choose to explore the depths of the Mystery in a way that enriches their overall life experience yet still allows them to function adequately in a social context, to live well among other egos. Does this make sense?"

"Perfect sense, Aunt Tara. Please go on."

"Okay. If we use simple imagery, your gift of extrasensory perception results from having "holes" in your ego. These openings allow you to access the hidden, unconscious realms more easily. Unlike those with weak or wounded egos, your ego's overall health and strength have enabled you to use the information that comes through these gaps – in your dreams, your empathy, your intuitions, your shamanic journeys – to guide you toward higher wisdom, but at a price.

"People whose consciousness aligns itself with a conventional sense of reality have not typically understood your offerings. Consequently, they have not valued them either. You have had to learn to value yourself;

you have had to ground yourself in a higher level of consciousness. Having Alethea's soul as your own explains how strong you are and how you have managed it."

Promise nodded her understanding and agreement.

Tara continued, "Having these gifts, you are really asking how to remember the wisdom of the ages while also currently learning how to present that wisdom in ways that modern humans can digest. The world will tell you that you really can't do this at all. It will tell you this because the collective mindset doesn't understand your gifts, doesn't believe that the ancients had wisdom, and often closes its purview to any other possibilities. Like most egos, the perspective of our contemporary world likes to think that it knows or can discover and then control all that needs to be known.

"If you listen to the world's viewpoint, you will be left living half a life, which is really no life at all, given the dimensions and intensity of your nature. If you choose to live differently than what the world calls normal, you will have to bypass its agenda and simply do what you love. Let what you love call you to your next step. As they might say of a dog using its instinct of smell on a walk, follow your nose. Or better, follow your heart. It's nothing defined, but it's full of life. What are your thoughts about that?"

Promise laughed heartily. "It's so freeing!!! Maybe expensive, but we'll see, won't we! My heart loves Lugh. My head loves learning. My perceptions dwell in seen and unseen realms, and, thanks to you, I have learned to tell the difference.

"I will go to Arizona, and I might even continue to major in psychology, but I will take every mythology course I can. I will also take some anthropology classes focused on human evolution, and maybe some religious studies courses to better understand ancient spiritual practices. You have mentioned Carl Jung a few times, Aunt Tara. I think that eventually I might like a graduate degree in mythology and folklore, or perhaps I will want to study Jungian psychology.

"It's clear to me now that I have to craft my own future. The ancients told the human story through their myths. I want to understand them better. Ancient myths have helped me these past two years. Maybe their message needs a wider reach. Maybe they will help others as well.

"I don't know the specifics right now, but that's okay. I will take every elective that strikes my fancy and likely minor in something relevant. I will enjoy my life! That's my new promise! This is perfect!" Promise beamed with joy.

Tara reached over to warmly embrace her goddaughter. This was perfect, indeed!

68

BRITTANY AND PROMISE DOZED next to each other on the plane taking them to Arizona. Two weeks after spring break, Promise had received notice of her acceptance as a transfer student. Her parents encouraged her to visit the campus so that she might experience its environment for herself. Their destination's April weather offered an enjoyable respite from the cold temperatures slowly leaving SMU's locale. Lugh had driven them to the airport, making suggestions along the way regarding some local restaurants and special places they might like to visit during their trip.

After they landed, Brittany and Promise drove a rental car to their hotel, less than half a mile from the university's grounds. They had an appointment the next day with Deborah Wilkins, Ph.D., Dean of Liberal Arts. Promise hoped their discussion would help her clarify her choice of major. Brittany also encouraged Promise to find her own place to live for her junior year. She had no illusions about Promise spending considerable time with Lugh, but she encouraged her daughter to establish a sense of individual presence in the community before she fully committed to living with him. Promise appreciated the wisdom of her mother's advice. They planned to explore housing options after Promise had her meeting with the dean, followed by a tour.

Dr. Wilkens, a warm and gracious woman in her mid-fifties, cordially invited both Brittany and Promise to join her in her office. Her desk, set in the corner alongside huge windows, provided a beautiful view of the campus quadrangle now in full bloom. They seated themselves in the armchairs and sofas surrounding a coffee table on the other side of the room. Filled bookshelves lined the walls, artistically bordering intermittently placed photographs of the university. The atmosphere felt simultaneously academic and welcoming.

After they completed the more formal introductions and information gathering, Dean Wilkins asked Promise about her interests. When Promise shared her fascination with mythology, her curiosity about human evolution, and her sense that the ancients had possessed a wisdom that might guide current social issues and concerns, the dean seemed especially excited. She asked Promise to describe what had contributed to her enthusiasm about these topics.

Promise hesitantly replied, "Well, to be honest, I've always had an interest in mysteries and hidden realms. My boyfriend, who will be attending graduate school here in the fall, hopes to pursue research regarding civilizations that existed prior to the last Ice Age. We've had intriguing discussions relating the content of my psychology and mythology classes to his significant concentration on ancient peoples. We've both explored shamanic workshops together as well. In the midst of all this, I've discovered that I really enjoy mythology even more than I do psychology. It invites me to wonder about our distant ancestors' access to the spiritual realm.

"I want to make a contribution to the world, and I strongly suspect that the ancients had access to a wisdom that eludes us in our current day. Trying to understand their consciousness through their pottery and cave paintings offers one approach. I suspect their myths offer significant clues as well. Even though I'm not thrilled with psychology in general, it may be helpful someday for me to understand the human psyche – maybe I will want to study Jungian psychology. I just don't know right now. I would simply like to position myself to pursue what calls me when I arrive wherever it is that I'm supposed to go! Can you help me identify the best academic major to pursue?"

Dr. Wilkins smiled broadly at this point. She replied, "Promise, we are in the process of introducing a new major course of study into our undergraduate program for the fall semester. It will focus on ancient civilizations and explore their religious, artistic, cultural, and mythological perspectives and activities.

"Having examined your transcript, I can see that with one more course you will have enough credits to qualify for a minor in psychology. You have also completed many of the basic requirements this university holds for general studies. You might choose to major in Ancient Civilizations. The program will be sponsored by the anthropology department, although its courses will involve interdisciplinary collaboration by necessity. We hope to have it listed on our website within the week."

Brittany listened to this dialogue between Promise and the dean, reveling in her daughter's depth of focus and intention, articulated so clearly and with such a passion for service. Brittany also observed the dean's delight in having the opportunity to impact a young person's future so profoundly. This new program in ancient civilizations sounded perfect for Promise. The eagerness on her daughter's face suggested that she thought so too.

Promise bubbled with excitement after their meeting, thrilled to finally have a sense of her future, at least on the shorter term. She and her mother toured the campus with a student guide who shared many little-known tips for how to negotiate various aspects of such a large institution. Afterwards, Brittany and Promise procured a map of the local environs and investigated rental apartment listings, hoping to get a feel for Promise's options. When they left Arizona that next afternoon, Promise felt like she could envision her future there with hopeful anticipation. She had her own discoveries to share with Lugh as well.

Lugh picked them up at the airport, this time late in the evening. He made his room available to Brittany and Promise while he slept on the couch. The next day, Brittany parted company with them, having enjoyed her time thoroughly but also eager to return to Peter and Lizzie. Promise sincerely thanked her mother for making all these wonderful adventures and discoveries possible.

Brittany returned home to find Peter eagerly waiting for her. They had conversed intermittently during that whirlwind trip, but he wanted to hear more about Brittany's impressions of the campus and Promise's reaction to it. He personally acknowledged his need for many positive indicators to compensate for the geographic distance that would soon come between them.

Brittany had obviously reflected on these very issues during her long drive home. She hugged Peter with great love, wistfulness, and excitement. He gazed directly into her eyes with understanding. She smiled in response to his recognition of her complex emotions. In that moment, she expressed what mattered most to her heart. "Peter, our daughter has grown into an amazing young woman!"

Peter nodded. He already knew as much, as did Brittany. To launch Promise into this larger context, which undeniably included her transition into adulthood, called them to the next phase of their lives as parents. Lizzie would graduate high school the following year, then follow in her sister's footsteps soon enough. Endless transitions, so full of life.

Peter and Brittany hugged again. With the resolve born of love, wisdom, and surrender, they pledged to each other: they would share their daughters graciously with the world, and with gratitude for the privilege.

69

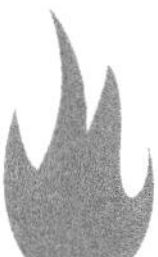

UPON HER RETURN TO SMU, Promise and Lugh concentrated on bringing their semester to a successful conclusion. Freed from all their previous strain and struggle, they joyously continued their runs together on the track, looked forward to Lugh's graduation, and imagined and planned their future together in the warm surrounds of Arizona sunshine.

Promise worked her last weeks at Dunkirk Hollow Medical Center and arranged to keep in touch with Kay. Promise still hoped that someday she might learn astrology. She parted company with Lydia without much ado. Promise acknowledged to herself that Lydia had played a role in this past year's drama, which had served the intentions of her own wise soul. Promise decided to be grateful and move on.

Even as the semester's end quickly approached, bringing with it the typically dreaded week of finals, Lugh and Promise opted to attend Dylan's Beltane celebration to mark the beginning of Celtic summer. The joy of May Day felt like the perfect way to ceremonially acknowledge their emergence into the next phase of their lives. Again, Lugh drove them to their destination, the converted barn surrounded by forest. In this new season, blossoms blazed with color all around them. The bare trees of winter had given birth to the green hues of springtime. Insects buzzed around them sporadically, reminding them that Nature belongs to all creatures.

After Dylan welcomed them, they set up their stations in a circle around the altar. Dylan explained that Beltane not only invited the commemoration of new life in Nature, but in ancient times its celebrants also enjoyed the making of babies in the wild darkness surrounding the Beltane fires. Their ritual that day would center around the beheading game, an old Irish myth in which a knight offered to be ceremonially beheaded. All parties understood that he would return the following day to similarly behead the one who had beheaded him.

Dylan explained that through their adaptation of this ritual, each participant would identify a specific form of suffering in the world that needed healing. Having paired with a companion, one member from each twosome would join the others to drum a trance-inducing rhythm while their partners danced, working to shamanically embody, then raise their chosen suffering into their crowns. Following this, the dancers would allow themselves to be symbolically beheaded by their partner, who would then ritually cleanse the polluted head of all its turmoil. The beheaders would then reunite the figuratively purified head with their partner's body, having completed the shamanic intention of relieving the planet of some of its pain. In the next round, the couples would switch roles and repeat the process to bring more healing into the world.

During their first journey, participants would each meet with their wise guide to discover what suffering they felt called to gather for cleansing. Their second crossing to the hidden realm would involve the ritual's garnering of that pain for its cleansing and release. Promise and Lugh agreed to be partners for this adventure, then they each prepared themselves for their respective otherworldly travels. They settled themselves on their mats. Promise reconnected with her lion, Lugh with his boar, as Dylan began to drum.

Promise and her lion stood at the edge of the forest and once again ran toward the interior. An eagle swooped down and carried them both across the waters of time and space. Promise and her spirit animal landed in a lush garden of exotic greenery brimming with flowers of every color, size, and shape. Not twenty yards away she spied a small hut with vases of blooms at the door. She approached to find Alethea waiting for her once again.

Alethea beamed as she extended her arms in warm welcome. She said, "Hello, Promise. I thought you might like to see where we lived in one of our lifetimes. In this place, we guided your Aunt Tara to become a priestess. I am happy to have you consciously join me again!"

Promise smiled broadly. "And I am thrilled to see you, dear soul. So much has happened since I last spoke to you so formally. I'm thinking you know all about it. I sense you feel satisfied. Am I right about that?"

"Ah, dear one, you most certainly are. You handled it perfectly. So did Lugh. Honestly, I am really pleased, especially with how happy you are. We have a chance to focus on other things now!"

"Alethea, I am glad you mentioned that. I am making plans to go to Arizona with Lugh and to study ancient civilizations. Who knows, maybe I will study a place I've already lived!"

"No doubt, my dear. No doubt," Alethea confirmed.

"Do you have a sense of what I might contribute to the world?" Promise asked.

Her wise soul responded, "Whatever you want, of course. However, I suspect your question goes deeper than the tangible. One can make an offering to the world that isn't perceived by the five senses, you know."

Promise looked puzzled as she replied, "Alethea, please say more about that."

"I'd be happy to, my dear. Creation as a whole, and the planet we live on in particular, is a tangible phenomenon known to us through our five senses and the machines we build to extend our perceptive capacities. We both have experienced the intangible realm as well. Even your ability to sit with me and have this conversation reflects an existence of something that reaches beyond Dylan's room and drum.

"Those who value tangible reality exclusively would call our conversation 'imagination' and maybe even belittle it as such. But how does one measure imagination? Even though its contents are not tangible, does that mean that the ability to imagine is not real in itself? Paradoxically, those who try to reduce the otherworldly to simple imagination have already taken a step toward acknowledging its reality.

"Consequently, both the tangible and the intangible have their place in the created scheme of things. Your extrasensory perceptions and journeying tap into these other realms. Your shamanic intention for today, in fact, is based on the premise that what you do in your 'imagination' has practical impact upon the world. There are those who would disagree, of course. There will always be those who disagree."

Promise nodded her reluctant understanding as she also noticed a tightening in her gut. She asked, "So, how does this relate to my contribution to the world?"

Alethea smiled, then said, "You have to decide if what you offer has merit. Will you base its worth on what others describe as valuable? Or will you allow yourself to make that determination and then honor your own assessment? You can begin this decision-making process with this ceremony today. If you decide that it is all silly and a waste of time, you will find those who agree with you. If you decide it is meaningful, you will have to choose when and with whom to share your experience. If others oppose you or criticize you, you will have to choose how to respond.

"If maintaining your pride becomes the priority – and pride always needs a witness – then you will have to denounce the value of any imperceptible contributions to the world. If you choose to give merit to those offerings that others cannot detect, and therefore cannot value, you will need the courage to stand on your own and hold true to your own self-worth, even if no one can notice or validate you.

"Many people have pride without courage. Our son, Mark Roland, provided an excellent example of this. He bolstered his pride with anger instead. Pride without courage is nothing more than arrogance. It marks the bully. It is pathetic, really. It masks an underlying shame. Only with courage can one make a meaningful contribution to the world, no matter if no one notices, and especially if they do see it and misinterpret it or disagree. The greatest courage is needed when the reactions of others turn angry, or worse. The challenge is to remain true to one's heart, where courage truly resides."

Promise nodded her understanding. As she reflected further, she chuckled and said, "Alethea, you remind me of Prometheus and Chiron. This time last year I wondered if, in the course of their trials, they ever felt disheartened. If they did, I questioned if their despondency had anything in common with what psychologists diagnose as clinical depression. Last year, I considered the possibility that a sense of purpose and meaning might mark the difference between the heroes and heroines of myths and a modern-day, clinical diagnosis. Was I on the right track with my question?"

"Absolutely, my dear. Purpose and meaning, to be recognized and lived fully, require courage. Your psychologists describe clinical depression as an illness. Truly, it reflects some wounding that has impaired a person's conscious access to their courage. When human beings have courage, they may certainly wish their dire circumstances were different, but they will deal with whatever comes at them with a willingness to endure, to persist in their efforts if they can, and to hope for success. Your Prometheus endured and waited, never sacrificing his commitment to the truth of his vision. Chiron recognized that his true calling did not require eternal suffering. By courageously agreeing to die on Prometheus' behalf, he became a light to all."

Promise gratefully reflected on her soul's words to her. She silently hoped she would have the courage required to pursue whatever path her heart and soul beckoned her to honor.

Alethea as her soul recognized these qualms. She consoled her human self, "Promise, my dear, you have enormous courage. Of course, one cannot rest on past accomplishments because life always demands more from us as it invites us to grow. If you let your heart continue to guide you, and you do not give in to any fears that might interfere with its calling, you will exercise your courage muscle and keep it strong. There are no guarantees, of course, and such choices do not ensure your safety. They do promise to keep us – you and me – aligned, however. In that alignment, you will know me. You will know that I will never abandon you. Never."

Promise quickly wiped the tear that escaped her eye covering. As Dylan began to call them back, she whispered to her soul, "I won't abandon you either. I promise!"

Epilogue

THE LARGE BANQUET HALL BUZZED with the voices of its two hundred guests for the evening. Professionals from various therapeutic backgrounds and lay people interested in alternative healing techniques gathered to acknowledge the courageous efforts of those who had made notable contributions to complementary healthcare. Twenty round tables, each hosting ten people, faced an elevated podium at the far end of the ballroom. As the meal concluded, the waitstaff worked to serve dessert before the official speeches and formal presentation of the award would take place.

Peter gazed at the multitude before him while still seated at his table. The director of the holistic association, Russell Wilson, N.D., had welcomed Peter and his guests privately before making more formal introductions when their gathering commenced. In his opening remarks, Dr. Wilson also thanked the manufacturers of homeopathic remedies, flower essences, percussion instruments, and massage equipment, as well as the patrons of other modalities, for their sponsorship of the event. He specifically directed the assembly's attention to the pamphlet at their individual place settings for a complete listing of these generous donations.

After his introductory comments, Dr. Wilson rejoined the other members of the holistic board seated at the next table. The waitstaff sprang into action at that point, serving each guest their meal. The room would hum with conversations until the presentation portion of the program began.

Now that the meal had concluded, Peter worked to master the anxiety threatening to rise into his voice. In minutes, he would finally offer the reflections that had gestated for months, only to finally birth on paper during the past week. He recalled his first speech to the staff at St. Raphael's more than twenty years ago and chuckled to himself. He had no idea then where that moment in time would take him. All the many moments between then and now, all the angst, all the work, all the decisions, had brought him here.

Peter concentrated momentarily on the guests at his own table. Brittany, who had offered her assistance from the very beginning, sat at his side. He had grown to love her more than life itself. Tara and Alex, now his close friends, had helped him in so many ways to formulate that initial, innovative, financial proposal to St. Raphael's board of directors. Their collaborative efforts provided the template for the Rainbow Healing Arts Center, which this holistic organization wanted to honor today. Promise, Lugh, and Lizzie sat eagerly awaiting the award presentation and his remarks. Promise's musings on Chiron and Prometheus, tales he had told his daughters often enough, had crystalized his thoughts for his comments this day.

Mary Lu Reynolds, the current administrator of the Rainbow Center, also joined them at Peter's invitation. Angela Rilken, Esquire, and her husband attended as well, having provided instrumental legal advice for the civil suit twenty years ago and all else since then. All of these people filled his heart with love and gratitude.

As dinner concluded, Dr. Wilson rose from his seat and proceeded toward the podium. Brittany reached for Peter's hand and gave it a gentle squeeze. Peter returned her love with a wordless gaze. They had developed their own silent communications over the years. She received his message and smiled.

After Dr. Wilson provided the background information regarding the board's mission and decision-making process, he identified the many reasons why they chose to honor the Rainbow Healing Arts Center on this occasion. The Center's innovative introduction of complementary healing methods to an inner-city community headed the list, followed by the challenges of such an offering in the backyard of a major hospital, the very one that had rejected the idea of taking on the proposal as its own. The financial struggles of the neighboring community and its residents, not to mention their relative lack of awareness regarding the potential benefit of such an endeavor, also challenged the Center's survival. Despite all these odds, Dr. Wilson noted how the Rainbow Healing Arts Center now serves as a model for other cities and towns to establish a complementary healing hub of their own.

Having summarized his understanding for why the Rainbow Center deserved the award, Dr. Wilson then introduced Peter: "To accept this award, I would like to present to you Peter Holmes, a financial consultant by profession. In the course of honoring his contract with St. Raphael's Hospital, he developed the initial idea for this holistic program and presented it to the hospital's board of directors. When they rejected his proposal, he decided to pursue the project on his own. I trust he will share some of the challenges that confronted him in the process. I have encouraged him to spend some time reflecting on his experience with us. We can only benefit from his wisdom.

"Mr. Holmes, we want you to know that we recognize your heroic efforts and applaud your fortitude and perseverance. It has served as a gift to us all. Please accept this award with our deepest appreciation."

Peter rose on cue as the room exploded with applause. Lugh mumbled to Promise, "No pressure here!" Promise worked to suppress a laugh. She sensed her father's mild anxiety, but she had known him too long to worry about his ability to handle a situation such as this. She squeezed Lugh's hand, then turned her attention to her father, awaiting his insights with delighted anticipation.

Peter took the podium and paused, gazing at his audience attentively. The room quieted as he expressed gratitude to Dr. Wilson and the members of the holistic board on behalf of everyone involved in the Rainbow Center's activities and services. Peter also thanked Dr. Wilson for his kind introduction. He acknowledged his appreciation for the opportunity to share his reflections on what had become for him a life-changing adventure.

Peter continued: "On an occasion such as this, the honoring of an established and successful endeavor like the Rainbow Healing Arts Center, it is natural to reminisce about its beginnings. It occurred to me that most new and significant ideas spring from a longing, the heart's desire for something greater than itself. A physical desire for an immediate comfort does not define a longing. Such desires, once satisfied, have little energy left to sustain any ongoing pursuit. In contrast, the heart's longing seeks completion, the kind that requires a determined commitment and an unwavering faith in the ultimate availability of Love.

"When I first signed on to that financial consulting contract with St. Raphael's over two decades ago, it was just a job to me. Then I took a tour of the hospital and met many, many people – patients as well as staff from different disciplines – all coming together with one purpose in mind: healing. Everywhere I turned, some new aspect of human vulnerability caught my attention and pulled at my heart. Even so, they had consulted me to help manage their budget.

"I quickly understood that monetary expenditures for the newest technology, along with rising employee healthcare and malpractice insurance premiums, had to contend with the limited reimbursements defined by managed care insurance plans. This clash has historically left little room to develop a more holistic perspective regarding the creative financial management of clinical care. Despite that, I was soon to learn that St. Raphael, the archangel of healing, had more in mind for me.

"From the very beginning, I had help – wonderful help, in fact. The CEO of St. Raphael's had assigned an intern to assist me. Brittany Thomas, who joins us this evening, has since become my wife and the mother of our two beautiful daughters, Promise and Lizzie. Not long into the project, Tara Lakelyn, a hospice nurse at the time, shared her expertise in complementary healing methods. Dr. Alex Haskins, an internist at St. Raphael's, helped me appreciate the struggles of current physicians and how to best approach them and their views on healing. Attorney Angela Rilken has offered her legal services throughout the years, especially when unsubstantiated complaints threatened to close the Rainbow Center's doors.

"So many others have played an enormous role, to include the two pastors who offered to host us initially, and the countless instructors who shared their expertise with various healing modalities – such as drumming, flower essences, Reiki, energy medicine, reflexology, art therapy, meditation, yoga, and other complementary methods as well – all to promote greater health and well-being. I cannot omit mentioning the community residents who participated in our offerings and shared their experiences of benefit with their families and friends. The teens in particular made astounding progress in their community involvements through the medium of drumming. They have grown into fine adults who continue to make important contributions to our world. I am grateful to their first instructors, Beat Marston and Bernie Jacobs, to this day.

"We now have also formalized our own board of directors. We remain a nonprofit organization, and our capable administrator, Mary

Lu Reynolds, keeps everything afloat. The Rainbow Center carries its own momentum now. The success of this program required an energy Source much greater than anything I could have ever provided on my own. I stand in grateful awe of what the Rainbow Healing Arts Center has become.

"Through it all, I have had the privilege to witness what it takes to help human beings heal, and to reflect more deeply upon the more essential meaning of that process as a whole. From the very beginning, my teachers have been mythic figures, first introduced to me by Tara Lakelyn. From ancient times, the Greeks told the tales of Chiron and Prometheus. These figures provided the inspiration for me to take on the development of the Rainbow Healing Arts Center before it even had a name.

"As you may know, Chiron was a Centaur – half-horse, half-man – and his father, the god Saturn, passed on to his son the status of deity as well. After Chiron was wounded through no fault of his own, he suffered terribly. One of Hercules' arrows, dipped in the blood of the Hydra – a many-headed serpent – had pierced Chiron's leg. This would have killed a mortal human instantly. Instead, as a consequence of his immortality, Chiron's wound would never heal. As an immortal god, he would suffer eternally.

"As a renowned healer, Chiron tried everything he knew to heal his own wound. When his efforts did not work, he experimented with different plants and other substances. He discovered beneficial effects that helped others, but nothing released him from his own pain. He began to face his destiny. Healing on this plane would elude him.

"In the meantime, Prometheus, also a god, had stolen fire from Mount Olympus for the purpose of bringing light and warmth to human beings, who were especially vulnerable in the dark of night and the cold of winter. Zeus did not appreciate this transgression, however, so he had Prometheus chained to a mountainside where an eagle would peck out his liver every day, only to have it regenerate every night.

"Prometheus could secure his own freedom if he told promiscuous Zeus the name of the consort who had birthed the son who would eventually usurp his throne. Prometheus refused. His integrity mattered more than his comfort. He began to face his destiny. The only other way he might ever be freed depended upon the unlikely willingness of another deity to surrender his or her immortality – in other words, die – on Prometheus' behalf.

"Chiron and Prometheus, two individuals in pain, neither one able to heal himself. Both dedicated to the well-being of others, but unable to free themselves from their own torture or confinement. When we are sick, this is us. The moments tick on in seemingly endless impossibility. We long for relief. That longing reflects the heart's yearning for completion. We would very much like to be made whole again.

"In this pursuit, we try one remedy after another. Perhaps we exhaust every intervention modern medicine has to offer before we turn to complementary or alternative care. We may explore every invitation that promises to eradicate the ills we suffer. Financial expenditures may mount because we all know that health insurance doesn't cover alternative healing methods.

"Sometimes, we may find something to which we attribute our healing success. If this triumph happens early on, we may forget our struggles. Or, we may appreciate our restored comfort and ceaselessly promote the benefits of that one thing that healed us. If healing eludes us for a longer period of time, however, we may begin to acknowledge our previously mistaken illusion. Our former lives have disappeared and can never be regained. We are no longer the same.

"Suffering changes us. Pain alters our perceptions. Values shift. Relationships grow deeper or they fall apart. And still the moments tick on. Traditional medical procedures and medications seem to offer a quicker fix, but at great price, typically. Physical pain, iatrogenic infections and other consequences, pharmaceutical side effects, financial expense, the stress of doctor visits and waiting for phone calls that are slowly, if ever, returned – we pay it all for the promise of renewed health. And sometimes it works out well. Surgery for blunt-force trauma can save lives, for example. No one can dispute these benefits.

"Still, we must ask ourselves, do any of those interventions actually heal us? I have met many a person who has had one medical problem treated successfully, only to suffer the side effects or traumatic consequences of that intervention for years to come. Others simply proceed to develop other, seemingly unrelated health concerns, one after another. This invites us to consider that what may initially present as a cure may not be a true, deep healing.

"Practitioners of energetic healing modalities recognize that most illnesses typically originate in the outer, more rarefied layers of our auric field. The methods for such holistic healing treat the primary cause of what may finally present as a physical or emotional ailment. These remedies function, first and foremost, on the subtle, energetic level; it can take time to penetrate the denser auric layers before physically manifesting the magic we long for. The client or patient of such care may think nothing is happening, nothing is working. The moments tick on and on.

"I have to ask us to reflect on our assumptions that nothing is really happening while the waiting for relief seems endless. By all overt observations, we may be tempted to agree that all has come to a standstill. If we content ourselves with such limited sight, however, we will miss the subtle unfolding of something greater. Chiron and Prometheus both came to understand this. The eventual deliverance from their pain and imprisonment impacted two very changed individuals.

"At a specific moment among all the other moments, Hercules informed Chiron of Prometheus' predicament and how Chiron might positively affect it. The solution would offer relief to each of them: Chiron would no longer suffer, and Prometheus would be set free. Chiron courageously chose to surrender his immortality. He agreed to die to all that he had known of this plane's existence, hoping to facilitate something that he considered meaningful. He accepted that his former life had come to its natural end. Perhaps something new awaited him upon his death. He didn't know. Just as we don't ever really know.

"Meanwhile, Prometheus had grown firmer in his convictions to uphold his own values, no matter the eternity of his current daily torture and the nightly anticipation of its return the next day. He also had to relinquish his previous notion that he could master his own fate.

"Both of our mythic figures had to surrender their belief in their own ability to control their circumstances and the outcome of them. When we are in pain, we must also do the same. There is Something Greater. Our awareness of the spiritual layer of the aura confirms this. The heart has always longed for It. If we are blessed to notice, we discover this Something Greater to be the spiritual Presence that is the essence of our wholeness. This is what we have longed for; this is what completes us. The beauty of holistic healing methods attends to the wholeness of our spirits, hearts, minds, and bodies in a way that traditional medicine cannot in our day. Holistic healing methods truly are beautiful.

"I conclude these reflections with the ending of their myths. Chiron, having died, moves on to the Underworld. Zeus has pity for such a great loss and elevates Chiron to the heavens as the constellation Centaurus. Meanwhile, Prometheus is freed, and he immediately resumes his commitment to give humans fire. Chiron and Prometheus bring light and enlightenment when their suffering has ended. The Presence within them shines forth. It is my understanding that the experience of that Presence, and the opportunity to consciously embody the Light of Its Radiance, constitute the real healing. I applaud all of you for engaging in this sacred work.

"With great humility, I accept this award on behalf of the Rainbow Healing Arts Center and on behalf of all those who truly, deeply try to heal. The Greater Light that comes with such healing emanates forth to benefit us all.

"Thank you for this recognition and for your kind attention."

Promise sighed, smiled broadly, then jumped to her feet, applauding, as did everyone else at their table, quickly followed by the body of the audience. Peter actually blushed in response to their tribute. When he returned to his table, Brittany kissed him tenderly. Promise went to his side and whispered in his ear, "That was wonderful, Dad! You really are guided by Prometheus! I will never forget this. Thank you!"

In that moment, consciousness of Presence permeated the banquet hall. Promise also sensed Alethea's smile quite keenly. Tara and Peter did as well. Together with Brittany and Alex, they reveled in the momentary communal experience of Something Much Greater than their singular human existence. They silently acknowledged the gift Peter's consciousness and comments had offered them.

Peter turned to Brittany and gazed softly into her eyes with his unspoken message: Let's see what's next!

Acknowledgments

WHEN I FIRST CONCEIVED of *Chiron's Light,* I had no idea how it might end, let alone that it might launch a series. Its plot felt given to me from a Source I could not describe or control. With the completion of that book, my publisher suggested that I consider a trilogy. It sparked a goal, daunting and mysterious. I gratefully tended the downloads as they came.

In and Out of Time went through a similar progression. The urge to begin writing required that I trust its evolution and let the ending reveal itself. Fortunately, it did as the chapters took form.

Finally, with *Prometheus Returns,* I could do nothing but trust once again. This time, the challenge included writing a story complete in itself while simultaneously bringing together all the loose ends from the previous two novels. I began with only the flimsiest sense of what might happen in the plot. The Mysterious Source guided the rest. I can only express my deepest gratitude for the privilege of watching this process unfold, typing as required by the pressure rising within me, editing with the joy of soulfully dwelling once again in a world revealed to me through the narrative. These characters live in my heart. I hope they come to enliven yours.

On that note, I would like to express my thanks to the readers of the first draft: Celeste Saunders, Melanie Moffat, and Mick Katch. Also, to the reader of the second draft, Laurel Leland. For drawing suggestions, my thanks to Anthony Smock. Their input has been enormously valuable.

Much gratitude also goes to Bobbi Benson, the inspiration for the trilogy and the designer of its three component novels as well as previous works. It's always fun to work with Bobbi, an artistic wizard in her own right. The soulful feel of each book's presentation is to her credit!

Source holds us all. It has made these books possible. I can only hope they serve a greater purpose in the coming years. May each reader be blessed. Amen.

Made in the USA
Middletown, DE
06 October 2023

40262916R00235